Pancardi's Pride

To Chris
Best Wishes
[signature]

Pancardi's Pride

Ron Clooney

Matador
9 De Montfort Mews
Leicester LE1 7FW, UK
Tel: (+44) 116 255 9311 / 9312
Email: books@troubador.co.uk
Web: www.troubador.co.uk/matador

ISBN 978-1-84876-011-0

A Cataloguing-in-Publication (CIP) catalogue record for this book is
available from the British Library

Typeset in 11pt Stempel Garamond by Troubador Publishing Ltd, Leicester, UK
Printed in the UK by TJ International Ltd, Padstow, Cornwall

Matador is an imprint of Troubador Publishing Ltd

For the One –
who said I should

Introduction

When *Pancardi's Pride* was unleashed on the 1st of October 2008, I was amazed and humbled by the reception it received. Within three months it had sold out, and thus reprinted in early 2009.

This gave me an opportunity to revise the novel once again. There have been no substantive changes to the first edition, save those errors which, sometimes, even with the best will in the world, creep in.

However, it has now given me the opportunity to thank all those who came to book signings; recommended it to others; critiqued it; hawked it; advertised it; joined the fan club; passed it to friends; sent it to the far corners of the world; gave it as a Christmas gift and sent me messages of goodwill on my web site. All of these were encouraging and remain very much appreciated. In particular I would like to thank the following:

Jim Warbrick and Ian Smith MBE who kindly provided some entertaining musical interludes at signings and the official launch. The staff of Waterstones bookshops, in Southampton, particularly; Robin Duke; Sue Dent & Emma Wearn for advertising and launching the book upon an unsuspecting public.

Louise Amond for designing the striking cover.

Simon Jones & John Cook, Waterstones, Winchester; Rob Verner-Jeffreys & Justin Gamblin, Waterstones, Fareham; John O'Connor, Borders Bookshop, Newbury; Matt Fennell & Katy Gledhill, Waterstones Portsmouth; Simon Collins, Borders

Bookshop, Southampton; Charlotte Ellis, WH Smith, Eastleigh; Paul Lynch, Waterstones, St.Helier, Jersey and Dee (Diana) Steed Waterstones, Poole...

For promoting me and my work at author signing events within their stores.

And to all the other bookshops that stocked it; critics that reviewed it; newspapers and magazines that profiled and promoted it across the country. A big thank you.

Ron Clooney
January 2009

Chapter 1

"Oh my good grief," said a voice from under the duvet cover, "Dolly chuffing Parton." The man propped himself onto one elbow and looked at the clock and the vibrating mobile phone beside it on the bedside table.

"I know," replied a woman's voice from the bathroom. "Isn't she great? Nine to five what a way to make a livin' gettin' by it's all takin' and no …" She was singing along to the alarm tone on her mobile phone. "Use your mind and never give you credit, it's enough to drive you crazy if you let it."

The shower was splashing and the combined noises of singing and water drove the man from the bed to his feet. He was tall, athletic and blonde; the muscles in his backside were taught and his waist was firm but his broad shoulders showed several scars; wounds which looked like the result of deep intrusive surgery or a dangerous life. He stood before the toilet bowl to relieve himself of the wine from the previous night of revelry. His head was clear and his mind sharp, without the slightest trace of a hangover.

Returning to the bedroom he reached for his wrist watch and clicked the metal bracelet into place, "Come on Alice," he blurted, "we're going to be late."

The woman came out of the bathroom towelling her hair which was long, red and unkempt – she was naked. Her body was lithe, her pert breasts were held high, her nails were highly manicured and painstakingly painted. She was a beautiful woman and she knew it.

"It's your fault, you know," she mocked. "If it wasn't for me we'd have been later still. It's my phone that got us up. There, that's one thing to thank Dolly for."

"Really?" he said sarcastically, "I thought we were already on the move. And as to your beloved Dolly I thought it was Porter Waggoner who we should really thank. Wasn't he the one that made her, in more ways than one?"

"You were still sleeping. Anyway it's not like they're going anywhere is it? And as for Porter Waggoner he was just a phase, her undergraduate love so to speak; and she has gone up in the world and well, how many people know about him now?"

She was towelling her hair as he was slipping into tight fitting black trousers and a black top.

"For the female of the species is more deadly than the male," he mocked. "Just like you, my little wayside Cobra."

"I cut the labels out," she sighed, "just like you asked and all the stuff from the cars has been removed – no identity and no trace back."

"I know you think it's crazy," he was moving quickly now, "but I don't want any trace if something goes wrong."

"Wrong?" she questioned, leaning over to kiss his mouth. "The only thing that can go wrong is that dozy American, I don't like the way he looks at me. He sort of undresses me with his eyes."

"And why not?" he said, slapping her pert backside as she bent to retrieve the towel. "He knows his trade though – he can blow anything," he smiled, "a bit like you."

"It was you who wanted to go to bed for a.....sleep," she laughed, "and we always do what you want."

She was dressing rapidly now and her hair, which was damp, hung in profusion about her shoulders. They exchanged quick phrases on rendezvous points and fine detail, checking and double checking times. She was lifting the valance around the bed before moving the pillows to the couch. Then she opened the wardrobe door before returning to the bathroom, speaking as she went.

"I'll sort the lock down when you and the boys are underway," she justified, her tone becoming serious. "Just leave everything, I'll clear the room down and check out."

"Right, let's go then," he said, reaching for the light switch.

"My shoes," she squealed, "where the hell are my shoes?"

Quietly, with a throaty hum a dark blue Mercedes drew into a parking bay at Piazzale Michelangiolo. The cold night air was crisp and clear, stars were shining over the city; the night was still young and intoxicated tourists were leaving the bars and restaurants which littered the small hilltop viewing area. The air was heavy with the sound of laughter and the scent of wine, as the dark Mercedes passed almost unnoticed, save for the small group of men who admired the line and style of the vehicle. The car stopped, the lights dimmed, but the occupants remained inside, they made no move to exit the vehicle, and clearly they were waiting. Ahead they gazed at the grace and beauty of Florence. Below them the panoramic view spread out across the plain and the sheer medieval grandeur burst into the darkened sky, but they were focusing on the task ahead. The marble of the Duomo, glazed like a huge iced wedding cake, was floodlit in magnificent beauty. The air was clear and to the untrained eye these men were merely foreign tourists taking in the unique vista.

Time passed slowly, accompanied by the ticking of watches and tapping of fingers.

One man lit a cigarette, momentarily signalling his presence to onlookers, and having finished it promptly lit another from the stub end of the former; he opened the rear window to let the smoke drift into the night air, threw out the butt and blew a smoke ring through pursed lips.

A second man dozed, his head back against the front passenger seat headrest, small purrs of confident heavy breathing emanated from between his clenched teeth. This man exuded confidence, the taker of quiet before the onset of the storm.

The third man, behind the wheel, chewed languidly on a stick of fresh gum, watching, alert, poised like a predator waiting for the chance of a swift kill. His face was pale skinned and framed by dark hair and a beard.

"Well fellas here we are again, but where the hell is he?"

The smoking man spoke distinctly; there was an accent in his voice – Southern American perhaps Georgia, Alabama, or some area which does not sound the ending "g" in words. His teeth were perfectly white and glowed from the darkness of the rear seats as he spoke.

He continued, "Poppin' I bet. One last chance of some tunnel before we get to the tunnel if you know what I mean, man."

The chewing man made no reply but started to slowly fold his gum foil into ever decreasing squares. His eyes scanned the darkness for any movement.

"For God's sake," said the reclining man, without opening an eye, "he'll be here. It's his score. Just relax a little." His voice was calm, clinical, Northern European; his appearance clean cut, precise.

A small Volkswagen Golf appeared at the crest of the hill, it slowed and began to crawl into the car park. The man behind the wheel of the Mercedes became instantly alert and tapped the leg of the reclining passenger, who sat up in response – both watched intently. The car carried two occupants, a blonde man with a face which looked hard bitten, aquiline, and almost cruel. The white of his teeth showed as the car passed making a precautionary sweep of the area. There was a woman at the wheel her face obscured with long hair which curled in profusion about her shoulders, she seemed tall but slender and elegant.

The Volkswagen passed the Mercedes for a second time and the headlights flashed once, showing the driver's distinctive manicured nails. As if to order, the men in the Mercedes became animated and exited the vehicle; hastily they grabbed four packages from the boot and walked toward the smaller car, which was now parked opposite them. The bearded man silently tossed a bag to the male occupant of the Volkswagen as he clambered out. The woman exited the Volkswagen and without saying a single word climbed behind the wheel of the Mercedes and drove it away.

"We thought you weren't comin', on the nest were you?" The smoking American lit another cigarette as he spat out his condemnation, his face contorted in a wicked, knowing smile. The brief illumination, as he cupped the flame, showed his eyes, which were keen, sharp and observant like those of a wolf.

"Did you indeed?" The blonde man replied with a very pronounced English accent. He was obviously well educated – probably public school. His eyes glistened blue in the reflected light of the street lamps and there was a cruel edge to the corners of his mouth; a cruelty borne of deception and hardship.

"Don't give us any of your bollocks," the Englishman continued, mimicking the Southern American drawl of his accuser. "This ain't no Yogi Bear picker nick Boo Boo."

The mimicry created silence and an accompanying deep draw upon the smoker's cigarette.

The men appeared to be dressed in identical outfits of close fitting black; they resembled wetsuits, accentuating the athletic physique of each. The impression was one of men accustomed to physical exercise and toil, or at least a diet of healthy food and the gymnasium.

"Nice night for a skinny-dip my boys?" said the American, looking toward the starry night sky. "It's gonna be a cold one too."

There were no replies.

Quickly the men walked toward a gravel footpath which led directly down to the river.

"Ah, the smell of the Arno." Again the voice of the American pierced the night air.

"Your loud mouth," said the Englishman, "will get us all; why the hell can't you shut up like Jock there. You don't see him blurting about like some God-damn Southern Belle do you - Scarlet?" The reply was spat out, loaded with venom in the expression of the words, "Southern Belle and Scarlet" sarcastic and yet controlling. It was clear from the tone and dynamic within the group who had the position of authority.

"I was only sayin' how," replied the American, "the stink comes up from the water like you'd not imagine. It's hard to believe that people think this is a wonderful city. It stinks like a trailer camp piss-hole to me."

"We're not on a bloody sight-seeing trip here so shut up," the Englishman replied.

When they reached the edge of the river they silently slipped diving masks over their faces, there were no flippers, or snorkels, but they entered the cold fast flowing river making their way down stream with the current.

Ten minutes later four bodies moved in unison and passed under the Ponte Vecchio before vanishing into the murky gloom.

The team of men moved as if well rehearsed with a clear purpose. To any casual onlooker they might appear a commando assault team, able, controlled, and working as a deadly unit. Pulling themselves through the muddy waters they moved swiftly along the wall, built to hold back the river after the floods of 1963. They halted, listening to the footfalls of the drunks on their way home, bobbing, and listening to the tumult as people passed overhead. A signal of thumbs down was given by the Englishman and they disappeared, as one, below the surface.

Before them, below the water line, stood a small iron grate secured onto the masonry with heavy bolts of chromed steel. The grate covered a circular opening barely large enough for a man to pass through. Just inside this tunnel stood a steel sluice automatically programmed to open when a sensor registered that the river might once again flood the city and destroy the precious works of renaissance art. Through this sluice and the sixty seven others strategically placed along the Arno's bank, water overflowed into the main drains and away from the city. The cost of construction had been enormous and the public debate which surrounded their installation heated and often tenuously close to civil disobedience. The Florentines resented the extra cost to local taxation and so the municipal administration had passed this directly on to the millions of visiting tourists, in the form of entrance fees and hotel levies and duties. But that had been nearly ten years ago and the average Florentine considered the issue dead, forgotten, and of absolutely no political interest. And the tourists, they still came, came in their millions from the four corners of the compass, came as never before in fact.

Water flowed through these tunnels from time to time, particularly in the spring melt when the rush and impact cleared away the myriad of rat colonies that had nested behind the sluices. Each year the rats built and each spring they were flushed back into the marshland beyond the city, it had become a ritual rather like the winter snows on the mountain tops.

To the average Florentine the sluices and the tunnels were of no interest – they simply existed, but to the four men in the water they constituted the path to paradise.

One man extended his arm above the water line and secured a water filled container over the sensor eye and the sluice in the tunnel below slowly began to crank open. Water began to rush through pushing the men against the wall. It was a sufficient signal to know that the tunnel might not be blocked but there was no certainty.

The submerged and muffled click of bolt cutters severed the bolts securing the grate to the wall and the whole cover was lowered quietly to the river bed; the four men passed into the tunnel opening with the stealth of hunting otters.

The propulsion was immediate, it was as if they had entered a water flume at a theme park and they were catapulted at high speed for fifty metres. Each man carried a water pack and a mini-tank with a small supply of oxygen; once in the tunnel there was no turning back. With the sluice now fully open water flowed at great velocity and the men were hurled down the engorged tube. If there had been an obstacle there would have been no escape and they would have been crushed one against the other as the Arno's water forced them along the passage; but the Englishman knew that there could be no obstacle, the flow of water was too swift and too intense for the tunnel exit to be blocked.

As they passed the first of three bends in the tunnel all switched overhead pot-holers lights secured to their foreheads to the on position; blue light bathed the slime covered walls which rushed past as the velocity increased. The speed of the water forced them toward their destination, they passed a second bend and then a third. The tunnel opened suddenly, divided, and each had to force their way into the narrower and rising right-hand option; once inside that, the pressure began to drop and the water slowly subsided. The men dragged themselves onto what might be mis-construed as a beach; a gravel ledge littered with condoms and the remains of rat feasting. Rats that had heard the slow mechanism of the sluice gate opening and had instantly scurried through the minor apertures to reach the safety of higher, drier ground.

"Jesus Christ what a ride man," said the American. "Nantucket sleigh ride baby."

The words were spat out amid a gasping for breath; he tore the diving mask from his face and instantly noticed the acrid, putrid stench of a disused drain. His face lost any optimism and he scanned the dark for signs of movement.

"I hate rats man – hate 'em," he said, "all shit and yellow teeth."

The large Scotsman spoke calmly, "They'll no eat ya," he said, as he wiped spittle from his beard. "They have better taste than that." His voice had no echo and the chamber into which they had crawled seemed little more than a pocket of a cave eroded into the rock.

"Well I hate the damn things, all disease and crap and they're worse than jus' about anythin' when protecting young or cornered. Got my brother's dog once and when we found him he was surrounded by dead rats. He'd bit some clean in half. But he was covered in bites and the things were still attacking him, must ha' been two hundred dead and they still kept attackin'. Reckon they'd kill a man down here iffen they was hungry and he was trapped." The American's reply was nervous and his eyes and light were darting into the obscure corners where the silent assassins might lurk.

The Scotsman scoffed, "So you're a Choochta then. All barefoot schooling, catfish fishing, and playing with your good looking cousin in the barn."

"Well what's a Choochta then jocko?" smiled the American.

"Why laddie, it's just a term of endearment."

"Well I ain't no Choochta, nor Yokel, nor no Appellation Albino neither," the American replied. "But I know what rats can do. Eat you right down to the bone like a God damn Piranha fish. That's what they are – Piranhas with legs."

In the dark void a clear English voice spoke with calm authority, "Right gentlemen, rats or no rats, we are under one of the greatest collections and," he paused, "as this is not an afternoon church outing, let's work the problem shall we?"

Chapter 2

That morning there was every possibility of a walk and Giancarlo Pancardi was intending to take Mostro for his morning constitutional. Being a creature of habit he would take his well worn route, down Via Vittorio Veneto past Galoppatoio and on toward Villa Borghese and the park.

As the heavy oak door slammed behind him he could smell the air of the Roman Spring and raised his coat collar in response to the morning chill; attaching the lead to his patient dog, he tucked his English Times under his arm and set off at a leisurely pace. This was his one great pleasure since quitting the Questura time to walk and observe.

Pancardi loved the routine of the stroll, though his knee caused him great agony at times, and the quick click of his now customary iron tipped walking stick gave him the air of a nineteenth century Victorian gentleman stalking a promenade; all he lacked was the frock coat and top hat for the illusion to be complete. His wants were simple, he lived a solitary life, despising television and filling his time with reading and the occasional good meal accompanied by fine wine and a close friend. In truth most people gladly avoided him as they found his manner brusque, terse, intense and some even said rude. Consequently, Pancardi had many acquaintances but few friends and chose those with whom he spent his time diligently, analysing them, their motives and their intellect. When speaking he still voiced the air of authority which grew with those who were accustomed to giving orders and having them obeyed. Sadly there were few "real friends" left alive and Mostro, despite his increasing age, filled the vacuum left by human companions still embroiled in the wage toil: Pancardi was content, or at least felt he was.

The trees of the park glistened as the early dew of the morning began to evaporate and the now customary tourists began to assemble to view the wonders of Bernini. Spiders re-span webs in the bushes which had been destroyed by the antics of the many teenagers who frequented the park at night, laughing away their youth with an endless ability to alleviate their boredom in vacant conversation. Many of his colleagues had talked of how lucky he was to leave at the pinnacle of his career.

Pancardi pondered on luck. The same luck which had made Michelangelo, the Florentine, a favourite of the Medici Popes; personally he had always thought Bernini the greater artist in marble and had marvelled at the skill he himself did not possess. Once he had harboured thoughts of becoming an artist, thoughts long gone in the reality of his police career. His father, like all loving fathers, had thought economic stability worth far more than the possible fame of a Bohemian artist and Pancardi senior had probably been correct. The death of his father had been a hard blow; it was from him he inherited his own love of methodical detail. It was from him he had learned tenacity, patience and the humility to accept advice and ideas from the most junior of his officers. It was these genetic properties which had separated him from his peers and had earned him the respect of his juniors, but it had also instilled fear in his superiors.

"Pancardi is always right," was often the call when investigations were stifled. "Pancardi knows the criminal mind like no other," became the war cry of office juniors when cases had baffled less able rising sycophants. It was Pancardi who could read the mind of even the master plotters as if he were connected to them by some form of telepathy. He alone seemed to understand them, think like them, and subsequently mirror their every move. But now those days were over, his famed years at the Questura had vanished like a morning mist and he was glad not to have to turn his brain to insurmountable problems which consumed his every waking moment. In truth he had loved the chase, as a panther loves to hunt, but the taste of victory had become less appetising as age and the consequent collapse of his arthritic knee became ever more painful.

Once there had been "the woman," as he referred to her. Pancardi knew that he loved her then and probably did still, though many years had now passed. She could have chosen marriage but circumstances of death and duty had driven her down another route and he had lost her. What a beauty she had been with striking red hair and emerald green eyes which grew moist in the afterglow of passion. Regret sprang upon him and Pancardi's face curled a scowl which then rapidly passed as he thought of Yeats; inwardly he recited the final two lines of Never give all the Heart. He had been lucky, more lucky than most.

He voiced a, "Buongiorno," to the flower seller at the corner stand and moved on toward the gallery of modern art turning a brisk left back through the trees toward Santa Maria di Popolo.

Taking a bench, he released Mostro from the leash, then opening his English Times, read quietly, absorbing the latest minute detail of English politics. Members of his old team were amazed at his ability to recall facts which had long since passed from their memories, the devil, Pancardi had always said, was in the remembered detail. Those small little areas which even the best of us fail to act upon, but the devil, he never forgets the detail.

After some half an hour he rose, called Mostro, who had made the acquaintance of another dog some hundred yards off, placed him gently on the leash, turned toward Trinita dei Monte and thought of fried eggs and bacon in the small café he habitually frequented. The owner allowed dogs and pandered to his quirk of the "English breakfast," even supplying some scraps of bacon for Mostro, who the waitresses genuinely loved and pampered.

Pancardi had developed a real taste for England after spending five years working with Interpol and Scotland Yard in London. His English had improved dramatically and Chief Inspector Michael Stokes had introduced him to the "fry–up." He thought of Stokes and a wry smile drifted across his face; they were both out of service now and Stokes lived a life of domestic disharmony and gardening, well beyond the clamour of London – and he hated it. Occasionally they spoke on the telephone but their friendship was more one of mutual respect rather than idle chit-chat. Two old silverbacks who had given over control to lesser men, each avoiding the true nature of their regard for one another. Stokes grew roses and seemed to live in his potting shed well away from his wife, whereas Pancardi walked and read.

Stokes had often ridiculed Pancardi in the early days giving him the prefix Tin Tin, but as time passed and mutual respect grew, the prefix became his affectionate office nickname and they became lifelong friends. Once at Christmas Stokes had bought him a gabardine raincoat to reinforce the ridicule and likewise Pancardi, in good spirit, had worn it for many years until he was re-assigned to Rome as part of a pre-retirement package. Pancardi in return had half a ton of ripe horse manure delivered to the Stokes' city garden household with a simple card which read, "This is shit Holmes."

The name of Mostro had come to Pancardi in a flash of sarcastic inspiration and remained a standing joke among the Italian officers of the force. Small and tenacious he was part poodle, part terrier, lively, thoughtful and Pancardi's constant companion and confidante. As they walked Pancardi observed the tourists, some of whom would be easy targets for the pick-pockets that worked these locations. Small time criminals who lived on the wallets of the Americans and English that had come to discover the hidden joys in Rome's art and history.

The door of the café opened with the customary creak and a small bell sounded in the kitchen.

"Good morning Inspector?" the waitress asked, as she patted Mostro and lead Pancardi to his table, a window seat looking back toward the park.

"I think it is, if a little cold," he replied in his normal aloof manner. "How is the bacon today?"

"Smoked and fatty, just as you like it." She patted the dog, "He will love it."

As Pancardi sliced the fatty bacon Mostro flirted with the waitresses and then sat patiently observing his master until the last mouthful had been devoured. Then he adjusted his position to lay under the table whilst the Times once again opened and the smell of strong coffee drifted into his nostrils.

Pancardi had loved his time in England but had never quite got used to the coffee. Weak and milky Americano style – he preferred his black and strong. Coffee that could grip a spoon and hold it upright so that it glided slowly to the side of the cup from the upright, rather than falling abruptly.

Time passed and Mostro drifted into the secure dozing which only contented and well-fed dogs can muster. Pancardi lost concentration and began to think of past cases, archaeology, antiques, and Westminster Abbey in a stream of consciousness which seemed totally unrelated and confused by the irrational manner of their appearance in his thoughts.

Glancing at the clock above the counter he read 11.34. He was later than usual and began to think of the things he had to do that afternoon. Dry cleaning to collect, ironing a shirt or two, and then the customary after tea stroll through the Foro Romano and into Villa Celimotana: Life was easy.

The door of the café opened and the small bell sounded in the kitchen once again. Pancardi paid no heed and continued to read the pages on Chelsea and Arsenal and the clash of fans in a local pub. He knew the area well, it had been part of his 'Manor', as Stokes called it.

"Inspector Pancardi?" A lithe man in a dark suit spoke quietly above the edge of the newspaper.

"Mr. Pancardi," he corrected.

"Thank goodness! I have been looking for you for at least half an hour. I've been through the park and the flower seller told me that you'd be here. My name is Alex Blondell," he offered his hand, Pancardi did not reciprocate. "C.I. Stokes recommended that I contact you." He blustered as he reached for a chair opposite, making his intention to join the Italian clear.

"Do I know you? I think not," the reply was aloof, wary and loaded with authority which communicated an air of menace to the younger man.

Mostro stirred under the table.

"So this is Mostro, I was told that you would have your little dog with you. Can I sit down please?"

Pancardi motioned the younger man to sit and then shuddered inwardly with disgust as he ordered a café Americano.

"I can't stand the Italian style coffee it's far too strong for me. I'd have tea but they always give you the yellow label stuff which is too weak and tasteless."

"Never mind your tea, what do you want?" was Pancardi's curt reply.

"As I said, C.I. Stokes suggested that I contact you, because in his view you were the best thief taker in the business and well the thing is…"

"And how is the illustrious old demon? Still growing roses in Suffolk? He wasn't such a novice himself."

"Well, very well I believe."

"Right then sunshine, why are you here and not talking to Stokes?" Pancardi's voice was sharp and lean, like a well prepared runner.

Pancardi resorted to the vernacular he had learned in London and took no time in establishing his authority over Alex Blondell, whom he considered a mere stripling boy. Pancardi had noticed his stained tie, which had a pull of haste on it. His ruffled shirt and a black ink stain on the index finger of his left hand; a stain which spoke of fountain pens, public school and bureaucracy. This was a man who had hastily travelled a long way to get to him, perhaps someone who had not even checked into a hotel yet. His speech was impetuous, quick, and he certainly was no senior officer, Pancardi doubted if he was force at all.

"Well as I was saying C.I. Stokes…"

"You said that already," Pancardi scoffed.

"Err um yes, well I was asked to find you. You see we have some notion that there is likely to be a major incident in Italy over the next couple of weeks."

"An incident. Really?"

Pancardi shot a wry look at the younger man combining it with a sarcastic inflection to his voice and then viewed the consequential disarming effect upon his verbal quarry: It worked.

Again he flustered, "Err um yes, well there is a little problem of what we, that is, Britain, that is our government, that is Interpol, are concerned that…"

"Concerned," he pondered, "an interesting word concerned, don't you think so, Alex? It is Alex isn't it? All these people are concerned and here you are drinking coffee with me, what an earth for?"

Pancardi had a completely disarming effect upon the younger man and revelled in the joy of verbal control. Mostro stirred, sniffed an ankle and nonchalantly resumed his silent vigil beneath the table, whilst the very agitated young man attempted to impart his message; his poise and public school education gone beyond his wit.

"There is likely to be a robbery of epic proportions," he said waiting for a sarcastic Pancardi response – none came, and the Italian merely smiled as he drew in a deep aromatic mouthful of strong coffee. "We believe," Blondell continued, "that this robbery is to take place in Italy. We are unsure of the location, but we are certain it's Italy and that you might be able to help us with our enquiries."

"In Italy, oh dear, oh dear my, my, me," his tone was almost mocking now, "you mean like the Italian job?"

"Mr. Pancardi….. Err um Inspector Pancardi," he blurted, his frustration shown in his reversion to formality.

"Italy's a very very big place Alex."

"Yes, yes but err um, we could do with your expert knowledge."

"Has Charlie Croker got another gold bullion robbery planned? Are the crown jewels likely to be snatched?" His voice was loaded with pure sarcasm.

"Inspector please! I am trying to be serious."

"I'm sorry but I find this sort of vague intrigue ridiculous. I've retired and I don't hold any authority with the Questura. Shouldn't you be speaking to someone there? Shouldn't your government be speaking to someone in the Carabineri? They are the boys for this sort of international incident."

Pancardi's sarcasm and lack of interest was beginning to irritate the younger man who drew in a large mouthful of coffee in a hurried tense manner. He became terse, "Inspector we," he faltered and corrected, "I, was sent to you precisely because of your past record. I believe the words of C.I. Stokes were get Tin Tin on the job he's the Italian boyo. I see now why they call you that." He nodded to acknowledge the dog that was blissfully asleep under the table.

Pancardi's face showed no reaction, no warm smile, no dislike, nothing. He sat as if made of wood, his dark eyes boring into the man he so obviously had no interest in, nor regard for. He disliked the errand boys of government and found that they were as steadfast as jelly in water. Tiring of his own cat and mouse antics Pancardi quietly withdrew within himself and like a psychoanalyst re-examined the young bureaucrat who was so obviously Foreign Office and, the ice-breaker.

Having made his observations and noted them, Pancardi suddenly beckoned the waitress and nodded for more coffee. As she came to top up both cups he smiled a reassuring smile at Alex and calmly, with absolute authority, said, "Go on then what information do you wish?"

Alex Blondell waited for the Italian to take a mouth of coffee and when their eyes met over the rim of Pancardi's cup he began, "Well the thing is," he said.

Chapter 3

The four men began to work systematically along the masonry which jutted onto the jagged beach-like projection. They carefully examined the mortar joints in the brickwork with an intensity which might belong to a Clerk of Works inspecting a listed building for defects. The consistency and strength of the mortar was tested using sharp tools as gradually they scratched what seemed to be an outline the size of a doorway through the joints.

"Get on the end of this tape." The blonde Englishman produced an extending rule which he forced into a projecting buttress corner, "Get the height, and get it right," he continued.

The same procedure was followed and two tapes converged approximately six inches from the centre of the roughly scratched door outline.

"That's about right," he confirmed. His accent changed in the excitement and an East London twang appeared. "Now Scarlet it's up to you. You're the bleedin' expert we need a hole large enough to get us some leverage, but right through got it," he said emphatically.

The American smiled broadly and produced a small package from his pack which resembled glazing putty. Quickly he kneaded the mixture into a small lump in the palm of his hand while his bemused companions winced at his blasé bravado.

"You see harmless," he began his confident running commentary, "work it into a nice soft mass the size of a golf ball and then slap." He slammed the mixture against the brickwork in the flat of his hand accentuating the word slap for effect. "Sticks like shit to a blanket," he laughed, "ha! This baby will get us in. You know people get scared, real scared of explosives. It ain't that easy to get it wrong you know. I seen this guy once near blew his cock off cos' o' his meanness." He turned to his companions, smiled and continued, "Why?" he paused, "cos he was a two faced chicken shit, a fucking piece of slime." He paused again kneading the mixture, "And the next time I see him I will blow his balls off," he laughed.

"Aye and your hand and us too. I don't fancy going sky diving with the angels. You're a right numpty," the Scotsman voiced his distain at the bravado.

"Listen my friend," replied the American, "this stuff is the safest high explosive on the market. This ain't no gelignite, sweatin' and oozin' all over your palm. This ain't no well greased whore." He paused, working the mixture into the mortar joints. "This is the real mother. Now pass me the DT."

Retreating as far as possible from the wall, back toward the waterline, the men placed plugs in their ears as the American introduced a small electrical detonator the size of a pen into the mixture. Once again he pushed heavily against the grey mass stuck to the wall, paying special attention to the joints between the bricks. Then retreating, he joined the other men, turned his back against the blast, and flicked a remote switch.

"4th July fireworks baby," he whooped, as the blast constricted the air in the confined space.

The resulting explosion was quiet, controlled and no louder than a car backfiring. In the subsequent silence the men sat and waited. They were some 30 feet below the level of the road above, which was covered with the flotsam and jetsam of tourists and vans leaving the Ponte Vecchio for the night. Their eyes stung and as they removed their earplugs they each experienced a ringing back-drop to their observations. As the dust settled they observed the breach created; it was approximately nine inches in diameter and a clear opening was visible behind the now violated wall.

Satisfied that the explosion had not been heard and that the traffic above had not even paused, the men sprang into action. They began to pull away the weakened masonry clearing a space large enough for them to pass through. Within seconds they were into what looked like a tunnel or ancient disused walkway. Steps which were hewn from solid rock, reminiscent of the winding stairway of an ancient castle, meandered into the darkness above them rising some ten feet before opening into another darkened chamber.

With the agility of gazelles the men jumped forward and up the stair into the small sealed chamber. Unlike the previous space there had been no repair work and the chamber looked as if it might have been an ancient dungeon. They scanned the walls with their lights, passing their hands over the stone as if appreciating the softness of female skin or the feel of finely polished marble; there were no marks, no alterations, and no clues to any continuation of a passageway either original or sealed. They seemed contented.

"Ok we all know the drill – by the numbers." The Englishman seemed more relaxed and the accent of the privileged reappeared.

Working quickly they emptied the contents of their packs onto the ground. Four collapsible graphite poles were produced over which they stretched a rubberised sheet. The corners were then secured by nylon ties, the American was heaved onto it at head height, like a trapeze artist on a safety net, and quickly he began to examine the roof of the chamber.

"How thick is it Paul?" he asked gleefully.

"I told you no bloody names," came a terse reply.

"Yeah, yeah, number one," he sarcastically accentuated the one. "Like anybody can hear us down here in this shit hole," he muttered to himself, "we ain't in public view; I don't see no CCTV," then more loudly, "how thick?"

"The old man reckoned two feet," came the reply, "but he doesn't know for sure. The drawings of the time give no real clue. We're dealing with variables here not certainty."

"Jesus Christ if it's that thick we are in deep shit man. When I blow this baby the whole damn room could come in."

"You're the expert, and now you lose your nerve, just get us up alive."

"Alive huh? I thought that's what I was doin', and I don't have no loss of nerve man."

"Anyway you know the problem, we've done it in the mock up, so do your bloody job."

The Englishman turned to the other men and raised his eyes heavenward in distain, whilst the sullen American began the familiar routine of kneading and palming the high explosive around the seemingly solid rock. He rolled the material into finger thick sausages which he carefully placed in the joints of an oblong shape overhead, pressing firmly to attach the explosive to the ceiling. Finally the detonator was pushed home and he seemed satisfied with his work. He alighted from the head high platform and joined the others below. They quickly disassembled the platform, which folded back neatly inside their respective packs. They worked methodically without hurry; they were neat, meticulous, and confident.

"Right everyone out, back down the stair, this baby is gonna be messy." The American exuded confidence as he spoke, knowing the control he had over the others. This was his arena – with explosives he was king, a God.

All four men retreated into the relative shelter of the stair, as once again the pouted kiss of a muffled boom rocked the air around them. This time however, the impact upon their lungs was all too apparent; they were breathless, choking, gasping in the vacuum, there was thick dust and shards of rock ricocheted from wall to wall accompanied by the heavy drum beat of masonry hitting the floor above. Then once again silence.

"Shise, sheet!"

The accent of the man's expletive placed him geographically – perhaps Dutch but more likely German. He clutched his upper arm when a small projectile embedded itself in his flesh perforating the black of his suit and creating an intense stab of pain. He raised his hand to cover the small wound and through his fingers small gouts of blood could be seen trickling over his knuckles.

"Shite, shise, shit!" he exclaimed again, exasperated.

Within seconds the small wound at the top of his left arm was staunched. It was neither deep nor debilitating, merely a flesh wound, the result of a small flying shard of limestone.

"Hell!" he exclaimed, "it's always me."

The other men rallied aid quickly – the blood flow was

staunched with a scrap of shirt tightly bound in strips. They then sat quietly alert and listening as the Dutchman casually wiped the residual blood from his hands with a remaining scrap of shirt.

"Bollocks!" he exclaimed, "bloody damn explosives."

"Ai," replied the Scotsman from the adjacent darkness, "we all have to take that risk my friend."

The wounded man snorted a guttural expletive.

"Ai, and we can all moan too, but we could all have died in that tunnel back there. After all no one tested it did they? A big gamble for a big pay off. Is it worth the risk?" His lilting voice trailed away into the darkness, giving off a ghostly air as it melted into the airless black.

Meanwhile both the American and the blonde man had returned to the upper chamber to examine the effect of the explosion. Above them in the darkness a perfectly oblong entrance was cleanly blown; the edges of the opening appeared crisp and sharp as if cut by a skilled mason.

The American hissed through his teeth, "Double one A man, fucking whoopty doo. Does this man know or does he know," he chuckled.

The English man gave no immediate reply but used his light to examine the entrance above them.

"Dalvin was right, the silly old bastard," he said.

At their feet lay the remains of a shattered stone cover which had been used at the time of the Medici to seal the night soil exit to the river. In the upper surface lay the corroded remains of two massive iron rings long encrusted by the ammonia of urine and the air of disuse. It looked similar to the entrance of a Cathedral's funereal vault. Both interlopers tried to imagine the strength of the men who crawled into these long disused sewers to drag this lump of masonry into place. They visualised them dressed in rags eager for the work, toiling like Egyptian slaves or English pit ponies dragging the stone on rollers and rails.

It had been anonymous men who finally sealed the exit which they had just blown open. Men who had purposely failed to backfill the stair, through which they had just passed, simply because they could. Men who had managed to put one over on their employer Cosimo di Medici, who would never check it anyway and would expect his house Marshall to do so. But these anonymous night soilers knew of the house Marshall's laziness and of his passion for spying on the ladies of the court. The same Marshall who would contrive to watch the lithe nudity within the dressing rooms, through key and spy holes as the ladies of the court washed and dressed. And so it was that the night soilers finally sealed the entrance with a tightly fitting slab while the Marshall was viewing one particular raven haired servant of the Medici who slept and rose naked. While he had been admiring the soft milky forbidden fruit, delighting and committing to memory her firm breasts and the triangle of her pubis for his future use. They, the night soilers, had laughed at their good fortune and cunning, the cunning of being paid for a job not done. The fateful consequence of the Marshall's voyeurism and the night soilers' deceit had remained hidden for centuries, until the new entrants pulled themselves up through the virginal opening they had so easily penetrated.

The intruders now lay in a final tunnel. An upward gradient of approximately three feet, a forty five metre narrow passageway known now only to the rat population of Florence. A forty five metre airless crawl under the Palazzo Pitti with the priceless artwork and furniture and then on to the Banko Rolo and their intended prize.

The men did not speak but replaced the breather tanks which they had carried through the earlier waterlogged section of their approach. In the silence hand signals were given and even the American observed the verbal curfew. Above them could be heard the barely audible click of ladies' steel shod high heels as they made their way along the very same cobbles over which the deceitful night soilers had stumbled so many centuries before; laughing and longing to spend their easily earned money on whores and drink at the now demolished Dragonetti tavern.

Swiftly the team of men passed minor entrances down which water and rats passed at will and to which they paid little heed. The Scotsman at their head and using forearms for propulsion they moved in unison, akin to snake hunting in a burrow for an unwary mammal. Their packs were pushed before them as the head height decreased and the tunnel narrowed. In less than two minutes the men had reached their final objective, the precise spot where this ancient waterway for royal faeces passed the newly constructed underground handling hall of the Banko Rolo.

This time there was no need for explosives, the wall of the tunnel was easily removed as the crumbling lime laid mortar disintegrated under the deft touch of the Scotsman's hand. Sealing the tunnel beyond them with the removed debris, all that finally remained was the thin layer of inch thick plaster which Miosh Calvini had spread only five years before.

As the fine drops of dust fell to the ground in the customer service bay nothing stirred in the Bank. The sweep of the CCTV camera inside the vault did not notice the movement on the upper wall. It was not trained to do so – for this was not the vulnerable area. It was not this area that was a risk, for here the rich and famous came to covert their goods, to add more, to become Smaug – this was a secure area.

The four lowered themselves silently from the opening and touched their feet to the non pressure sensitive floor. A floor which could, even now, have saved Banko Rolo embarrassment, but by not being installed at the time had saved hundreds of thousands of Lire.

Breathing apparatus removed, the team of four intruders moved quickly to work.

The Scotsman to the CCTV exposed control panel, to re-chip the programme, enabling the camera to replay a continuous empty image. In seconds the matter was accomplished and apart from the momentary interference blip not even the most diligent observer would have noticed any variation. Indeed the security services guard in the belly of the bank above had lost the power of observation years before, replete in his knowledge that this Bank, Banko Rolo Italiano, was one of the best and most secure banks in the world. His heavy lidded eyes barely registered the alteration on the monitor screen and his breathing pattern remained at a steady purr as his chin nodded forward onto his chest.

Silently the team moved into position. Before them stood one steel grate, locked centrally by a Mauser combination time sealed key lock, beyond that, stood twenty feet of pressure sensitive floor; further still another German built Mauser treble combination steel vault door. All of the expensive security devices so carefully laid in the bank above and in all the possible known entrances to the vault had been totally worthless, thanks in the main to voyeurism, laziness and greed.

Their roles had been repeatedly rehearsed and they now worked at an unhurried pace. Any casual observer might have considered them a team of engineers inspecting the premises, or a security test team inspecting the possibilities for robbery. They worked at a pace which exuded confidence and gave nothing but hand signals in the silence of their movements – but their objective was clear.

Chapter 4

Alex Blondell took a mouthful of his weak, milky coffee and continued.In an unnecessary and habitual precaution he lowered his voice as if he were suspecting the conversation might be overheard. His tongue nervously lapped the side of the coffee mug as he swallowed hard at intermittent intervals, much as a lizard laps the air for occasional insects. The fingers of his right hand nervously drummed the cup handle as he played with the residual dew on the table with his left – he traced lazy figure of eight shapes. Pancardi observed closely the lack of rings, the well manicured cuticles and neatly cut, clean nails, a man who took time over at least one thing he thought, perhaps that was his personal obsession.

Blondell's voice became coldly robotic, measured, considered and he spoke as if he were speaking to himself rather than another human being.

"Some time ago Interpol intercepted," he began, "a telephone conversation on the subject of the Romanov fortune. At first nothing was made of it as it was part of a routine surveillance. In fact the details were subsequently passed to me much later, almost a month later in fact, at the Foreign Office."

Pancardi noted the reference, he had been correct in his first evaluation, Blondell was no policeman and he was nervous, nervous enough to be repetitive.

The robot continued, "I had produced a paper on the missing jewels for Scotland Yard and therefore seemed the natural choice for further information. That routine surveillance ended in the breaking of a group which was established in London; this was all in the course of the investigation on the Brinks-Mat robbery. You know the bullion boys," he quipped flippantly, smiling, hoping to receive an acknowledgement or some flicker of a smile.

Pancardi reacted by looking through Blondell and smiling at the passing waitress in an attempt to hide his now aroused interest.

Blondell continued, "We all thought it casual banter and nothing more. The problem was that very few people seemed to take the whole issue seriously, indeed there were many members of Scotland Yard who had long since thought the notion of the missing Tsar's millions a myth. Some of the best Inspectors in...."

"All very interesting Alex," interrupted Pancardi, "very Charlie Croker, but what on earth has this to do with Italy and more precisely me?"

Pancardi was not in the mood to receive flippancy; his mind was already trawling the years of his experience, searching for a jewel specialist. He was beginning to be irritated by the younger man who seemed to speak in tangents and who had disturbed his morning routine, but once his mind was alert he became a machine, the perfect thief taker. Pancardi was a creature of obsession, once hooked he could fight like a Marlin for the final breath of freedom, and this boy's banter was rapidly becoming that hook. He was intrigued by the research and by the whole idea of buried millions and unsolved crimes, so he listened, sifting the information into useful compartments for a case.

"Well surprisingly," Blondell chirped, "the Romanov diamonds and an extensive collection of other priceless stones had been deposited in London for a considerable time, since 1918, I discovered that much from my research. It appears that the Bolshevik revolution was not as communal and egalitarian as many at first thought and some of the new hierarchy including Trotsky and Lenin managed to squirrel away personal fortunes under a variety of names; mostly Russian nobility that had been caught and slaughtered in the blood bath of the revolution's aftermath. How do you think Mexico became so easy for Trotsky to escape to? This was a man who supposedly fled with no more than the shirt on his back. That is nothing to the saintly status he now has, I mean how many people know about his affair with the married Frida Kahlo?"

Pancardi realised then that Blondell had done his personnel research thoroughly. Pancardi loved art, Kahlo would be known to him, and Blondell used it with subtlety, and the Trotsky link was cleverly orchestrated into the conversation too, just enough detail to open the door of thought. Perhaps he had underestimated the young man he was now examining.

Blondell continued, "Doesn't that seem strange for a man who was the most likely successor to Lenin himself? There were ways, even then to hush things up, to squirrel away fortunes. Stalin may well have outmanoeuvred him with control of the red army but Trotsky was no fool now was he?"

Blondell waited for a reply, none came, and instead Pancardi drew a deep draught of the strong dark coffee into his mouth. His eyes were alive, and Blondell sensed, rather than saw, interest. At least he is listening he thought.

He continued, "The Romanov fortune had been presumed lost at the time of the 1917 revolution. The family were slaughtered at Ekaterinburg and the secrets of the cellar executions and the disposal of the bodies became the stuff of legend until the re-emergence of the so called crown Princess Anastasia. It was she who claimed that she had bought her way out of the execution, and after being wounded had escaped simply because of the diamonds and gold which the Tsar had so carefully stored to finance the counter White Revolution. Many royal assets were seized, but some, mostly the portable items, made their way out through Siberia and into the West, usually sewn into the coat seams of fleeing nobility and minor aristocrats. After the royal family were slaughtered the trail, as it was, went cold, until Anastasia, who was promptly disowned and denounced as an impostor. That grand old Duchess had far more to lose than the gaining of a granddaughter. So it would seem the custody of the diamonds and assets, whilst not available to Anastasia, did make their way into the coffers of some very important people. It seems that some or all of the pieces had been in the care of the, failed, white counter revolution; some of the collection had been dispersed to a variety of locations – Switzerland, Amsterdam and Italy. That in itself is rather ironic don't you think, the gnomes of Zurich holding in safe deposit boxes the amassed collections of Capitalism, side by side with the ill-gotten gains of Communism – viva la revolution and all that?"

Blondell paused to see the reaction on the Italian's face. There was no flicker of emotion but Pancardi's mind had begun to tick like a bomb which had been primed for action. His eyes sparkled in the morning sun which streamed through the café window; the bright sun of Rome, clear, crisp and sharply illuminating.

Blondell continued, "As I have already said the collection disappeared and some believed that the items were sold to finance a variety of Royal projects or monies dispersed to the crowned heads of Europe. Some said that the Communist murderers…" Pancardi noted the inflection and choice of language analysing Blondell's possible political leanings, "Of the Russian Royals disappeared with the jewels, others that it was the Romanov fortune which financed the space race with the US in the 1960's. Some conspiracy theorists even said there was a financial pact between Khrushchev and Kennedy prior to the bay of pigs, going right back to Joe Kennedy and Stalin during the war; others that Castro and Guevara had both built their revolutionary armies for the invasion of Cuba on the Romanov jewels. The paths of dispersal were complicated and…."

Pancardi interrupted, "All very very interesting to any historian of the Russian revolution, but to me it is tiresome and to be blunt totally irrelevant." Pancardi now seemed irritated. "Can you get to the point? Is there a point?" he asked.

He too had heard the far fetched stories of the Tsarina's Faberge eggs worth millions of dollars which had vanished during and after the revolution. He like no other human knew greed. That was his forte, the one constant in his world; he could smell it in the sweat of a bookmaker at the race track, he could sense it in the face of a fashion model, but more importantly he could taste it in opportunity.

Blondell caught Pancardi's keen eye and smiled a knowing smile, "Well we now have reason to believe," he said, "that the collection has been regrouped. Why we do not know, how we do not know, but we believe it is housed in one location here – Italy, and we also believe that there is going to be an attempt on them."

Pancardi burst a laugh, "Wow what a lot of if Alex. You know the story of if do you not? If your granny had balls she'd be your granddad," he smirked, as he continued showing his small, perfect and yet false teeth. "Italy, my my," he snorted once again, but the keen interest in his eyes shone through, beyond the doubt.

"The results of such a robbery," Blondell's voice was serious and methodical, "would have wide reaching repercussions on virtually all of the European Royal households, particularly Britain and Sweden. This sort of thing could destabilise Europe and have repercussions in America if a connection could be established. Think of Cuba, Kennedy and any other conspiracy theory you care to name, they would all pale in the light of this one. For that reason alone it could have a very de-stabilising effect, in short it could be cataclysmic disaster."

Once again the young Englishman waited for Pancardi to react. Once again Pancardi did not, but his eyes shone with intrigue.

"Your part in this, Inspector" he continued, "would be to both locate the jewels in question and also prevent the theft of such items."

Pancardi stared wistfully out of the café window at the motor scooters carrying young lovers toward the fountains and commuters to the offices. His mind began to think of the red-haired woman who had slipped from his grasp so many years before and as he did so a smile stirred in the corners of his mouth. Blondell read this as an affirmation of consent while Pancardi thought of picnics on Capotoline Hill and the staggering Barolo walks home to the small warm apartment which for so long now had been his home, his castle, his sanctuary; and now this was all being disturbed by a boy who seemed to thirst for glory. He suddenly looked at Alex Blondell and wondered if he had a woman who could inspire him to acts of al fresco passion, a woman who could make him smile when the entire world caved in upon him. Pancardi noted the excited grin, the slightly dishevelled look of a poorly ironed shirt and a jacket which would benefit from a dry clean and brush. He thought that no Italian woman would allow her man to wander the streets so style-less, he was so obviously single. Pancardi also noticed the slightly worn cuffs and the small speck of blood on the shirt collar which spoke of airport waiting lounges and snatched attempts at freshening up and he knew Blondell was absorbed by his work. He sensed obsession and a thirst for glory, a younger version of himself.

"You need to find a woman to keep you warm at night Alex," he suddenly said.

"I'm sorry Inspector?"

The younger man was completely unprepared for the statement which totally disarmed him.

"A woman Alex. One of those soft things that hang on your arm and keep your bed warm. Something to make you feel alive. Don't carry on waiting," his tone became serious, "or the mistress of career will stifle you and by the time you discover your mistake it will be too late and life will have passed you by." He laughed and then mocked, "Wouldn't you like someone to iron your shirts and nag you about shelves?"

Blondell was bemused by the totally unrelated stream of consciousness which he was now witnessing, a stream which centred on him and not this investigation. His eyes opened wide and his jaw fell and he began to wonder if this old Italian was precisely that, old, and as others had warned, bordering on the insane.

"Inspector Pancardi, we, that is I, would like to work alongside you. To learn from your methods and hopefully find both the Romanov jewels and the team that have obviously got some insider knowledge."

"You want to learn from me, and what would you learn," his voice was tinged with bitterness, "how to mess up your life? How to waste your great chances, and for what, momentary glory? If that is all you can learn then I pity you." Pancardi laughed so heartily that the waitresses turned to see the commotion. "Alex, Alex, Alex, there really is nothing to learn and being a sycophant will not get you any further. Let's be honest with each other, you seek the aid of a broken down old cripple to give you some chance of advancing above the others in your Foreign Office department. You, the one who believed in the Romanov hoard, when others had long since consigned it to legend. I have no doubt you have done your research. I suspect that you are very good at it but you want me to help you in advancement, am I correct?"

Blondell considered, "You are very perceptive Inspector but I have a professional pride more than anything else."

"Do you? So do I, I too have pride. So who owns these jewels Alex? Have you considered that, not just thought but considered?"

"Of course, they are the property of the crown."

"Which crown – the British crown? Are they not already wealthy enough? I believe your Queen is one of the wealthiest people in the world is she not, and yet she wants more?"

Blondell's face contorted, once again his politics were shown to Pancardi.

Pancardi thought to warn him never to play Poker for money but toyed with him a little longer attempting to raise his hackles and unbalance his equilibrium.

"I intend to do my duty and should you be unable or unwilling to help I will seek help from elsewhere."

"Ready aren't you I should imagine? But, and I stress the word but here, you have got to a dead end and you so much want to succeed you can taste it. In your Foreign Office you have the chance to make more of yourself, advance from your middle class origins to the big league. Perhaps your father did not quite make the chances you now have. This is your big opportunity and so you are clutching at the straw of Pancardi." He paused, his head titled to the left as he winked his right eye, "And they in their turn will use you Alex, give you some advancement, but look out for the glass ceiling over your head, aristocrats are clever people are they not? They dangle the chance before your eyes like a shiny bauble on a Christmas tree, and oh how it sparkles, oh how it delights. And then they will abuse you, you who will never really be allowed to rise among them, know this, Pancardi knows this, knows this to his cost for he gave all his heart and lost."

Pancardi's voice resumed the hollow tone of painful recall and Blondell felt the cruelty of every analytical observation. In the Foreign Office he was precisely that, one of the "poorer" boys looking through the sweet shop window while others could enter and buy; the bitter words of the Italian stung like a wasp at a summer picnic.

"Inspector Stokes spoke of me and no doubt you picked over his carcass too." Pancardi was almost sneering at Blondell now, "But that was not enough for you and so now here you are."

Blondell remained silent; his mind was racing, paddling rapidly, much as a swan appears to glide on water with onlookers unaware of the exertion beneath the waterline.

"So in this café in Rome you hope to seduce me one last time – am I right?" Pancardi continued in the same mocking tone. "You think that Pancardi is like you, after some prize." Pancardi's tone suddenly changed and his voice softened, "Well Pancardi has grown tired of the chase and he wishes to grow olives and tomatoes in Sicily and bathe his skin in the lemons of Sorrento. Have you been to Sorrento? Napoli? She is the woman of Rome the man. And you my young friend need that woman, that at least Pancardi can teach you."

"Inspector I need your help."

"I now, and not we, that is more like it. You are slipping Alex, remember the small mistakes cost you dear." Pancardi's face broke into a broad grin, "No style, but balls of steel and guts, you'll go far – I like."

"Then you will work with me, guide me?"

"Work, ah do not run my young friend, we shall see, we shall see, walk with Pancardi before." Pancardi turned to the waitress and called, "Due distretto."

She replied questioningly, "Due?"

"Si due," he replied with a broad smile. Pancardi turned to the young man opposite and changed the subject, "Have you eaten?" he asked, "first we feast and you tell me all you know and then Pancardi thinks about this working."

Mostro stirred beneath the table replete in his dreams of further bacon. His senses told him that the routine had changed today, something unusual was happening. This young interloper had caused Pancardi to stay in the café longer than normal and Pancardi was drinking even more coffee. Pancardi stroked Mostro's head in reassurance; the dog turned a full circle and then lay once again at his master's feet.

The waitress brought the coffee.

"And you learn the art of Pancardi, drink, revive, Prego?"

The Italian Inspector motioned Blondell to drink the strong coffee and then took a huge gulp of his own. Replacing the cup to the table he smiled a broad smile and asked, "Well what did you learn so far from this phone tap conversation, tell me now and be precise in the detail?"

Chapter 5

The impact and subsequent squelch of the suction pad was barely audible as it passed through the gaps between the metal bars of the high tensile steel security gate and attached itself to the vault door beyond the pressurised floor. It hit the smooth steel of the vault door with a slavering slap and stuck fast. The soft puff of the air pistol which delivered the pad to the door was as sudden and swift as a stolen kiss. Rapidly the fine nylon of the trailing draw-chord was replaced by a dual cored steel cable; cable which carried an electrical pulse which in turn converted the suction pad into an electro magnet strong enough to suspend a car from and yet allowed it to remain as flexible as spider silk.

The team of cracksmen worked steadily and methodically. The four men moved in a well rehearsed but regimented manner, they showed no anxiety and gave off an air of unhurried quiet reassurance, professional, calm, cold and calculating and yet somehow urgent.

"Like takin' candy from a God-damn baby. I love this shit!" the American chuckled as he prepared two small charges which were intended to detach two bars from the steel gate before them. "Man these security gates suck and I tell them time and time again, but do those arseholes listen. Might as well be talkin' to a daug. The manager here will be shakin' like a daug shittin' peach stones when the TV gets hold of the story." His fingers worked the explosive quickly with reassurance. "The secret is," he muttered as he worked, "not to let any debris fall back on the floor or we are screwed man, screwed."

He kneaded the explosive putty, this tin.
the size of woollen thread, rolling it on his knee h
cigar; then he wound the strands around the steel bars w
now the only remaining obstacle between the men and the
door.

"One little puff and it's there man. I love this bank robbery
shit!"

Wrapping scrap cloth around the set charges he quickly
detonated them .The sound was no more audible than a verger's
cough at Sunday church – there and then gone in the instant. The
bars shook as they severed and then two men working together
could rock the clear end back and forth creating enough warmth
within the metal to lift it no more than nine inches or so. That
simple gap would be enough for all of them to pass through in
single file.

The European was the first to enter; climbing through like a
cat he arched himself as he reached above his head to haul his
body weight onto the inner side of the steel grating. He was lithe
and quick and yet his upper arm strength was clearly apparent.
Like a ballet dancer he clung with one hand on the gate whilst the
other deftly attached a pulley and harness to the cable. A harness
customised from the standard issue hang glider harness so often
seen and so easily purchased, but more importantly almost impossible to trace after it would be left behind. In one swift motion he
slid into the harness and hung suspended. He turned to his
companions and grinned broadly.

The Englishman followed with the same balletic movement
and took up position on the inside of the steel gate. Attaching
another harness at the cross bar point he gave himself free arm
movement; his body suspended, he began to winch the pulley
with both hands and the Dutchman began to fly toward the vault.

The next through was the Scot and finally the American. All
three clung to the steel gate watching as the Dutchman began to
work on the vault locking system. He produced two small half-
filled vials from his breast pocket and pouring the contents of one
into the other he shook the mixture, as he did so he felt a small
trickle of blood run down his arm and dampen his cuff. He cursed
at his own stupidity.

The problem was a simple one, burn a hole through the lock

d then simply trip the few sequenced door inward. Design was all, and in oor the design fault was the inward . the arrogance of the designers to under- ity of the locks and timers required. His and apart from the small wound which ie warm blood to his wrist he felt totally confi- se had been freely acknowledged by the team when ioved a ring from the Scotsman's finger using acid without le g a mark or breaking the skin. He worked methodically as he dripped the now activated acid, via a pipette, onto the lock tumbler outer. The effect was almost instant; as the dissolving process began he dripped a constant stream of fluid onto steel and as he had predicted the inner workings of the locks became exposed. Once the vault door began to open he would simply slip from the harness to the non pressurised floor of the inner sanctum and then nothing more remained. A simple case of opening the deposit boxes inside possibly with no more than a drip or two of fluid.

"How's it going?" the Englishman called across.

"Fine – just like I said the design is crap. The lock innards are too close to the surface and any second now we shall be there."

He worked more acid into the growing opening of the lock timer. Inner contacts became confused by the melt down process and the timer, in consequence, sent the relay message to the microchip of jammed mechanism – override clock.

"The clock is now disabled," he called over his shoulder, "I'm starting on the lock tumblers."

Once again more acid was introduced as one by one each tumbler dissolved. These tumblers were as the Dutchman so clearly stated brass and as such too soft to withstand the acid which simply melted them as if they were butter. Resealing the vials he again placed them in his breast pocket and producing a small electrical screwdriver he worked within the now open wound of the vault door.

"Hey Dutch how long?" the American drawl echoed across the cavernous space.

"Nearly there or I was until you opened your big mouth. I need some silence for this part."

Beads of sweat grew on the Dutchman's forehead as he listened for the two dull clicks which would signify the vault was open and disarmed. He had heard one but the godforsaken yank had disturbed his concentration and he now fought hard to regain it. The wound on his arm pained him and he noticed small spatters of blood on the vault door which appeared as he feverishly worked the screwdriver.

An audible click!

Pushing his legs against the massive vault door it swung open with consummate ease. Like a cat he landed on all fours, attentive, listening, and watchful.

"Ok boys we're in," he called across the void.

Within seconds the other members of the team crossed the cable and all four were standing amid a sea of individual numbered lockers and safes.

"Right we take them all but only the good stuff and nothing too bulky." The air of the smooth English commands was once again interspersed with the twang of the excited East–End lad. "You two," he motioned to the American and the Scot, "blow the larger safes and we'll concentrate on the individual ones. And try to do it carefully, we don't want any burning stocks and bonds setting off the fire alarm now do we?"

"Yes sum boss we's jus a powder nigga, we do as the masser says." The disdain of the American became apparent in the now Southern Alabama Negro drawl he adopted as he pulled the hair at his brow.

"Let's move like we have a purpose," the Dutchman interceded, "I for one want to be out of here before any security people get suspicious."

"I love this part of the job, it's so interesting to see precisely what the rich and infamous have tucked away in their greedy little vaults where only their eyes see it." The Scotsman spoke seriously disregarding both commands and barracking alike.

"Hey Jock you're not turning all commi on me are you?" The American mimicked the man's accent.

"Well you Yanks have no concept of Socialism, with all your get rich quick notions, we have a little more understanding of…."

The American interrupted, "Well Robin Hood how much of this is going to the poor then?"

"Ye dunnae get it!"

"Yes I duuu," the mimicry accentuated now, "you're just a greedy bastard like the rest of us, and only yuuu won't admit it, yuuu filthy, grasping, shit-bag Capitalist yuuu," he laughed.

The charges now set on the heavy duty safes the American issued a warning. The team lay face down and the doors popped ajar as if they were sealed with jelly.

"Bingo! Pass me a sack Jocko mate," instructed the American, "time to go fucking shopping baby."

The opening of the various inner vaults allowed the men to comb through the contents of each as they came to them. Stocks, bonds, and money orders were left, far too easy to trace. Some cash was taken, in pockets, gold left behind, because of the weight. These men knew their trade and focused upon pearls, jewels and only the most expensive ones at that. Diamonds, Rubies and Emeralds were taken, complete with settings and those which were attached to heavier gold objects were crudely prised away. Each man carried a small sack no bigger than a ladies handbag and each knew precisely what to look for.

"Jesus H. Christ almighty somebody loves us. Take a look at this shit." The American's profanity resounded as the other three members of the team turned to see the contents of one of the larger units revealed. The area was crammed with items but not items of usual jewellery these were far beyond that.

" Fuuucking 'ell!" there was no affected accent now. This was pure Brick Lane.

"Man, oh man the English crown jewels baby, the fucking crown jewels," the American whooped with amazement at their good fortune.

A silence descended as if they felt they might be overheard and some fearsome Knight guardian might leap forth to dismember them.

The Dutchman was the first to speak, "These my friends are not English they are Russian. And this," he reached into the hoard, "if I am not mistaken is a Faberge egg the sort given by Tsar Nicholas the II to his bride Alexandra as a simple Easter gift."

He continued to paw rapidly, assessing items as he went, "What we have here are the Romanov jewels, the Russian crown jewels – the ones so many people have sought and never found."

"What the hell are they doing here? How come Italy? Just who does this safe belong to? What do we do now?" The American voiced his train of questions freely.

The Englishman, having regained his composure, spoke with a huge grin suppressing impending hysteria. "Let me take those queries one at a time if I may," he said. "Number one who gives a shit they are ours now," he laughed. "Number two refer to answer one; number three, again refer to answer one," by this time he was audibly chuckling, his eyes sparkling with good fortune, "and what we do now is – we steal them, every last one"

"We'll never get this lot away it's far too heavy," replied the canny Scot.

"Right," he agreed, "so what we do is take the largest stones from any of the pieces. Just a few of these will set us up for the rest of our days. And we're going to fill all of our bags and leave the crap behind. Let's not be hasty or greedy chaps. Let's do this carefully. No mess ups now, we have another two hours before the cleaners arrive so we can comfortably work this for an hour and still be in Rome for breakfast."

Steadily the men worked, sifting through the items and removing only those jewels of the highest quality, rubies, sapphires, diamonds and emeralds.

"Jesus Christ look at this man – I mean Jesus," the American twang was delivered by a sucking through teeth much as a drowning man might seek a gasp of vital air. "What the hell?"

Wrapped in a crude hessian cloth was an exposed bundle which now lay at the feet of all four men. Freshly exposed there seemed to be a crown although it seemed distorted, squashed out of shape; within that was a smaller crown obviously a female version and within that an orb topped with a Russian Crucifix.

"Fuuck me backwards gently boys," the drawl of London's East-End piercing the air.

The Dutchman spoke again almost in awe of the majestic pieces before him.

"It will be a shame for these to be broken up," he said, "they are some of the finest jewels in the most historical settings. They ought to be in a museum where everyone has a chance to view them. Magnificent truly magnificent." He held the squashed crown to the flouresecent light which refracted the hues of a rainbow.

"Museum, are you totally fucking crazy these are our ticket out baby. Somebody stored these for a rainy day, who the hell do you think that was – the fucking tooth fairy, Santee Claws?" the American sneered.

"But we shall never be able to sell them unless they are re-cut and they are perfect now."

"Yeah and they'll be even more perfect when they are converted into American Dollars and paying for my villa full of pussy and Champagne."

The American whooped away any sentimentality as he prised four enormous emeralds the size of pigeon eggs from their settings. This was followed by half a dozen rubies slightly smaller and ten diamonds, Russian cut, sparkling like a child's eyes in a candy store.

The men worked swiftly. After fifteen minutes all the satchels were full and the floor was littered with priceless gold and minor stones which had been discarded. Half of the individual safe deposit boxes remained unopened for which many owners later thanked providence. One which avoided the greed of the intruders contained some five years of Nazi genocide pay-off diamonds amassed into a biscuit tin sized bag. Easily transportable and the financial resources of the Alte Kamaraden now based in Argentina. Years of Jewish blood money gathered from those willing to try and purchase their freedom from the death camps only to be betrayed and sent to their death anyway. The box also contained a small book of new aliases and post boxes to which money could be wired worldwide, as and when the periodical need for cash arose. It would have signalled the death of the Nazi movement worldwide had the vital safe deposit box been opened. As it was, when the robbery was reported, the apoplexy caused shortened the lives of many on the South American continent, until one white-haired man with his blood group unobtrusively tattooed under his left armpit personally met with the manager of the Banko Rolo to withdraw the bag and carry it to Geneva. A little old, white-haired tourist passing through the Florentine crowds, anonymous and un-noticed and yet armed with the standard issue Luger pistol mounted in a holster at the small of his back. He walked unhurriedly toward the Duomo and on toward San Marco and the waiting car which sped North away from the city. They cared little for the detail of the robbery and their involvement ceased immediately.

Full satchels slung about their necks and with pockets stuffed by greed the men made their way back across the cable. The vault lay in carnage as if a large mammalian kill had taken place and the prize cuts eaten, with the remainder scattered for would be scavengers. The harnesses were discarded too, left to swing gently as the men re-entered the tunnels. Down again into the empty chamber and on toward the flowing water.

The most dangerous part of the whole daring do plan was yet to come – the exit.

There had always been no possibility of returning the way they had come. Their exit required a rapid headlong rush, some 150 metres in length. This time with the water forcing them through a final tunnel and out into the now obsolete electrical substation which once housed turbine generator blades. They sat once again on the false shore with the water rushing by.

"Right lets get organised," the Englishman spoke quietly, his composure regained after the excitement of the kill. "The breathers have less than a minute left and we have to get out or we are all done for," he continued, "Jock you're first up."

This time the frame which had made the hop-up platform was converted into a cigar like tube which served as both a canoe and submarine. Once inside the first two men would have no escape and if the tunnel were blocked it would mean certain death as the second two were hammered into them at high velocity. The cigar like projectile was loaded with the satchels and first the Scot and then the Dutchman slid into the condom like structure. In an instant it vanished into the darkness. The American followed and finally the Englishman was catapulted into oblivion.

Less than a minute later the men were climbing up a rusty ladder attached to the side of the disused turbine tank, having been spat forth below the water line. At the edge of the tank they paused to allow their eyes to adjust to the darkness. Here they shed the canoe allowing it to sink deep into the turbine tank filled with bricks from the derelict walls which surrounded them.

"Fresh air man," the American spoke the relief of all.

"Silence," the Englishman snapped.

Lights on a distant car flashed once and silently they made their way toward it. Passing through what appeared to be a small, freshly cut hole in a perimeter mesh fence they crossed a deserted quadrangle now a mass of idle machine parts and scrap metal, where children explored by day, avoiding security guards, and cats hunted rats at night. They moved quietly now, fearful of any overly diligent security guard that might hastily arrive with an Alsatian in an attempt to justify his existence – none appeared. Over waste ground, through a second fence and down a rude slope, they plunged for freedom. Out under the edge of thick laurel bushes, emerging among park pines; across some open ground, past newly planted flower beds and over the silent early morning road, they slipped unnoticed by all, save the odd urban fox who wondered at their early morning ritual and then returned to scavenging the bins.

The engine on the car started as they approached, and as it drew away the lights remained quenched, half a mile into the suburbs the lights suddenly flamed as a dark blue Mercedes swept out of Florence.

Chapter 6

"Pancakes – food for the thinking man are they not and maple syrup ah ambrosia? Personally I like the German crepes with Zimt they always remind me of snow and Christmases long ago when I was a boy." Pancardi was excited, and his voice became more insistent, "America has little to commend itself to we Europeans, but pancakes -now they are commendable are they not?" He did not wait for a reply but continued his disjointed ramblings. "Trees with candles and the smell of pine and the glitter of glass, and then there is always gingerbread." He paused leaning his head to one side and smiling asked, "Did you enjoy your youth Alex?"

Blondell looked carefully at the older man, he found his questions and reactions almost impossible to read. Pancardi spoke in confusing tangents making his criss-cross thoughts seem like incoherent ramblings. He asked unrelated questions as if he were on the verge of senility and yet they all seemed to make perfect sense. Blondell was beginning to see that as he probed, searched and dug beneath the guard of formality he pieced together evidence which others might miss. Alex did not want to answer the barrage, but he felt that Pancardi's razor sharp observation would find unwanted clues, would discover and deduce more, so he found himself answering with more than he ought.

"Yes it was very secure," he replied, defensively.

Pancardi pounced! "Secure, an interesting choice of word Alex. Did this mean you were loved or unloved, but safe? Were you really happy?"

"I was loved if you must know and yes I was a very happy child."

"Then why are you so defensively guarded and resentful of my questions?"

"Inspector I am not resentful, I just don't see the relevance of my childhood Christmas experiences to our investigation."

"Everything is relevant at some stage Alex, and when did it become our investigation?" He stressed the our.

"Inspector really, why do you continue in this manner either you will help or you won't?"

Pancardi continued by changing the subject, "Eat your pancakes, good?"

"Very good actually."

"Language is a funny thing actually Alex, because it actually, tells you much about both the speaker and the listener. Strange is it not how few people listen," he paused and quizzically tilted his head to the side yet again, "when there is much to learn they simply miss it. What is our most valuable resource?" he asked, with sudden fury.

"Are we on to riddles now?"

"No I merely wish to see if you...."

Blondell interrupted, "Can think?"

"Precisely."

"Time," he paused, smiled, and then asked, "do I pass?"

"You see there is much to be learned from simple questions. It is these that give away the thoughts and feelings. The deeply buried ones which make us an individual. The garbage we cannot shed – our programming."

"So my answers tell you things which you can use in your assessment of me?"

"Precisely, and do you not think that criminal minds are not programmed? Are we not made up of our past? Are you not the result of your parents? In this Larkin was truly correct. Your parents fuck you up, they don't mean to but they do." Pancardi laughed triumphantly and then simply gestured for Alex to eat.

As Alex ate Pancardi thoughtfully observed his mannerisms. Blondell had spent time in America, that was an obvious deduction, but he held his knife and fork like a true Englishman. He was careful, precise and most respectful in his approach to food and Pancardi liked that.

"Have you ever been to Köln in winter Alex?" He didn't wait for an answer and continued, "I have and those markets full of happy shoppers buying for their friends. The faces of the children all oblivious of things going on around them. We humans are indeed a very feeble animal don't you agree?"

The younger man replied through his food, he was eating heartily and gesticulating with his fork, orchestrating his views. He knew that the Italian had been hooked when he talked of the criminal mind, the psychology and programming, and all he, Alex Blondell, had to do now was carefully reel him in. Pancardi was correct, a leopard cannot change its spots and Blondell smiled at his success. Pancardi too had been programmed, by his years of police work and father before that, he too had trip switches which set the wheels spinning and Blondell had flicked them to on.

"Bullion robberies as you are well aware Inspector require patient planning, precision, timing and most of all clear team work. Particularly with the removal and sale phase, so that was where I started on surveillance."

Pancardi took another deep gulp and finished his coffee motioning for the younger man to do the same.

"We spent many hours on the surveillance and drew a complete blank. It would seem that all the known teams were not involved in this, except one name did appear that I thought you might be interested in, James Folsen-Drecht."

Pancardi's eyes lit up as if a fire had been placed behind them. "This man is known to me," he said.

"I thought that he might be of interest to you." Blondell continued, "Well on his list of telephone calls made, it would seem that two were made to an office in South Africa, to the office of one Smithart and Verrison solicitors and estate agents."

"These I do not know."

" Well, it would seem neither does anybody else; except if I said that there is a rather shady character known to South African police for some past history of illegal diamond smuggling, one Michael Vaughan, who also happens to be a sleeping director on the same Smithart and Verrison company, does that help?"

Pancardi's mind was trawling his personal Rolodex for Vaughan, there was nothing; he shook his head.

Blondell continued, "Well he was not known to me by that name either but how about Michelangelo Verechico?"

"My oh my Alex, what have you stumbled upon when all others missed the clues? Michelangelo Verechico now there is a name to conjure with. A very able adversary and a man who knows how to cover his tracks so that all traces lead to someone else. A very clever mind indeed."

"Inspector you speak as if you admire him," Blondell's voice was muffled by a final mouthful of syrup laden pancake.

"Alex you have no idea of your enemy. Never underestimate your enemy; look at Napoleon and Hitler they did that and see where it got them. This man is extremely able, he is a chameleon, clever and the best of all the logisticians. He sees what all others miss, how do you say, if there are fifty ways to mess up he sees forty nine of them. He plans robberies from a distance; he even scopes a job for the team but he never takes part. He is always there in the background – where the wealth is, he is. Michelangelo never gets caught because he never gets greedy. At this he is excellent; he never believes he is infallible, he never underestimates a problem and any money which is used as the basis for the set up is laundered through legitimate companies such as these solicitors and land agents in South Africa. He uses off shore accounts or Swiss banks where money becomes untraceable; he does not let himself be photographed and he is always changing tack. Many times people have been close to catching him but he always quietly slips away. He is calm, cool under pressure, an iceman. That is why despite being known to Interpol, the FBI, Scotland Yard, and other assorted bodies he remains free. He has no face, this he changes as he needs to and he has never served, and never will serve, a custodial sentence. He moves from country to country unrecognised, living on the very best of everything anonymously. He is the very best and a ghost."

Blondell saw the look of wonder in Pancardi's eyes, saw the glint of steel at the pupil and knew he was hooked.

"You do admire him Inspector?"

"No it is worse – I am in awe of him. He is the best planner I have ever encountered and I believe he will never be caught," he paused thoughtfully, "alive."

Blondell almost choked spluttering coffee as he gulped a mouthful.

"This man is untouchable Alex, he is the best there has ever been."

"Well if he is behind this then I intend to catch him."

Now it was Pancardi's turn to splutter. "You would be better to focus on Drecht," Pancardi said with a wry smile.

"Well that trail has gone cold," Blondell snapped at Pancardi, "and they have both gone to ground or there is someone else involved in this – someone far more clever, far more cunning, someone we have not come across yet."

"Trust Pancardi on this one there is no other – he assembles his team."

"Who? Where?"

"My young friend, the money has been moved and they are somewhere, thinking, watching, and waiting. They are true predators, but I do know how to catch him."

"Verechico?"

"No my young friend he will never be caught, but Drecht. This one does have his personal way with things, his foibles and he will be our first quarry."

"How? When?"

"So hasty my young friend, we must slow down to gain some speed. How does the saying go," he paused, "welcome to my parlour said the spider to the fly."

Then with sudden movement Pancardi rose, threw some Euros onto the table and began to instantly make for the door, Mostro followed alert and awake.

"We can walk and talk in the sunshine can we not?" he chirped. Calling "Arrivederci" to the waitresses and receiving the customary "Ciao, Inspector." Giancarlo Pancardi stepped into the street beside a young Englishman busily wiping his mouth on a restaurant napkin. "Lire were better – I liked the Lire, like you English love your pounds sterling."

They walked along a noisy boulevard choked with Roman traffic. Motor scooters buzzed past in the clear crisp light. Blondell had no idea where they were going until they crossed the Ponte Cavour toward Via Crescenzio. Pancardi bent to place a leash on Mostro and the click of his cane was audibly quicker than it had been earlier in the morning. His pace was also more purposeful and Blondell sensed that Pancardi was already on the hunt.

"Are we heading toward the Vatican Inspector?"

"Yes, an old friend of mine is there and I think we should speak to him urgently. He knows how to throw stones at glass houses, ha."

"Why what has a priest got to do with this?"

"He is no priest, he is a security guard and a damn fine one too."

"Then what has he got to do with us Inspector?"

"You will see my young friend, you will see. Come we can cross here. There ahead are the museum entrances."

Pancardi briefly let the traffic pass and then gesticulated at a young couple who sped between the cars narrowly missing his dog and making him check his stride. Blondell noted once again the quickened pace and a renewed sense of urgency, Pancardi was obviously impatient to get started. Passing between the tourists he moved quickly down some worn stone steps to a heavy Spanish oak doorway. He looked up at the closed circuit camera above his head and punched a five digit code into the security panel set in the impenetrable stone of a massive column adjacent to the door. Blondell briefly wondered if Pancardi, like most Italians, was a Catholic, but this was far more impressive than the right of passage for a common church goer. The sound of the entry buzz was barely audible over the chatter of the excited queuing crowd expectant for a glimpse of the works of Raphael and Buenorotti.

Once behind the heavy oak door the silence became almost eerie and a dark suited man approached quickly; Blondell noted the smart click of steel heel savers. Pancardi had said virtually nothing and Blondell now knew the walk and talk had been a smoke screen. Pancardi spoke quickly and quietly to the suited man and then all three were continuing down a long dimly lit tunnel, the far end guarded by two halberd bearing Vatican guards dressed in the gaudy costume of centuries past. The click of Pancardi's cane and the shoes of the suited man making a rhythmical jazz counterpoint on the ancient stone flags.

"Traitors walk they call this Alex," Pancardi said gleefully. "This is the way the heretics came on the way to their excommunication or execution."

They turned sharp left, walked across a courtyard with a fountain and on toward a smaller but no less imposing door. Passing through, they turned left again and then right, before crossing another open courtyard bathed in the trapped sun of spring and lined with olive trees set in massive terracotta pots. Their suited guide turned right and motioning them to continue straight ahead turned sharp left, departing as swiftly as he had arrived. Lounging on a bench was a balding man in shirt sleeves, around his feet were the tame Vatican doves which he fed daily out of habit. Blondell noted the slightly greasy appearance of a man who ate well and sweated too much. Hearing Pancardi approach the man stood up and extended his hand smiling broadly. Pancardi approached the man with both arms outstretched and the two embraced. Blondell noted the height of the man and his shoulder width and his former power and presence now diminished with the onset of age.

"Alex Blondell this is Roberto Calvetti," Pancardi's introduction was swift and business like.

"Buongiorno signor Calvetti."

The man wiped his palm in his trouser pocket and Blondell noticed the restrictive belt at his waist. Alex proffered his hand and it was taken in a rather moist grip, firm and plump with the feel of a warm skinned chicken breast.

"Sit down please," the man motioned to the bench in perfect English, sweeping away crumbs from the wooden slats with his handkerchief as he did so.

"Roberto how goes it with you?" Pancardi asked as he sat.

"I grow fat on the security of the Cardinals," Calvetti jovially replied.

"We are not as young as we once were eh Roberto, and as you grow plump I grow lame. Did we ever believe it would come to this? How is that fine wife of yours still making those wonderful meatballs?"

Calvetti patted his stomach in reply and hunched his shoulders with a wry grin.

"We are here on a fact finding exercise," Pancardi's tone

became serious, immediately Calvetti perked up in attentiveness. "Ah, I forget myself Alex, Roberto and I are old colleagues," continued Pancardi, turning his head and tilting it quizzically once more.

"I thought I recognised the name from the files of the Questura," Blondell remarked.

"Pay no attention Roberto he is English and from their Foreign Office, but he is very polite." Pancardi snorted, "And he knows all about us, you see he has researched us all."

"The Foreign Office, what have our Cardinals been up to now? Are we looking at a diplomatic immunity problem?" Calvetti laughed.

"No it is far better than that," Pancardi smiled as he spoke, "one of your old friends is up to his old tricks." Calvetti frowned wistfully. "Mr. Blondell has some very interesting news on Verechico," Pancardi nodded, "up to his old tricks no?"

Calvetti clenched his teeth and gave a slight but barely audible hiss.

"This young Englishman has some interesting news on Michelangelo and a link with Drecht."

Calvetti made silent eye contact with Blondell, gave him a look which penetrated to his soul, lingered and spoke of ancient knowledge. His dark eyes showed a deep intelligence.

Pancardi spoke directly to Alex, "Roberto was so close to this man, so close that we nearly had him. He above all others knows how good he is," he laughed, "but that was long ago eh Roberto?"

Pancardi urged Blondell to repeat all that he had heard during the conversation in the café. Interjecting with his own comments the story was relayed with very little comment from Calvetti. Blondell noted that the man was a superb listener.

He lit a cigarette and proffered one to Blondell, who refusing, continued to give a truncated account of the Romanov connection. Calvetti then quizzed him on that connection and Blondell quickly realized that editing information was pointless and wondered precisely what his man did at the Vatican that he could be absent from his work for so long. As Blondell concluded Pancardi smiled.

Pancardi then spoke excitedly to Calvetti, "Maybe he has made his mistake, maybe he is more greedy than we ever thought?"

Calvetti's reply was measured, thoughtful and cutting, "Carlo, Verechico is a ghost and I am an old fat man who takes away the troubles of His Holiness – I am a humble security man. I deal with diplomats and eat too well at dinners where nothing really happens."

Blondell noted the affectionate shortening of Pancardi's name and the reference to the Pope. Did this man's connections go that high? Was he more than a mere security guard? Was he -The security guard?

"Roberto you mistake our visit," Pancardi reassured, "we are here to learn from you, we want to know about Drecht, his habits, his likes, his weaknesses and his connections, teach us, help us catch him."

Calvetti drew deeply on his cigarette and smiled broadly, "Carlo we have been friends for a long time and both you and I know that Verechico is the brains, Drecht is merely the fixer and he...."

Pancardi interrupted, "You can help, you have connections here at the Vatican. Connections that we cannot know about but ones that only you can use. You can find out about the money laundering and where we go to next, is that not so?"

Calvetti shrugged.

"Give us some help as to the target, if it is here in Italy then someone must know. We can do the rest. For old times?"

Calvetti rose and silently shook Blondell's hand firmly.

"I will see what I can do Carlo," he said, "but I promise nothing. Now I must go to His Holiness to discuss security on the trip to Poland."

Calvetti embraced Pancardi and as if by magic the click healed guide simultaneously reappeared. Blondell caught a glimpse of red and black robes at a window high above as they were led away by another route. He thought Calvetti was among them in shirt sleeves but he could not be certain and all too soon they were in the tunnel and out once again into the thronging street.

Chapter 7

"Blimey is this the place Alice? It looks like a real hovel. Not much for a Professor of archaeology and a really famous one at that, and it's in bloody darkness too."

"Well this is the place, if Jimmy gave us the right address."

The man was tall, blonde and athletic and spoke with a pronounced English accent. The woman beside him was slim, verging on the slight, with a profusion of red hair which hung loosely from under a complimentary maroon cap. They parked a small inconspicuous white van, which advertised floral deliveries on its panelling, a hundred yards from the house and locking the doors walked back toward the suburban home set back from the road and shrouded by Rhododendron bushes. The garden was ill tended with a gravel path which crunched beneath their feet as they entered through a rotten wooden gate.

"Good Lord this really is neglected and such a nice building too!"

"Give it a rest Paul," the woman retorted.

"Oh fuck it!" the man quietly exclaimed as his foot made contact with something soft. "Dog-shit that's all I need and the place looks deserted to me," he said, as he wiped his heel on the overgrown grass verge.

The woman chuckled.

"It's no good you laughing missy these are Feragamo and what the hell are we doing here?"

"Shit up Paul, sorry shut up," she snorted playfully in reply. "We're here now so let's see what the chancer has to say."

Alice rang the doorbell – there was no sound.

"See no one here," said the man, "let's go."

The woman tried the knocker and was greeted with a cacophony of noise, principally the baying of dogs. Lights came on and a voice could be heard from the bowels of the building shouting at the dogs to be quiet and calling to the door that he was coming. The sound of chains and bolts being unfastened followed and then both were bathed in bright light which contrasted heavily with the growing dark of the outside. A small growling Jack Russell terrier appeared closely followed by a large Doberman both of whom seemed intensely interested in the woman. At the door stood a middle aged man in his forties, spectacles on the end of his nose and worn carpet slippers on his feet. He wore khaki corduroy trousers, a pale shirt and a cardigan, all of which would not seem out of place on a man twice his age. His hair was greying at the temples and too long for his years, all in all his appearance was tired and fashion-less.

"Don't worry about my boys," the man said, "they are only there to keep intruders at bay. See they like you," he continued, as he patted the Doberman and bent to pull the Jack Russell inside. "They both have an eye for the ladies."

"Professor Dalvin? I'm Alice, Alice Parsotti and this is my associate Paul West, we are advocates of Smithart and Verrison and represent their interests in Europe. May we come in?"

The Professor looked at the couple, and stepping out beyond them, quickly scanned the street and bushes for passers-by and parked cars. The street was empty and only a white delivery van was visible in the distance, satisfied he turned.

"Come in? Yes please do."

Standing behind them now he ushered them toward the back of the building where a room stood well lit.

"Just follow my boys they'll lead you. Don't worry they are quite harmless once you're in, but those other bastards don't know that thank God."

They entered a well lit and comfortable work space with high ceilings and a large oak table strewn with papers, maps and books. Around the walls were over laden book cases and near the fire one large dog basket in which the Doberman now sat surveying the interlopers. The Jack Russell leapt into a leather arm chair which had seen better days.

"Alfie's the boss you know," said the Professor, nodding at the smaller dog. "Frightens old Freddie there, terrorised him when he arrived as a pup."

The Professor laughed and motioned the couple to sit down in the large enveloping sofa which did not match any of the other furniture in the room. The room was old with the assorted junk of past generations strewn about it. There were photographs of a wedding but not the man sitting opposite them and there was the hand of a woman in the décor. Above the large fireplace hung an oil painting of a young woman, she was slim and her features resembled those of the Professor but her clothes were Victorian, dark and imposing. A French mantle clock ticked, its pendulum of gold encased in red tortoise shell and a rack of used pipes sat in an inviting pose. There had been money in this family, ancient money which had now faded like the expensive heavy curtains which draped the windows.

"I want ready cash you understand. That's what I told Mr. Folsen."

"Professor we are fully aware of the monetary arrangements what else would bring us out on such a frosty evening? However, we are here to satisfy the conditions for our senior partner Mr. Vaughan who wishes us to check the detail of the information and its origin before we release the cash," Alice smiled as she spoke.

"It's not that we are unsure you understand, but we must be clear as to the nature of your research and the authenticity of ...." The Englishman was interrupted as he spoke.

"Authenticity?" the Professor burst in, "I can assure you that my research is perfect."

"£500,000 is a large sum Professor," West continued, "and I am sure you are aware of the possible...."

Once again the Professor interrupted, "But what I have found out will be worth far more than that, far, far, more."

"Absolutely, but we need to hear the complete detail for verification. The devil's always in the detail, as my grandmother used to say," Alice remarked sweetly, sensing the growing tension between the men.

Dalvin shot a look at the portrait above the fireplace and both West and Parsotti placed his link to the painting.

"Your mother?" asked Alice.

He nodded, "She was striking in her youth, but first can I offer you both a drink? A coffee?" he asked.

"Thank you, both black if you please with sugar," she replied, smiling broadly.

The Professor left the room.

"Nice one Alice, why did you accept?"asked West, "this place is disgusting, it stinks of dogs and age, it needs a good clean, how can you drink here?"

"Come on Paulie-if Jimmy's right."

Her reply was curtailed by the re-entry of the Professor carrying three large mugs.

"That was fast Professor, thank you," she accepted the mug, smiling again.

"I always keep a pot on the warm stove, cowboy style; like in the old John Wayne movies it reminds me of my American heritage. Mother likes it too, sorry liked it too."

"When did your mother pass on Professor?" Alice asked sympathetically.

"Two years ago now, the strain of it all destroyed her you know," he became reflective, "the neighbours and the press and the foul things they said. It was all a pack of lies, a crock of shit, but it killed her nevertheless, drained her life away and for that I shall never forgive them."

"I am sorry for you it must have been dreadful," Alice increased the sympathetic tone.

"You know what they said, they said I was a paedophile, a molester of girls, a monster. That's what those idiots said." The Professor's tone grew bitter, "Those girls knew what they were doing. They weren't children were they? They were eighteen." Anger grew in his tone of voice, "Just because I made them suck cock and fuck a little they said I gave away degrees for pussy. Said this house was a house of sin, where young girls got their tutorials in the black arts. It wasn't like they didn't want to." He paused and his eyes became vacant, "So what if I arse fucked the odd one they knew what it was all about, and they liked it too. So what if one of them is a politician's daughter they're all corrupt in Italy anyway. She loved it too – a real wriggler." He smirked, "Daddy ought to proud of her she was a real user just like him. Got her degree and just because I had a few others, and jealousy kicked in, she turns to daddy for help to save her from the wicked nasty Professor and all the time she's got her mouth on my cock."

"The issue is simple." West attempted to turn the conversation, but Alice placed her hand on his forearm to stop him and smiled sweetly at the Professor.

"It must have been so unjust," she chirped.

"Unjust, I'll say. They fired me because of the scandal. Fired me after all I had done for them. Public opinion is fickle don't you think?"

"Awful," Alice agreed.

"Those sods at the University drag me and my mother over here from the States to sort out their mess on the Medici research and then because I fuck some students they drop me. Bastards, all bastards, liars and corrupt shits."

Alice could sense that the ranting was subsiding and wanted to draw the Professor's attention to the fact that his position of power had allowed him to act like a pariah. Students often fell for their teachers and it was his own weakness and stupidity which had caused his downfall, but she thought better of it and continued to smile over the rim of her coffee cup. Nobody forced you to come here from the States she thought. She noticed that he was like a small boy constantly blaming others for his mistakes-constantly raving. It was he who had destroyed his mother and it was he, who had fucked those girls, and why, because he wanted to. He enjoyed them too much.

"It must have been such a trial with all the publicity," she increased the sympathy in her voice.

"It was hell but I've got them now."

"Well let's hope so," she replied.

"They have kept me out of The Academia, but I have done some of my own research this time and I know it's perfect. I'll sell this house for a tidy sum and with that and your cash I'll retire and they can go fuck themselves. Cocksuckers !"

And you'll be chasing other young girls Alice thought as she smiled at him approvingly. You are so angry that you want us to succeed, you want revenge. You're not a truly bad man, just one driven by sex and for all your intelligence you can't even see it. You poor deluded old fool. With that she turned the conversation accomplishing what her colleague could not.

"So would you like to share your research with us now then, so we can do business together?" she quipped grinning broadly.

"It's all there on there table," he replied in triumph, "the whole thing."

They all rose and walked to the oak table; the dogs stirred but lost interest as the three bent over a large medieval map of Florence.

"There you see," said Dalvin.

"You'll have to talk us through it I'm afraid, it's a little too complex for me, I don't have your brains Professor," Alice said in a mildly flirtatious manner, while moving closer to the man.

Alice could smell the stale sweat in his hair and noticed the grubby collar of a shirt worn one too many times. How on earth he had such a lady-killer reputation she could not imagine, but for the kind of money they were likely to net she would force herself to pleasure him right now if she had to. She wiped the thought from her mind lest nausea take her.

Professor Dalvin began to explain, in minute detail, the routes of old sewers in Florence, his research into the Medici, and the records of payment made to night soil men, builders, masons, and others of the time who undertook building alterations. He produced court diaries regarding Cosimo's Marshall and yet failed to see any similarity between himself and this man; though oceans of time separated them they were driven by the same desires, the same obsessions. Alice noted that this one simple fact was lost on him. Like all intelligent men, she thought, he fails to see the obvious and looks for the more complex solution.

"This is very interesting I am sure Professor," West interrupted.

"But you want to see what else I have found out?"

"Exactly"

The Professor smiled and continued on about public works alterations following the flood destruction caused by the river Arno in 1963. Producing documents from the public records office in Florence he outlined the interlocking tunnels and overflows which had the complexity and spontaneity of a rabbit warren. Using the Medici Marshall's original map as a base he overlaid the 1963 public works plans, re-scaled onto acetate, over the medieval original.

"You see one route passes close or under the Banko Rolo," he said, jubilantly.

West's expectations rose when the two items clearly showed a navigable route through which he could get a team of men into the bank. His mind began to race.

"And finally," the Professor said in absolute triumph, "two small bits of seemingly irrelevant information."

West looked at the Professor, making clear eye contact as he did so. In an instant he saw the sparkling glint of revenge shining through the haze of the man's disjointed sexual aberrations. He liked what he saw, revenge meant honesty; Dalvin had much to gain by the robbery succeeding so the chance of the information being dud was less likely.

The Professor stopped suddenly, "Have you the money with you?" he casually asked. "I see neither of you has a bag."

"I'm sorry Professor," replied West, "but business is not done that way anymore, we're not gangsters and this isn't the movies, this is for real. I have here in my pocket the numbered bank account for a Swiss bank. If you call this bank and give a security code £500,000 will immediately be deposited into any account of your choosing, anywhere in the world. I have here the code required for the credit Swiss transfer; the whole transaction will take less than five minutes. So please continue."

"The first piece of information," the Professor continued, "is this." He made eye contact with Alice who smiled reassuringly. "A record of an arrest under Medici law; the arrest of a man who was so drunk in a tavern that he spent two days in the stocks in Piazza Signoria where he was urinated upon and pelted with rotten fruit and vegetables, as was the custom at the time. In his record of arrest it was noted that he bragged about getting money for not doing a job. That he was violent and offensive to church law, and that he insulted Cosimo's Marshall, accusing him of being a pervert. I believe that this, job, was the sealing of a night soil chamber which remains without back fill to this day." He pointed to the exact location on the map.

"Can you be certain?" West interrogated.

"As certain as any man can be with ancient research." The Professor continued, "The second is from when I was arrested on those ridiculous charges."

Alice sensed that he might begin to rant once more and moved herself closer to his side, slipping her arm inside his provocatively at the elbow.

"You're far too intelligent for them though aren't you Professor," she seductively giggled, "please continue I am excited to reach the finale."

She smiled and the Professor visibly rose in stature. So easy, she thought, so damn easy. The smell of his hair stung her nose but she played her part to perfection. She had been manipulating men since she had been fourteen and knew that men wanted her, it had always been so easy. Her craft came from upbringing; her mother had died when she was an infant and she had been shipped off to live with grandmamma. After her death, she went to live with a rather cold, stern, uncle and his superbly manipulative second and far younger wife. Alice learned her craft there and observed that hints and veiled sexual promise achieved far more than honesty.

"Yes – where was I?" the Professor continued.

"The second piece of information?" she almost pouted her reply at him.

Paul West watched her, admired her. There was no room for jealousy right now, she was working.

"Well after I was arrested and had to appear in Court I was transported in a police van with another man Miosh Calvini. As we passed the Banko Rolo he blurted out that the walls of the vault were as thin as paper. He told me that they hadn't even reinforced the vault because it was so far below ground and that he had plastered it. He was a drunk." The Professor walked to the window, "He re-plastered this for me you know, poor deluded man. Rather ironic don't you think? Nobody ever believed him but me. Everyone thought he was mad and that he would drink himself to death and then one night he did. Still the best thing for him really; I hoped that case of Scotch would help him."

"You mean you…." Alice interjected.

"Killed him? No, he did that to himself. I merely gave him the means."

Alice wondered at this man who was a strange mixture of intelligence and sociopathic anomalies. Perhaps he was harder to read than she at first thought. What if the tunnel were back-filled? What if the research were a myth designed to con them out of the half million? If it was she'd have got her revenge before they started anyway, but she wanted to get her hands on some real cash not just a paltry half million.

The Professor looked at them both, "Do we have deal?" he asked.

"I've just the one thing to say Professor," replied Paul West.

"A question?"

"No more of a statement of fact."

He looked directly into the Professor's eyes and spoke calmly, "If you have deceived me and this is all a hoax I will hunt you down and kill you."

"Mr. West I wouldn't expect otherwise. May I remind you however, that you did say you were not gangsters," he replied with a laugh; a nervous laugh which nonetheless exuded confidence.

Alice looked at West and nodded. West produced the necessary bank details and passed them to Professor Dalvin, who promptly excused himself to leave the room.

Alice looked at the detailed map on the table, while West gripped the edges of it with both hands-pondering.

"It's going to have to be a good team," he said.

"Jimmy thought so too," replied Alice, "any ideas who?"

"The vault has to be scoped yet and then we decide."

"I suppose," she confirmed, "we'll need a mock up for a dry run. No it's not a poor joke, before you start."

"Yep," he replied seriously, "and on this one there is no we, you are not in the water tunnel, it's too risky and besides if it all goes tits up I want you to kill him, slowly. I want you to bleed him real quiet where no one can hear him scream. Can you do that?"

"You know I can; I'll cut it and his balls off and cook and feed them to him if this is a con, but I think somehow he's on the level. It's his hatred that drives him on. He wants revenge so bad he can taste it and he knows who and what he's dealing with, so I actually trust him for some strange reason."

"So do I love, so do I. Let's hope both our judgements aren't wrong, eh?" West replied.

Professor Dalvin re-entered the room, "That's extremely reassuring Miss Parsotti. I can assure you, however, that I have no intention of eating my own testicles and penis when the world is full of willing young ladies only too eager to do so," he said laughing. "More coffee or something harder?"

Ten minutes later they were in the florist van waiting for the blower to defrost the windscreen, complete with the plans of the sewers and copies of diaries and manuscripts.

"You know he'll be gone from here as soon as he can be," said West.

"I hope so," replied Alice, "harder to be traced if he is."

"Let's move like we have a purpose then. You better let the man know."

Alice sent a simple text from her cell phone it read: – *Trans. complete satisfact. Item acquired. A*

Chapter 8

James Folsen-Drecht was leaning on the parapet of the Ponte Vecchio casually flicking ash from his Cuban cigar into the Arno below and idly watching the flow of the river. The neon signs for Buon Natale were everywhere and the sky was heavy with snow clouds. He was humming bars of Rudolph the red-nosed reindeer to himself as excited children passed on their way home from school. Turning he fixed his grey eyes on the expansive windows of the Banko Rolo building beyond the Palazzo Pitti. It was bedecked in festive garlands and gaudy lights ready for the customary office parties. It was the 18th of December.

"Ah, there you are Jimmy," said Paul West as he approached. The men embraced.

"Have you taken care Paul?" Drecht asked.

"Yes."

"The transfer too?"

"Of course."

"Good, good." He puffed on the cigar and grinned as he spoke.

"That Professor gave us all we need for the logistics of entry, but what I need now are details of the inside. It needs to be scoped. I need measurements, fine detail and photographs."

"That my young Englishman has already been done. We are not idle for our percentage," he chuckled as he spoke.

"Percentage or no percentage it's me in there not you and I don't want to get caught with my dick in my hands now do I?"

"Paul, Paul, Paul, don't be so crude, you trust me don't you?"

West caught Drecht's eye and smiled a toothy grin, "Nope," he replied. "Don't trust anybody, especially you Jimmy, that's why I never get caught. I can't afford fuck ups and simply walk away like you can."

Drecht looked at the flow of the river below. Without looking at West he sighed, "Paul you always select your team and I don't even need to know when it will happen I just want it done." Drecht handed West a large brown envelope. "Happy Christmas," he said, "it's all in there including photographs. Enjoy your holiday and I'll see you in Amsterdam when this is over. Good luck."

"Luck has nothing to do with it," West quipped, "it's all in the planning."

Paul West looked at the Banko Rolo building ahead of him and began to walk toward it, then abruptly he turned left down Lungarno Torrigianni and walked along the river bank. He did not open the envelope nor draw attention to himself. He flipped his coat collar against the cold and listened intently for footsteps beyond and behind him. At the corner of Costa di San Giorgio he turned and walking behind the Boboli gardens stopped at Via di Belvedere. Casually he looked to see if he was being followed, but sensed he was alone. He continued to wait, surveying the view of the city like a tourist. His actions were calm, methodical, almost languid; he exuded confidence and yet possessed the patience of a waiting predator. Then with what seemed a quick and violent contrast he made a strike at his mobile cell phone. This accomplished he once again resumed his patient stance with only his eyes constantly scanning the parked cars and bushes.

A few moments later a dark blue Mercedes appeared at the corner and waited with the engine running. West watched the vehicle and occupant, a large powerful dark-haired man – he sported a beard which was full.

Time passed.

Satisfied, West moved with a quick, sudden step. He walked to the car, and once inside, the vehicle moved up the hill and vanished into the dusk.

"Nice to see you Paul," the driver said after a mile or two.

"I thought Alice was coming," West replied.

"Well apparently she had an emergency, gone to Pisa to get the Yank or something. Flight problems or some such. Though why you want to use that gob-shite I'll never know."

"Because he's so damn good Jock, that's why. How are you anyway, how is the Scottish weather – still raining?"

The man at the wheel shrugged, "You know me Paul I love the islands and my boats. Why would I want to live anywhere else?"

"And that my dear boy is why you'll get caught one day, sentimentality, too many ties. Never have anything you can't leave in an instant that's my motto."

"And Alice?"

"Her too."

The two men looked at each other for a few seconds, there was mutual respect between them and yet each was wary of the other.

"So why did I bring you over from your lovely fishing village and that lovely raven haired beauty of yours? You are still with her aren't you?" asked West.

The driver nodded.

"How many years younger than you is she Johno?"

"Twenty," the Scotsman laughed.

"Twenty, well to each their own that's what I say," he paused, "need your expertise on this one Johno, it's a water job."

"Boats?" was the enquiring reply.

"No, worse, tunnels. Submerged tunnels."

"And the take?"

"Diamonds and safe deposit boxes."

"Pounds?"

"Dollars, if we're lucky. I need you to work on breathing gear, the exit method, and a way to get us out fast – logistics."

"And if the Yank is in on it there has to be explosives right?"

"Right."

"Under water?"

"No that comes after, once we get there."

The Scotsman checked the rear view mirror, "The score?" he asked.

"Big enough for you never to leave those lovely islands again. You can spend the rest of your days making babies and eating home made jam. Get that young beauty to fuck you into senility,"

West laughed. "Take the next left and stop the car over there," he pointed to a lay-by.

The Scotsman turned off the engine and the two men sat motionless. There was no need to speak each knew what the other was doing. The Driver scanned the rear view mirror while West scanned the parked cars. There were no vans and the vehicles he could see were unoccupied. He scanned windows for movement – there was none.

"Clear," said West.

"Clear," replied the Scotsman, restarting the engine for the last three hundred yards of their journey.

As the Mercedes approached, the metal security gates swung open electronically.

They were being watched from within, though they were oblivious to the fact. The car hummed as it edged up the secluded driveway and on toward a modest rented property which blended quietly into the trees which surrounded it. There were no lights showing and the building looked empty, dark and forlorn. It was in need of repair and had clearly seen better days before its reincarnation as a holiday home. In front of the house stood a small Volkswagen and tucked neatly under the branches of an overhanging tree stood a motorcycle covered in polythene. The two men parked and walked quickly to the rear of the building.

"This way," said Alice Parsotti, as she approached from the darkness of the trees.

"The others are here then?" questioned West, in reply.

"Inside, in the dining room straight down the hall."

The Scotsman had not seen the woman half-shrouded in the darkness of the trees but he caught the glimpse of a hand gun as she passed ahead of him. He noticed her perfume which was sweet and musky; despite this he knew she would have a far more steely soul than her perfume promised.

"Good evening gentlemen," said West, as he entered the dining room.

Two occupants stood and smiled, placing their bottles of beer on the floor.

"I think we should start with introductions don't you?" he continued. West turned to the Scotsman, "Let me introduce John McDermott. John this is Duane Rightman. I think you know each other and this is Klaus Meine. Oh and this is Alice Par...."

Parsotti interrupted, "Alice, just Alice will do for little old me. Can I get anyone some drinks, more beer?"

She left the room and closed the door behind her as she went.

"So what do we go ask Alice when we're ten feet tall?" asked Rightman in a heavy American drawl.

"Fuck me he's started!" McDermott said, under his breath.

"Nice to see you again too Jocko," returned Rightman.

Alice returned with more bottled beers – the room broke into gentle conversation. It was obvious to Meine that the others all knew each other while he had been recruited for a specific task. There seemed to be badinage around past achievements and all three men exuded confidence. Alice, he surmised, was not known to any of them except West. Meine wondered if they were business partners or lovers, his observations of the couple were inconclusive.

"Gentlemen," said West, "I have brought you here because you are the best in your field and I have a target which I am sure none of you would like to pass up. You have, none of you, any criminal record. Like myself you are invisible." He paused looking at the others, "I want to tell you a little story about a Professor and some research. About how this academic came across, by sheer chance, a series of tunnels which lead beneath one of the richest and reputedly most impregnable safe deposit banks in the world. We are going to go through those tunnels and empty the vault."

Duane Rightman could not resist a quip, "Like Alice," he blurted looking at the woman, "down a fucking rabbit hole man, this is real Wonderland stuff." He laughed and then began singing, "One pill makes you smaller and one pill makes you taller, and go ask Alice."

Paul West then placed the maps and research materials on the table, inviting the others to look them over. Finally he produced the brown envelope which Drecht had provided earlier that afternoon.

"So you see gentlemen," he said, "it's all rather simple – any questions?"

Chapter 9

When the door knocker boomed and roused the dogs into a frenzy of barking Professor Dalvin's blood froze, "Fucking journalists, fucking pests," he mumbled, as he tried to block the noise from his ears. Now he had the for sale sign prominently displayed at the foot of his drive he thought they might return for one last wheedle before he vanished into obscurity.

"Won't they ever give up?" he spat, as he rose from his chair.

The knocking continued. The barking turned into a whine of familiarity – the dogs knew the caller.

"Professor Dalvin?"

A voice was coming through the letter box– a voice he recollected, but one without a remembered face. A girl's voice, sweet, innocent and full of promise. At the door stood Alice Parsotti.

"Hello Professor," she said, provocatively.

"Err hello again," was his hesitant reply.

"Can I come in? I'd like to continue our chat." Alice lingered on the word chat.

"Of course, um are you alone?" The Professor habitually stepped beyond her at the threshold and surveyed the street, there was no movement and satisfied he gave a broad smile to his visitor.

"You know I'm alone and anyway I thought it best if we were, private," Alice replied, smiling coquettishly.

"I was just about to open some wine, you caught me at just the right moment," he lied.

The dogs began sniffing her legs waiting for petted recognition. She stroked their faces and pouted at them and Dalvin noted that she liked dogs and was fearless of them.

"My boys seem to like you," he said, "they can smell excitement in your moisture, come on through and make yourself at home," the Professor continued.

Alice Parsotti walked ahead of the Professor at a pace which allowed her figure to be fully framed in the light of the oncoming doorway. She wore a small pleated skirt above knee high black leather boots, with heels that clicked confidence on the parquet flooring. Halting to frame herself in the doorway she turned to allow the Professor a full view of her breasts encased in a tight low-cut sweater. Dalvin noticed she wore no brassiere and this accentuated her nipples which were pertly erect. A profusion of auburn hair hung tousled over her shoulders and her face glowed with the freshness of youth. Dalvin's mind began to fantasise. As she sat down the Professor could not help but notice the merest glimpse of stocking top and the hint of a suspender belt above a flash of enticing lace.

"Let me get the wine," he said.

Dalvin disappeared into the kitchen as he had done when providing coffee, only this time he took far longer. The noise of a cork popping could be heard accompanied by the clink of crystal glasses being placed on a tray. A tap ran and the door to a refrigerator opened and closed.

He returned to see Alice on the couch with the larger dog at her feet and the Terrier lounging with his head in her lap. She was casually stroking his back and cooing and pouting gently into his ear – he had been seduced.

"Goodness me," said Dalvin, "my boys do like you. They don't usually take to people so quickly," he laughed, "they're a bit like me, very open to a gentle touch and soft words."

"Dogs and other beasts always like me Professor – it's sort of instinctual don't you think?"

"I don't know about that, but some women do seem to bring out the beast, sorry Freudian slip, best, in wild things."

Alice smiled at him and leant her head to one side her eyes moist in the soft glow of the dimming lights, "Are you flirting with me Professor?" she asked.

He laughed nervously and showed boyish teeth, "You don't mind me dimming the light do you?" he asked. "It's just that poring over books and papers makes my old peepers a little fragile and its nice to rest them by looking at beautiful things in softer tones."

Alice felt slightly sick as she smiled at his lame chat-up approaches; they might impress young sixteen year olds but to her they were tired, boorish and obviously the product of aberration.

Carelessly scattering his papers Dalvin placed the tray over those that remained and poured two glasses of champagne, passing one to Alice.

"Champagne Professor?"

"Why not – it's time for me to live the high life. I'm going into retirement on all that money you arranged. Going to write and eat and…," he was going to say fuck, but thought better of it and said, "enjoy the finer things."

"Oh Professor there's no need to be so obtuse with me. I expect you'll be fucking quite a few young ladies too won't you?" Alice laughed. "I mean it's not like you don't enjoy the tight young things is it?"

Dalvin spluttered his reaction to her bravado.

"That doesn't disturb me you know," she continued, "after all we are grown-ups now aren't we? We all like something to play with." She caught and held his eyes with hers, "You like small soft moist things, while I like," she paused, "I like big, hard things."

She saw small beads of sweat appear at his temple and sensed a growing unease her presence was having as he shifted in his armchair opposite her.

"Champagne makes the girls dance," she giggled, "and squiffy girls then drop their pants, isn't that the old adage? You are a very naughty man aren't you?"

Alice took a large gulp of champagne and smiled at the repugnant man before her. Moving her hips she allowed her thighs to part slightly so he could appreciate the white lace of her thong and the soft promise beneath before readjusting. She knew how easy it would be to gain entry to his home with the promise of entry into her and she manipulated him as easily as a baker kneads bread.

"Do you mind if I take my boots off Professor and make

myself more comfortable?" she continued, standing once again to give him full view of her tight thighs and flat stomach.

He imagined the gap at the top of her legs and wondered if she were moist with anticipation.

Sitting once again she tucked her heals onto the couch and gently persuaded the dog to the floor.

"Why don't you come and sit here?" she asked, patting the seat beside her. "We can be more friendly if you like."

Dalvin required no second invitation.

"I've always liked older men," she continued, "men with a brain, powerful men and you like me don't you Professor?"

"I find you stunning Alice, absolutely stunning. But why are you here?" he replied lamely.

"I think we both know the answer to that don't you? If not, you might have guessed by now surely? You must have noticed I was drawn to you," she replied.

Her hand casually stroked his upper thigh as she tried to ignore his odour of stale excitement. His hand fell to her thigh and she smiled as it travelled beyond the suspender belt and on toward her lace thong.

"You like that don't you, would you like to be inside me?" she didn't wait for an answer, "I think I would."

Dalvin's agitation became apparent as his fingers found the edge of her lace panties and fought to enter her now moist femininity.

She grasped his wrist, "Not here though, with the dogs," she chuckled, "I prefer a bed with plenty of room to play, don't you?"

Dalvin pushed Alice before him up the stairs closing both dogs inside his sitting room so they would not be disturbed. He watched the roll of her hips as she languidly mounted each step before him, his fingers toying with her orifices which he could easily access as she discarded both her skirt and thong. Letting the knickers fall to her ankles she casually stepped out of them in a series of fluid movements. He could smell the scent of her sexual arousal mingling with the perfume she wore, and as he touched her she responded with a coquettish giggle which spoke of animal promise.

Laying herself naked on his bed, he watched her while he

hurriedly undressed. She rolled provocatively from her back to her stomach and back again, spreading her legs and arching her back so he had full view of her womanhood. Her hand strayed to her crotch as he joined her on the bed.

"I shaved for you," she said, moving his hand to her sex, "see."

His hand found her moist mound of Venus and revelled in the depilatory nakedness which she knew would arouse him. His fingers were bathed in her warm moist fluid as they entered her and she gave a sharp gasp. She responded bending her mouth toward his arousal flicking her tongue to tease him mercilessly.

Disengaging she asked, "Shall we play a game Professor? Do you like games?"

"What sort of game?"

"Oh a really good one – I'm sure you'll love this one. Have you got a belt?"

Dalvin's last waking memory was a mixture of ecstasy, fear, and intense sexual pleasure as Alice Parsotti tightened the belt around the bound Professor's throat, while he simultaneously entered her deeply as she sat astride him. His lungs were gasping for air as his erection sought to penetrate the depths of her femininity and then everything went black.

When he woke Alice Parsotti was fully clothed sitting on a chair observing him. She was smoking a cigarette being most mindful to get newly applied pink lip-stick onto the butt end. Having extinguished one after a few centimetres, she lit a second, a third and then a fourth. The air in the room was thick with tobacco smoke as they burned collectively in the ashtray. Dalvin struggled to become conscious through the haze.

In her surgically gloved hand she held a champagne glass and pouted pink lip-stick onto the rim. Dalvin could not move, his hands and feet were securely bound and the leather belt which had caused him to pass out was now loose around his neck. His groin was moist and tacky, soaked in his own drying semen.

"Ah you're awake then you foul little man," said Alice.

Dalvin could not speak – his mind swan. Alice patted his lower stomach.

"Did we have a good time did we?" she mocked. "Did we come? Don't worry Professor you did, I made sure of that, but not in me I'm afraid, just all over yourself. Quite a lot too, you seem to be very healthy and have no prostate problems."

She held his left testicle between her finger and thumb and squeezed lightly. Dalvin began to wince and then attempted to scream only to find her white lace thong being forced into his mouth to muffle his madness.

"Does that hurt?" she mocked, "oh, dear, just nod if it does. It's your turn to bite the pillow now isn't it Dalvin? You really are a fucking piece of slime. And for the record, you stink of stale sweat and your cock is small, no wonder you like impressing young girls and then breaking them in. I wouldn't sleep with you if you were the last man on earth and mankind depended upon it."

Dalvin's eyes grew wide at the insults – he was genuinely frightened.

"I'm going to ask you for your bank account number, and the name and location of that bank Professor and you will tell me won't you?"

She smiled and squeezed harder – his legs thrashed aimlessly in pure agony.

"Then you will give me your personal identity code, all six digits. You see I'm not here to fuck you, just rob you, and it can be easy or it can be painful. Which will it be?"

Dalvin shook his head. His mind struggling to understand the things being said.

"Tut tut Professor just think of it as a learning curve. Like those young students learning from you. They didn't mind the pain of being fucked did they? They enjoyed you forcing your meat into them, didn't they?"

Dalvin nodded frantically.

"Now, I'm going to fuck you over in much the same way."

Alice grasped both testicles and squeezed hard. Dalvin writhed and his mouth sought to scream but nausea overtook him.

"Feeling sick? Oh dear now that's a shame, wouldn't want you to choke on your own vomit just because you have my panties in your mouth would we." She slapped his face to keep him awake and then inflicted more humiliation upon him as she probed his anus with her fingernail.

Dalvin nodded and then shook his head. He couldn't understand. He didn't deserve to be treated like this. He tried to wriggle free but could not.

"Oh, you're confused, bless. Shall we start again? Your Bank account location, our money, your security number. See that's all I want."

Dalvin shook his head.

"Stubborn aren't we, how about if I cut these out?" Alice Parsotti ran her fingernail between his testes. "A small cut here," she smiled, "you'll hardly feel a thing. Then I just pull them out slow and easy and snip snip they're gone. Perhaps your two boys would like one treat each. We have to be fair now don't we?"

Dalvin's eyes lit up in blind panic as he again struggled against his bonds. He could not move and the red-headed witch was going to castrate him, take away his one pleasure.

"Or," she was toying with his testicles as she spoke, "you can give me the number; it's all rather simple really. So I'll say a number from one to ten and when I say the right one you nod. When I have all six numbers I leave and you can keep these, understand." She squeezed his testicles once again and his nausea overrode his fear.

He nodded.

"One; two; three....." she began.

He nodded rapidly.

"Is it three then? Good boy. You see you're learning very quickly. Looks like you're going to keep your balls Professor."

He nodded and then shook his head.

She started again, "Not so hasty now, one; two."

Chapter 10

The journalists who hounded Dalvin for his sexual proclivity were more respectful in death than in life and left out much of the lurid detail.

Richard George Dalvin renowned meritorious Professor dies in bizarre accident.

Once known as the leading expert on the Medici family and famous for his research into the medieval library of Florence. Professor Richard Dalvin was removed from his post at the University of Florence following a notorious sex scandal involving the daughter of right wing Austrian politician Gerhardt Teupner. It was Teupner who claimed that his daughter and other female students had been groomed by the Professor to become willing victims in bizarre satanic sex acts.

The court case ended in acquittal but the allegations cost the Professor dear, he claiming they had contributed to the premature death of his heart–broken mother.

Professor Dalvin had constantly proclaimed his innocence and vowed to leave Italy for good. He was planning to return to the United States .The last book in his series on the Medici remains unfinished, "Cosimo's Sewers-A study of renaissance waste".

It is believed Professor Dalvin died accidentally during an asphyxiation ritual with a prostitute in a bizarre sexual game which went tragically wrong.

He and his two pet dogs were found dead at his home on the outskirts of Florence; it is believed he had been dead for some weeks before being discovered by a local estate agent.

The closed casket funeral takes place on Friday 23rd March at San Miniato Al Monte with an internment in the adjacent cemetery thereafter.

Chapter 11

When the phone on the bedside table rang Pancardi looked at his watch, it was 8.30am and his head swam. He coughed and picking up the receiver answered brusquely, "Prego?"

"Carlo it's Robe."

Pancardi came awake instantly, disregarding the savage headache and the arthritic ache in his limbs, he sneezed and reached for tissues to clear the phlegm from his nostrils; his breath came in gasps and snorts.

"You sound terrible my friend, can you talk?" Calvetti enquired.

"I have the flu but I will be fine. Been in bed for four days, it's one of those sweating ones which lays you low," Pancardi replied, "but I am on the mend."

"I am sorry to hear that my old friend but something interesting has come up and I thought you might like to know. Can you come to the Vatican or shall I come to you?"

"To be honest Roberto I think I should try to get to you, I could do with some fresh air to clear my lungs," he sneezed loudly. "Besides Mostro needs some exercise, the little girl from the café, Lorena, she could do with a break too. She loves him but it is not easy with her shifts and she is young."

"Prego, but I think it best if I come over to you my friend, you sound terrible. I can take the monster for a walk, it will keep my fat down. Maria, she always moans that I grow fat for the Cardinals, but I say I grow fat on the Cardinals," he laughed. "Old is a terrible thing my friend, how is the leg without the walking?"

"Stiff."

Pancardi had no further will to resist and in truth he was thankful not to have to face the human traffic of Rome, despite his earlier suggestion of fresh air Mostro could wait he thought, and Roberto could manage one walk. He looked at his dog that lay so patiently at the foot of the bed and wondered at his unflinching loyalty, to just lay there in a darkened room day after day.

"I'll be with you in a couple of hours Carlo," the voice said down the phone. "I have some phone calls to make. Take a hot bath and some lemon and honey my friend; I think you will find this news interesting."

Pancardi knew that Calvetti seldom used the word interesting unless he had something to impart of which he was certain. Calvetti was a man who kept his own council until he could confound or amaze and it was a quality which Pancardi secretly admired; it cut through niceties and made him a trusty friend and in turn a terrible adversary.

Pancardi rose gingerly from his bed, which was strewn with tissues and empty ibuprofen packets; half empty glasses of fruit juice and water clustered on the bedside cabinets. He kicked over the dog's bowl of water he had made Lorena place near the bed and cursed his own forgetfulness. Lorena had come to find him when he had not appeared for his routine breakfast one morning. She was a comely girl, broad hipped, pretty and sensual and far too young for him. She loved Mostro and pampered him with all sorts of scraps at the café, but she was often tired and walking his dog was a chore even for her.

The flotsam and jetsam of flu clung to him and the smell of his stale perspiration filled the room. He needed a shower and was glad that Calvetti was not going to get there immediately. He rubbed his hand across his chin and felt the stubble. How Lorena could stand that he simply could not comprehend. Why would a young girl in her twenties want a broken down cripple such as he was? Pain, he thought, women are drawn to men in pain; he had seen it so many times in his career and Lorena's need was to be needed – to be useful rather than ornament. He parted the curtains, and opening the windows wide, looked out into the chill morning. The bright light stung his eyes. It was at times like these that he wished for a wife, not just any wife, but more and more for Margarite. As age crept up on him he realised that the mistakes of his youth would always haunt his dreams. In the half-world of his recent flu induced delirium he had spoken to her, she had been there standing at the end of the bed smiling. When she had smiled and laughed he too had been young again. He could smell the freshness in her hair and taste the soft sweetness of her kiss upon his lips. He recalled the colour of her red hair as it danced upon her shoulders when she walked; and he could see the line of her naked hips as she mounted the stairs before him and he knew, in that instant, that he had loved her – she had been his one.

He sat on the edge of his bed and his mind became wracked with remorse. His head swam with muddled recollections of their passion and intensity together. Mostro nosed his side requesting a stroke in return for his sickness vigil – and got it. Her mother had opposed the union thinking Margarite could do better than a mere policeman, she had been destined for greater things. Margarite was part of the Alsetti family, descendants of Italian aristocracy, and Pancardi well, he was nothing more than a lower order irritation. Often his thoughts strayed to what if. What if they had married, what if they had produced a child, what if, he Pancardi, had been accepted by the mother. He coughed, rasping his lungs to clear the detritus of flu which clung like a canker to an oak. But her mother had seen to it by placing the highest mountains in his path, and slowly furrow by furrow the seeds of destruction had been successfully sown. Margarite had been whisked away from him, seduced by the opulence of opportunity and he had been too proud to chase her. His pride had forced him inward and he had withdrawn, precisely when he should have declared his love more fully, the result was a simple death on a roadside. The oh so fashionable young men and their oh so fast cars, which Margarite's mother favoured, had stolen her from both of them and it had been a very bitter pill to swallow; one which had an aftertaste that lingered daily on the palate of Pancardi.

In the shower he felt his body revive. His senses were invigorated by the warm mist which swept a clearing vapour into his lungs. Pancardi remembered the funeral and how his eyes had swelled and how his tears had been masked by the drizzle as they lowered the casket. Even then Margarite's mother had shown no glimmer of warmth or regret and in fact her bitterness toward him had deepened; shunning his condolences she allowed him only marginal attendance at the internment. He had kept his distance for Margarite's sake, even though she was dead, and reserved his tears for the solitary car which he drove from the cemetery. Many times, over many years, he had returned to leave flowers on the dates they, as lovers, knew and treasured, and he was always pleased that he avoided meeting others at the site. He noted with pleasure the flowers which seemed to be freshly placed for her birthday, even after her witch of a mother had died herself. Water ran down his spine and his mind began to clear. He had loved and been loved and was thankful. Lorena did not deserve to be his nursemaid and waste her youth on him and he would tell her so. Go find a young man to love, he would say, a man to make you laugh at life and swell your belly. A man who will drag you under him every time you try to leave his bed. He could feel his melancholy dispersing like a morning mist as he forced his reason to thank providence for his brief, dreamy, kind delight.

He spat out water as the phone rang a second time. He ignored it and the answer-phone kicked in.

"Inspector? It's Alex Blondell, pick–up if you are there."

Pancardi stepped from the shower and dripped his way to the lobby rapidly towelling down as he went.

"Pancardi!" he barked hoarsely into the receiver.

"It seems that we are too late Inspector. Last night in Florence the Banko Rolo building," Blondell hesitated waiting for a reply.

Pancardi was silent busily towelling himself – he switched to loudspeaker.

"Banko Rolo's safe deposit boxes," Blondell continued, "they were systematically stripped and only the precious stones taken. It would appear that some of the Romanov jewels were in the vault and they must have been the target. I am on my way over to..." The line crackled and then went dead.

Pancardi replaced the receiver and returned to the bathroom to carefully hang the towels over the radiator. The young English man was on the way over to where Florence or to him? He cursed his luck.

He cleaned his teeth – his mouth felt like the bottom of a bird cage. He examined his face in the over-sink mirror as he shaved; the sound of the cut-throat razor rasping as it cut through the three day growth of grey hair on his cheeks. His eyes were blood-shot and dark blue bags had appeared below them. I'm getting too old for this he thought when he nicked his chin. He reached for a styptic pencil to staunch the bleeding and winced at the intense stinging sensation.

When the doorbell rang Pancardi answered fully dressed in a suit but without a tie.

"Inspector, good morning." Blondell stepped into the lobby without further niceties. "I know I have not been in contact for some days," he said, "but I have been pursuing many lines of enquiry, and to be honest with very little success."

Pancardi snorted into a tissue.

"As I said on the phone," Blondell launched, "the Banko Rolo has been hit and it would seem that the intelligence of the thieves is better than our own. It would seem that the vault contained the substantive part of those jewels and ornaments which formed the Russian crown jewels and some of the lost Faberge Eggs."

Pancardi sneezed.

"Bless you!" exclaimed Blondell.

"Continue," mumbled Pancardi, into a handful of tissue.

"It was a very precise operation. They entered through a maze of tunnels from the old sewers. They could have got into those via a hundred different places; then they used highly volatile acid, high density explosives and then vanished back into the sewers complete with their booty. Military precision, fast effective and seamless."

Pancardi blew his nose loudly.

"They totally disregarded stocks, bonds, cash, and lesser quality items. They even took the time to remove stones from settings. It was first class – they did not hurry; they held their nerve and took a small fortune in the process."

"Come through to the kitchen and I will make us both a coffee. You could do with some. You look as if you've been travelling through the night; and let me guess you want me to go to Florence with you?" Pancardi did not wait for a reply but continued, "Well this I can do," he said, "but first my friend

Calvetti wishes to see me so we wait for him first do we not?"

"I think the sooner we get there the better Inspector."

"Why so impatient to be gone? Do you hate my coffee that much?"

"Inspector I would like to get to Florence as quickly as possible so that we can investigate the scene of the crime."

"And what good would that do? You said they were very good. I am sure the locals will find all they can and we can follow on after that can we not?"

"Yes, yes, I agree but the sooner we get on to them the better – don't you think?"

"Alex that is extremely untrusting of you – don't you think? They will be long gone. I expect they are not even in Italy anymore and we may be like the tortoise or the hare. You be the hare if you choose," he paused quizzically, "I however, shall be the tortoise – the slow lumbering tortoise, and I shall win the race. So tell me what you know before we go on your wild goose chase."

Blondell then began his narrative on the many enquiries he had undertaken since they last met. It was Calvetti who had guided him and given him pointers, but the adversaries were, as Pancardi had predicted, slippery. Pancardi listened intently only stopping to clear his throat and blow his nose. He drank deeply from his supply of coffee, replenishing his cup several times while Blondell sipped insipidly. Time passed and when the door bell rang and Mostro barked, Pancardi excused himself from the room to return swiftly with Roberto Calvetti at his heel.

"Come Robe and listen to my friend he has some interesting news on a robbery in Florence. The game is afoot is it not Alex? Continue if you please."

The conversation which followed was methodical as Pancardi acquired the names of the officers investigating in Florence and the precise involvement of both the Italian Government and the British Foreign Office. He listened carefully to the details which Blondell imparted on the method, all the while sifting the facts and interjecting where detail was scant.

"They were very professional then," was the only evaluative remark he made.

He turned to Calvetti who had helped himself to coffee and

had remained patiently silent like a waiting predator before a strike. He took a deep draught of coffee.

"I too have been investigating," he chuckled, catching Pancardi's eye, before continuing. "It would seem that one of my Cardinals, who is extremely interested in archaeology, has some interesting thoughts on a bizarre suicide which came to his ears from a priest in Sienna. I think he too should have been Questura and not a Holy Father of the cloth."

Pancardi sneezed.

"This Cardinal," continued Calvetti, "who I will not name, passed to me a newspaper clipping, an obituary of a Professore Dalvin. He was an American who came to teach and research at the Academia in Florence. He was disgraced and dismissed from his post for having relations," he stressed the word relations and laughed, "with his studente. He slept with many it would seem, but he chose badly and one was the daughter of an Austrian politician – Gerhardt Teupner. When the news broke this politician immediately accused Dalvin of being a pariah, a paedophile."

"How old were these girls?" asked Blondell.

"Oh they were eighteen or over – young women. Dalvin claimed that he had been seduced and that he had not authenticated degrees for sex as Teupner's daughter claimed. The politician pressured the authorities, had him dismissed and also forced a prosecution. Teupner looked after his daughter's reputation rather than her virginity."

"So the man takes his life?" Pancardi shrugged.

"Well so it would seem, but here is the interesting part, he was an expert on Medici Florence and he was working on an in depth study when he suddenly died." Calvetti took another mouthful of coffee. "It seems that a priest in Sienna received a letter from this man Dalvin. A man who he neither knew nor met."

"Intriguing," interjected Pancardi.

"Ah, it gets better still Carlo and more mysterious. This letter said that someone was trying to kill this Dalvin. The letter was written in his own hand and had been forwarded on the instruction of Dalvin's solicitors. To be forwarded to the priest unopened one month after his death."

"But what has all of this to do with us?" Blondell asked.

"Maybe nothing. Maybe something," Calvetti shrugged. Calvetti turned to Pancardi, "Teupner has Mafia connections, the Marcosi family."

Pancardi smiled, hissing through his teeth.

"Shall I go on?"

Pancardi nodded, while Blondell shrugged, perplexed.

"Well Dalvin is now dead. Then the letter arrives to the priest and he passes it to my Cardinal and then the Holy Father passes it to me. He says I should take this to the authorities. So I get this letter and here I bring it to you."

Calvetti reached into his breast pocket and produced a small brown envelope with a small hand written note inside. He passed it to Pancardi who read it aloud; written in English the message was clear. "Holy Father, please excuse my writing to you. My name is Richard Dalvin and I write to you because I cannot trust the authorities in Florence. As a man of the cloth and one of the highest integrity I turn to you.

I am dead I have been murdered. I ask you to take the key which is enclosed and use it to open a security box at my home. The box is under the floorboards of my mother's dressing table in a bedroom at my home. The contents of the box must be passed to investigators you can trust. I thank you in advance for this act of humanity. He then signs it R. Dalvin," Pancardi finished reading. "There is no key?"

"And the Holy Father says there never was," quipped Calvetti.

"Strange, very strange," replied Pancardi. "Why write a letter and then not put the key into it?"

"So, this Dalvin was sleeping with a politician's daughter whose father has Sicilian family connections and he turns up dead. Hardly surprising is it?" questioned Blondell. "What," he continued, "has that to do with us now?"

"Always the hare Alex, be calm there is more no?" Pancardi nodded to Calvetti to continue.

Pancardi could sense that a revelation was about to come from Calvetti. Something strong, something irrefutable, he too knew his man and smiled when his deductions were right.

"Professor Dalvin," began Calvetti, "was a Medici expert. The foremost Medici expert in fact. He had been working on a text which examined the public health works of Florence. It was to be groundbreaking. Then he was shamed and dismissed and he cited the academic rivalry of his new research as the real grounds for his dismissal. He claimed the Medici were far more socially advanced than historians had previously assumed. He claimed that renaissance Florence had been the birth place not only of art but of medicine too. The Medici were far more paternalistic than history had given them credit for. He claimed they were philanthropists and not just hedonistic money lenders and slave traders."

Calvetti sensed he had heightened the tension and then delivered his punch line as Pancardi had expected. Pancardi smiled at his timing, some things never change he thought.

"He was working on a history of sewers," Calvetti concluded.

Blondell's silence spoke volumes.

"I think it is time we went to Florence Alex," said Pancardi. "Is the box still at the house Roberto?" he continued.

"We three and the Holy Fathers are the only people who know of it," was his reply.

"But what about Mafia involvement?" asked Blondell.

Calvetti smiled, "That we shall soon know," he said.

Chapter 12

Throughout the long drive to Florence both Pancardi and Calvetti spoke in rapid Italian while Blondell struggled to keep pace with the conversation. Calvetti made three telephone calls each with an air of authority which Blondell had not seen him exhibit previously. Clearly he was well known to his callers and his tone of command was one of being accustomed to giving orders and having them obeyed.

The Banko Rolo building on the banks of the Arno glowed. Fine shafts of deep red and translucent gold pierced the clouds giving the building the aura of a firebird ready to take flight into the sunset. Outside the building cars of white and blue stood like peacocks on a lawn, their blue lights flashing in a defiant display. The paparazzi were held back by the Carabineri making the whole vista seem a fantasy. The car containing Calvetti, Pancardi and Blondell approached.

"It's a media circus," exclaimed Blondell.

"Ah, this is Italy my friend and not England, our ways are not yours," replied Pancardi grinning, "there is no stiff upper lip here. You see the reporters there - they have become like wolves baying for blood. I am so glad that I am not the investigator here. After the shock waves, someone will call for his head and the chief executive of the bank is probably clearing his desk as we speak."

Calvetti wound down the window, flashed his identity card and spoke to one of the Carabineri in swift Italian, and in return received a motion to park inside the cordon barrier of red and white tape-which was rapidly parted to allow them access.

Blondell had thought Calvetti a mere security guard, he became intensely aware of his error at this point. Cameras flashed as the car passed.

Exiting the car the three passed unhindered through the cavernous red tiled mouth and on into the belly of the Bank building. Mostro trotted beside Pancardi without a leash, his step almost haughty. He had stood on the rear seat of the car as the cameras flashed and Pancardi had threatened to rename him – media tart. His presence alone would have signalled to all, that might notice, Giancarlo Pancardi was definitely out of retirement. Calvetti strode ahead with confidence, passing the inert uniformed security guard he approached and spoke to a man in a blue pin-striped suit who had come up a staircase to meet them. Pancardi had been tardy to follow; he gazed at the frescos which lined the walls of the foyer and Blondell had been trapped by his own indecision of whether to follow the rapid footfall of Calvetti or linger with the slower click of Pancardi's stick.

"Beautiful is it not?" Pancardi enquired looking at the ceiling.

Blondell halted, "I'm sorry Inspector?" he said.

"The ceiling, look. This was once the home of a great family and now it is reduced to this. The grandeur of the past wasted on the people who come here to change their travellers cheques and…."

"Inspector I hardly think this is the time to be site-seeing."

"Why? Do you think that by being quick you will solve those vital clues, remember the tortoise and the hare?"

Calvetti had begun to descend the stair with the suited man and Blondell moved as if he was about to follow, but checked his stride; Blondell was caught in his own no mans land of indecision.

"You see Alex very few people look at what is around them. They see what they wish to see. Tell me my friend, have you looked at the roof line above your shopping streets of London or are you just seduced by the things that flash and sparkle and delight your eye line?"

Blondell was about to issue a frustrated rebuke but thought better of it and instead moved rapidly to follow Calvetti.

Pancardi raised his voice, "The men who undertook this were men who looked in other places." He pointed heavenward, "They were not obvious. Like our robbers don't you think? Artists! We too must not be obvious, think outside the box as the Americans say."

Blondell reached the top of the stair as the pair ahead descended rapidly. He hated American speak as he called it. Hit the ground running and pro-active action. Either a person was active or inactive, he thought. The verbosity of having a nice day had now become have a very, very, nice day. Thank you, had become a kind thank you, with pretty bows attached. He realised that Pancardi thought much as he did about language but was toying with him and he hated that.

At the foot of the stairway Calvetti was deep in conversation with the pin-striped suit; Blondell approached and they fell silent waiting for the almost nonchalant arrival of Pancardi. His stick clicked on the terracotta tiling as he finally approached.

"This gentlemen," said the suit, "this is the entrance to the lower chamber which houses the safe deposit vaults – beyond those doors." He pointed into the gloom ahead. "I must ask you to take the necessary precautions as our forensic team are very fastidious. Alaina will provide you with the necessary equipment."

Out of the shadows a young woman appeared carrying shoe covers and surgical gloves. Her hair was netted and she wore a white boiler suit over her clothes. Blondell noticed her figure and the precise well formed teeth which glowed as she smiled.

Mostro's tail began to wag – he recognised her.

"Buongiorno Inspector," she said approaching Pancardi. "Buongiorno Mostro."

She bent to stroke the dog – his tail wag quickened in pace.

"Alaina how are you – well I see?" the Inspector asked.

"Quite well, but I thought you had retired," the woman replied.

"And I thought you had left forensics to make babies?"

"I made marriage and then I unmade marriage-no babies and then back in the Questura. Have they dragged you back too, on your hands and knees, or were you just bored with retirement?"

Knees, thought Blondell, knees, and then smiled at the subtle lunacy of language.

She handed the men shoe covers and sets of surgical gloves as a second woman appeared with white plastic boiler suits. All three men removed their jackets and cast them over a nearby chair.

Blondell removed his mobile telephone and placed it in his trouser pocket, Calvetti smiled.

"Like snowmen?" he said to Alex. "There will be no signal down here." He pointed at the mobile phone.

Mostro was left on guard with the jackets, a role he took seriously, and they were ready to proceed.

Alaina spoke rapidly to Pancardi in Italian giving as much detail as possible while Blondell struggled once again to glean all of the information. He was glad that Italians animated as they spoke for this gave him the opportunity to fill gaps in the colloquial phrasing. The forensic team had covered all of the vault area and several had moved into the now floodlit tunnels through which the raiders had approached. Thus far they had found nothing not even a single hair.

"So they were good?" Pancardi spoke to Alaina in English.

"Better than good, they had all eventualities worked out. Come down to the vaults and see for yourselves."

The woman moved gracefully ahead of the men and Blondell noticed the confident swing to her hips. She had grace and power combined with a smiling intellect and Blondell knew she would be the equal of any male. He pondered on what her husband had been, a lawyer, a doctor most likely; a professional who had not devoted enough time to her and he realised in that instant that this woman demanded time. Even through the surgical gloves he noticed her fine and elegant nails which were painstakingly painted. He caught the brief scent of Samsara and the musky pungency spoke of sexual promise and intrigue, this was a woman who could command attention from any man and her eyes knew it. Blondell felt sorry for the man who had lost her.

Calvetti and Pancardi remained silent as she took them through the process of entry outlining the explosives used on the bars and the acid used on the lock mechanism.

The hoist was still in place and two men were busily dusting every centimetre on it for fingerprints. Both Calvetti and Pancardi knew, as did Alaina, that this exercise was a waste of time. The hole in the wall through which the team had entered was now like an ants nest with men entering and exiting with various samples and polythene bags.

"My team have traced the route back into the sewers. They

got in and they got out. You can go down there if you like though it's very narrow and very claustrophobic," Alaina said.

Pancardi silently shook his head and Calvetti declined citing his girth and patting his stomach as the debilitating reason. Blondell thought he might like to see the route but felt his best option was to remain with Pancardi whose eyes now exuded a predatory gleam as he scanned all angles of the room.

"So they came through the sewers in through the wall, blew the bars and used the hoist to avoid the pressured floor?" Blondell reasoned.

Alaina nodded.

"It all seems so simple and yet so precise," he continued, "they worked above the eye-line." Pancardi's previous comments struck him mid-sentence as he continued, "And then dropped down once they had disarmed the alarms?"

"No," replied Alaina, casually contradicting him. "They did not disarm the major circuits they by-passed them. The precision was inch perfect. The explosives were placed methodically and the acid was the same. The equipment used in the hoist is standard issue and can be bought at any hardware outlet."

Blondell noted the phrase, "Standard issue," and wondered if the woman had military connections. He noted once again her athletic physique and saw her in his imagination as an officer in the Italian army.

At the entrance to the vault Pancardi halted at the door examining in fine detail the mechanism burnt open by the acid. "There is blood here," he said.

"Ah yes," replied Alaina, "I knew you would spot that."

"Blood where?" quipped Blondell.

"You see," said Pancardi, "a fine smear which has been wiped. Look at the way it shows a stain in the floodlight when you stand to the side."

Blondell noticed nothing more than a residue, a fine smear as one might find on a hand smudged mirror. Calvetti nodded and said nothing.

"Was one of them injured then?" Blondell asked.

"This is indeed blood and the finest of smears. We have taken samples and we believe we have enough to get a DNA finger-print," replied Alaina. "My team are now working the tunnels," she continued, "if there was an injury then it may have occurred there."

"So if we can get DNA then we can trace them?" Blondell's reply was loaded with expectation.

"DNA is one thing," replied Pancardi, "identity is another matter."

"But it is a half chance?" Blondell retorted.

The vault floor which lay ahead of them was strewn with many items. Money of various currencies lay in discarded bundles alongside stocks, bonds and share certificates scattered underfoot.

"We also have a partial footprint on one of the papers," chirped Alaina.

"And I expect that too will be standard!" exclaimed Calvetti.

Pancardi turned his attention to fine detail as the small group moved into the centre of the room. Various security boxes lay open and the horror of desecration stung Blondell when the first of the Romanov pieces lay at his feet. He picked up a discarded Faberge Egg which had the larger stones prised from their settings. Carefully he replaced it to the floor. He noticed a crown – distorted out of shape by the pressure of a foot. It seemed to him like a crushed skull.

"This is unbelievable," he said, "how could they know this was here when we could not?"

Calvetti and Pancardi had not heard his mutterings and had moved to the rear of the vault to examine two small piles of jewellery which lay glowing in the floodlit cavern.

Pancardi called Alex to him, "What do you make of this?" he asked. He pointed to the piles of jewellery.

"Well I suppose they could not carry it – perhaps they were not prepared for the wealth in here."

"Not prepared? They were prepared for everything," he snapped.

"Well they could not know how many of the Romanov jewels were here. Perhaps they had underestimated."

"No my friend – they were lucky."

"Lucky?" he questioned. Blondell failed to grasp the significance of the small piles of jewellery that Pancardi was studying- his mind raced to keep up.

"It is so simple and yet you do not see what your eyes tell you," said Pancardi.

"I fail to see what these...."

"Precisely," Pancardi interrupted, "you look but you don't see .You listen but you don't hear. Explain to him Robe."

"They did not know the Romanov jewels were here," he said on command.

"But they must have known."

"How so?" Calvetti replied.

Pancardi had moved to examine the open safe deposit boxes and then quickly examined those that remained unopened. His movements had now become intense and almost balletic, as he moved from one side of the vault to the other, and then finally to the repository of the Romanov jewels which now lay stripped bare, yawning at the onlookers. Blondell moved to join him.

"I don't understand Inspector. How can you know this?"

"Deduction," replied Pancardi.

"Deduction, how can you deduce that from this? It doesn't make the least sense."

Pancardi sighed and straightened himself from a crouch where he had been examining the floor, much as a hunter of animals seeks tracks of his prey in the wood.

"Some excellent news gentlemen." The man in the pin-stripped suit chirped loudly as he entered the vault. "We have found an interesting item weighted down at the bottom of a disused expansion tank. It's a very short distance from here on the old electricity generator site – an abandoned site."

Blondell wondered who the man in the suit was, he didn't seem to be a bank official, Questura, or Carabinerri and he had not introduced himself. It was clear he was senior to Alaina the forensic specialist and Blondell reasoned Government or Italian Secret Service.

Pancardi, now fully erect, smiled knowingly at Calvetti and said, "Shall we take a look?"

"I have an escort car for you," the man said, "please follow me."

The suited man then turned on his heel with body language that said they should follow immediately.

"No time to lose then," replied Pancardi, "the pieces are all coming together."

Blondell, overawed by the sudden change of pace in Pancardi, attempted once again to ask the question of precisely what might be deduced from the piles of discarded items in the vault. He received no reply and instead Pancardi turned his back and busied himself with removing the shoe covers and gloves whilst chattering in rapid Italian to Alaina. She, in turn, laughed and petted his attention seeking hound.

Chapter 13

A diver's head bobbed in the water and was caught in the spotlight of the police beam. An arm was raised as it gave a thumbs up signal .There was no need for language as the slack ropes tightened into a strain and they winched the sodden and distended make-shift structure from the water ; it began to empty like a colander.

The escort car pulled through the security fencing followed by the car carrying Calvetti, Blondell and Pancardi. Calvetti was at the wheel, his eyes red from the day's exertion of being the perpetual chauffeur. Men were moving to place crime scene tape around the area and lights were being installed rapidly around the compound.

Generators were whirring into life, giving the area a sound of past glory before its present dereliction.

A site security guard was being interviewed by local officers in the lonely illumination of his temporary terrapin as they passed. Another white suited forensic investigator greeted them.

"We have to follow the path," he said, "we cannot have the area disturbed. Leave the dog in the car please."

Pancardi nodded. This time there was no familiarity. Evidently Pancardi did not know the man. There were no names and no small talk as they passed in the direction they were bidden.

"We sent our men into the tunnel and it merged into a maze of channels which are impossible to follow." The man spoke as he walked.

Pancardi nodded again.

"So we sent small tracers through the channels. There were five exit points for the water. Some were too small for a man to pass through and this was the last one to be checked. We've had a diver here all afternoon and finally we've found something. It's being lifted now."

Blondell noted the sharp edge in his voice and tried to place the dialect.

At the edge of the tank lay a beached mammal or something that could be mistaken for one. A deer perhaps that had haplessly wondered into Florence and fallen into the tank and slowly and agonisingly drowned, or so it seemed to Blondell. The smell of rotting putrefaction stung his nostrils, this however, was no corpse it was clearly man made, but the mud which caked it stank. Blondell saw the diver climb up the rusted ladder, the very same ladder which West and his team had used and which had probably not been used for years before that. The diver then walked toward the group of onlookers. He was small and agile and Blondell wondered if he had traversed the dark tunnels to reach the tank; it was a task he could not envy. Removing the oxygen tank and then the mask Blondell realised the diver was a woman. She appeared to have no breasts no hips and her face was sharp, with an aquiline nose and his first thoughts were of her as a Lesbian. She was, he noted, singularly unattractive-hard bitten even. He brushed the thoughts aside as she spoke. Her voice was a total contrast to her look, it was warm, soft and sumptuously inviting; the kind of voice a man could listen to in the dark of a bedroom and fall in love with. When she spoke it felt like someone were pouring warm oil into his ears and he could not resist her, he had to listen.

"It's black as night down there. This," she pointed to the carcass, "was in the mud. I thought it might be a body but its polypropylene and it's been weighted. Well it was until I took some of the bricks out. I've been down several times in the last two hours and I know it might be nothing. It's not been there very long either."

"Magdalene these men are the investigators they've been inside the bank and they may have some questions," the white suited forensic guide spoke swiftly.

"Is there anything else down there?" asked Blondell.

He noticed the woman's eyes which were almost black as coal

and strangely hypnotic. Her voice continued to play a harp in his head, he fought hard to concentrate – hear her reply.

"Nothing except a couple of dead animals, a fox I think and maybe a badger. A lot of thick silt and rotting leaves."

She smiled as she reached toward her wetsuit zip behind her neck.

"So where does that leave us now?" asked Blondell, as he turned to Pancardi.

"Investigating!" Pancardi blurted in exasperation. "Which is what Robe has done while you my friend make your English eyes." The diver smiled. "See he has already found the hole in the fence," Pancardi continued.

Blondell turned to see Calvetti some distance away examining the fencing and discussing with another white suited officer a route across the compound.

"You see, but you don't see do you?" Pancardi was stooping toward the object at the edge of the tank.

The diver was now in a bikini having removed the wetsuit and Blondell was amazed by the sudden transformation. She did have breasts, small but well formed and although her hips were slight they were the hips of a woman. Her olive skin was totally without blemish, glowing, except for the tattoo which ran across the small of her back. It ran from hip to hip like the pinion tips of an eagle's wing with a point which lead provocatively to her coccyx tip. She began pulling on a track suit. She was lithe and alive and moved with a feline grace which Blondell admired. Her whole being oozed into the tracksuit along with her body. Blondell was drawn to her – had to watch her.

Pancardi studied Blondell as Blondell studied the diver. His mind was alert and he perceived attraction in both.

"This looks like some form of boat to me," he said, breaking the silent observation.

"Just what I thought," the woman replied, "it could just be something kids played with and dumped."

"They cut through the fence in two places and then went out over the park that way," Calvetti said loudly, as he strode toward them.

"So Inspector what can we deduce from all of this?" Blondell enquired sarcastically.

"Very simple conclusions my friend," he replied. He then fell silent.

"Please go on Inspector."

"If you insist Alex Blondell."

Blondell could sense that Pancardi was about to launch into him and began to regret his use of sarcasm. Pancardi began, "Sarcasm is a low form of wit. Is that not what you English say? Second you do not see that which is before you. Third you have an eye for the ladies."

The diver was towelling her hair which hung in a moist profusion about her shoulders. She smiled at Blondell and this he knew was not the smile of a woman who craved the company of other women, it was the smile of a woman in need of a man.

"You see, even now a pretty smile and you are lost. Magdalene she is," he tapped his head, "in your thoughts and in your loin," he laughed in triumph.

The woman turned away as if she had not heard Pancardi's last comment. Blondell knew his face was reddening with embarrassment and wished for a sudden power cut to quench all the lights.

"That will not happen," Pancardi laughed again, as if reading Blondell's thoughts.

Magdalene had now moved off to speak quietly with one of the many white suited forensic officers.

"She is a pretty woman, no? Then you must give her your hotel, no? And then maybe we can concentrate on the task in hand no?"

Calvetti was suppressing a chuckle and the female diver had now turned her back to the group. It was obvious to Blondell that she could hear their every word and he wished the ground would open up and devour him.

"Hotel yes, I think it is time to eat and feast and then we discuss what we know, come."

And without further ado Pancardi turned and began to return to the car with the white suited guide. Blondell was hesitant, but as he moved he felt a soft touch on his forearm. Magdalene passed him a slip of paper with her other hand. Catching his eye she spoke liltingly, "Call me if you want to. Florence can be a lonely place," was all she said.

At the car Pancardi noted, "She gave you her number then, you must call her tonight, or at the latest tomorrow – it will be good for you. You are hungry and she is hungry you should feast together."

"How on earth did you know she would give me her number?" Blondell asked shocked.

"What else would she write down with her back to us? I saw the pen. You see Alex I see when I look," was Pancardi's solemn reply. "Make sure you call her, she is Sicilian."

"The holy fathers have rooms at the Hotel Brunelleschi behind the Via Calzaiuoli that is where we are staying tonight," said Calvetti as the car engine spat into life.

"So being in the employ of the Vatican does have its perks," said Pancardi, "a very fine hotel indeed."

"Why is the Vatican so interested in this robbery and why have we not been met and been challenged by the Questura, don't you find the whole thing odd?" asked Blondell.

"Odd? No?" replied Pancardi.

"Well I think it very strange."

"We have been given carte blanche on this," said Calvetti, "everyone will be more than eager to help us. You see the Vatican owns the majority holding. It is in their interest to discover the perpetrators and everyone here owes a great deal to the church- including the politicians. The Holy Father does not have faith in the Questura but he does have faith in me, and I in turn have faith in Carlo. So you see it does make some sense after all."

"So we are here because of the Pope?" Blondell sounded incredulous.

"Precisely," replied Calvetti. "Well the Pope's bankers actually."

"And perhaps now you can tell me what you deduced in the vault?" questioned Blondell.

He turned to face the rear seat and Pancardi, who sat imperiously stroking the top of Mostro's head, which lay in his lap.

"The floor," Pancardi replied, "did you notice the floor?"

"Yes of course," Blondell replied.

"And what did you see?"

"Scuff marks and piles of jewellery."

"Precisely- but why?" Pancardi toyed with the Englishman,

"You have no idea do you? It is as I said, you look but don't see."

The following few seconds of silence in the car were interspersed with traffic horns as Piaggio scooters shot around corners and wove among the stationary vehicles. The tension in Blondell was akin to the excitement of a child opening a Christmas present.

"Well," Pancardi continued, "the men in the bank on that day, and here I assume they are men, because the physical strength required would be too demanding for a woman. They were very busy, they had planned everything and they were after the jewels."

"Yes, the Romanov jewels, we know that," interrupted Blondell.

"No, that is where you are wrong they did not know they were there. That is why they are lucky."

"I don't understand."

"I know," said Pancardi, "so if you listen I will explain. There were four men. One for the acid, one for explosives, and two others. At first I thought three but I have revised that."

He looked at Blondell quizzically expecting a question-there was none.

"Good now I continue. These men they enter the tunnels, one of them gets hurt or has been hurt before they start – there we have the blood. If he was bleeding at the vault door it was because he was straining in the harness – so he must have been the first. The first man was the vault cracker. He used acid. So this much we know.

Once in the vault they start opening the deposit boxes. They only take the very best and start to fill small bags. Then, and now we come to the interesting part, one man opens the deposit box containing the Russian jewels; this then becomes the centre of their attention so much so that they discard the contents of the bags they are filling. How do I know this? Because as they go they throw useless things to the floor they scatter randomly, so we have our foot mark, as they hurry. But the bags are emptied in orderly piles they are not thrown, why? There are three such piles. Two small and one larger. The larger pile is a double pile. So from this I get four bags- one per man. From these piles they take only the best. One man sorts these and he is tidy by habit –so in this he gives us another clue. The other men – three, start to strip the Russian jewels, this takes time. One uses a pen knife another has a divers knife and the third breaks open items with his foot so the other two can work fast. Why so crude, if they knew what they had to do they would have had better tools no? They would be ready for the problem. The crown of the Princess was crushed and the shapes of the scoring on this are deep and sharp, the scoring on the Faberge Eggs is blunt like it is made from a chisel. Two different knives? Then they give us the last vital clue-the unopened deposit boxes. After all their trouble they leave without opening them, why? Simple, they have more than they can carry and they do not waste more time. They do not bother because they know that there can be no better in them. So they leave."

"So there are four men?" Blondell questioned.

"Of this I cannot be certain, there may be a woman."

"But that is unlikely," interrupted Calvetti.

"Why?" Blondell sensed he was out of his depth.

"Upper arm strength," replied Calvetti, "they pulled themselves through the steel caging. They were upside down as they did this so they must be very strong. Very strong and agile, like gymnasts, there were no more than a few centimetres between them and the pressurised floor."

"But a woman could do that couldn't she?"

"Yes true, but they would have to be powerful and powerful women tend to be broad hipped are they not?"

Blondell turned to face the forward direction of the car. His head swam and his mind raced. Had he been wrong? He thought of his intelligence in London.

"I still don't believe it was luck with the Romanov jewels," he stated.

"Quite so – your intelligence," replied Pancardi.

"What if the team didn't know, but others did?"

"I agree."

"What about this Professor and the Sicilian connection?"

"So many new questions Alex!" exclaimed Pancardi. "Ah, the Sicilian connection that is what you need to explore thoroughly and…. deeply. That is your next challenge is it not?"

Calvetti roared with laughter at the inferred implication and swung the car into a sharp bend which threw Blondell against the door and made him reach for the hanging strap above.

"Steady," he said, involuntarily.

"Ah, this is Italy," replied Calvetti, "the home of the motor car. He complains about my driving Carlo," he shrieked loudly, as the car swung hard left.

Pancardi was chuckling in the back seat, "And why not you are one of the most dangerous drivers in the whole of Italy."

Blondell sensed a conspiracy.

Chapter 14

Alone in his hotel room Alex Blondell stepped from his bath. He felt refreshed and ready to examine the photographs which Calvetti had handed to him after dinner. From his jacket pocket he extracted the slip of paper with the quickly scrawled number – Magdalene's number. He toyed with the notion of phoning her and then glancing at the clock noticed the time, 9.45 pm and thought better of it. All the while his subconscious called to him, tomorrow maybe tomorrow.

He emptied the contents of the envelope onto the bed and spread the images before him. They showed a man in his forties or fifties, he could not be certain, inside a chest, no a wardrobe, around his neck was a belt and in his mouth was an orange. The man was naked and splashes of what appeared to be semen were visible on his thigh and pubic hair. Blondell shuddered and felt a surge of disgust. He examined the paper commentary describing the scene. It was bland and lifeless – non judgemental and precise. The commentary described the finding of the corpse and the approximate date of death. The body lay undiscovered for some time, but the cold of winter had slowed decomposition. Asphyxiation was recorded as the cause of death. Blondell looked again at the photographs and now noticed the belt secured to the rail above the man's head. He had heard of such things but had never seen …The phone rang and Blondell answered with a swift, "Hello."

"It is Magdalene I am in the foyer can I come up?"

Without considering he blurted an involuntary, "Yes of course."

Five minutes later there was a soft tap tap at his door and Blondell hastily pulled on his trousers to answer it.

"Good evening Mr. Blondell. May I come in?"

He wondered how she had got his name. It was not given at the water tank site.

"Please do," he said.

Blondell stepped into the corridor to scan for activity and thought he saw the heel of Pancardi's boot entering a room some distance away, but he could not be certain. Bastard, he thought as he closed the door and re-entered the room.

Magdalene was sitting on the bed examining the photographs her legs crossed provocatively. She had applied make-up which had softened the features on her face and she smiled as she perused. Her voice poured like molasses, soft, rich and warm into his ears.

"Mmmmm these are bizarre," she said, "sick even."

"Yes they are rather aren't they – they're part of this case. Not very nice, a man dying in a bizarre masturbating ritual."

"Oh dear that is sad," she said, her voice oozing into him.

"Not really the man had some sexual practices which included the defloration of young virgins."

"How young?"

"Seventeen and eighteen I believe."

"Really, well we all have to lose it sometime don't we?"

There was a painful silence.

"Well I suppose if you look at it that way then, erm, yes," he replied.

"I got the hotel you were in from the Questura. I'm afraid I told a little white lie. I said I had some further information for the Inspector and he gave me your room number. That was rather naughty of me wasn't it," she giggled.

"I don't know…. was it?"

"Oh I think it was. I just wanted us to have a chance to get to know each other a little better." She giggled again and shot a look at Blondell which would have made the ice in his drink melt if he had one.

"Aren't you going to offer me a drink, especially as I've come all this way to see you?"

"Yes of course."

Blondell went to the mini-bar.

"I seem to have everything including some champagne, but no glasses."

"Oh yummy, I love champagne – can I have some of that then please? There must be some tumblers in the bathroom I'll get them."

She pouted the word please at him like a little girl begging from her idolising father.

She bit her bottom lip as the cork flew into the air and hit the ceiling and offered a glass to be filled, first from her left hand and then her right.

"It's so nice when a man pops his cork, its music to my ears – I bet you like it too?"

Blondell felt his reason begin to evaporate in the face of the most advanced coquettish flirting he had ever encountered. He smiled at her and she smiled back. He cracked a joke or two as they talked and she laughed, but not so much with her mouth as with her eyes. Her whole being spoke of the promise of sex. She was the most overtly sexual woman he had ever encountered.

"I'll clear these," he said, as he removed the papers and photographs from the bed.

He placed them on the night stand and sat on the edge of the bed beside her.

"How did you become a police diver?" he asked blunder-ingly.

"Oh, I was just good at it and they offered me the post," she replied.

He was about to ask another banal question in his attempt to steer the conversation when he could not believe his ears.

"I thought we should go to bed," she said coolly.

Blondell spluttered his champagne.

"I'm not usually like this but I saw your need in your eyes when I got out of the water. Did you like my bikini?"

Blondell was dumb-struck. He gulped a mouthful of champagne to give him vital time to think. His mind raced for a reply but she beat him to it.

"Mutual sexual attraction I call it, don't you agree?" she said.

"Well yes, I suppose so."

"There is no supposing about it."

The negotiations and niceties had been closed and Blondell felt as if he had no further say in the matter. She stood up and started to undress. There was no shame, no feigned embarrassment and no need for further posturing. Naked she slipped under the covers of the bed and motioned Blondell to join her.

"Some people say that Italian girls are staid," she giggled, "but I don't think that's true do you?"

Her lilting voice drew him on and he felt the warmth of her nakedness beside him as he disrobed and joined her beneath the covers.

"Your Christian name is Alex isn't it?" she asked.

"Alex... mm ... yes, short for Alexander"

"Ooooo that is lovely, shall I scream it when I come?"

Then without waiting for a reply she kissed him full and hard, and taking his left hand in hers she guided him to the moist pubis between her legs and Blondell knew he had lost. As she touched him she hypnotised him with her voice and he became her willing slave. First her hands and then her mouth hardened his delirium and, as she had foretold, she repeated his name coaxing and imploring with every thrust of his engorged loins until his grunting climax coincided with her whimpering giggle.

When the wake up call sounded he was alone and for a moment he thought the activity of the previous night had been a fantasy. He felt his groin and the hard stiffness of dried body fluids met his touch, and he knew that they had been.

He glanced at the clock 7.40 am and then noticed a small note beside it.

The message was simple. *Thank you for a wonderful night,* it said, *I have to work today but you have my number and I am sure you will call.* He could hear her voice in the words as he read them aloud.

The phone rang and he was snapped back into reality much as the hypnotised react to the click of the hypnotist's fingers.

"Blondell," he said into the receiver.

"If you are not otherwise engaged," laughed Calvetti, "perhaps you might care to join us for breakfast to keep your strength up. Pancardi has arranged for us to visit Dalvin's house at 10 o'clock."

"I'll be down in ten minutes," he replied.

In the shower and washing the nights toil from his skin he thought of what he should say to Pancardi. He wanted to admonish him, but his mind could only think of thanking him. He thought of Magdalene wrapping her legs around his waist as he entered her, and he heard her velvet voice imploring him to force his manhood deeper. He saw her sitting astride him her hands on his knees as she thrust her pelvis to his and he knew in that instant he would phone her again

At the breakfast table Pancardi and Calvetti were deep in thoughtful conversation.

"Ah, Alex come and join us," said Calvetti.

Pancardi motioned the waitress to bring more coffee and he ordered scrambled eggs and bacon for Blondell.

"Sleep well?" he asked. "Of course you did," he replied to his own question. "Today we go to the house of Dalvin and there if I am not mistaken we will find ..."

"The plans of the sewers," echoed Calvetti, "and if we are luckier still this Dalvin will have some information for us from beyond the grave."

"Did you get a chance to look at the crime scene photographs," enquired Pancardi smiling toothily.

"I did."

"And what did you see my young friend. What did you notice?"

"Inspector I'm growing tired of these guessing games can't we just get to the crux of the matter?"

"Patience, did you hurry last night? I think not, so humour an old man just a little and answer this. Why would a man who has so many young women at his fingertips, quite literally I might add, be found asphyxiated whilst masturbating in a wardrobe?"

"Then he was murdered?"

"Maybe, maybe not. Maybe he was playing sex games that went wrong and somebody just left him there dead," said Calvetti.

"Ah, here come your scrambled eggs, excellent to improve the sperm count and repeat capacity I believe, it's all the albumen apparently," chuckled Pancardi.

"Ok let's get it over with-the ribbing," replied Blondell.

"There is, how you say, no ribbing my friend only admiration for our young stallion and his Sicilian mare," Pancardi laughed aloud.

"Well I was left a note this morning which may be the kiss off. It's what you might call a one night stand." Blondell felt himself becoming strangely defensive and wondered why such a brief encounter might spark such a reaction within him.

"I think not!" Pancardi was emphatic and continued, "Magdalene is diving to find the way our thieves entered the tunnels. She is much respected as a professional and she likes you." Pancardi's tone became dark, "If she cannot find the entry point no one can. She will go through the maze of tunnels if it takes her weeks – she is methodical." He paused and then suddenly asked, "Do you believe in love at first sight?"

"That's a strange question coming from someone like you?" was Blondell's terse reply.

"Why so? That you answer one question with another."

"I'm studying the technique from Pancardi, you – my teacher."

"And so you should. But do not mistake, love is more important than anything, of this I am certain. When you are as old as me you will know this as a fact. No Sicilian girl, who is normally so cautious, would act with such abandon. Do you not believe in love at first sight?"

"Love at first sight? Now that is an absurd notion Inspector."

"Absurd yes, but true yes, do you not think so Roberto?"

Calvetti nodded and Blondell caught the merest glimpse of sadness tinged with loss deep behind Pancardi's eyes. In a fleeting second it was gone and the cold eyes of the predator returned.

"Come we have discoveries to make," the Italian said, with enthusiasm, rising from the table before the others had finished their food.

Chapter 15

"What is that smell?" asked Blondell, as the three men entered.

"That my young stallion," replied Calvetti, "is the stench of death."

"My god it's awful."

"I know but you must remember that three corpses were found here."

"Three? Who else?"

"Not who ...what."

"Have you forgotten the dogs?" asked Pancardi.

"Of course there were two of them," Blondell remarked, "they were locked in a room. One of them had been half eaten by the other but both were dead when the Questura broke in."

"Quite so. No water, dehydration."

Calvetti left the front door open behind them as they moved toward the large room at the end of the corridor which had served as a reception room and study - he turned the key. The door swung back with a heavy laboured creak. The room was empty and the curtains drawn. Calvetti drew them apart and threw open a window. The effect was to create an immediate through draught and Blondell sensed the oppressive stench lift, he felt he could breathe again.

"All of the personal effects were shipped to America some time last week," said Calvetti.

"Shipped?" Blondell questioned.

"Yes to a cousin of the dead man. And the furniture and other effects were sold at auction and the house is now up for sale."

"These personal effects?" asked Pancardi.

"They were checked," replied Calvetti, "they were in two crates - books and family photographs mostly, of his mother and father. It would seem that his family had little regard for his plea of innocence. They wanted to get the business side tidied up quickly, and run away from any social stigma."

"When the carcass is down how quickly the vultures gather," quipped Pancardi, "one life in a box of photographs."

Blondell noted the tinge of sadness in Pancardi's voice; a sadness which only those who have moved toward the final stage in their life can contemplate. He looked at the two men in the room. Calvetti, fat, sweating and breathless and he pondered on his ending; Pancardi clicking through his latter years with a cane, until his body, crippled by arthritis, would eventually buckle beneath him. Their minds were sharp but they no longer had time on their side. He thought of Magdalene's lithe youth impaled and writhing; then, in the instant, he understood Pancardi's melancholy and regret and his regard for both men quadrupled.

"Jesus, what the hell is that?" he said, pointing at the carpet.

A set of brown stains of varying sizes were scattered across the floor.

"Looks like blood to me," replied Calvetti nonchalantly.

"This is the room in which the dogs were found – locked in," said Pancardi.

"But why would he lock the door, in his own house?" asked Blondell.

"Precisely!" replied Calvetti.

"So what do you say Alex?" questioned Pancardi.

"Well perhaps he was not alone on the night he died. Perhaps there was someone here who was scared of dogs."

"Perhaps."

"But he was found alone, masturbating," Blondell concluded.

"Masturbated no? Past tense – he was dead," Pancardi replied.

Blondell's mind was racing to deduce, and from one simple fact a myriad of possibilities sprang to his mind.

"Tell us what you see?" said Pancardi, encouraging him to explore his own thoughts.

"Well he would not have locked the door to masturbate in that wardrobe, he would have simply closed it. Unless he was intending to commit suicide. But then he would have made provision for the dogs, or poisoned them or something first. He would not have left them to die a slow agonising death surely?" Blondell knew that Calvetti and Pancardi were already way ahead in their reasoning but he continued, "So he locks the door, goes up stairs and the masturbation goes wrong and he dies. But why lock the door in the first place? It doesn't make sense. Unless, unless somebody else locked the door to keep the dogs out of the way, killed him, and made it look like a suicide or an accident."

"And the mistake?" asked Pancardi

"Who ever it was forgot to unlock the door when they left."

"There from Foreign Office researcher to detective in one easy leap," laughed Calvetti.

"But how can we be certain?" Blondell asked.

"We can't," said Pancardi, "but we can deduce – no?"

"And the letter to the priest?" Calvetti quipped.

"Then it was murder?" replied Blondell.

"And now for the upstairs," chirped Pancardi, triumphantly.

Mostro trotted up the stairs glad to be free of the foul stench in the rooms below. He padded from room to room assessing the various smells as he went.

The Bedrooms on the first floor were as empty as the rooms below. Only one or two pieces of furniture remained. The wardrobe which had housed the corpse had long since been removed for forensic analysis and the wallpaper showed the yellowing of age - where pictures had once hung.

"It's all very dingy," said Blondell, as he entered Dalvin's former bedroom.

"Hard to believe he was a sex god isn't it?" said Pancardi.

"It's tired," replied Blondell, "and it smells of neglect."

"Did you look at the crime scene photographs?" asked Calvetti.

Blondell sensed the two men were having sport as they toyed with his inexperience.

"He was busy last night Robe, very busy," said Pancardi, smirking.

"But I did see them," replied Blondell.

"So what did you see?" asked Calvetti.

Blondell's mind threw the images before his eyes and he attempted to reconstruct the room in his head.

"There was the bed," he pointed, "a chair here and over there was a table. An ash tray and glasses - two glasses." He reflected and as if he were Archimedes, then announced triumphantly, "There was an ash tray and two glasses: two glasses?"

"Dalvin did he smoke?" asked Pancardi

"Good grief," exclaimed Blondell, "there was somebody here otherwise there would only be the one glass."

"And they drank champagne," said Calvetti.

"Is that not a strange drink to have if you are alone?" asked Pancardi.

Blondell's mind returned to Magdalene, "There was a woman here or a girl," he said, "there was a seduction?"

"Yes and?" Calvetti asked.

"They drank champagne, she smoked, and they played some sex games that went wrong. Dalvin choked and she panicked and left the house and because she was afraid she did not go to the police."

"That is what we," Calvetti remarked, "are supposed to think and that is what the......"

"So why was the door locked?" Blondell interrupted. "Surely she wouldn't have locked it before she left, would she? And what was he doing inside the wardrobe with a belt around his neck anyway?"

"You tell us," said Calvetti.

"Good grief!" exclaimed Blondell, "what was this man into?"

"How do we know that there was only one killer and that it was a woman?" asked Pancardi.

"The body, did it have had signs of a struggle, bruises and such?" Blondell questioned.

"There were none," Calvetti said.

"But there were some marks on his wrists and ankles. I read that in the file."

"Yes, but they may have happened at another time," Calvetti concluded.

"The key here is the man Alex," Pancardi interjected, "what was his crime?"

"He liked to deflower girls and he abused his position of power."

"Yes continue."

Blondell's mind raced, "So why would a man who liked to dominate play the submissive?"

"Exactly!" exclaimed Pancardi.

"Maybe he was trying something new?"

"With a young and inexperienced girl," Pancardi deduced, "who became so frightened she ran downstairs locked the door and then ran away: Teenagers talk. What is the point of sleeping with someone important if you cannot tell a friend?"

"It doesn't make sense when you put it that way," Blondell mused.

"That is precisely what we thought Alex," Calvetti confirmed

"So now," Pancardi began, "we have a Professor, dead, and a wardrobe and a sex game and….."

Blondell's mind played the sexual encounter that had taken place in this room in vivid colour. As Pancardi spoke he thought of Magdalene again. One word kept coming into his frontal lobe – seduction. Dalvin had been seduced and somehow he had been persuaded into the wardrobe and then he had been killed. Sexual promise, maybe someone had offered to scream his name when she came. This sex game required privacy, because Dalvin had been taking a gamble. This was no young girl willing to part her legs for advancement. He thought of the letter to the priest; perhaps this perverse Professor was far more astute than his killer had imagined. If he felt he was in danger he would be vigilant, but what better way to get him to lower his guard than his need for sex.

"Holy Mother of God," he blurted aloud, "it's a woman, not a girl and a very clever one at that."

"And more I think," said Pancardi, "she was no stranger to him – he knew her; why else would he let her tie him up? He must have trusted no? Maybe she played a game in the wardrobe. His hands and feet were tied and she makes him ejaculate and then she strangles him. She removes the ropes and places the orange. She leaves it all for us to find, the glasses, the ashtray, but she forgets to unlock the door. That is her one mistake."

"How do we find the compartment – in the letter to the

priest?" asked Blondell, "it could be in any of the rooms."

"Deduce my friend deduce," said Pancardi.

Blondell went from room to room while Calvetti and Pancardi took their joy in watching him reason. Even Mostro studied him, sitting bolt upright between the two detectives his head moving quizzically from side to side as the strange Englishman scurried.

"It's this one," he said after a few moments.

"Why?" asked Pancardi.

"Because it smells of an old woman."

"It smells of piss to me," said Calvetti.

"And look at the decoration," Blondell continued, "it's definitely the taste of an older woman. The window is there so the dressing table should be here. There look at the marks on the carpet. The feet have left their impression. So Dalvin's secret must be under here."

Blondell went to the edge of the carpet and lifted it, rolling back an old underlay to get to the floorboards below. He felt like Carter at the mouth of the Tutankhamen tomb. The warm excitement of discovery was in his blood as he removed the carpeting back further. Mostro barked encouragingly as if to say get on with it. But both Calvetti and Pancardi watched him nonchalantly from the doorway as he worked.

"Look the floorboards are not secure here and they have been cut short to make a trap-door."

There was tension in his voice. He lifted a board and then another and finally a third – the void was empty.

"Damn," he said. He sat back from his knees to his heels as he spoke, "Bollocks it's empty."

He threw himself forward again and groped shoulder deep into the void, his face turned to the doorway and as he did so his eyes were greeted by the vision of Pancardi and Calvetti roaring with laughter.

"You bastards," he said.

At that same instant Pancardi's mobile rang and he answered swiftly.

"That was Alaina," he said, "time for us to return. Enough of this tomfoolery. Come Alex we have played enough with you. It is time for us to get serious."

Chapter 16

A Dash 8 – 400 touched down on smooth tarmac. The morning was sharp and clear. There was a puff of smoke at the wheel and the plane lurched hard left in the wind which pushed the light people carrier toward the grass verge. The pilot corrected and slammed the air breaks into place, and then the silence of the passengers, subdued by fear, broke into a cacophony of noise and chatter. The plane was virtually empty on the run between Gatwick and the islands.

At the rear of the plane sat a blonde woman, her hair cut into a neat mid-length bob; her eyes were obscured by heavy sunglasses which also partially covered her face. She wore heavy foundation, which gave her skin a pinkish glow, she stared nonchalantly into the distance as other more nervously relieved passengers jumped to their feet before the seat–belt sign had been switched off. She smiled to herself and wondered at the lunacy of standing as if that in itself would serve to save someone from a speeding wreck; were they able to jump if needs must?

She walked down the steps slowly, deliberately last to leave the plane, her hips rolling languidly as she passed from step to step. She wanted to be noticed and she was. Baggage handlers momentarily stopped to admire the turn of her long legs and the tightness of her waist above the rounding hip-line. She smiled coquettishly at them and they returned to their work knowing they could never possess anything comparable; their wives and girlfriends could not measure up. She was a trophy on legs and both she and the men who saw her that day knew that simple fact.

Their unsung desires evaporated in the fleeting seconds it took for her to pass through and out of their lives.

At immigration control she showed a Dutch passport, was asked the usual questions, on business or pleasure for her stay. She said pleasure, stating she was on holiday for a week. The official behind the bullet–proof glass toyed with the fantasy of giving her his phone number and then as rapidly thought of his career and mortgage and said, "Have a nice stay," instead. In her bag she had another departure ticket for that same afternoon. From the baggage carousel she collected a small suitcase before taking a taxi into the centre of St. Hellier.

To the teller in the foyer of the bank she introduced herself as Miss Rose Dalvin and the response was immediate.

"Come this way, our manager is expecting you," he said, with excessive politeness.

She swung her hips as she followed him through a set of double doors and into a confined office.

"Can I get you some tea or coffee?" he asked.

She gave a polite yes to black coffee no sugar and the teller disappeared.

He re-appeared in seconds with the coffee which she accepted with a gloved hand, she noted it was instant and cheap. Upon removing her sunglasses the teller was immediately transfixed by the striking deep blue of her eyes which were moist and inviting. He left the room. A few minutes passed and she busied herself with a handheld compact by applying a light coating of pink lip-stick.

When the manager came in he rushed forward to greet her – his hand outstretched, "Good morning Miss Dalvin," he said.

"I am so sorry that my uncle could not come himself," she replied softly, "but he has been unwell for the past few weeks. However, I hope the security codes tally and that once I have given you these numbers," she pushed a typed list of six numbers across the desk, "the money can be prepared."

The manager gazed at her and thought of his nagging, grasping, social – climbing wife and then had the deepest feeling that this niece and uncle relationship was a far better arrangement than his own. Lucky bastard he thought.

"As per instructions we have prepared the money in Euro," he said.

"I love Euro," she giggled, "uncle says it sounds so much more like that."

The manager laughed with affectation, "Well your uncle is right," he said, "at the current exchange rate it works out at 705,000 plus the 112,800 which was already in the account. Making a grand total of 817,800 Euro."

"Well we can leave the account open can't we?"

"Of course."

"Shall we say that I will take the 815,000, and the rest can be left?"

"I am concerned that so much cash may put you at risk though." The manager's tone became serious.

"Oh don't worry about little old me, I have a friend, well," she lowered her voice to a whisper, "a guard-dog man, outside." She opened her case and produced a folded rucksack, "It can all go in here," she said, flashing her lashes.

"I expect you'll want to check it though?" asked the manager. "Count it?"

"Not really uncle can do that when I get back to Florence – I'll trust you."

She drooled the word, "Yooouuu," and the fine hairs on the back of the manager's neck stood to attention. He could smell her rich perfume and once again he thought of her as a toy: A pure sex-toy.

Minutes later a taxi headed toward St.Aubins Bay where she checked into a hotel overlooking the sea. There the woman removed the blonde wig and flushed the blue contact lenses and her Dutch passport into the toilet. Then she washed her face clear of make-up, making sure to use the cheap soap provided by the hotel; her face looked bland, pale, almost dull. She threw the wig, clothes, sunglasses and expensive Prada shoes into the suitcase and sat on the bed in her underwear. She removed her up-lift bra and tossed that into the case too. Her long red hair was unwashed, greasy and looked neglected – she did not brush it. The rucksack sat on a chair. She wondered if it might be overlarge for hand luggage, but then thought better of it. From the case lid she pulled a sweater, this seemed old, stained and baggy. The jeans were unwashed and the plimsolls she had selected for the transformation were riddled with holes. She platted her hair into a pig-tail donned a beret and finally placed a pair of spectacles on her nose. Looking into the mirror she smiled and her green eyes sparkled with intense glee: She was a true frump.

On the bed she placed her new identity British passport, the flight details to Southampton and the train ticket to London, complete with a student rail card.

Then taking a pen-knife from her jean pocket she made multiple puncture wounds in the case – the attack was quick and frenzied.

Passing unnoticed via the fire escape and carrying the suitcase she slipped down to the waterside via the narrow walk-ways between the plush houses. An old man walking a dog passed in the opposite direction without giving a second glance toward her face. On the edge of a short mooring she placed two large boulders into the case, and checking to see she was alone, dropped the item into the sea where it bobbed twice and then sank.

Within minutes she was back in the room unnoticed. She ran the shower and dampened the towels then ran them along the skirting boards to give the impression of use before throwing them casually over the back of a chair. Then she lay in the bed and made indentations in the pillows and rolled crumpling the bedcovers and sheets into an unsightly heap. All this would give, she surmised, the impression of a tourist checked in to use the shower facilities and then a doing a moonlight flit to avoid payment.

The bus journey to the airport was unpleasant, twisting as it did through the rural lanes which served as roads on the island. A gangly youth with acne had attempted conversation as he sat next to her but a scowl was enough to stall his hopes.

Check in was smooth save that this time her passage went completely un-noticed. To the untrained eye she was just another back-packing student travelling in a gap year. Her eyes down and using a slovenly slouch she passed through the nothing to declare exit at Southampton and walked out of the airport unhindered.

The train to London was late.

Chapter 17

"That was a shitty thing to do!" Blondell looked out of the car window as he spoke. "Bloody well made me look a fool!"

Calvetti was driving at high speed, following two motorcycle outriders as they sped back toward the city and the offices of the Carabineri. Pancardi was in the front seat beside Calvetti talking rapid Italian into his mobile phone. Blondell had taken the rear seat in protest, even if it did mean that Mostro would treat him like a pillow all the way back. He wondered why the dog had to go everywhere that Pancardi did; he even got to sleep in the hotel room alongside the grumpy old bastard.

Calvetti ignored the remark.

"Really shitty," Blondell repeated more loudly, so they could not pretend they had not heard it.

"Just a bit of fun Alex, a laugh no?" said Pancardi, snapping his phone shut.

"But it's still shit."

"Come Alex, forgive us our jape, we have much to do and I will explain."

The car banked and threw the passengers left and then hard to the right.

Calvetti was in a hurry, something had happened which had made a dramatic difference to both of the detectives – that much Blondell could tell. Pancardi was excited and was gesticulating as he spoke.

"Late last night," Pancardi spoke solemnly, "while you were…. sleeping, Robe and I went to the house to find the compartment of Dalvin. It is a sorry place no? Here we found papers, copies, plans of the sewers, also there was an overlay of the modern building works. These were all in a strong box which we took back for Alaina to work on. She has been in the lab all day."

Calvetti continued the narrative, "There was also a note written very neatly by Dalvin. This we had to check was his hand – it is."

"Now the plot thickens," Pancardi continued, "the note has some names; Smithart and Verrison, these you know of – they in South Africa. There is mention of a Mr. Vaughan, and we know who he is. Our friend Folsen-Drecht, though to Dalvin he was merely Folsen, and two interesting others, Paul West and a woman – Alice Parsotti."

"Crafty old devil!" exclaimed Blondell, his embarrassment gone, "he really did cover his back."

"And it gets better still," said Calvetti, "he describes the two people who came to his house. Paul West – English, tall and blonde, athletic, well spoken, and a woman."

Pancardi resumed the narrative, "And the woman, she is tall, slender, Italian, with long red-hair and very striking green eyes. Dalvin he says she is attractive and sexy. It would seem that this professore sold his plans for £500,000. He places the money in an account in Jersey – he even gives us the account number and the secure code."

Blondell began to replay the murder scene in his head. He saw Dalvin stepping into the wardrobe and then allowing himself to be bound. He could see the red hair and the fiery green eyes set in a pretty but cruel face. Suddenly the face turned into that of Magdalene as he visualised her with an orange stuffing the throat of Dalvin until he choked. She was mocking the man, calling his name repeatedly.

"That's her then," he said, his embarrassment totally forgotten, "our killer – the red head."

The car screeched to a halt in a courtyard and heavy steel gates were clanged shut behind it as they stopped at the foot of some well worn medieval steps. A uniformed officer was waiting and they were ushered through a maze of corridors before entering a rather dimly lit office and laboratory area. Mostro was the first to recognise the sole occupant and he rushed forward to greet her with his tail wagging ferociously. At the far end they saw Alaina, sitting, bespectacled, poring over some large pieces of paper laid out before her. Mostro had already managed to clamber onto her lap to receive a petting. She flicked his ear and placed a kiss upon the animal's head.

"The plans gave us everything," she said, without looking up.

"So what do we now know?" asked Pancardi, without the civility of a greeting.

"Magdalene has gone through the tunnels from the Arno overflow grate precisely where the entry took place. She has worked her way right through the route and up to the bank vault. In fact she should be joining us shortly."

"This I already know, she has told me," replied Pancardi.

Blondell smiled at the merest thought of her. He wondered how Pancardi could know, unless the excited phone call had been from her. He pondered, but why would it be? Surely she would report to the Questura first. And then he remembered what Calvetti had said about faith and power in Italy. This certainly was not how he envisaged the investigations would go.

"It seems that this team," Alaina continued, "blew open an ancient sealed sewer which the old pervert had discovered in his research. The Questura have already been in contact with Interpol and the bank on Jersey – the money has gone. It went some time ago, probably just after Dalvin's murder. There is another woman, one who called herself Miss Dalvin; she emptied the account, supposedly for the Professor."

"So now we have two women?"chirped Blondell.

"It could be that the whole team are female, have you considered that Mr. Blondell? Would that be so incredible? Women can do amazing things too," she mocked.

Alaina raised her head, caught Blondell's eye and smiled at him. For a brief second he wondered what she knew of Magdalene, of him; were they friends, confidantes, or had they laughed at him together, as only women can when they discuss a man. Her look seemed to pierce him and he felt a distinct unease in her presence.

"The blood smear is useless for DNA, it's been corrupted," she said.

"So all we have are the names?" asked Blondell.

"The South African Police," said Pancardi, "alongside Interpol have already raided the registered offices of this Smithart and Verrison. And as you might guess they have shut up shop and vanished. The premises are deserted. It looks as if they have been empty for some while. The phone has not been used for months and it may well have been a postal safe drop only."

"Vaughan, Verechico?" asked Blondell.

"Who knows, vanished, a ghost, as I said. He could be anywhere right now. We could pass him in the street and not know him," Pancardi sighed.

"West? Parsotti?"

"There are no criminal records in England of this man and forces all over your country are checking every Paul West, via tax, national insurance and employment records, as we speak. We here are doing the same on Parsotti. But let's be truthful we are wasting our time – they have flown."

"Drecht ?" asked Calvetti.

"Gone, if we ever had him," sighed Pancardi.

A hushed silence descended on the room as it seemed that all leads on the crime had suddenly dried up.

"What now?" asked Blondell.

Pancardi stared wistfully into space, "We start the leg work," he said. "We must assume that the team of cracksmen did not know about the full value of what was in the vault, but the financiers did. If they did, someone must have given them this information, so somebody else must know – no? Who is that person? This person we must find."

"And just how are we to do that?" asked Blondell.

"We must go back to the Holy Fathers and his Holiness himself to find the connection we seek. That is a task for Robe and his Cardinals. They have the political connections – we do not. Also he and the Questura must talk to those people whose deposit boxes were opened and get any information they can. Maybe one of the information providers is a deposit box holder too. We need to check any new accounts opened in the last year."

"I think it unlikely that the bank will give us this information," said Blondell, "confidentiality and all that."

"You forget majority holding and the power of the church in our land. I'll get what I can Carlo," confirmed Calvetti.

Pancardi paused as if immersed in deep thought, "Alaina and her team will work on the explosives and the acid. Chemical analysis, purchasing, anything to give us a minor route to enquire on," he continued, "you Alex must go to Jersey and try to follow the tracks of this woman. She arrived from somewhere, she also left, but how, when and where, maybe she will have left us a clue in a mistake she has made? That mistake must be found if we are to find her."

"And while this running around like blue-arsed flies goes on what are you going to do?" asked Blondell sarcastically.

"Me, I will do no more than attempt to trace the owner or owners of the safe deposit box in which the Romanov jewels were held. They were there, but who put them there?"

Footsteps could be heard approaching from the corridor, a woman's step. The door opened and Magdalene entered, her face was flushed, and her eyes showed the strain of working long hours. She came straight to the table holding a small polythene bag in her left hand.

"Found in the tunnel," she said triumphantly, "just below where the explosion on the ceiling took place. It was covered in some shingle but it looks too clean and fresh to have been there for a long time. I think it might be a piece of a shirt. It has been cut with something sharp and there is some dried blood on it."

Chapter 18

The two aircraft touched down simultaneously but they were separated by the waters of the English Channel. The larger of the two landed at Schiphol, Amsterdam, it carried an eclectic mixture of passengers; tired lovers, families on connecting flights to the warmth of the Caribbean, and two rather dishevelled men who might be en-route to the red-light cabins of Voorburgwall. The men, who sat separately at the rear of the plane, did not speak to each other and paid no attention to the other passengers. Instead they stared out of the porthole windows at the baggage carts and refuelling trucks. They were slow to leave the plane and carried nothing more than computer lap-top bags.

The smaller plane landed at Jersey and the single occupant left quickly, passing unnoticed through immigration

Amsterdam was warm on that afternoon and the two men passed through immigration slowly. The first, a tall dark man with a beard, carried a British passport, the second an American one. They walked out separately toward the taxi rank and stood patiently several metres apart in the queue. At the corner of the newspaper stand stood an elegant, athletic, well-dressed blonde man; at the café opposite sat a smaller man in spectacles nonchalantly watching their arrival too. He raised his eyes above a newspaper to scan the many passengers as they moved in a variety of directions; none seemed to be making for the taxi rank. Screaming children, anxiety ridden lovers, exasperated parents and the desperately late passed him totally oblivious of his quick evaluative eye. Satisfied with his observations he moved from his table and left the building – walking briskly. Taking separate modes of transport all four vanished into the hub-bub of traffic heading in the direction of Rembrantplien.

On Jersey a young man was in a taxi heading toward the Jersey bank which had once housed Dalvin's revenge money. The plane had bumped down in heavy winds and he felt slightly queasy, he much preferred the larger, slower and more cumbersome planes which gracefully slid onto the tarmac. His driver was asking him all sorts of questions about his visit, was he in finance, or on holiday? How long was he staying? The passenger's mind flashed and he wondered how shallow the taxi driver might be, did he just talk for the sake of it and not notice, just as Pancardi had observed shallow people do? For his luggage he carried a small hold-all, so obviously he was not staying for long and they were going to a bank and he was dressed in a suit. You don't need rocket science deduction to put two and two together here, he thought. He wanted to admonish the driver for chattering aimlessly, but thought better of it, and simply gave curt replies designed to stifle further questions.

At the bank he paid the driver and admonished himself for failing to remember to request a receipt for his expenses claim. His superiors had given him carte-blanche on everything and he had been amazed at the level of communication between the Foreign Office and the Vatican. It seemed that he could now travel first class to anywhere in the world, stay in any hotel and everything could be charged without question. A far cry from the previous position of only six months ago when he had been considered an expensive eccentric, a liability who should be checked at every opportunity. His credibility had risen within the department and the Banko Rolo raid had made him somewhat of a celebrity. Even the young secretaries showed him more respect; some of them even knew his name now. He smiled and scanned the roof-line of the buildings around the Bank of Jersey. Pancardi had taught him to observe and he was not going to hurry. He glanced at his wrist-watch, he was early. He scanned the street and made for a small coffee bar which would still give him a full view of the bank entrance.

At Rembrandtplein a car turned right then left and disappeared into an underground parking facility. Simultaneously two taxis were disgorging their passengers in the main square. A small motor cycle passed both taxis and parked on the pavement; the rider, a woman, watched two men as they walked casually toward the rendezvous point inside a building which appeared to be made of blue tinted glass and small metal strips. The building was ultra modern and the security guard was checking credentials and asking visitors to sign the book. The bearded man flashed an identity card which he had received the night before by special delivery, the second man signed into the visitor's book and asked for directions – he cracked a joke and the security guard was laughing and pointing to the escalator.

Without removing her crash helmet the woman watched both men – one taking the open glass elevator and the other the escalator. She scanned the street for any other observers before dismounting and placing the crash helmet and her gloves into the secure box at the rear of the bike. She ruffled her hair to release it from the confinement of the restrictive helmet; it tumbled in a thick profusion of auburn which cascaded like a waterfall onto the black leather of her jacket. Her hips were invitingly accentuated by the tight leather trousers which confined her; it was her waist to hip ratio which lit lust and she knew she would be noticed by every passing man once she had started to walk. She sat on a bench and watched intently as the smokers strolled outside and the visitors came and went; her green eyes were constantly scanning, evaluating.

Inside the building the elevator had returned to the ground floor as empty as a discarded chrysalis.

Alex Blondell sat and observed the bank before him. He was sipping a small strong coffee. It was an unimposing building, dark, cold grey stone with tired wooden sash windows painted a dreary brown; it reminded him of the small southern market town he had grown up in as a boy. A place where broken biscuits were sold by weight and pensioners shopped at dawn and the hush of boredom descended at 5pm on a Saturday afternoon. He had hated it – wanted to get out.

Dalvin was a clever man he thought. A clever man to seek such a backwater, a place where young girls craved excitement. Then he remembered Dalvin's potential return to America, cursed Pancardi, for making him over-evaluate, and then wondered if that had been Dalvin's double-bluff, his track covering. No doubt if he had settled on Jersey he would soon have found his local Lolita or imported a young European girl eager to leave the poverty and penury of Bulgaria or Romania behind.

Wealth gave privileges beyond the law and here Dalvin would have been one of the privileged few. His mind raced to Magdalene and he thought that a nice little town like the one of his childhood would suit him now. He no longer craved excitement and he had tired of London long ago.

Across the street a man came out of the bank and lit a cigarette and Blondell's stream of consciousness was snapped – he looked at his watch, it was time.

James Folsen-Drecht sat at a large desk in what appeared to be a virtually empty office. He sat patiently his elbows on the desk, his hands clasped before his face, giving the impression that he was deep in prayer. He was smiling broadly.

"Paul you cannot be serious?" he said.

"Absolutely bloody serious, as you are about to see."

"There is no need to be like that Paul we have to consider our future don't we?"

"Consider our fucking future? Don't think you can roll us over like you did that cunt-struck Professor." West's voice was harsh, cruel and carried a heavy east-end twang, a real Brick Lane drawl. The niceties of affectation were gone. He appeared to be very angry. "Don't think any of us are going to end up in a body-bag," he concluded.

"Now, now, Paul you're getting paranoid. I can assure you that it was none of my people who took care of Dalvin."

"So who was it then? The four fucking horsemen of the apocalypse?"

"Sarcasm doesn't become you Paul. Have you considered Teupner and his Sicilian connections? The Marcosi family? I can assure you we, that is I, did not order his execution. I can also assure you that if he did die accidentally – well I, for one, will not shed a tear for the vengeful old nonce."

"So you want me to believe the Marcosi's have the money, the £500,000? Payment for Teupner's daughter's virginity. Fuck me, how they love their kids, but they love the money more. You seriously want me to fall for that crap – it's a crock of pure shit. And you know that if for some bizarre reason," he paused, "there is now a murder to add to the …….."

"But you won't get caught. The money – well that I think we must write off. And you never get caught, now do you Paul?"

"That's not the fucking point. I have a team who will be implicated.You know my rules. Hell's teeth man, I don't want to be watching my back for the rest of my life for some fucking Mafioso."

The door opened slowly and three men strode confidently into the centre of the room.

"Come in gentlemen," said Drecht. He motioned with an accentuated sweep of his arm.

"We already are," replied Duane Rightman with his customary American twang.

Rightman was followed by John McDermott and finally Klaus Meine. The three men stood looking directly at Drecht who once again had resumed his supplicant posture behind his hands.

"No introductions necessary gentlemen," Drecht spoke quietly, "usually I don't meet with Mr. West's teams. It's a sort of unwritten rule. But on this occasion we have a little problem, well two problems actually. A dead Professor and of course the jewels which are going to take time to cut and disperse. Once we have them all that is."

There was a pause in the conversation and the air filled with tension.

"It's nay bother to me – I just want my money and I'll be on my way," said McDermott confidently.

"Sounds fine man – up, up and away," Rightman agreed, spreading his arms to emulate an aircraft.

"What do you mean?" asked Meine, "all of them."

"Well it would seem that someone is being a little less than honest with us gentlemen," replied Drecht. "You see we have a quantity of emeralds and diamonds unaccounted for."

"No fucking way baby!" Rightman's voice rose in pitch, "what we got, you got, so don't start this ground zero shit with.........."

❧

Alex Blondell crossed the street. He passed the smoking man and entered the bank. Inside the manager was waiting, nervously pacing and observing the entrance hall, clearly he had been briefed.

He approached Blondell, his hand outstretched, "Mr. Blondell?" he enquired. "I'm the manager and we have been expecting you. We will do everything we can to aid the Foreign Office in this most important matter."

Blondell analysed the greeting. No name given, clearly the manager was hoping that Blondell would not have a name for a report-back. Foreign Office? Clearly the manager was panicked; perhaps he had been told that Blondell was far more important than he actually was. Blondell was glad that he had worn the new suit which Magdalene had chosen with him. It was Italian cut, stylish and he thought it made his shoulders appear wider and his hips narrower.

The men shook hands.

"Thank you," said Blondell. "As you are aware I am making further enquiries, as are Interpol, into the theft of monies assigned to accounts in the name of Dr. Richard Dalvin, late Professor."

The manager's mind began to race. He heard the words Interpol and Professor and began to sweat despite the air-conditioning. Had he made the greatest mistake of his managership? Should he have been more careful? Had he been duped by the pretty blonde? Was this the end of his career?

"The woman who came to collect the money is the person we are most interested in," said Blondell.

"Yes, yes, the very attractive blonde woman," replied the manager nervously, "most striking. Our teller was here on the day too. He is in my office now, please allow me."

Blondell followed the manager to his office and calmly took a seat, exactly the same seat which Alice Parsotti had sat in.

"Would you like a drink, a tea or something?" asked the teller.

"Coffee would be nice," replied Blondell.

The teller left the room. Unlike the manager he was perfectly calm. For him this incident was not likely to prove a threat to his future with the bank; in fact it had proved to be the opposite – a valuable learning experience.

"The flight in," asked the manager, "was it a little bumpy?"

"Yes it was- it's quite windy up at the airport."

"It is for most of the year and in the winter it gets foggy too. It's in the wrong place on the Island really."

The teller returned with the cheap instant coffee which Blondell found weak and wanting.

"The blonde woman?" he said, "She called herself...."

"Rose," the manager interrupted, "Rose Dalvin."

"Quite so," Blondell stated and then continued, "she was blonde?"

"Yes."

Blondell turned to the teller, "Her eyes?" he asked.

"Very blue, intense blue deep and very ..."

"Yes, very blue," confirmed the manager.

Blondell took a mouthful of the coffee, not to enjoy it but to give him time for thought, "Her eyebrows," he asked, "were they blonde too?"

"I think so," the teller replied.

"Think carefully, were her eyebrows the same blonde as her hair? Or did she have that Marilyn Monroe look, slightly darker ones?"

"Come to think of it," replied the teller, "they could have been darker. She was very pretty anyway. She put on pink lipstick and her face was heavily made up. That much I do remember."

"Pink?"

"Yeah, a very soft pink, classy, and she sort of pouted it on. And her eyes were deep blue like they had been painted."

"That's probably because they were!" exclaimed Blondell.

He talked with both men for a considerable length of time, his mind cross-referencing the detail in Dalvin's descriptions of both West and Parsotti. He asked which way she had come and gone. How she sat, how tall she was, and her nails – were they neat, painted, cut, and manicured? The manager talked of her having a bodyguard but Blondell sensed, more than knew, that this collection job was accomplished alone.

"Did you see him, the bodyguard?" asked Blondell. Hoping against hope that it might be West.

"No, sorry, she said he was outside, waiting."

"Did anyone meet her then?" he continued, "a tall blonde man-well dressed?"

"I'm sorry Mr. Blondell but..."

"No one met her," said the teller, "she had the cash in a rucksack and got into one of the taxis on the rank outside and then she was gone. I watched her go."

Blondell was aware that the teller had more likely fantasised as she left, leered more than looked, but he was thankful for that. More thankful than the teller would ever know.

As he left the building he knew he had a long shot but he thought that luck might finally be on his side.

꧁

Drecht's hands had not moved, his face was calm and his eyes were cold.

"We believe gentlemen," he said, "that some of the diamonds and especially the emeralds have not been accounted for. I believe there are some emeralds known colloquially as the green lights. They seem not to be among the items which we now have."

"And you think," said McDermott, "that we have them somewhere – is that it?"

Rightman was out of the blocks and leaning over Drecht with both hands clasped to the desk edge in order to restrain himself.

"Listen to me you sack of shit," he said. "I crawled through that tunnel, risked my life and got you your fucking diamonds. I didn't see no separate bags, we took what we took. Maybe those emeralds weren't even there."

"But they were Mr.Rightman." Drecht spat the name at his accuser.

"How.....How....," Rightman stuttered, "do you know my

name?" Then he stepped back, stood erect, and attempted to continue, "What the fu..."

"Rest assured Mr. Rightman we know all of your names. In fact we know all about you."

Rightman suddenly reached across the desk and grabbed Drecht's collar.

"Well you should know about my fucking temper then you sack of shit. I want my cut and if I don't get it I'll give you the biggest fucking enema you've ever had, you fucking slime ball. I'll blow your arse all over this city, they'll be wiping you off the sidewalks with a rag you chicken shit."

"That, I am sure, is a very fine fantas..."

The sentence was cut short by Rightman's heavy blow to Drecht's nose, which exploded like a peach being hit with a hammer. He yelped and rolled from his chair to the floor. Blood flowed copiously as he held his face in his hands.

"You stupid hot–head," said West, blocking Rightman's intended kick to Drecht's ribs.

At that moment a side door to Drecht's office opened and Michelangelo Verechico casually walked in. Dressed in a light blue shirt and a pair of dark blue trousers he looked every inch a security guard, minus the uniform jacket.

"I abhor violence – so unnecessary," he said, "so unnecessary."

West instantly recognised him as the security guard from the main lobby below.

He was followed by two men in dark suits. Motioning with his left hand one of the suited men lifted the moaning Drecht back into his chair and passed him a white handkerchief to place over his nose. The butt of a hand gun protruded from the fold of his jacket.

"Perhaps we should try again?" said Verechico.

Chapter 19

Convinced that the blonde woman calling herself Rose Dalvin and Alice Parsotti were one and the same Alex Blondell crossed the street toward a row of stationary taxis. There were a group of cabbies outside the first car smoking and in the last cab sat a man with a newspaper and a coffee. It was clearly not a busy day. As he approached the group broke up and one man opened the door to the first cab in the rank.

"Excuse me, I need some information," said Blondell.

The cab driver closed the door, disgruntled.

"Do you chaps always work this rank?" he continued.

The cab driver nodded and lit a cigarette, "Pretty much," he said, through the smoke. "Sometimes we're in other places, but pretty much here, why?"

"Some weeks ago a friend of mine came to the bank over there and then left and I was wondering if you might have seen her?"

The cabbie stared at the man in incredulity, "Some weeks ago?" he said.

"Yes but you might remember her. Tall blonde, late twenties, legs all the way up to her chin."

The cabbie looked hard at Blondell and wondered if he was a private investigator on the trail of an adulteress. No man would refer to his friend as having legs up to her chin, nor his wife or girlfriend for that matter. The cabbie pondered – he had seen it all before. Old man, loads of money, young girl loads of life and the affairs of the heart. He stared at Blondell and noticed the expensive

Italian suit, his mind leapt suddenly; he might actually be a husband looking for a runaway wife. He turned to the other drivers and called them over. One man tapped on the window of the cab which held the solitary reader and he too joined the group.

"Blonde, tall, with a bob hairstyle. Long legs, pretty big blue eyes."

The cabbies laughed collectively.

"Big blue eyes eh?" said one, clasping the front of his shirt. "I've always liked big blue eyes," he laughed.

Blondell laughed too, to humour him, "She might have seemed odd," he said. "She had a case and a rucksack. A strange mix for a classy woman. I'm trying to trace her."

The cabbies shrugged and claimed not to remember her. Except for the more thoughtful newspaper reader. Thank God for beauty and lust thought Blondell.

"Yeah," he said, "real good looking girl. I thought the rucksack a bit strange, took her out to St. Aubins Bay."

"Can you take me there?" asked Blondell.

The other cabbies looked at each other. Clearly as the newspaper reader's cab was the last on the rank, he, by rights, should not be the driver. Blondell produced a fifty pound note from his pocket.

"There's a drink in it for all your help," he said and passed the note to the first cabbie of the group.

Moments later Blondell was heading toward St. Aubins with the same driver who had taken Alice Parsotti along the same route. He sat in the front of the cab and talked freely, asking questions about the woman passenger and about St. Aubins.

"Morning it was," said the cabbie, "pretty girl dropped her in the bay area near the yacht moorings."

Blondell's heart sank, "Did she go to one of the boats?" he asked.

If she did, thought Blondell, then there was no hope of tracing her, finding out where she had gone next. He pondered the rucksack full of Euros; surely she would not risk customs. It had to be a boat off the island but where to, France?

"Don't know, didn't see. She might have, she wouldn't have gone far if she did. It's all cobbles down there and she had some real heels on her."

Blondell stepped out of the cab, dropped his holdall at the kerb and gave the cabbie a £20 tip. Standing at the roadside he looked out to sea, turned toward the bay moorings, saw the yachts and his heart sank. He looked at the skyline, he needed a shower and a meal and some time to think – he needed a hotel.

~❦~

"It still appears that some of our items are missing Mr. West. Of course we may be wrong in our intelligence, but we have reason to believe that our sources are correct. They have not been wrong so far." Michelangelo Verechico spoke at the four men, "You know if I wanted, you could all be dead," he said, "but that does not do any of us any favours."

"Fuck favours and fuck you," retorted Rightman.

"Please Mr. Rightman we are all friends here. I am merely attempting to ascertain whether you or other sources are correct. I do not wish us to fall out." He spoke to the man supporting the groaning Drecht, "Larry you can leave Mr. Drecht now." To Drecht his tone became friendly, a false friendly, "Jimmy I think your nose may be broken, I am so sorry please allow me to have it fixed."

Drecht grunted a reply and leaned his head against the high back of his chair.

John McDermott watched carefully. His anger was rising. The feigned politeness and soft cruel voice began to grate on him.

"I dunnae care what you think is missing," he said. "I know what came out of that vault, and if, if we don't get our money we..."

"Oh the money will be deposited one week from today, as agreed and I am sure all of you have done well. You can enjoy the sights for a few days or simply go home. But the nasty fact remains that someone is being less than economical with the truth and I don't like to be cheated."

"Well it ain't us," chirped Rightman.

"Fine. We understand each other perfectly then. I just wanted to say, in person, that if by chance these little items do find their way onto the open market then of course we would have to take appropriate action."

"And what would that be exactly?" Meine asked, "I don't do threats."

"Neither do I Klaus, I can call you Klaus can't I, as we are friends?" Verechico's face opened into a broad toothy smile.

In his hotel room Alex Blondell showered, ordered pizza from room service and considered the information of the day. Had there been something he had missed? He pondered on the cabbies and the fact that Parsotti had been so noticeable. His mind ran through items time and time again but it kept returning to the rucksack. His mobile phone rang – it was Pancardi.

"Alex how are you in Jersey? Have you tracked down our thief yet?" he said.

"Well it's definitely the woman Parsotti."

"This we suspected no? Not two women but one in disguise no?"

"And none too good a one at that. It's almost as if she wanted to be noticed."

"A good way to vanish into the crowd no? Mis-direct your watchers."

Blondell's mind cleared in a flash. Mis-direct, that was it; Parsotti had not wanted to vanish she had wanted the opposite, to be seen; seen arriving at the bank and seen leaving it – leaving for St. Aubins Bay. Why take a taxi from there unless you wanted someone to know where you had gone? There were companies that could have picked her up in other places. She could have hired a car. Why a taxi? So that anyone on her trail would think she had taken a boat to France and vanished along with Paul West. Maybe she thought Interpol would be scouring all the little bays and ports and hideaways on the South of France and the Mediterranean. Looking for that little luxury yacht – but they would be looking in the wrong place. The Rucksack? Why ? Because that was part of her actual disguise. His mind was racing as the deductions and postulations exploded onto his tongue.

"She left by plane and went north – the UK," he blurted.

"How do you know this?" asked Pancardi.

"Because of her real disguise," he replied. "After she left the bank she took the money and she changed her disguise that's why she had the rucksack. Otherwise why have that, she could have

134

used the case, unless there was something else in it?"

"Good – but this is guesswork."

"So she changes clothes - where did she change and when did she leave?"

"She needed privacy no? She needed quiet no?"

"Good grief!" exclaimed Blondell, "she checked into a hotel."

The side of Drecht's head opened like an orchid in full bloom. His eyes went wide in startled surprise and small gurgling noises bubbled from his nose and throat. He wanted to scream but his body crumpled from the impact of the single silenced shot which had pierced his temple. His body twitched liked a landed fish, his eyes glazed and became opaque, and then he was still.

"I do hate thieves and liars don't you," said Verechico calmly. "And as I always say, if you sup with demons make sure you have a very long spoon."

He started to remove the silencer from the pistol which he held firmly in his left hand. His eyes were cold, passionless and bright and his small perfect teeth were shown in a broad grin.

"There always has to be one and I just had to be sure which one it was," he continued. "Greed is such a terrible thing don't you think?"

"Fuck," was all that Rightman could say.

"A right little fuck I'd say," mocked Verechico.

"So he was holding back?" asked West.

"Oh absolutely," replied Verechico.

"But you just shot him," squealed Rightman.

"And I believe you were going to kick him to death just a few minutes ago?"

"As long as we get our money I really don't give a tinkers cuss," McDermott interjected.

"And that," said Verechico, "has been taken care of Mr. McDermott, precisely as was arranged with poor deluded Jimmy here. You merely have one week to wait while the items are re-cut. We have to make sure everything is authentic don't we?"

Alice Parsotti watched the security guard come down in the glass elevator. He was flanked by two large men in suits and to the untrained eye he might have been leading them to a meeting. The three walked across the lobby and out into the sunlight of the square turned left and vanished into the crowd.

"Now that's just fuckin' great, fuckin' fine and dandy," said Rightman.

Paul West was deep in thought, "John give me a hand here," he said to McDermott. "Let's roll Drecht into the carpet and leave him along that wall. This office looks empty anyway. That way the blood won't soak through several layers. With the air-conditioning the smell might take a few days to drift through."

"Murder man, fucking murder," said Rightman, "that's the chair baby, the fucking chair stateside."

"Well we had best be invisible then?" replied Meine. "I'm going back to my homeland, disappear into the Teutoburger Wald."

"I thought you were home Dutchy!" the American exclaimed. Rightman, like the others, had been convinced that Meine was Dutch.

"Well not quite. I'm no Dutchman – Deutsch baby, pure Aryan master race," Meine said, mocking the American accent. "That's my insurance," he continued, "my little cover. Like Jock here I'm away."

"And that is precisely why Drecht was shot." West interjected. "If we try to sell any of those missing items ,even if they do exist, then bam the cops have us. We are screwed. A clever insurance policy."

"So this guy Drecht," asked Rightman, "did," he paused, "was he on the take?"

"Who gives a shit?" Meine was nervous, "It was a warning for us and I for one understood it loud and clear."

The carpet rolling accomplished West looked at the desk, "Against the opposite wall," he said, "now the phone line."

McDermott pulled the cable from the socket and smashed the plastic connector under his heel, "We don't want any unnecessary noises to attract people to this office," he said.

The chairs stacked neatly, the men left the office, locking the door behind them as they went. The first down the escalator was Meine, followed some fifteen seconds later by Rightman and McDermott. All three vanished into the crowd outside just as Verechico had done fifteen minutes earlier.

Alice Parsotti stood astride the motorcycle waiting on the pedestrian square. As West approached she kicked the engine into life and handed him a helmet.

"It's all turned completely crazy," he said.

Chapter 20

Paul West reached inside the grey room safe in room 717 at the Hotel Doupelein on Kloveniers-Burgwal. It was registered to a Mr and Mrs. Diamond, his feeble joke as Alice called it. He had programmed the safe with his mother's date of birth so no one would have been able to reset or open it. Over the upper left corner he had placed a thread of Alice's hair. It had not been disturbed – no one had been in the room. He was satisfied that his caution had paid off; he checked two of his other traps, they were also undisturbed.

Looking out of the window onto the canal below, which ran next to the hotel building, he planned his escape, if he needed it. From the second floor it was just a slight drop into the murky water and a few strokes of swimming would see him across the canal and into the maze of streets which made Amsterdam so quaint for tourism. Light danced across the water and he was reminded of his prize. The package inside the safe containing the emeralds and diamonds was tucked behind two Canadian passports. The package appeared no bigger than a coffee mug wrapped in bubble wrap, it looked like a cheap souvenir but the contents were priceless, unique.

"You know Alice," he said, "we have one chance on this one. Jimmy got blamed for these. We have to stash them somewhere just in case." He threw the package onto the bed. "It was too easy to get him stuffed," he continued, "he had been a greedy little shit in the past and Verechico knew that and that had been his downfall."

"In case of what thieves?" she said loudly.

Water was tumbling down her torso and her ears were straining to hear. Alice Parsotti was in the shower with the bathroom door open. Her naked form shimmered behind the screen and West could just make out the well trimmed triangle of her pubis as she soaped and lathered her legs. She seemed calm.

He walked to the doorway.

"Did you hear what I said?" he asked. "You are one fine woman Alice, so where can we stash the stuff. I don't like having things where we are. It's not our style – just in case," he repeated.

"Oh Paul you are so careful, sometimes it verges on paranoia. No one is going to trace us. We're just a couple of wealthy tourists and we're lucky," she replied.

"Well yeah but I'd like to know why that dumb smuck of a Professor was topped; and if Verechico thinks we cheated him and not Drecht we'll both end up floating in that canal out there."

"Perhaps it was Teupner or one of those families. He wasn't very careful after all," her calm reply echoed off the Italian marble.

"The fucking Mafia always the Mafia. They're everywhere like flies on shit, you just can't get rid of them and if those bastards found that Professor they could find us. We need somewhere safe, somewhere we can always get to easily." He became reflective, "Jimmy was not on the take, but he took a bullet for….."

"For being dumb?" Alice interrupted.

She was shaving her legs now and he could see the line and form of her buttocks as she twisted to reach all angles. He was lucky to have her and at this moment he knew it.

He returned to the bed and tore open the package of jewels and poured them onto the counterpane. He held one of the Russian cut emeralds to the light and rays of multi-green refracted into the room. They were the colour of Alice's eyes.

"Got to be easy access," he muttered, "day and night. Somewhere that even the cops won't think about."

He sat back against the headboard and drifted through locations in his mind.

"Makes me jealous," said Alice.

She was standing in the doorway-naked. The warm glow of

her reddish skin contrasted with the bright green of her eyes. She was towelling her hair.

"So Jimmy and the Professor was there some kind of link?" she asked casually.

"Christ I don't know but this cupful," he pawed the haul, "will give us our insurance."

"But we can't do anything with them, can we?" she said.

Alice had always admired West's ingenuity. He thought when others reacted and that was what made him a good planner, the best. He chose his teams well. It had been his idea to take a side order of green salad, and she had merely encouraged him. She knew he could find a clear pathway to disposing of them if anyone could. It was risky but they had taken the jewels anyway and Drecht had paid the ultimate penalty. She was not intending to do the same.

"That my little green-eyed love doll is where you are wrong," he was almost laughing. "You see," he chuckled, "they will have Europe covered. But there is a place that will cut diamonds quietly. So we go there when we need to. It might be a year, it might be ten. The others will go to ground, John on his little island; Duane to some shagging palace in the Mohave Desert; and Klaus to some log cabin in the German woods. All wurst and wild boar hunting."

"You've thought of everything," she pouted, "that's why I love you."

"Now let's not get too dramatic my lovely. It's safe and the team are clean. No records, no trace. You'd need to be a bloody mind reader to find those guys."

"Oh Paul," she advanced toward him, "this is perfect. But how do we get them out of Europe?"

She lifted an Emerald to examine it. She could see the value in every glint of light.

"Not we Alice," he replied, "you."

Alice Parsotti was standing naked full frontal to West; her navel was in line with his eyes as he sat on the bed.

"You smuggle them out," he repeated.

He touched the soft moist mound of well trimmed pubic hair, twirling shapes and patterns with a fingernail. She shuddered as his thumb brushed gently over her clitoris, simultaneously his index finger toyed with her labia as he slowly opened her. The dew of her sexual arousal ran to his knuckles and he slid a second finger into her.

Her mind was racing and she had visions of cigar tubes and items inserted inside her.

"Won't it show on the x-ray?" she asked, pushing herself onto his fingers with a seductive moan.

"Will what show?"

He lifted his lips from her lower stomach and withdrew his fingers from inside her.

"Having things inside me," she said.

West laughed, "The only thing that is going inside you," he said, "is me."

He leapt from the bed and retrieved her woollen hat from the workspace desk.

"This is where the jewels are going to go," he said.

"But they will be shown won't they?"

"Not if we do it right," he replied. "It's all a matter of misdirection."

Paul West lay in the afterglow of an intense sexual union. Beads of sweat clung to his forehead and his lower stomach felt sticky and bruised from being pounded by Alice. She lay curled beside him, purring as she slept. He lay on his back, one arm tucked beneath his head. His mind replayed the events of the afternoon. Drecht questioned him about the jewels that much he had expected. He could easily bluff that one, but the Professor. Drecht brought that one up why? If he had ordered the assassination why would he bring it up and Verechico had also been cagey. His mind wandered to the Marcosi / Teupner connection and he began to think that perhaps he needed to cover his tracks more carefully. Someone knew what they had done. He would have to change his identity again and do something for Alice. He rolled onto his side and casually threw his arm over her waist spooning her.

Gradually his breathing patterns changed and he slipped into a fitful slumber of vivid chase dreams in which he barely got away. He was a little boy and there was his bloody brother's dog ripping up his shoe, and old Mrs Jenkins at the corner shop cursing him for shoplifting, and his father's belt, and his mother's tears as she put a cold flannel on his back to ease the bruising. Then the trap door opened and he was falling, falling and…

"Come on then sleepy."

A distant voice was calling him back into the room. Snow White and he was a dwarf. A man with a gun, standing about to shoot…

"Hey sleepy."

Alice Parsotti was standing by the side of the bed. She had running shoes on and a tee shirt which was damp and stained with the salt of exertion.

"Hell, what time is it?" he asked.

"It's 8.30 and I've been for a run. Got myself all sweaty, though after last night I shouldn't have the energy. Do you want to lick it off?" She laughed, pulling the tee shirt over her head and exposing her pert breasts which she joggled at him.

"Like two pink nosed puppies in a bag," he said, rubbing his eyes and yawning. "Why the hell didn't you wake me?"

"Well you looked so asleep that I thought you could do with a rest. Mind you your eyes were twitching like mad, so I hope she was good, but not as good as me," she laughed. "I'll have a shower and we can get some breakfast, want to join me?" she asked coquettishly. "I think I've found a hiding place for our lovely, lovely, jewels. Come into the shower and I'll tell you all about it. It's a corker of a place."

West had always hated the London knee trembler, as he called it, and declined the obvious offer of sex but agreed to the shower. Alice rubbed herself against him and he knew that was why they made such an effective partnership. He placed his hands on her soapy hips and knew she was a trophy. He could feel the eyes of other men burning into her, stripping her and fuelling their fantasies whenever she walked past them. Even Dalvin had been seduced by her in an instant and why wouldn't he? She was a fine woman, ruthless, intelligent, sexual, calm and his. West began to wonder if this was what love was like. He had known many girls in the east end; some who would be only too willing to drop to their knees in an alley way and give him pleasure, usually for the price of a good night out. There were the others too, good looking at sixteen and by the time they were twenty they looked like a sack of shit tied with a belt; bloated by childbirth, trapped in the poverty of menial work and stuck with a dead-end man they despised. Men who spent their whole life in the boozer or down at the match. Men who grew fat, old and impotent before their time. Alice was not like that, she was firm to the touch; her body was smooth and her Italian nature made her his perfect partner – a Cleopatra to his Mark Antony.

"Let's do something touristy," he said, kissing the back of her neck.

"Like shopping?"

"No let's go to a museum."

"Yeah a jewellery one so you can scope it."

"No I'm serious," he said, "I fancy Van Gogh."

"Oh you poor man," she teased, as she stepped onto the tiled floor. "He only had one ear, would you cut off an ear for me?" She pinched his ears sharply.

"Fuck me Alice!" he exclaimed, as he winced at her cruelty.

"Maybe," she laughed, as she fled the scene of her crime.

He flicked a wet towel at her in return. She was teasing him, allowing him to see the full view of her sex as she bent over to lift a shoe from the floor, her legs slightly parted.

"Let's do that – fuck it were nearly millionaires," he said.

"But," said Alice, looking over her shoulder at him and wiggling her bottom, "and it's a big but. Shall we fuck now or……. after breakfast?"

"Let's order room service and then we'll fuck and fuck."

"What about Van Gogh?" she giggled.

"Later!" he blurted, as he made a lunging grab for her hips.

Chapter 21

Mostro lay on his bed snoring while Roberto Calvetti and Giancarlo Pancardi drank coffee at the small table in the kitchen of Pancardi's home. The smell of warm pastry filled the room and both men were buttering Italian toast and taking bites in quick succession. They were hurried in their movements and they spoke with their mouths full.

"Nothing, we have no soft information at all," blurted Calvetti. "There was a rumour that one of our Cardinals had been involved with the Mafia but that has nothing to do with the safe deposit boxes in Banko Rolo. Teupner may be a fascist but even he respects the Holy Father's emissaries. Nothing, not a single whisper, even the Holy Father himself could glean nothing from the foreign dignitaries who come. Who ever or whatever this was, the people concerned wanted absolute secrecy and they got it. What about the English Royals or the Swedes? We know that MI6 had one of the safe deposits as part of their safe house back-up facilities. Why not the Royals too?"

Calvetti took a large gulp of coffee. "I have let you down Carlo," he continued, "I can find no more though I dig and dig and dig."

Mostro readjusted and thinking carefully decided to go for a drink from his water bowl. The lapping of his tongue disturbed the silence. He caught the scent of pastry and ambled toward the table in the hope of a scrap or two.

"We two were out late last night," Pancardi remarked, nodding toward the dog to acknowledge his slow stiff movements. "He is retired and not so young as he used to be, hey Mostro?" He patted the dog on the head as if to signal his affinity, rubbed his own knee, which ached, and then took a large gulp of coffee. "The Israeli Government," Pancardi broke his sentence to take a bite of toast, "the owners of a safe deposit box, is that news?"

"But that is ridiculous Carlo. The Russian crown jewels in an Israeli owned safe deposit box."

"No. Not… the, safe deposit box. But one of the boxes.

"How can this be?"

"That my old friend is something we may never truly know," Pancardi's tone deepened, "but we can guess," he paused, "Mossad. We should phone il fidato stallone."

The two men laughed at their own in-joke.

"Let us surmise, my old friend," Pancardi wistfully continued, "a bank in Florence houses the lost Russian crown jewels, and nobody seems to know they are there. The legend carries on, such that people say perhaps they no longer exist. In the same bank MI6 and Mossad why? Well," he paused, "I go one step further." He paused again for a mouthful of coffee, "In Argentina there is a meat company called *Magentosa* and they own this box, only they don't know they have this box because they are a small family business."

Calvetti nodded.

"In fact they have never heard of this box. But they are in Argentina and the people who own this box in their name are in Argentina too."

Calvetti's face remained thoughtfully dour, "I don't see, who are these people?" he asked.

Pancardi looked as if he was in a trance, his mind was piecing together a jigsaw with many missing parts and he could not afford to lose his train of thought. Any outsider viewing the two men might think Pancardi a medium communing with the dead, or a conjuror entering some phase of self-induced hypnotic state. His eyes stared at the wall behind Calvetti's head and he began to slip into a monotone.

"Well every so often," Pancardi's tone was hushed, "some money is needed in Argentina. But who needs it, who and why? Why not move the jewels? Why Florence?"

Pancardi was speaking to himself now, wrestling with questions and answers with the hyper-speed of a computer. Calvetti was following the wild logic. He had seen Pancardi do this before; piece together seemingly unconnected information which would eventually form the basis of a theory. The fine details were often wrong or the rationale not always absolute, but the general idea opened up a world of possibilities.

"Why Florence why Italy?" Calvetti asked.

Pancardi was looking at Calvetti now and the trance was lifting, he was beginning to think and notice outside influences. Mostro too had seen this, he licked Pancardi's hand in reassurance and the moment snapped.

"And now I guess a little," chuckled Pancardi, "and maybe our stallion Alex he would follow me here, after all he is the historian."

Calvetti knew something magical had taken place inside the old Inspector's head, something which set him apart from his contemporaries.

Pancardi's voice lowered to a virtual whisper, "The Russian jewels are taken during the German campaign in 1941. Maybe they are even a pay off to get the Nazis out. Or the Communists think they might lose? Who knows – we are guessing. So the jewels are taken and the deal goes wrong or the Russians are lied to and the jewels they vanish. Where do they go?" he paused with a rhetorical question, "Italy-but why?"

Pancardi took a deep draught of coffee and gave Mostro a piece of pastry under the table. "So Italy," he continued, "they cannot go to Berlin …and pay for the bomb? No that cannot be. That would be madness, even in their eyes, and it is not safe, not safe from the fanatics and Hitler. They are the spoils of a Nazi faction who must have a new leader and make peace to survive. But they lose the coup and the war is lost too, so they must hide the jewels where – here, and wait for safer days and they are helped by Italians." His mind moved in swift tangents, "We too had our fascist black shirts," he continued, "and they are still here now. You know that the Ponte Vecchio should have been blown during the German retreat, like all the other bridges, but it was not. Ha!" He slapped the table in a gesture of triumph, "Perhaps the jewels were already here," he repeated, "already here."

Pancardi sighed, and refilled his mouth with coffee. He paused and thought of the German commander who had refused to demolish the Ponte Vecchio and wondered what he looked like and what he had thought of art. War sickened him and he knew that his father's generation had experienced horrors which others could barely imagine. His father, like all men who have seen the carnage of real warfare, do not thirst for glory, nor medals, nor acclamation, they thirst for peace. His father had wanted him to be more than an artist, to become what he himself could not and Pancardi understood at this moment, more than ever, precisely what that meant. That German commander, whoever he was, had single-handedly saved a piece of the past which would live on long after he and the petty conflict had ended. He probably didn't even survive the war. Pancardi's mind strayed to the ever moaning, ever anxious public and he thought of Rome and the Coliseum and the howling masses baying for the blood of gladiators. He wondered how he would have fared in war, would he have been able to kill and still sleep. His mind was wandering he had to stay focu...

"This is too fantastic for words Carlo, it is almost ridiculous." Calvetti's voice broke the silence and the chain of Pancardi's subconscious meanderings.

"Is it though? Just suppose," Pancardi replied, "just suppose the jewels were then broken up piece by piece over the years to finance the Alte Kamaraden, the old SS in hiding, and the new rising ones like Teupner in Austria. Then the new bank is built and the Vatican have the majority shares – what a safe storage place. Except Mossad and MI6 they are always looking, searching, war crimes, they narrow down the field to this bank. They make the phone taps and they trace the jewels."

"Carlo this is madness, it is too incredible for words."

"But Blondell he intercepts phone taps from the Foreign Office and he has MI6 and they..."

"You mean these robbers are MI6?"

"Why not?"

"Well they could be Mossad then or not?"

"Yes, they could be, but I think not." Pancardi smiled a toothy grin as he spoke, "Is it not a strange coincidence that Blondell he comes to us with the knowledge of the jewels?"

"Ok, so what about the Mafia?"

"Maybe they are just agents of knowledge. Everyone wants to stop the fascists. You know that Mussolini destroyed the Mafia on Sicily when he was in power. He wiped out the families – had them shot, the leaders. He was truly anti-Mafia and it worked better than anything before or since. "

"Carlo this is the wildest notion we cannot prove anything."

"But the fact remains that a company in Argentina owns this deposit box. If we can find this out so can others. Information can be bought at the right price, even from your Cardinals."

Calvetti buttered a third pastry and added a thick smear of Strawberry Jam, "And Dalvin how does he fit in?" he asked, filling his mouth. "Was he fascist too?"

Pancardi considered his response, "Just a pawn caught by his own need for young girls and sex. And when all goes right and they have the plan someone wants him dead, so he dies."

The two men sat in silence. Calvetti was unable to comprehend the full extent of Pancardi's reasoning, it seemed too far fetched for words. There was no real proof but somehow it all made perfect sense. That was Pancardi's forte, his special gift, stringing together unrelated facts and making perfect sense of seemingly disjointed nonsense. He passed some pastry to Mostro who was now awake and sitting near his feet.

"We must phone Young Alex," he said.

"I have some great news for you Alex."

Blondell recognised Pancardi's voice instantly. His own investigations had stumbled and faltered - now they had ground to a halt. His hunches about Parsotti had been innovative and following Pancardi's method he had transposed himself into the personae of Alice rather than trying to guess how he might trace her. If he had been her he might have checked into a hotel somewhere in St. Aubins – it did not take long to find out where. If she wanted to be seen and noticed he guessed somewhere with lots of guests rather than a bed and breakfast guest house. She wanted to be noticed that much was obvious, she was leaving a trail which was far too easy to follow; she wanted to be followed.

As he had walked across the little lawn at the front of the hotel he had realised this had to be a likely place. He had passed the pool on his left and smiled at two young women who were busy drinking and laughing; he had noted the colour of their hair, both were a non descript mousy brown. He had climbed the steps and entered the bar. It had been quiet, well appointed and plush though some of the furnishings did look tired. He had scanned the room - two pensioners reading books. They were obviously a married couple who having spent many years together had run out of things to say.

"Parsotti was at the Somerville Hotel, but I've lost her – she's vanished," Blondell spoke loudly into his palm.

"Now that is a surprise," replied Pancardi. "The signal is weak, I can't hear you very well, can you use a land line?"

"Ok I'll call you back. I'll be at my hotel in ten minutes."

Blondell both hated and admired the way in which Pancardi always assumed he knew the answer before the question had been set. If he was so sure Parsotti would vanish why had he specifically sent him on a wild goose chase, any gumshoe could have done the job. He cleared his mind and evaluated - cunning old bastard he thought.

When he called ten minutes later Pancardi's line was engaged, "Typical," he said, aloud. When he tried two minutes after that, it was still engaged. "I bet he has forgotten to put the receiver in the cradle." After the fourth attempt Blondell cursed and decided to take a shower.

As he stepped out of the shower the phone in his hotel room rang and he had to cross the floor dripping onto the carpet.

"Hello lover boy," said a sultry voice, "have you missed me?" It was Magdalene. Her voice was warm, soft and inviting, almost hypnotic.

"You know I have."

"What are you doing?" she asked.

"Just taken a shower," he replied.

"Lovely. So you're all warm and slippery....mmmm...nice."

He could feel the erection beginning between his legs and was powerless to stop it. He felt like a teenager with a crush and yet he craved the insistent voice. He wanted it to continue, wanted it to entice him.

"When are you coming back to Florence?" it asked.

He wanted to go immediately as his now firm body would substantiate. He wanted to be inside her. Wanted her to gyrate and pound against him. He could smell her scent in the room.

"Soon," he lied. "Just as soon as I get things sorted out here on Jersey."

"You know about the DNA sample we got from the blood?"

"No, when?"

The fantasy died instantly.

"A couple of days ago," she confirmed. "Hasn't Pancardi spoken to you yet?"

Blondell felt slightly foolish, "You're the first person I've spoken with for two days," he replied. "I've been trying to trace this woman."

Magdalene laughed. It rolled from her throat and into his ear like molasses from a spoon, "Another woman already my tiger," she said. "Am I not enough for you?"

"Oh you're more than enough for me," he replied, "more than enough."

"You had better phone him then," she said, sensing his unease. "You can phone me back later. When you're in bed all tucked up and ….ready."

"Pancardi," the reply was terse.

"It's Alex," he said. "I hear you have some interesting news. It would be nice to be kept informed."

"But you have been, no? She has told you, no?"

"Why must you always play games?" Blondell's voice was tense.

"Tell me what you have and I will tell you what we have and then we sort out, no?"

Blondell relayed the story of his pursuit for Parsotti. The trail which he diligently pursued had suddenly dried up. She had checked into the Somerville Hotel for one week under the name of Brenda Mitchell and on the following morning all of her luggage had gone and she had disappeared without paying the bill.

The Hotel had assumed it to be moonlight flit and despite being a four star had only just discovered that the credit card given had been false. The whole trail had been carefully laid to lead straight up a cul-de-sac.

"So what did she do next?" Pancardi asked.

Blondell remained silent – his brain ticking like a bomb.

"Really, you pursue this woman for two days and you cannot second guess. You must think like her Alex," he paused, "become her."

Blondell's mind cleared and it came to him in a flash of inspirational cunning, "She made sure she was seen all the way here," he said, "then she checked into a Hotel, apparently staying for a week. She is gone within hours, minutes, maybe. The credit card is false so she does not have long. She disposed of her clothes, passports and in the case she has another set, another identity."

"Good." Pancardi could sense the blind guess evaluation coming.

"She has a rucksack with the cash."

"Yes."

"Christ alive that's it," Blondell exploded, "she changed into an identity which no one would notice and dumped the other stuff in the expensive case. She arrived as one person and left unseen as another. She wants to be seen arriving but not leaving. So where is the case?"

"And where would you place it?" asked Pancardi.

"The ocean of course."

"Precisely."

"So simple and yet so effective. Lead us out here and then keep us running around while she quietly slips away," Blondell halted engrossed – he was thinking.

"Go on …reason," said Pancardi, his voice sharp.

Blondell voiced his thoughts, "She has a rucksack full of Euro. She needs a small airport where she might not get checked."

"England my friend!" Pancardi exclaimed impatiently.

"Southampton twenty minutes away."

The silence that followed expressed the dejection in Blondell. He had pursued his quarry and she had taken him down a blind alley; he felt slightly stupid.

"But there is hope," Pancardi's voice was elated, "they have made a mistake and we have been lucky."

Blondell was still reeling from the complexity of his female quarry. His tongue was dry and stuck to the roof of his mouth. He gave no reply.

"In the tunnels, that rag, the scrap of cloth, which Magdalene finds.... Alaina tests it. We have DNA. We have Interpol check out details; and this DNA it belongs to a petty German thief called Udo Richter. He has a record. We have a lead. Good news no?"

"You said he was a petty thief." Blondell checked the excitement in his voice, "Surely they would not have him on any team. It's far too risky he'll be too easy to trace."

"Yes, but what if they do not know the risk and it is a long time since he was last arrested. Nine years in fact. Nine years of a clear record. Only he has no tax records in Europe anywhere. So what does he live on?"

"Well it could all just be a red-herring, a careful plant," Blondell was wary, "another blind alley for us to rush up."

"It could….. maybe. Only this thief he has not been taken for years by the police. He is out of Germany. He has no tax records anywhere. And he has his mother in an expensive nursing clinic in Köln. All this the police know because they think he is evading tax – working abroad or using another identity. But as you English say, once a thief always a thief, no? And this mother she has Alzheimer's and she cannot say anything to us. But the staff at the nursing home they say he comes to visit many times a year. Good no?"

Blondell hissed through his teeth, "My God, he thinks he's safe," he said. "He thinks he's covered his tracks."

"And sooner or later he will..."

"Visit her." Blondell interrupted. "We've got him," he laughed, "and if we get him we get them all."

Chapter 22

Alex Blondell replaced the receiver in the cradle. Eighteen minutes later he was stepping into a taxi and heading for the last flight off the island to Southampton.

With luck, he thought, he'd get a connecting flight to Düsseldorf and be on a late night train to Köln. If he could not get a connecting flight he'd stay at the Park View Hotel opposite the Titanic memorial – he knew the area well. Often as a student, complete with battered rucksack, he had come to Southampton for the boat show and stayed in an old pub where the Mayflower Pilgrims had set sail...

"Shit that's it," he said aloud. "Why didn't I see it? So simple, so bloody simple?"

"Are you alright mate?" enquired his quiet driver. "You ain't left nothin' behind like yur ticket?" He laughed and turned sharp left.

Blondell laughed too but thought- twat.

"She's changed herself into a student and melted into the crowd," he whispered to himself.

He imagined Pancardi nodding wistfully and heard his dry laugh ringing in his ears. It seemed so simple, so easy, and yet so fool proof. That was why she had the rucksack. Why didn't he think of it earlier? Such an obvious clue and he had missed it. This was a woman who thought of every detail. The rucksack had not been a randomly chosen bag and yet she used it in full view at the bank. Even she was not infallible; if she made this mistake she could make others, and if she makes mistakes, he thought, I can catch her. His memory ran wildly through the fine detail of his investigations – looking for any small clue or mistake, anything he might have missed. Imagination gave him a vision of Alice Parsotti dressed as a student with the rucksack, passing the customs men. Had they even been on duty that day? Her gamble had paid off and she had slipped by unnoticed. He wondered if even one man had noticed her as she passed. He could see her dressed down for the task and once in the UK she could take up another identity and vanish. She was good, he mused, very good in fact, better than most, but not good enough.

"Four days and not a sniff of the man," Pancardi voiced his frustration. "He pays for the medical care via bank draft, half yearly in advance, and he visits fairly regularly. No one seems to know when he's coming or if he's coming, business keeps him away." Pancardi sighed heavily, "There is an emergency service number which transfers and re-routes calls, rather like a mailing service. We have tried a trace but it goes through the Cayman Islands and we can not get further information. I think Roberto needs to get one of the Mafia boys on the case. To make him an offer..."

"That he can't refuse?" interrupted Blondell. "Ha bloody ha, this is not a movie you know and you are not Marlon Brando."

Pancardi lowered his voice and became serious and thoughtful, "Alex I am not joking," he said. "Roberto can have these connections through his Cardinals and if we lose Richter here we may have to use them yet. But he will come to visit again of that I am certain, unless the old lady dies."

He handed Blondell an old photograph. It showed an athletic young man with a dark pony tail and goatee beard. His right ear was pierced and Blondell knew that the man they were looking for no longer dressed like this. He focused on the face and tried to make impressions of age and fashion which might fit Richter now. His mind strayed to the steel grate which the whole team had scaled like inverted spiders and he felt, rather than knew, that Richter had not gained weight, though he might have become more muscular.

"How old is this?" he asked. "It looks like 1980's Goth to me. Look at the velvet frock-coat he's wearing."

"Too old, far too old, but it is the only thing we have. Taken from his mother's photograph collection and there is nothing more recent. In that he was very careful. Sometimes the old woman sits and looks at them but she does not really know what she is looking at. Do you know anything of this illness Alex?"

"No." He was curt. "So we sit here and wait for this Richter to show. It could be weeks, months, and if he thinks we are on to him he may never turn up."

"It is like your brain rots inside your head, like a bulb in a pot with too much water. It is the worst of all illnesses. This is the one Pancardi fears - this is the one he could not endure. To lose the mind, the personality, this is indeed hell." Pancardi reflected and then changed tack, "You could not find more on Parsotti. She is clever no?"

"Very clever but I never understood why she would risk the possibility of being caught by us or customs and why that small amount of money could cause her to take such risks."

He looked at Pancardi and hoped that the older man might throw some criminal psychology into the mix. Something which his experience alone would allow them to understand and have an edge - he was disappointed.

"Greed," was Pancardi's smiling reply.

"But they have the jewels, it simply doesn't make sense."

"Each one of us has a weakness Alex, why should hers not be greed?"

"But to jeopardise the whole caper for £500,000 is madness, its crazy." Blondell reflected before continuing, "Put yourself in their shoes; you have just taken one of the largest hauls of jewels ever, and you go back for £ 500,000. It just doesn't make sense."

"You think there is something else then?" Pancardi tilted his head quizzically much as Mostro did when perceiving there might be a scrap of food on offer.

"Oh I don't know," sighed Blondell, "I'm just clutching at straws I suppose. Greed is greed after all. But it just seems unlikely that all the planning, all the risk, might be wasted in a simple customs security check."

"No, this is good," he laughed in reply. "You look for more.

You know that they can make mistakes like….. the Professor, so maybe there is more in your thoughts. So this is good, very good."

"Good it's terrible, bloody awful in fact."

"Why so? Because you would rather be in Florence with the lady of the dark eyes, rather than Köln with your friend Pancardi? Greed is a weakness my friend just like lust." Pancardi laughed heartily and then suddenly stopped as if stricken. "She is human," he said stoically, "and if she is human she will make mistakes; precisely her greed makes it so, and we, my lusty young Englishman," he clapped Blondell on the back, "we will catch her?"

Blondell's face reddened, "Well anything would be preferable to being stuck here in this foul smelling place with nobody but you and Mostro for company."

"I agree, Magdalene is far more comforting than me and she is more interesting no? To have a warm woman is more joy than any conversation and puzzle with me and Mostro." Pancardi laughed again and clasped Blondell's shoulder, "But it will be worth it when we get them, no?" he said, convincingly.

"If," retorted Blondell, "if - and it's a big if at that."

Mostro heard his name in Pancardi's voice and immediately rose to stretch his limbs. He yawned and Blondell sympathised with his dilemma of waiting. He wondered how many times this little white dog had been forced to wait as Pancardi patiently moved in for the kill. Blondell noted with envy that the ability to sleep almost anywhere was a marvellous gift which most dogs enjoyed – Mostro was no exception. He had found a comfortable end of bed to lie on and he was content, though any quick movement brought him to instant readiness. Blondell noted that he rarely barked except as either a warning or a request. His economy of effort was the perfect compliment to Pancardi; it was almost as if he had adopted Pancardi's personality.

"Look even he is bored," blurted Blondell, changing the subject.

"Bored no, he is never bored with Pancardi, he is tired. He has been very busy, he has been studying, and he knows what to do if and when it happens."

"Do what if it happens? That's if anything happens at all. Studying? What an earth has a dog been studying?" Blondell felt that Pancardi was toying with him again. "Should we go downstairs, to at least be part of the stake out?" he asked.

"And if this man thinks we are close," Pancardi replied, "or have any idea of him, he will vanish and we will..."

"I know," Blondell interrupted, "lose the one and only solid lead we have."

"Yes, precisely," snapped Pancardi. "The paparazzi have covered this story and your face and mine may be known to them. They read the papers too. We must wait - until we get the call. Anyhow there are beds here."

He pointed at two iron framed bedsteads which looked as if Noah had rejected them for the Ark. Blondell remarked that they looked and felt uncomfortable enough to have been in use then. Pancardi shrugged, his resolve was absolute; he could taste blood in the water and although his knees were weak his heart was strong and his mind as sharp as a tack.

"And," he continued in the same stoic manner, "we can come and go via the delivery entrance at the rear. He must suspect nothing. He must think he is safe; if he shows up we have enough officers to take him."

"Won't he think it strange that most of the nurses have changed?"asked Blondell.

"No I think not. The girls here change often, they come to Germany to get a start in the west - Russians, Poles, Romanian. Once they get established they move on or go back. He will not remember their faces. Anyway all of our officers are..." Pancardi stopped mid sentence.

The phone on the desk rang, Blondell instinctively moved toward it.

"Leave it!" Pancardi snarled abruptly. "It will ring three times if he..."

Blondell counted, two, three, "Bingo," he said, "he's here."

Roberto Calvetti had not been idle, his trace on the fascist black shirts had proved valuable and his use of the Sicilian Cardinal with his obvious Mafia connections had come to him in a flash of inspiration. There were still many Italians who longed for social and political stability; Cardinal Capresse was one of these. As long as the church remained the focal point of Italian society he had little time for the fascists. His connections extended into the Mafia, who unlike the fascists, wanted to enhance the Catholic faith rather than usurp or destroy it. Capresse had given Calvetti the name of the underground Italian fascist organisation, the location, the principal officers and the names of bankers and brokers who laundered money in various corners of the world. For that information he had turned to the Mafia who were constantly watching. There could have been covert assassinations arranged but too many fascists were prominent citizens and the Mafia could no longer afford the wars of the past; there was an uneasy truce with the political hierarchy and a few fascists could be dealt with when the tide turned. The Mafioso played a watching game ready to pounce if and when the time was right.

The fascist tentacles extended across Europe and into South America. Argentina had figured quite prominently but the name of *Magentosa* had not appeared. Calvetti wondered if the name had merely been usurped and the owners knew nothing of the use. The family company was run by an old man but he had three sons, sons of the right age; one of whom had political aspirations and connections. Whatever the true connection it was most probably at the highest level and well hidden. The youngest son might well be no more than a pawn; a pawn promised advancement; a pawn to be used in the wider game, and expendable if the time came. Calvetti had passed this information on and the resulting raids had shown, as Pancardi surmised, older connections to Hitler's former SS and a new, far more sinister, faction. Young men who glorified the history of which they had no direct experience – these were the real danger. Calvetti had little doubt that the youngest son of the *Magentosa* meat business would meet with an unfortunate accident and the strands of the web would suddenly sever.

The Cardinal's Mafia connections ran deep, so deep that the Holy Father himself was not fully aware of them. To Calvetti they had proved an asset but they had not given him any real leads on the robbery team. Paths of enquiry had led up alleyways which in turn doubled back into dead ends. The tangents were crossing at all sorts of angles and he knew that he might as well try to unpick a bowl of spaghetti with tweezers. His report on progress had been inconclusive and was not going to get them any closer to the gang. Pancardi had suggested he join him in Köln. Blondell was on his way from Jersey, with some information after tracking down Parsotti. That had been four days ago now and he knew that the tedium of a dreary stake-out lay ahead of him and he was in no real hurry to participate.

On the plane he tried Pancardi's mobile phone, to tell him he was on the afternoon flight-it was switched off. He tried the nursing home direct line - the number Pancardi had given him. He punched the number into his palm. It rang three times before the stewardess reminded him that all mobile phones needed to be switched off for the duration of the flight. Cursing he snapped it shut and pulled a pillow under his head so he could lean against the fuselage in comfort.

The train from Edinburgh was slow and the clanking and creaking of the carriages as it crossed the Tay Bridge set the imagination of John McDermott racing. He thought of the icy waters below and the haunting screams of those who had plunged into the deadly water when the original bridge collapsed. He tried to recall the date and settled on 1889, the same year as his mother's prize French mantel clock had been made, but he knew he was probably wrong. He thought of his little daughter who clung to him when they swam together, her arms gripping his neck like a vice and he thought of the poor little girls who might have clung to their fathers as the train carriages plunged into the river bed that December night. He saw the smiling face of a six year old girl, his girl. He was in a half–dream state, his head nodding forward, first to the left and then right as his mind replayed nonsense verses of McGonagall before being flipped topsy-turvy into the world of Spike Milligan and the goons; simultaneously the voice on the speaker above his head announced.

"The next station is Dundee. Next station Dundee in 5 minutes."

McDermott raised his head, looked at the overhead luggage rack and then gazed listlessly out of the window. The run from

London to Aberdeen had always made him tired but he knew that there was no way to trace him once he had landed back in Scotland. He could have taken the city to Dundee flyer which would have been quicker but airports kept records and he did not want to leave any easy traces to follow. Slow but sure had always been his brother's motto and it had always worked.

He had come into Gatwick from Amsterdam as Jonathan Landis and almost immediately destroyed the passport and any items which could link him to the job.

His share of the money would, as it had always done, go directly to the untraceable Cayman Islands account, then on to the Isle of Man and finally be transferred to his Royal Bank of Scotland account as fictitious monthly salary payments. The Inland Revenue demanded their tax, and he paid it; thus his cover was complete. He was simply a man who worked from home for an anonymous, non-existent, non traceable company on the Isle of Man. Nobody at the Inland Revenue cared what he did; his tax records were complete, he owed nothing and so he was just another meaningless statistic in a mass of statistics. McDermott had evaded being caught by being careful. He was never greedy and the only contact he ever allowed close was Paul West and even then only on neutral territory. He chose his jobs carefully and discussed nothing; the only other human being who had his confidence was his wife. At one time it had been an older brother, who had been a partner and mentor, but since his early death at the hands of cancer, his circle of associates had dwindled and he "worked" less and less.

The train pulled out of Dundee and the carriage was now empty.

"1879," he said out loud, "28th December 1879."He thought of his brother again.

At Aberdeen he alighted from the train carrying his holdall and passing the ticket collection barrier he walked into the main station area. His ears were greeted by a small voice shouting.

"Daddy, daddy," it called, "over here." A small dark haired girl was waving frantically before running through the crowds to reach her father.

McDermott swept the child up into the crook of his arm and she in turn threw her arms around his neck and cuddled him as she was joined by a dark haired woman who was obviously the child's mother. The facial resemblance between them was uncanny and they could have been twins save for the distance of time.

The ticket collector had seen it all before. A man who worked on the rigs come home to be with the family he risked his life for, and smiling he turned to continue collecting tickets.

"She's missed you John," said the woman.

"And what about you?" he asked in reply.

"Me too."

"It's good to be home princess," he said.

"All clear and no hitches?" she asked, reaching to take the holdall. "Golly this is heavy."

"Presents - I can't come back to my girls without presents, now can I?"

The little girl shook her head as the woman caught her eye with hers, "We don't need presents," she said smiling, "it's just good to have you back in one piece."

They kissed briefly and without putting the little girl down he said, "That's it for me now, the last one. For the stronger we our houses do build the less chance we have of being killed. Let's go."

"You still miss him don't you?" the woman asked, after hearing the verse recited and allowing McDermott to take the holdall in his free hand.

"Yep, every time I cross that damn bridge I think of that school project. All the help he gave me; ridiculous but Jimmy and that bridge are sort of linked. I think he haunts it."

"I'll drive," she said, "you must be tired."

"That's it now princess, never again," he replied, "I'm home for good this time. No more risks, no more chances, I've retired, we're made in the shade, home and dry."

The woman smiled and the engine burst into life.

Chapter 23

The warm afternoon sunshine made the outside of the modern museum building glow. It had become one of the jewels in the crown of Amsterdam and the paintings it housed drew people from the four corners of the globe. West and Parsotti were seated at a café table and Alice wore heavy sunglasses which gave her an air of Audrey Hepburn. As they waited for their coffee to arrive, West toyed with the idea of taking some of those famous paintings which were now so prominently housed. He was certain it could be done, despite the modern security. His mind strayed to the notion of fashion and he marvelled at the fact that so many paintings had been destroyed, used for target practise at the asylum.

"It's the strong colour that makes it bold and expressive," Alice said, snapping his train of thought.

"Funny but they look different close too, and amazing that he never sold a single one in his life and now, well they go for millions," West replied.

"Paul it's not all about money you know. It's about a passion for life, for beauty, for art."

"Well when you have no money and you're hungry, beauty and art takes a back seat, little Miss Privilege."

"You're not going to go on again about how poor your family were are you?" she asked. "How your father left you. How your mother had a breakdown and you were grown up.... no a man at 13. It gets tiresome you know, tiresome."

"It's all right for you," he replied wistfully, "you and your Italian moneyed routes, I came up the hard way."

She could sense the familiar bitter edge coming into his voice. His life had been hard she knew that, but his bitterness was powerful and sometimes all consuming. He had learned quickly that boys from his background simply didn't advance, because they weren't meant to, in fact they were held back. Quashed, squashed and sat upon as he put it.

"I'm their worst kind of monster," he said, "the bastard demon they fear. The one that sits in the dark with a sharp knife and a whetstone; a knife ready to cut their throats and steal their silver," he paused, "a working class kid with a brain."

"Oh, Paul," she made a face which mocked him. "They? Just who are they?"

"Every shit and advantaged bastard that ever stopped me getting on."

"Well you big demon monster you, you're at the top of the dung pile now." She smiled broadly at him defusing his anger, "And you're mine all mine," she continued, "and we are so lovely and rich it's marvellous," she giggled, "so marvellous it's obscene. I just love obscene wealth."

Picking up on the change of mood in her banter, he started humming an old pop tune, returning full circle to the beginning of their conversation.

"Art for arts sake," he sang, "and what's the next line? Money for God's sake," he chortled, with a broad smile on his face.

"Philistine and that old 10cc tune won't let you off the hook," she laughed back at him.

"And you my little beauty," he retorted, "are worth a million Van Goghs any day."

He kissed her, reaching across the small table and placing his hand behind her head to draw her into the embrace.

"You always go for the renaissance and the Florentines why don't you try extending your palette," she was taunting him now, as they broke from the kiss, knowing what his reaction would be.

"Oh my," he said, with mock sarcasm, "we'll be looking at Chagall next. Now that is real robbery. It looks like an eight year old painted it. Where's the talent, the skill, the verve? At least Van Gogh had a sense of moving things on. Hey if I had some talent I could have done this rather than be a cracksman."

She laughed at his reaction and the way in which she could

virtually push his thoughts in any direction.

"Chagall is total shit," he said loudly.

"Sssh there are kids about," she chided.

Then reaching across the small table she pulled his head toward her and kissed him hard on the mouth; this time it was her hand which held them fast.

When the waiter arrived with the coffee they broke from the embrace and Alice looked at the man with her moist green eyes and in return the waiter's spine tingled in delight. He like many men before him had noticed the rampant sexuality hidden behind those green orbs but he knew that she was beyond his acquisition.

The passing tourists mistook them for a young couple, madly in love. Touching, talking and laughing, content in each others company but Alice Parsotti was also scanning, watching them just as carefully as they moved into the museum. Security was high and the idea had come to her in a fit of inspiration as she jogged along the tow paths and over the canal bridges. A simple idea, as Paul West had said to her, almost too simple.

"It will work Paul," she said. "It's the perfect place."

"I know," he replied, "I don't think I could have thought of that one."

"Well our stuff is there now and it will only be there for a few days at the most. Have you still got the passports on you?"

He tapped his breast pocket. "As soon as the money is transferred," he said, in reply, "we'll be on our way. I don't like all this hanging around. I'd like to get well away. It's been what..... four days? Jesus we should be up and away by now."

"What shall we do for the rest of the afternoon?" she asked.

"How about a tour of the red-light cabins?" he joked.

She scowled at him, "Well, I'd like some lunch soon," she replied, "and a canal boat ride, something romantic."

"Fine by me," he said. "I can do romantic."

"Since when?"

⁓❧⁓

"The Questura have found a red Volkswagen in Michelangiolo, just above the city. It's been parked there for days. It might be abandoned but it seems too new and it's not a hire car.

They've got something on it. I'm going over to take a look at it right now. We might be able to tie our man into the vehicle if he…"

"Have you phoned Pancardi?" Magdalene interrupted.

"If he left any traces of DNA. I need you to come with me. I'm told there's some sort of equipment in the boot and if it's what I think it is."

"Have you phoned him?" Magdalene insisted.

"Yes, but I can't get through. There might be a problem with the signal. I've tried Alex too but he seems to not pick up."

Magdalene was quick in her response, "Alex? Why do you have Alex's number?"

Her reaction was sharp, pithy and tense. Magdalene was wondering why Alaina should refer to her Englishman by his Christian name and not as Blondell. Alaina sensed the sudden rush of jealousy and wished she had not mentioned the young Englishman. She didn't find him attractive but Magdalene clearly did and moreover she was protective of that attraction.

"I don't, well I do, but that's not the point," replied Alaina.

"It's a point to me."

"Look Magdalene I do not have an interest in Alex. We have been friends too long a time you and I; I need to speak with Pancardi. Maybe if you try to phone your man you can get a message to him."

Duane Rightman had a passion for live sex shows and Amsterdam was the perfect place to indulge his fantasies. He loved the sordid squalor of the whorehouse because, as he said, it gave him anonymity. This club, *The Apollo*, was a classy outfit, a little more expensive than the usual but the on cost gave privacy and he was in a booth with a young coloured girl who looked no more than nineteen or twenty. She was naked, and there for his personal use during the show. He could see the stage clearly and on his face he wore a huge grin as his eyes became transfixed by the sweaty glow of female flesh on the podium. The young coloured girl came as part of the entertainment package and Rightman knew he would enjoy her. It was mid-afternoon and his growing excitement was suddenly interrupted by the double vibration of his mobile phone which was in his left trouser pocket. It was a message. He thought about taking a look but decided it could wait and he encouraged the young girl's head toward his loin while the intensity of a faked orgasm was shrieked from the stage. As the young girl moved her mouth methodically, he admired her and knew she would work rapidly to ensure that another client could take his place quickly. He wondered how old she was, what she really thought of men and how she had ended up working as a whore in Amsterdam. She bobbed steadily, forcing him to fight for concentration. He tried to slow her with his hand but the floor show had changed and his excitement was reaching its peak. Desperate to lengthen the intensity of the moment he forced his hand into his pocket and digging out the mobile phone flipped it open. One new message - it read, "WMG."

His reaction was instantaneous, "Stop," he said, pushing the girl away from him.

She looked perplexed and didn't understand how her skill had not achieved physical recognition. Jumping to his feet he readjusted his clothing as a burly security man poked his head around the booth screen.

"Everything ok?" he asked.

"Yeah fine," replied Rightman, "absolutely fucking doodly pip."

The girl looked at the bouncer and shrugged her shoulders and then gave a nod.

He retreated back out of sight. The American wondered if the guard was her pimp and if he watched her working, or if he used her himself. The squealing floor show continued as Rightman reached into his jacket and threw the girl 500 Euro; it cascaded onto the couch. He was feeling generous and as she bent to collect up the cash he was sure she would have seen to his every need if only the text had not arrived.

"Got to go honey," he said, as he patted her behind. "Nothing personal just gotta go."

He left the girl and pulling on his jacket he passed the bouncer making eye contact as he did so.

"You're a lucky boy working in a club like this, all these lovelies," he said. "But if I come back and you wanna see my show, be careful man, be very careful or very brave." He smiled a toothy sinister smile, "Or I'll stick my fucking knife right down your throat man."

The bouncer stepped back amazed by the sudden aggression and what he perceived as insanity; he considered breaking the man's nose to teach him some manners and then thought best to let him simply slip away. He had the air of a madman anyway and he didn't need a knife in his guts to prove his masculinity to anyone.

Outside the air was clear and Rightman looked at his phone again. "*WMG*," was clearly displayed; the message was from a withheld number but he understood the sentiment immediately. As he scrolled down, two more messages came in rapidly, one simply said, "*Away J*" and the other, "*WMG, P.*" The signal had been designed to warn others if there was imminent danger. Who had raised the alarm? Rightman thought that perhaps the Italian authorities had the girl and then reasoned that she would not have been able to text if she had been taken. Still no text from the German either, he lit a cigarette and waited until he had finished it.

Suddenly at a brisk pace he set off toward his hotel. In his mind he churned the scenarios over. Someone had got to them – they had made a mistake. He checked his phone – there were no more messages. The German, they've got him, he thought, and then he reasoned on the time he had to get back to the hotel pack and leave. When he turned the corner of Dam Square his ears picked up the sounds of sirens and a distant megaphone. He stopped a shopping tourist who was walking toward him.

"Hey buddy do you speak American?" he asked.

"Sure do," was the curt reply. The man was Dutch but he spoke as if he had learned the language in America; his accent was strongly New Yorker.

"What's going on, all these sirens and all, it's kinda spooky?"

"The cops, they got that hotel sealed off." The man pointed toward the Doupelein. "Some armed thieves or sumthin' the place is closed off. Where you from?"

"Denver, but I need to get back to my room."

"Hell buddy I don't think you'll be in there tonight. They're checking all passports and they're moving people to different hotels as they come back. Checking all the rooms too."

Rightman wondered if Parsotti and West were trapped inside the building. If they were, there was no hope of getting out. He flipped open his phone and then sent a simple text, "*S when?*"

The reply was almost immediate all it said was, "*Now.*"

"Oxygen tank, filler tubing and a filter," Magdalene, was taking stock aloud.

"Why would they leave that here?" asked Alaina, "they must have known that we would find this car eventually."

"Maybe one of them is a spy," Magdalene joked in reply.

"It was the same with Dalvin and the clues there." Alaina was puzzling, "They take all this trouble, think of all the detail and then they leave equipment in the car - why?"

"Alex says that even the best, how do you say, screw up the fine detail."

"But this is not fine detail it's basic, everyone knows that much, it's out and out screw up."

As the forensic team started to arrive the area was cordoned off and the two women once again turned to their respective mobile phones. Again there were no answers.

"Why the hell aren't they answering?" exploded Magdalene. "You think he would pick up for me, what the hell is he doing?"

"Don't you mean who?"

Magdalene missed the quip and Alaina decided to let it pass. It had probably been a poor joke anyway. Magdalene tried for a fourth time before becoming disgruntled and stuffing the phone into her bag.

"Cretino," she said under her breath.

"They're all the same, aren't they?" Alaina laughed, attempting to defuse the anger.

"Even the English so it seems," Magdalene replied, a slight smile creeping onto her face.

The sight-seeing tour boat drifted around the corner of

Herengracht and under the arch at Koningsplein. It was heading for the bridge, and providing that was not carrying the high speed cyclists who traversed it as a short cut across Kloveniersburgwal, it would be down. They were en route to the lagoon area where boats turned in the canal complex to take to the narrower quaint routes which the tourists, especially the Americans, loved. The pilot of the river barge was pointing out land marks while West and Parsotti were laughing and joking along with the other tourists on board. An old woman asked how long they had been married and they lied and said they were on their honeymoon. The woman clapped her hands in front of her face in delight. She smiled and talked of her husband and his love of Amsterdam; he was off at some show or other and she had gone out on the boat for the afternoon. Alice Parsotti imagined the man this woman had been married to for thirty one years and how right now he was probably holding the hips of a girl half his age and pushing himself into her. She smiled and looked at the older woman who had trusted her husband so easily; the thought of him being with a young girl somewhere had not even crossed her mind. Or conversely she knew full well what her man was up to and yet turned a blind eye to the matter. Alice asked herself if she could do the same and concluded that for love she probably would. If that was the only issue in their long marriage then it was a small price to pay for happiness and security. Meaningless, mindless sex, she thought as she smiled at the older woman, who was now imparting the honeymoon discovery to all who might listen aboard the boat.

As the boat passed under Raadhuisstraat the Doupelein Hotel came into view.

Both West and Parsotti were unprepared for the sight which greeted their eyes. The streets were closed, the small iron swing bridge was raised and armed police had obviously sealed the hotel. As the barge drew closer and momentarily slowed armed police waved it on. West scanned the confusion and moved toward the driver under the camouflage of a canopy.

"What the….?"he asked.

"A robbery," said the pilot loudly.He was speaking Dutch into a radio receiver, "Apparently the police are raiding the hotel looking for a gang of jewel thieves and armed robbers. It's all over the local radio news," he called to his passengers.

Alice Parsotti gathered her hair together and placed it under a cap and casually turned to face the opposite side of the canal. Her eye immediately found the snipers on the roof tops and she knew in an instant that the quarry the police were hunting was them. Marksmen, there was no need for that she thought, and she turned toward the prow. West looked back toward her over his shoulder and their eyes met. Then seating himself near to the driver, so as to remain under the canopy, he made a hand signal to imitate the use of a telephone and Alice Parsotti reached into her bag.

Roberto Calvetti was tired when the plane landed and he had to wait for what seemed ages for a taxi. It was mid rush hour and the traffic was heavy. His driver had been a sour faced man who didn't want to get embroiled in the one–way system and suggested that Calvetti could get to the nursing home from the corner where he would leave him. Calvetti was glad to see the car pull away and he looked up toward the growing clouds in the sky above the city. He stretched his hand out to the elements as he walked, palm up, and thought he felt one or two light spots of moisture hit it; we're in for a stormy night he thought.

"I'm getting too old for this gallivanting around," he said, talking to himself.

Pancardi had told him to come to the rear of the building and use the service entrance, but the sour faced cabbie had dropped him now and he could see the place a few yards ahead. He needed a shower and as he entered the front doors of the nursing home he could smell his own stale sweat. That was his first and last mistake.

Udo Richter turned at the reception desk as the doors creaked behind him and Calvetti entered – he recognised the detective instantly. His reaction was swift and deadly and Calvetti flew back through the doors as his feet were lifted from the ground by the sudden weighty impact against his chest.

"Put the gun down," Pancardi yelled from the stairway.

Richter gave no reply but turned and sped down a corridor, pushing one of the nurses to the ground as he passed. A single shot rang out behind him and he felt a tingling pain at his left side and stumbled into a vacant room. Crimson syrup was oozing from the wound - it was superficial, irritating more than debilitating, and he knew he only had seconds and no choices. He threw his full body weight against the reinforced glass French window and the frame gave way with a splintering rip. Richter fell onto the rose bushes outside and his face caught a large scratch, needlepoint spots of blood burst into life on his cheek and above his eyebrow. Cursing his luck he crashed into the gardens before any of the surveillance team could arrive. Disappearing through tall rhododendron and azalea bushes he sped toward a high wall surrounded by benched enclaves where the inmates could sit and watch the wildlife while they slipped quietly into oblivion. He could hear the confusion of his pursuers and the voice of the Italian issuing orders. Richter clutched his left side as blood began to spurt through his fingertips from the exertion of running and he knew he needed to stop to take stock. He threw himself against the wall as if to climb it and once over would drop down into the street behind, but he could hear police cars approaching and so dropped back down into the gardens and vanished under some trees. Passing compost heaps he sped toward a greenhouse heavy with a vine and benches bedecked in bedding plants; deciding it was too open he entered a garden shed obscured by overhanging branches and threw himself onto the floor panting in his exertion. He could hear no close followers just distant confusion.

His mind was racing and his left side was beginning to burn. Looking at his watch he calculated three and a half hours to darkness and if he was lucky they would think he had scaled the wall and was away. They would have a city wide search out and he would quietly slip back to his bolt hole and rest up, he did not have far to go just three streets, and he could stay there for a week or a month if he had to. First he had to find something to stem the bleeding; he settled on an old sack.

He calculated vocally, "One third of a litre per hour maybe less if I can lie still. That's four hours maybe five and I'll be too weak to move. Six and I'll pass out. Got to slow the bleeding."

His voice was hesitant, and he fell into thoughtful silence as he reached into his pocket for a knife to cut the hessian into strips thick enough to bind around his waist. The gun which had blown Calvetti through the entrance doors was gone - lost as he crashed through the French window and he cursed his misfortune. His finger prints were on the weapon, there was no turning back now. Murder of a cop was a guaranteed thirty years in Germany.

He reached into his pocket for his phone and fumbled a text message though his hands were sticky; it was just three letters long. Then switching the phone off he slid it under some old flower pots and crawling to where he could have a full view of the door without being seen, he half lay and half sat, propped against the wooden wall behind him. His breath was short and he left a slug-like trail of blood in his wake. Glancing at his watch he noted the time 3.32.pm - if his calculations were right he could get away under the cover of darkness. He closed his eyes and allowed both his heart rate and breathing to slow.

"Robe!" Pancardi slapped his friend's face. "Come on fight!"

Roberto Calvetti lay in the street with blood bubbling from his chest and mouth. He was coughing and as he did so Pancardi's face and shirt were spattered with blood.

"Robe!" Pancardi was screaming now, "fight it, fight."

A pool of dark red had appeared under Calvetti's shoulders and was rapidly soaking into Pancardi's jacket which was folded beneath his friend's head. As the paramedics arrived Calvetti's vice–like grip on Pancardi's hand loosened and the spurting of blood ceased.

"You're too late," he said to them, "he's dead."

Blondell appeared at the doorway breathless from the chasing of Richter and looked at the sorry scene. Pancardi standing and wiping Calvetti's blood from his hands and face and Mostro squatting near the dead detective's feet as if in silent homage. The little dog sat motionless, his head lowered as if in silent prayer, it appeared he knew he would never see the detective again.

"I want that piece of shit," said Pancardi, through clenched teeth.

"He's gone over a high wall at the rear and he has disappeared into the rush-hour crowds; I think he went in the direction of the

Cathedral. We have the area being cordoned off now, he won't get far," was Blondell's encouraging reply.

"He's hit," Pancardi hissed, "I caught him in the left side and he fell into that room. How far can an injured man go?"

Pancardi discarded the surgical wipe and looked into Blondell's eyes. Blondell thought he saw a tear forming.

"Yes, you did hit him, there's blood on the window and across the lawn and on the wall too," replied Blondell, breaking from the eye contact.

"Show me," said Pancardi, and he lifted his stick into his palm and broke into an ungainly limping trot. "Mostro," he shouted over his shoulder and the little white dog obediently broke from his reflective vigil.

Chapter 24

Alex Blondell moved swiftly, too swiftly for Pancardi to follow and he could hear the cursing of the older man who was some feet behind him desperate to keep pace. They entered the room through which Richter had escaped. Blood and medical equipment lay on the floor where he had tripped and fallen over it, beyond that the shattered French window was in pieces on the rose bed and lawns outside.

"Stop!" exclaimed Pancardi.

"What is it?" asked Blondell, "your knee?"

Pancardi spoke in gasps, "No look!" he said, pointing at his dog.

Mostro was sniffing the ground intensely around the window frame and under the rose bushes and ground cover plants. All that could be seen of the little white shape was a tail and two rear legs which protruded from the undergrowth as if he were excavating a tunnel. Suddenly from under the bushes he gave one sharp muffled bark, his tail wagging in triumph.

"There, see he has found something," Pancardi was elated.

Blondell reached beyond the half buried dog and pulled a pistol from the undergrowth. Mostro barked once more in triumph as it was bagged by an officer in the guise of a nurse, who had followed both of the running pursuers.

"So now he is unarmed," said Pancardi. "He is shot and bleeding; he crashes through the windows and loses his weapon. In his panic he has no time to search for it. So he runs across the lawn and tries to find a way out."

"Yes," replied Blondell. "Then he scales the wall and disappears into the city crowd.

I followed this track while you were with Roberto. Look beyond the bushes there is the wall." He used Calvetti's Christian name to soften the impact of discussion. "The wall is covered in blood," he continued, "there are hand prints there too. I've got the local police searching the far side but there is no sign of him yet. I think he's gone to ground."

"Let us go to this wall. But we must walk and talk Alex, I can run no more. This damn knee…. Come Mostro."

"I think we can take our time. The local police have the area sealed off – he won't get far," Blondell reiterated in reply.

The little dog was sniffing the ground intently, as if he were searching for another artefact and then suddenly he rushed under the bushes and, on the precise route that Richter had taken, led both men to the base of the wall.

"Look at the smears, he climbed here and then dropped into the road behind," said Blondell.

"We have lost him then?" asked Pancardi.

"Well he has not been picked up yet but he cannot have gone too far. He's wounded - it's only a matter of time."

Pancardi stooped to examine the ground but Mostro was eager to lead the men away from the wall in a totally different direction. He sniffed the ground for some thirty feet and then returned to Pancardi. Blondell noticed the dog returned agitated when he was not being followed. Once again there came his rare single bark for attention.

"I think he wants us to follow him," said Blondell.

"Of course he does he has learned his study."

Blondell suddenly remembered the piece of cloth which Pancardi had painstakingly retrieved, despite Alaina's objections on the grounds of corrupting material evidence. The piece of cloth from the tunnel that would have scent on it. That was the study which Pancardi referred to. Mostro was following the scent-Blondell knew that now.

"If you have the officers check the other side of the wall there will be no blood….."

"Because he didn't go over the wall did he?" Blondell interjected, "he just wanted us to believe he did."

"Now you are seeing things Alex, misdirection is the real magician here."

Two police officers leapt up without instruction and examined the top of the wall and the street below on the far side. Their radios crackled but the communication was clear – no blood.

"You can call off the search," said Pancardi, "he is still here in these grounds. Are there any other ways out?" he asked, turning to more of the uniformed officers, who were arriving rapidly.

"No the only other way out is through the front entrance," a female officer replied.

"The rest of the property," she continued, "is surrounded by high security fencing. Almost impossible to get into and even worse to get out. Alzheimer patients and all that."

"Good, good," Pancardi was almost smiling now, "so we must search every inch of the grounds. Come into my parlour said the spider to the fly," he whispered.

Within minutes the police officers had fanned out and were beginning a sweep pattern through the undergrowth. Pancardi, however, seemed content to squat next to his dog and rub the animal's face with what looked like a handkerchief. It was only Blondell who knew the origin and purpose of the cloth. True to his training the little white dog followed an obscure path, passing compost heaps and bins and a greenhouse. He knew not to rush ahead; sniffing the ground he also knew not to announce his presence with a bark. He passed under some over hanging bushes and then lay motionless in the long grass, his bright eyes fixed on a shed which was partially obscured in undergrowth. As Pancardi arrived he patted the small dog, and silently raised his left index finger to his lips in a motion of silence to Blondell.

A small shed was clearly visible. Pancardi pointed to the ground, the grass was depressed and there were stains of crimson on some of the blades. Blondell nodded and then pointed to the shed indicating he would check to see if there was an entrance at the rear. Pancardi gave him a thumbs up sign, took a small .38 calibre pistol from his pocket and checked the chambers.

"Alive," whispered Blondell.

Once again the finger demanding silence was raised and Blondell nodded, his face crimson from his own stupidity.

As Pancardi pushed the door of the shed open Richter sat motionless on the floor his back propped against the side of the building. His right hand clasped his left side the fingers crimson with the steadily oozing syrup. His left hand, hidden beneath some sodden sacking held a small knife, which evidently was his last intention of defence. Richter sat in a pool of blood, his eyes closed, and his shirt and jacket and all of the hessian sacking which he had crudely wrapped about himself to staunch the bleeding was soaked in blood and his face was ashen as if powdered with white lead.

"Like the poor fly in the web," Pancardi whispered, "he is caught in the spider's parlour."

Pancardi moved in closer to the motionless figure and as he did so Richter lashed out; the knife slashed across the back of one of Pancardi's hands. Pancardi's reaction was swift and decisive, his cane struck out and the sharp crack of breaking fingers sounded like the snapping of twigs on a woodland walk. Richter's knife fell to the ground and simultaneously the back of Pancardi's hand opened like a rose in bloom; the cut was deep and the bleeding profuse.

"This fly stings like a wasp," Richter coughed, as his last resistance ebbed away.

"Bloody hell, that's bleeding well," exclaimed Blondell reaching into to Pancardi's jacket pocket for a handkerchief, as he appeared behind the detective.

Pancardi took the cloth and wrapped it around his hand, "It's not that deep," he said.

Richter smiled in triumph at the wound but said nothing. It was clear his strength was ebbing away.

"What hotel are you in?" Pancardi hissed at him. "If you don't give us the name we'll leave you here to bleed out."

Richter coughed his inaudible reply and laughed, a gurgling guttural laugh which he saw as a final act of defiance. Pancardi searched the man's pockets and finding a key fob threw it to Blondell.

"There is nothing else," he said, "no ID, no wallet, and no money, not even small change. Ah a speed loader, for the dropped pistol I presume."

"It says Ursula 7. What the hell does that mean?" asked

Blondell, examining both sides of the key fob.

"Well what does it mean?" questioned Pancardi turning to Richter. "And remember no answers we leave you here to bleed out."

"I'm dead already, or as good as," the man replied.

Pancardi felt a sudden urge to ram the point of his cane into the wound which Richter was still nursing with his right hand. It would be so easy to make him talk and who else but Blondell would know what he had done. He had his chance but decency got the better of him and he held Richter's chin and forced eye contact instead.

"Listen to me you piece of shit," he said, "my friend is dead outside and he was a cop and in Germany that's throw away the key time. How old are you thirty five tops? Well you'll be spending the rest of your days in some rat-hole jail trying to avoid being fucked in the arse and wanking like school boy over catalogue underwear pictures. By the time you get to die you'll have forgotten what a woman looks like. If we get some co-operation maybe, just maybe, we can protect you from those horrors. But we want some answers."

Richter opened his eyes as if to speak and lifted his broken left hand in an attempt to give a single finger salute. Seeing the damage to his hand he coughed and the blood landed on Pancardi's lips.

A faint, "Fuck you," was all he could muster.

Pancardi wiped Richter's blood from his lips and face as he stood up. Then with lighting speed he delivered a heavy kick to Richter's wound. Richter's eyes opened and he screamed one long scream, while the whites of his eyes rolled like marbles in their sockets.

"No fuck you, you worthless piece of shit. He was my friend," Pancardi hissed.

"Inspector!" Blondell indignantly squealed. He then placed himself between the two men. "Inspector, no," he repeated.

Pancardi turned and walked three paces out into the fresh air, while Richter slumped to his side as he passed out. His hand fell from the wound and the pace of the bleeding markedly increased.

"I hope the scum dies," hissed Pancardi.

He spat on the ground and cursed under his breath in Italian.

Blondell could only make out the words for Hell and damnation but he sensed the seriousness of the blasphemy more than understood it. Looking back into the shed he saw the slumped figure struggling for breath but had no inclination to proffer aid.

By the time the stretcher arrived to collect Richter he had passed out and the paramedics were quick to install a drip so that he could be moved. Both Pancardi and Blondell had left the bloody heap for collection and were on their way back across the lawns with Mostro strutting ahead of them. As they moved back into the building over the shattered door Pancardi was still nursing his hand and one of the nurses at the home offered to clean it up and stitch it. Pancardi noticed an elderly woman banging at an upstairs window. She seemed distressed and two male porters removed her quickly from sight.

"Is that Richter's mother?" Pancardi questioned, "she can't be that crazy she seems to know what's going on."

"Yes," replied the nurse, "she is lucid today but by tomorrow she will be back into the loss of memory which is part of progressive Alzheimer's. Please follow me to the nurse's station. It's just down the corridor a little, we need to get your hand cleaned up."

"How bad is her disease then?" Blondell asked.

"Better than some and worse than others. Sometimes people think that Alzheimer's doesn't exist – but it does and it's dreadful," the nurse replied, compassionately.

"So could we question her today?" asked Pancardi. "Would we get any sense?"

Blondell picked up the inference immediately, "I'll do it," he volunteered, "maybe we might get a lead on location."

Pancardi winced as she removed the cloth which was wrapped around his hand.

"Good heavens!" exclaimed Blondell, noticing that the cloth binding was not a handkerchief but the piece of shirt which carried Richter's scent. "It's the evidence from the tunnel," he paused, "and now it's got your blood on it. How the hell can we use this as evidence now?"

"Don't worry about that minor detail. We need to find out where Richter was staying. See if you can get that out of his mother," Pancardi replied.

Disgruntled, Blondell left and immediately made for the

upstairs landing where he accosted a nurse who was on her way to sedate Mrs. Richter who had become quite agitated by the change of routine.

"That's a very clever dog you have there," said the nurse, attempting a diversionary tactic as she administered a local anaesthetic. "Is he friendly?"

"Very," said Pancardi. "It was he who found our man out in the shed. Not bad eh?"

"Oh so he's a police tracker dog?"

"No he is my dog, my friend actually," he became reflective, "my last true friend now."

"Yes, the man who was shot was he a friend? I thought he was a visitor who just got in the way."

Pancardi looked at the girl who was examining his wound. He could feel the emotion choking in his throat as he replayed the entry of Calvetti into the building in his memory. He wanted to ask his old friend why he had used the front door. Had he been turned away from the rear entrance? If he had been a minute sooner or a minute later Richter would not have seen him and Roberto would still be alive. Fate, luck, chance, whatever it was it had been against them all today. He knew Richter would rather die than have a long prison sentence. He'd remove a tube or two when he became lucid enough to do so and then simply die. All the leads would dry up and the case would remain unsolved. He felt a twinge in his hand.

"I'll have to tighten this up, it won't hurt," the nurse reassured, "but it may sting a little. Seven stitches should hold it. That's the first in."

Blondell reappeared at the doorway of the nurse's station, "Total waste of time," he said. "She doesn't even know it was her son on the stretcher. Can't even give me her own name."

"That's not unusual with Alzheimer's," said the nurse. "They get all flustered when anything out of the ordinary happens. Loud noises, people shouting like you get with autistics."

Another stitch went in and Pancardi winced as he spoke, "He had no money, no credit cards, so what does that say to you Alex?"

"Local – he was local. He walked here or he left things in a left luggage facility."

"And where is the nearest place?"

"The train station."

"So should we not start there? Let me have a look at the key and fob again."

Blondell produced the item from his pocket and handed it to Pancardi.

"The thing is the key doesn't look like the key to a deposit box," he said.

"I agree it looks like a door key to me. Ursula 7 now what the hell does that mean?"

"That's easy," said the nurse, without looking up from her stitching. "Ursula Platz is on the other side of the Cathedral from here, just a few streets away. There are loads of little apartments there."

"What sort of apartments?" Blondell asked.

"All along the street – little apartments. Some of our nurses rent places there."

"We have to move fast," said Pancardi, "find that place and shit."

The nurse smiled as the needle bit into Pancardi's flesh for the seventh and most awkward stitch.

"I'm afraid we are going to be a little while yet," she chuckled. "You have got to have your tetanus shot and antibiotics and I have to dress the wound before you go. You will have to change the dressing every few hours as the wound is likely to weep and then in ten days the stitches can be removed, maybe eight if you are a good healer."

Mostro sat at the door way and avoided entry into the Vet area. He knew the smell of disinfectant and wanted to purge it from his nostrils. Seeing a large couch in the corner of the waiting area he left Pancardi to his needles and leapt into the corner of it, oblivious to the movement of white coated people all around him.

Pancardi sighed at his lack of sympathy, "Well what are you waiting for?" he asked, looking at Blondell. "Get over to Ursula Platz and find number 7. I'll join you as soon as I am done here."

"About an hour," said the nurse.

"Can't we hurry it a little," snapped Pancardi. "I feel fine and the thing has stopped bleeding."

"That may be the case," replied the nurse, "but if infection sets in, you could lose your hand."

Blondell was already at the door talking to the German police and two of the undercover agents dressed as nurses.

"I'll send someone back with the location once we have found the place," he called over his shoulder.

Pancardi was about to call a reply but thought better of it as Blondell moved right and disappeared out of earshot.

"I suppose your colleague will have to take over the investigation now," said the nurse as she dressed the hand.

"I suppose he will," replied Pancardi, unwilling to go yet again into the detail of their relationship.

"English isn't he?" she continued to probe, "and you, you are Italian?"

"Yes."

"I was in England once, I worked there in a hospital in Cheltenham."

"Yes I too was in England."

"Ah you see it is a small world. And your English colleague is he married."

Pancardi was taken aback by the question, "Married?" he laughed, "no he is not married; well not unless you count the Foreign Office. He's a res….." he hesitated, "diplom…… well actually I don't know what he is but he is British Foreign Office."

"He is well spoken and very good looking," remarked the nurse.

Pancardi had no immediate answer to offer but watched the nurse as she walked to a cabinet to collect needles and vials of liquid which would be shot into his arm.

"Can you roll your sleeve up please," she called over her shoulder.

Pancardi did as he was told. His mind raced and he wondered what women saw in Alex Blondell. He thought him a little too English, a boy, shy and rather non descript, clearly his evaluation had been totally wrong. First Magdalene, he reflected, that had been a prank, but they ended up in bed; then the under cover policewomen who always talked to Blondell and now this nurse. He looked at her as she worked, she was a young lithe woman, full breasted and broad hipped, no more than twenty five but he could not help seeing her as a girl.

"I suppose he is good looking," he said, "though I have never noticed it."

"Oh there is no supposing Inspector."

"Really that good looking? I don't see it myself."

"Now this is going to hurt I'm afraid," she said, defensively changing the subject and pumping fluid heavenward from the end of a filled hypodermic syringe.

Chapter 25

7 Ursula Platz was a small studio apartment on the third floor. There was a circular stairway which led up past a narrow and confining glass lift which rose and fell inside a tubular cage. Closed circuit television cameras watched each bland entrance and gave the occupant plenty of time between the buzz and the arrival to make preparations.

The door man could give no clue about the owner except he knew that the man travelled and that the flat was empty for long periods throughout the year. He was always well dressed – a business man of some sort who rarely spoke but always gave a handsome Christmas tip once a year; a gentleman in the old fashioned sense of the word. Mostly he was there at Christmas and sometimes Easter but mostly in the winter months. He could not recall if the man had visitors, or lady friends? Never, the door man had said with a wry smile of intimation. Blondell found him next to useless for detail and impossible to talk to as he spoke in unrelated tangents. He was obviously a man who spent long hours behind a desk during the cold winter months, studying TV soap opera, which he probably considered real-life, and in the summer standing in the doorway gossiping with anyone and everyone that passed.

Blondell entered after the policemen, stepping over the pieces of door frame which lay shattered on the ground. The door had a heavy deadlock with a security steel pin brace which locked into a steel frame at six points. It was obviously meant to be burglar proof and in the event of forced entry was there to maximise sound and give valuable warning to the occupant. The hinges had also been reinforced in steel and locked behind a solid metal rail which was discreetly hidden behind the architrave. It would have been impossible to force the door from the frame. Blondell looked at the devices and understood in an instant that the owner did not underestimate security.

To the right there was a door that led to a balcony with pot roses which overlooked the paved square in front of the Cathedral. The left hand side of the balcony had a draw down fire escape which could only be operated from above. The item was well greased for ease of use and when extended led on to a roof gully twenty feet below which had several exit points over various adjacent roofs.

"Very nice," muttered Blondell, "classy but compact, very clever, several exit points and no entry points," he said aloud.

On the opposite wall, behind a curtain, was a wall mounted bed. Blondell pulled it down and the legs splayed automatically as it lightly touched the floor. It had been slept in and simply lifted back up to clear some space. So Richter had arrived and slept and left in a hurry. Blondell was trying to piece the scenario together as he had observed Pancardi do. He looked into the fridge and found it stocked with beer, milk and fresh fruit.

"A short visit Udo?" he said. "But you went shopping."

Richter was a man who ate out or who ate simply. There were fresh vegetables, no freezer, and the cupboards were stocked with simple but wholesome canned goods.

In a sealed plastic container, which was stacked neatly behind some rice and pasta storage jars, Blondell found two passports one in the name of Klaus Meine and the other for a Marcus Tonyelle. Both had the same photograph and each was a clear likeness of the man Blondell witnessed shooting Roberto Calvetti. He began to wonder at the meaning of identity and how easily it could be changed. At the bottom of the same container lay 1000 Euro, $800 and a series of numbers scrawled onto the back of a business card. They could have been phone numbers or bank accounts, Blondell could not be sure. He took the whole container as evidence.

The décor was modern, expensive and sleek with a colour scheme in pale blue and silver. All the items in the kitchen area were chrome and a small glass table in the corner beyond the unmade bed had a vase of high quality synthetic flowers in the middle - white lilies. Blondell liked lilies but he instantly thought of death when he saw them. Next to the vase lay a wallet, and passport in the name of Udo Richter. The photograph here was unlike the other two, it was older, less careful and rehearsed, more spontaneous; he surmised that this was genuine, the sort which the average holiday maker might make in a department store booth. Over the back of a dining chair draped a fine quality hand-made Saville Row suit, a Van Heusen shirt with a grimy collar, the cuff links still at the cuffs. Blondell examined them carefully; they were platinum, distinct and clearly belonged to a man of excellent taste. They spoke of wealth without the need to constantly over emphasize the matter by being over the top; the single diamond mounted in each was enough to signal money without the flash of a see-me-now spotlight.

Blondell looked at the walls which had black and white photographs of famous landmarks. He could make out the Chrysler building in New York and the Duomo in Florence, somewhere in Hong Kong he thought, but he could have been wrong as he often muddled Asia; the locations of the others eluded him. The apartment was neat, controlled and had the air of not being lived in. Like a designer home without the homely touches, it was a masculine space and clear to Blondell that the delicate hand of a woman had not been evident anywhere. Richter would have to brew coffee and bake bread every time a prospective buyer came around - it would be a difficult place to sell.

The bathroom had an electric Braun razor on a glass shelf and a toothpaste tube in a cup - there was no brush.

In the kitchen a coffee mug sat in the bleached white plastic sink with a cereal bowl and a spoon. The cupboards held a variety of canned goods ranging from meats to desserts. It was obvious the owner needed to keep food stocks for emergencies or late night arrivals – there was no freezer; Blondell noted this for a second time and began to puzzle as to why. The only reason he could devise was power cuts. If Richter did not live at the location food could be defrosted and then re-frozen without his knowl-edge. One mistake and there could be major issues for a man who needed to be mobile and fit; he simply could not afford the incon-venience of food poisoning.

Blondell smiled at his reasoning and continued his scrutiny of Richter's mind.

There was a small bark which served to announce that Mostro had arrived and that his master would only be a short stride or two behind. The dog walked directly to Blondell, received his reciprocal recognition, and then sat waiting for Pancardi to climb the stairs.

"So this is his little hideaway," said Pancardi as he entered. "Nothing too ostentatious, just enough to allow a bolt hole."

"And it seems he left in a hurry," replied Blondell, "left the dishes in the sink and not in the dishwasher and didn't even make the bed. Clearly he was coming back, his passport's on the table and a wallet. How's the hand?"

"I'll live," Pancardi replied, "nothing else?"

"Not that I can see."

Pancardi walked over to the table and looked at the wallet and passport. He glanced at Blondell who was busily searching through drawers of clothes. He tried to see the attraction for women in the Englishman but had to admit he could not.

"This is not a fake the picture's too old," said Pancardi.

"There are a couple more in the container there and some money, US dollars and Euro. Get away money I suppose," replied Blondell.

"Have you checked the bin too?" asked Pancardi. "People always throw things away that give vital detail."

Blondell felt a fool as he lifted the bin lid but only found three unopened pieces of junk mail addressed to Udo Richter and a toothbrush covered in green mould. There was nothing else.

Without thinking and acting purely on instinct Pancardi searched the pockets of the suit which lay over a chair.

"This is interesting," he said, producing an e mail ticket from the inside breast pocket, "a return air flight to Amsterdam, dated for the day after tomorrow."

He threw the jacket onto the leather sofa which was the only soft furnishing item to sit on in the room. Blondell turned to see the detective search the trouser pockets and cursed his own stupidity. He wondered why he had not thought to do so when Pancardi had achieved more in seconds than he had in an hour of observation. Then realisation dawned, the man had left in a hurry after arriving late. He hadn't made the bed nor stacked the dishwasher. He had simply thrown items over a chair when he arrived and slept, then in the morning he went to the nursing home first. Richter was not the spontaneous type, so where else might someone who was in a hurry leave items, but in his clothes. He watched the older man search each pocket by turning it inside out. Then he remembered the fresh foods and was about to draw that to Pancardi's attention when the detective exclaimed triumphantly.

"Interesting ! At last !" Pancardi had clearly found something important.

"What is it?"

"I think you might like to see this Alex. It was in the back pocket. I don't think our boy even knew it was there."

Blondell crossed the room, "It's a dry cleaning tag," he snuffed, "probably took it off and put it in his pocket rather than in the bin. He's been well trained by his mother then!" he added.

"No, no," laughed Pancardi, "the tag says in fine print, see look, co. Doup. H, and the rest has been torn off. If he knew this was here then why keep it. No he just stuffed it into a pocket without thinking, or he didn't even know it was here, and why would he?"

"That could be anything!" exclaimed Blondell.

"But it could be.... care of Doup Hotel."

Blondell turned white and cursed his naivety in not having searched the pockets himself.

"The Doup Hotel?" Blondell asked. "The suit was sent out to be cleaned and then returned to the Doup Hotel. Is there one in Amsterdam?"

"If there is, then we must get it sealed off now and we must go there," Pancardi was excited.

"It could all be nothing."

"Or," replied Pancardi, "it could be the most meaningful mistake yet."

Pancardi spun on his heel and spoke to one of the uniformed officers quickly. There was a flurry of activity on the radio in German, which Blondell caught the gist of. The police were going to seek from the Dutch authorities if there was a Doup Hotel.

The Police helicopter was going to land in the Cathedral square and both of them were to be on their way to Amsterdam in a matter of minutes.

Blondell marvelled at the efficiency as he was escorted through the cordoned area holding back the crowds. Only in Germany would the populous allow a machine to land in a public square in order to increase speed.

"How long to get there?" he shouted at the police escort leading them under the still rotating blades.

"Forty minutes no more."

"You know what to do?" shouted Pancardi as they boarded.

"It's already been taken care of," came the loud reply from the uniformed Inspector.

"They will seal off the Doupelein Hotel so that no one leaves if they are there then we will have them trapped."

In the instant that the door had been closed and the Inspector jogged back out of ear shot, the surveillance helicopter rose vertically and Blondell's stomach sank to his shoes. He had always hated the vertical take off and as the tips of the twin spires appeared beneath them he thought he might be sick. Then the helicopter tilted forward and the motion changed to one of forward propulsion and the feeling passed as the machine sped off northward at high speed. Pancardi's initial words into the radio, of low key and caution, were lost in the sudden and violent increase in volume within the helicopter.

"Maybe we can get them all," said Pancardi hopefully. "Maybe they are all in Amsterdam, selling the jewels, what a piece of good fortune that would be. That's why Richter would come to visit. He was close and he had time and opportunity to visit mum. Let's hope they are all there, all the rats in one nest." He laughed loudly with a broad grin on his face. "We may get them all in one sweep," he smirked and rubbed his hands together almost gleefully. He was laughing so loud that Blondell struggled to hear his words.

"Yeah, but maybe they have all gone their separate ways and Richter was just unlucky," he shouted.

"Then why did he have a return ticket. Why did he need to go back to Amsterdam?"

"Maybe that's his home?"

The two men were shouting now, "What, in a hotel?" asked Pancardi, "no that's temporary, we don't have much time."

Blondell nodded, he had lost the will to shout a reply.

Chapter 26

Blondell's phone rang loudly in his pocket and he pulled it open.

"In a car on the way toward the Doupelein Hotel, Amsterdam," he answered. "I know but all hell has broken out and I haven't had a chance." There was a pause, "Maybe later on today or tonight." Another pause, "Of course I will," he said, "as soon as the pace slows a bit."

He snapped the phone shut, stuffed it into his pocket and said nothing.

Pancardi considered again the young Englishman's status as a lothario. He tried to imagine precisely what any woman might see in him. True, he was well educated, well mannered and probably interesting, but for all of this study Pancardi could not find the key factor which made women notice him. Deduce as he might the key factor simply eluded him.

"Magdalene?" he asked.

Blondell nodded in silence. It was clear he did not wish to discuss it further.

Mostro sat on Pancardi's lap, he seemed almost excited by the mention of Magdalene's name.

"Get a dog my friend," said the Italian, "less trouble and far more loyal," he laughed.

"Sometimes I think you may be right!" came the reply.

"And he likes the chase. See in the helicopter how he scans the ground, fearless my friend, fearless." Pancardi rubbed underneath the dog's chin and he raised and stretched his neck in response. "See how he tracks his quarry?" he quipped.

Behind the Heineken brewery in Stadhouderskade Duane Rightman punched a code into a key pad and waited for a rusty security gate to open. The gate was old and disused and it groaned as it opened almost as if to say, "Not you again." He passed the security hut, it was empty, but a sign saying guard dogs might be on site was emblazoned on the rough cut exterior. He listened – he could hear no barking and presumed that the guards came and went on a rota. There was nothing worth stealing and the signs were only there to discourage children from playing and getting injured.

The whole site looked as if it was ready for demolition. Weeds grew in the cracks of concrete long since abandoned by the transporters carrying beer from the small family brewery. Selzetten beer had been one of the best in Amsterdam and Rightman remembered the taste of a rich malt which they made. His senses were on high alert as he moved stealthily through the growing gloom of the oncoming evening.

Tucked away in a corner of the site was the entrance to a shabby office block - dark brown, dismal and typical of an old Dutch house which had been converted into small offices for private detectives and escort agencies servicing the local hotels. Even they had gone now and the latest development plans showed what the new luxury apartments would look like, when they were constructed and sold to the in-crowd of cosmopolitan yuppies. Rightman stopped to listen for footsteps and the rasping breath of a panting dog – there was almost total silence, except for birds which were beginning to roost amid the exposed roof trusses and sheltering voids of collapsed ceilings.

Inside he flicked a light switch beside the door – nothing happened. In the semi-dark he could just see a half-glazed door ahead with a white number 2 visible in the dusty gloom and he headed toward it. Passing the wall mounted light he checked for the bulb, it had been removed. Someone did not want the lights to work. He reached into his pocket and found the handle of the automatic which he grasped and withdrew flicking the safety catch with his left thumb as he did so.

At the door he stood stock-still barely breathing, listening intently for any sound in the room beyond. Through the obscured glass panel he could see no movement, no shadow. His mind raced and he wondered why he remained; if it had not been for the money, he thought, I would have already left by now. McDermott had gone but Rightman lacked his faith and trust in West – so he waited.

The click was barely audible but as he entered he heard the hammer being drawn back on a standard issue .38calibre Smith and Weston. Instantly he froze.

"Hey man," he said. There was no reply but he caught a glimpse of movement in the darkness to his left and raised his gun. "It's me," he continued, waiting for the reply to give a true location before he fired into the darkness.

From the dark a woman's voice he recognised asked, "Are you alone?"

"Of course I'm alone, what do you think this is some fucking three ring circus?"

"Just making sure," said a male voice from a pool of shadow to his right.

The room was then plunged into light. Paul West was sitting on a deck chair and Alice Parsotti was on a wooden bench a .38 calibre pistol laid next to her.

"So what happens now?" asked Rightman, shielding his eyes and lowering his weapon.

"We wait," replied West.

"Wait for what, for hell to freeze over?"

"Well we can't go back to the hotel our cover's been blown. The whole place will be crawling with the filth by now."

West's voice had resumed the cockney twang, which usually signalled anxiety and stress. His face was drawn but his eyes sharp – he was angry.

"What about our money?" asked Rightman. "I ain't goin' nowhere until I know we got that covered."

"Safe," replied West, "we'll get the nod on that, but we are not going to get out of this city now. They'll have the place sealed tighter than a duck's arse. That arsehole German!"

"So who sent the buzz?" asked Rightman. "If it wasn't either of you two and it wasn't me it must have been that hairy faced Jock."

"No, it wasn't him he had the guts to pull out early, and I trust him," replied West.

"And why would he alert the police to us?" piped Alice. "There's nothing for him to gain, and loads to lose - all the money in fact."

"So it's the German then?" Rightman seemed a little dubious. "Then why would he send the warning? That doesn't make sense either unless someone was on to him – but how?"

Paul West was toying with the set up, "Simple, so fucking simple," he reflected, "that shit's got a record or something which can trace him." He looked hard at Rightman. "Where is he?" he questioned. "You're his fucking buddy. So where is the bastard?"

Rightman shrugged nonchalantly.

"Don't give me that shit. He was supposed to be with you. Out with some classy ladies you told us. So don't bullshit me you mercenary piece of slime." West raised the pistol as if to fire on Rightman. "You told us," he continued, "that you were going to be close by, so that when we needed to move we could quickly. I ought to drop you right now. You're here, where's he?"

Rightman looked at the loaded pistol pointed toward him and clenched the one he was holding tightly. He wondered if he would have enough time to raise and fire once if West pulled the trigger; just once he thought as he imagined his body flying backward through the door he had just entered. Thinking better of it he relaxed and his tone changed.

"I ain't no baby sitter," he proffered. "Yeah he spends some time with me but I ain't his big brother or nothin' and he's his own man. Told me he was off to see someone."

"Who?" West's voice was sharp.

Rightman squirmed and Parsotti's hand drifted toward the .38 laying beside her on the bench. He knew that if any firing started he certainly would die.

"Listen you stupid fuck," West's voice was loaded with venom, "if you don't tell me right now I'll kill you right here."

"He said somethin' about a mother in a home and a quick visit." Rightman looked at West and then at Alice. "I don't know whereabouts but how the hell did they know where to look anyway?"

"So is he here in Amsterdam?" asked Parsotti.

"No I think he said he was goin' for a couple of days."

"How far?" she continued.

"Edge of Germany or some such."

"Well that gives us a little time Paul," said Alice as she turned toward him.

<hr />

The Doupelein Hotel was crawling with police as Dutch detectives met Pancardi in the lobby. A large square man came up and shook the Italian's hand and then Blondell's. He introduced himself as the Inspector in charge.

"No dogs I'm afraid," he said, looking at Pancardi.

"This is no dog," replied Pancardi, accentuating the word dog. "This is Mostro one of the best detectives on the force."

"Well he may corrupt evidence," replied the square set man.

His forensic team, he told them, were already examining the rooms which had been isolated - there were five in all, four singles and a double. Pancardi's face was scowling and Blondell noticed the distain creeping into a sneer which was appearing at the corners of his mouth.

"Five?" Blondell checked.

"Yes. The double is obvious as the woman had red hair and the guest in there has red hair. We are very interested in the man. Tall, sharp dresser by all accounts, blonde, English and well spoken. They went out this morning and have not come back. I think they've flown the coop."

"Hardly surprising," replied Pancardi, "all this police show; if they are anywhere nearby they will have had plenty of warning. Nothing like warning everyone is there? And boy is this a warning. The dog goes where I go by the way!"

Pancardi was clearly angry that the whole stealth operation had been blown wide open in a typical Dutch thirst for openness. His voice had become terse and his eyes began to show a flame of passion.

"I want my forensic team on this," he said, accentuating the my, "and I want this shambles cleared. Get your detectives stationed in the hotel and get all of the uniforms gone. I could do a better job alone with just this little dog. He has more sense than you."

The Dutch Inspector began his reply but the little dog sat at Pancardi's feet and tilted his head knowingly to one side and the big square man was momentarily transfixed by what he perceived as a knowing stare.

"Never mind your ambition," ejaculated Pancardi, "and you are ambitious, but foolish too. The dog stays." He turned to Blondell raised his eyes heavenward and said, "Alex the airports and all other exit points?"

Blondell nodded.

"There's absolutely no need," said the square Dutchman, "we have all those covered already."

"Show us the rooms then, all of them," was Pancardi's clipped reply.

The Inspector moved forward and as if to challenge the presence of the dog one last time but his actions were cut short by Pancardi's voice of command, "Come Mostro," he said.

"Right you boys," called the security guard from beyond the half panelled door. "You know this place is off limits and if you don't come out now I'm sending in the dog. I don't want any more of your dope smoking and drinking going on here. Go to a café or something."

Duane Rightman spun on his heel and reacted unconsciously by raising his pistol and firing a single shot. The time span was less than a millisecond and the loud explosive sound rang in the confined space. The world moved into slow motion like the recollection of a traffic accident; the odour of cordite was strong and a plume of smoke left the end of the gun barrel. A single cartridge case fell in the recoil and landed on the uncovered floor, ringing with the clarity of a church bell on a clear summer morning. The bullet penetrated the lower panel of the door and entered the Alsatian dog through the left ear and as the dog's legs buckled beneath it, the bullet passed out and through the knee of the security guard, who let out an almighty scream. West was at the door in a split second and opening it Alice Parsotti fired from the bench – one shot from the Smith and Weston .38. The bullet entered the forehead of the guard and there was immediate silence.

He fell back, his eyes and mouth still open in a wide eyed silent scream. The back of his skull and most of his brain lay spread like a carpet of raspberry jam behind him.

"Check to see if there's another," said Alice.

Rightman stepped over the corpse making an imprint of his sole in the gore as he sped into the open air. He saw a van with bright red writing parked some distance away near the security gate. He scanned for movement, first the van and then the hut window, which though lit, seemed empty. His heart beat in his chest and he raised his pistol before his eye line. Waiting he could hear his heart beating, rapidly at first and then slowing to a dull thump; there was no movement, the guard had been alone.

"Jesus Christ," said West, as Rightman re-entered. "We have to split up and get out of this city. There's bound to be a radio in his van or whatever he came in and he'll have to check in."

"It's a van and it's empty. Let's take the thing and head out, they can't have the whole city covered," said Rightman.

"No!" exclaimed Alice. She turned to Rightman, "Look the security guy is about your build, take the uniform and use his van and get out. Paul give him his now."

West handed Rightman an e booking reference code written on a scrap of paper.

"We organised these today," he chirped, "one for each of us. You have to memorise the code. There's no way to trace these however hard they try and they will now. I used an encrypted service so they can bust their bollocks for all we care. But you're gonna need this code at the check in desk." He laughed, "They're fuckwits anyway. Who ordered that surveillance on the Doupelein? It was shit." He laughed again, "Montreal flight leaves in three days. So you have to lie low, and I mean low," he concluded.

Rightman studied the reference, it read REW 383 C – 10:25 am.

"It says Stockholm man. Stockholm?" he commented nervously.

"Yep, we'll see you there in 3 days," replied West, "for that flight. No show and we go. Got it?"

"But Stockholm man …… Stockholm. Why there?"

"Just in case they had Amsterdam covered – diamonds?" Alice replied quietly.

"OK and after that we go our separate ways yeah?" Rightman's voice was anxious now.

"Until this is over I want to know that you are locked in to us man," said West with a sneer. He accentuated the word man in mimickery and caught Alice's eye as he did so.

"So either we all go together or no one goes," said Alice. "We have some lose ends to tie up and to check. We'll see you in Arlanda."

"Loose ends what about the body here?" asked Rightman, as he pulled the security guard's jacket over his arms.

"Leave it they'll think it was kids and get rid of the van as soon as you can. They might even think it was joy riders. So make it look good, torch it on some waste ground or something, make it big and bold something we would never do. Like kids trying to hide their misdemeanours. "

"Right," came the reply. "Christ look at that!" exclaimed Rightman as he pawed the man's trousers. "There ain't no way I'm wearin' those." He wiped his bloody hands on the guard's shirt.

Loading his handgun and stuffing it into his belt Rightman walked quickly across the weed strewn concrete toward the van. Once inside he wrote the flight reference and time on his cuff, before screwing up the small scrap of paper which West had given him. He lit a cigarette, clipped the safety belt into place and firing the van's engine into life he fought with the gear lever, crunching the gears as the clutch thrust-bearing engaged and then winding down the window he waved once and was gone.

"Right Alice," said West, "we are going to have to rough it tonight. We'll need to find somewhere to kip, the cops will have the whole area covered as soon as they realise that the security guard is not answering, and we can't use a hotel. They'll be checking all of those, and we can't leave without our stash now can we? We go for those in the morning, we can't get in there tonight. Anyhow they'll have all the roads covered. That American can be our decoy. If he gets away fine - if not we can get out without him."

She nodded, "There was one of those little 24 hour corner shops a couple of blocks back. I can go and get one or two things," she said. "I'll wear my cap and ditch the make–up they'll think I'm a late night doper with the munchies."

She started removing her make-up with a clean wipe and as she did so her natural paleness began to appear. She always knew that the lack of paint made her look almost drawn.

"I'll buy some booze too that way they might think I'm a right waster," she continued, "but where the hell are we going to get some sleep, I don't want to be outside in a park?"

"I've got an idea about that one," he replied. "I hope that American has got the common sense to dump the van as quickly as possible."

"Don't worry about him if he gets caught then we..."

"Move to plan B," he chuckled. "Ever the optimist eh beauty? The trouble is we ain't got a plan B, C or any other."

"So we move to scheme F," she smirked at him in reply.

"Now that's my girl," he snorted. "Scheme fuck-up is probably much nearer to the mark."

"How many Euros have you got, come on hand over?" she requested holding out her hand palm up and clicking her fingers.

He searched in his pockets for coins and poured them into the hand.

"Notes too," she said clicking her fingers rapidly to indicate more was needed. He passed her some notes. "Is that it?" she asked.

"Fuck me," he said, "don't you ever..."

"Cut the crap," her tone had become serious.

"Right girly," he interrupted with sudden earnestness. "You get over to that shop thing and I'll follow about fifty yards behind. We'll leave this piece of shit," he tapped the dead security guard with his toe, "just like this."

That above all else was what he liked about Alice. She thought clearly and was his equal when it came to being ruthless. He tapped the corpse again and a soft gurgle emanated from the lungs and open mouth.

"Poor dumb bastard," he muttered, "probably got paid peanuts."

Chapter 27

"I want Alaina here tonight!"

Pancardi was becoming anxious as he checked the rooms in the hotel. Blondell noticed he was becoming tired and his hand, which he claimed was no more than a deep scratch, troubled him. He was even disregarding Mostro when he sought attention which was most unlike him.

"You ought to get that looked at again," he said, pointing to Pancardi's hand.

"Oh this," he said, lifting it to his eye line, "perhaps when we have gathered all we can then ..."

"And what else do you expect to find?" interrupted Blondell. "Some laundry ticket maybe or something for Mostro to chase."

Pancardi turned and smiled and now knew he had made the younger man smart when he found the location of the hotel in Richter's trouser pocket.

"Well laundry ticket or not we have nothing to go on," he said. "Richter's room tells us nothing and the room for the couple well we know it is theirs but who are they. Where are the passports? There are just clothes and nothing else. They are thorough and the best I have seen. All we have are names and they are worthless. If it had not been for that ridiculous charade which the Dutch laid on today we might be closer still, we might have them right now."

Pancardi's back was toward the door and as he spoke the square Dutch Inspector reappeared silently behind him. Blondell nodded to the Italian to acknowledge the fact but Pancardi continued unaware.

"Marksmen on the roof and five rooms, ridiculous, totally ridiculous. Mostro here could have done a better job." He patted the small head at his feet, "And there we are looking at a room and a Japanese tourist turns up, more confused than we are, hopeless, totally hopeless. Lots of show, lots of noise and not one piece of hard evidence to show for it."

There was a cough behind him and Blondell expected Pancardi to show signs of embarrassment - there were none.

Instead he simply said, "It's all a bit of a mess is it not Inspector?"

The Dutchman was so taken aback that he found it hard to speak.

"Do you know Inspector?" continued Pancardi, "that today one of the best men in Italy was shot at point blank range. One of the best and my friend? He made a mistake which cost him his life and me a friend."

There was an uneasy silence.

"You are a fool," continued Pancardi, "the people we are after are not petty criminals, they are experts and see they have now flown. All your show has achieved nothing. It is all over the TV news and papers and had it not been for you we may have had them all. Now what have we to show but some soiled clothes and empty rooms?"

Eventually the Dutchman blurted out words to the effect that a police jet was bringing the requested Italian forensic experts to Amsterdam and that they would arrive within the hour. Rooms had been set aside for them on the ground floor and that bedrooms had also been made available for Pancardi, Blondell and the whole forensic team on the third floor. All the roads were being monitored and the ports too. The airport was also under heavy surveillance and it was only a matter of time before they were caught. The doctor that Mr. Blondell had requested was due in twenty minutes and his double room was definitely not a single. There was now no objection to the dog being at the crime scene either, because the Chief Inspector of Amsterdam was aware of who the Italian Inspector was.

The Dutch Inspector expected the fawning and flattery to have an ego stroking effect but Pancardi simply ignored it.

Pancardi's ears pricked up at the arrangements, "Ah ha," he said knowingly. "She comes too, to Amsterdam mmm."

"Purely business Inspector," said Blondell, formally

"And what business Alex eh, what a busy business?"

"I think Magdalene has some interesting ideas on the equipment found in the car," he replied defensively.

Blondell knew he was floundering, searching for any excuse to see her. He tried to sound convincing but knew that Pancardi had already drawn his sordid conclusions.

Turning back on the uneasy Dutchman Pancardi simply asked to be shown to the last of the five rooms so that no more time and opportunities would be wasted.

As they walked the length of the corridor he barked orders. Blondell was amazed by the sudden personality change to ruthless hunter. Pancardi could smell the blood of his quarry and any obstruction was being torn down in his tenacious pursuit. Blondell noticed how easily the Dutch policeman had fallen under his authority and that he was now desperate to please. He wondered precisely what his seniors had said to him to inspire such a change of heart.

"I want all the phone records for the double room and any web access used through your machines," Pancardi said curtly. "All of the rooms. Not much show in that." He grinned broadly, "I also want any room service records, any computer consoles which guests can have access to need to be marshalled. We don't have time for niceties. They know we are here. They know they must get away but maybe they have left us some trace?"

"This is the final room," said the Dutchman, as he ushered the uniformed police away from the door.

"So," said Pancardi, "one double and two singles. A four man team?"

"Well three men and one woman," quipped Blondell, as they stepped over the threshold.

"No my friend, four men and one woman."

Blondell stood firm, "Surely three?"

"Five rooms that is a mistake no?"

Blondell looked bemused and the Dutch Inspector had developed a sudden silence in the presence of the greater intellect.

Pancardi continued, "One double, for the man and the woman posing as a couple, no? West and Parsotti?"

Blondell nodded.

"One room for Richter who we know in Germany, yes? The one who goes to see his mother with the diseased mind?"

Blondell nodded again.

"This room no?"

Blondell shrugged and then nodded.

"Then the other two. One which is the Japanese tourist?" He shot an interrogative look at the Inspector, who shifted his weight from foot to foot in his unease. "But that room was mixed up with another room which was booked, not used and then reallocated."

"Sorry," said Blondell "you've lost me."

"One couple," Pancardi repeated, "and three other rooms."

"But that's four."

"Yes, but the Japanese she is the wrong room. Because there is confusion in the rush to make the public show." Pancardi looked at the Inspector once more, "One man does not come to Amsterdam – though there is a room for him."

"So the room is reallocated?" Blondell confirmed.

"That will show on the bookings no?"

"So where is that man?" Blondell was now following Pancardi's reasoning. "Was there some form of dispute? Is he dead?"

"This we will not know," said Pancardi, "unless Richter gives us the information and he is so ill that it is many hours before he can be interrogated, and we have a trail gone cold." Pancardi walked confidently to the window and looked at the canal below, "Clever, very clever, simple, thoughtful and so so easy," he said, with his back to the room.

"What's clever?" asked Blondell.

"That," replied Pancardi, pointing at the water thirty feet below. "All their rooms back on to the canal, if they had to they could jump."

"But that's insanity that canal can't be that deep."

"Deep enough my young Englishman. How many strokes would you need to be across and gone?"

Blondell calculated, "More than a few," he said.

"But not that many more, no?" was Pancardi's quick reply.

Maid service had cleaned the room, changed the towels and folded the toilet tissue into a little point on the roll. The soaps had been recharged and the bed linen freshened. On the dressing table lay a cutthroat razor and a small carton of milk. There were clothes in the drawers and Pancardi examined them carefully.

Next to the bed in the cabinet lay some chocolate and sweet bars and a packet of cigarettes.

"There are no laundry tickets here!" exclaimed Blondell sarcastically.

"But there are clues," replied Pancardi.

Blondell could sense a test was imminent and he racked his brain to think of the simple things he might have missed.

Pancardi continued, "We have four men and one woman, no?"

Blondell nodded in reply

"Dalvin he gives us the Englishman, West, and the Italian girl Parsotti. We have the German Udo Richter or Klaus Meine-he we have no? There is the mystery man, then there is the American here."

"How so American?" asked Blondell.

"American," Pancardi confirmed. "His clothes are from New York, look at the labels. He smokes Marlboro but not in a European packet. In the drawers there are Hershey bars and his underwear is all labelled Macey's own. If this man is not an American then he has been in America recently."

"How can you be so sure?" asked the Dutch Inspector speaking for the first time.

"The underwear, the underwear," Pancardi repeated. "How often do you buy underwear and when you do you buy only that which is comfortable. We are not women we are men. None of this is new it has been well laundered and it is all Macey's. I would say he is American."

The room fell silent as the two listeners digested the notion fully.

It was Pancardi who broke the silence once again, "Now this American," he asked, "what if he wants to get home, where would you fly Amsterdam to New York?"

"This is a wild notion – there's no basis in fact," replied Blondell.

"Maybe, maybe not."

"You mean," said Blondell, "on the basis of some Hershey bars and American cigarettes..."

"Which you cannot get in Europe," Pancardi remarked.

"You think this man is an American who will wish to get a flight out to America."

"Yes," replied Pancardi persuasively. "When you are ill where do you go?" He did not wait for an answer, "Home, you run for home," he said. Pancardi waited for a reaction there was none except attentive listening. "So they come here to Amsterdam," he continued, "why? To trade the jewels. They think they have time, we are nowhere near. They relax and they go mother to see. They go for meals to enjoy and they trade and then they fly away. Maybe they argue and one man he is dead or maybe he has left, maybe he has just gone home?"

"What, he has done the job and gone home?" asked Blondell.

"Why not?" Pancardi was now reasoning at lightening speed. "Perhaps he trusts this West and he knows his share will get to him, they are friends, so he goes."

"Or he is dead like Dalvin?"quipped Blondell.

"This is also a possibility no?"

"My god they didn't know we were on to them until this farce today."

"Precisely," Pancardi confirmed.

"So," Blondell was reasoning, "they will want out and one of them will try to get back to the States. He won't be able to use Schiphol because it's sealed tight as a drum."

"Yes?"

"So if I was him I'd make for any airport near enough to here to get a flight back into my own territory."

"Precisely," replied Pancardi triumphantly, "precisely."

Convinced by his own reasoning Blondell turned to the Dutch Inspector and made a series of simple requests. He wanted details of every flight out of a European airport to New York or any other North American airport for the next seven days. He wanted the direct contact with Dutch booking agents for bookings made today.

"How do we check them all?" asked the Dutchman, moving to exit the room.

"We don't," affirmed Pancardi, "we use logic."

The Inspector scuttled away pulling uniforms from the door as he went.

"Buffoon," hissed the Italian after him.

"Which room do you want my team to start in Carlo?"

Alaina stood in the doorway as the policemen passed into the corridor. Her face was drawn and she looked tired and in her arms sitting bolt upright was Mostro.

"He came to say hello," she smirked.

"You may as well start in here," he replied "anything to give us?"

"A fighting chance?" she injected. "I heard what you said from the doorway, I hope you're right, or at least half right."

"Ah," he replied, "here is the trainer scent for Mostro before I forget."

He handed her the shirt which Magdalene discovered in the tunnels under the Arno.

"Your material DNA evidence and Richter's scent, returned for safe keeping as evidence," he said.

"But this is heavily blood stained and useless."

"It's not Richter's either," interjected Blondell, "I used it stem the flow of that." He pointed to Pancardi's hand which was now leaking blood through the bandage.

"Richter's parting gift," Pancardi said, handing over the evidence for bagging. Pancardi's voice became thin as if he were no longer able to articulate his thoughts and his voice lowered to a hush, "There is much to tell," he muttered, "and still much to do and Robe he..."

"There's a doctor on his way up to see you," she interrupted. "That wound needs to be dressed and Mostro would like some food I expect. Though that doctor looks like Count Dracula, all thin, drawn and hungry – like he needs a good feast of blood." She patted the small head, "Magdalene's on her way up too. I thought you both might like to hear about the equipment in the car at Michelangiolo. The woman Parsotti was the driver and we have a good DNA sample. She broke a nail and left it in the driver's foot well. It's not much but it's enough to give us a match to Dalvin's killer and I expect this hotel. Ennio is going to work the rooms through the night - I must get some sleep. Just a few hours will do, I'm exhausted and I know about Roberto and I am very sorry for you." She blurted her words out in a stream of tangents, short and pithy.

"He was a good friend," Pancardi replied, "and we must find his..." His voice trailed away, "They have rooms for all of us here, some even have double beds." He laughed and linked his arm through Alaina's as he moved into the corridor, "So Magdalene she will smile yes?"

Two white coated men entered as they moved out.

"Dracula?" Pancardi said suddenly, "we must all feast and then we can talk through all we have so far. But first I must see to this," and he lifted his hand. "Where is il dottore?"

Chapter 28

The warmth of her mouth brought him back to life. She made him feel alive again and as her tongue flicked around his lips the softness of the touch took his breath away.

"Have you missed me?" she asked, disengaging.

"Do you really need to ask?" was the most he could muster.

"So Pancardi he works you hard?"

His mind raced and he could not think of anything to say and blurted the only picture which was solid in his consciousness.

"I saw Roberto get shot today. Was it today? I can't even remember if it was today. It's like a dream or something, a film. It's like everything is being concentrated down and all the water is being drained out. I can't explain it." Blondell sat on the bed. "It's like hell," he lowered his voice. "I've never really seen a man being shot – and it was all in slow motion. He turned, he fired, and then his body was going through the doors and he was running and then the shot." He paused, "And the blood so much blood, it was bubbling out of his chest and his mouth and his eyes, they were cold, glazed. Then he stopped breathing, just stopped and Pancardi was wiping the blood off his hands with a rag."

Standing before him, he had his hands on her hips and his head rested on her stomach as she caressed him. She stroked the back of his head and let him drain of emotion before she spoke.

"Go shower, we need to eat and you need to rest," she said.

Without questioning he rose and made his way to the bathroom. His mind was a blank suggestible canvass and she was the artist. Noticing that his shirt was spattered with blood and his skin stank of perspiration he realised he had no clean clothes. The thought of dressing in clothes spattered with Calvetti's and Richter's blood revolted him and he shuddered.

As water cascaded over his body and his mind began to revive he called from behind the curtains of water, "I've no clean clothes."

"Yes you do."

He could not hear the reply and as he returned from the bathroom wrapped in the courtesy robe he saw Pancardi at the door.

"Your clothes Alex!" he said, "from the nursing home in Köln. They came up with some of our people. "

"Come in," he gestured in reply, "how's the hand?"

"Well it seems to have stopped bleeding, but it hurts like hell. Can't even pet him now." Pancardi pointed at Mostro who had found Magdalene and was wagging his tail profusely. "Ladies man? That dog gets more attention than I do," he joked.

"Ah but Inspector," chided Magdalene, "he is the handsome one no?"

"What I really came to ask," said Pancardi, "was if you were coming to dinner? I would like to talk over the issues here and what you," he looked at Magdalene, "learned from the car. Alaina says you made a discovery in the boot."

"Well it's more of a hunch, based on what I found and know," Magdalene replied.

"The restaurant in half an hour?" he asked.

"Make it fifteen," said Blondell, who was facing away from the Inspector and pulling a pair of jeans over his naked behind.

He turned to face the Italian and Pancardi noticed for the first time scars on his torso. They were just above his waistline and clearly showed two entry points less than six inches apart. Pancardi nodded toward the marks as Blondell rapidly sought to cover them with the action of tucking in his clean black shirt.

"Bullet wounds?" he asked. Strange for a Foreign Office bureaucrat Pancardi thought.

"Accident when I was a boy," was Blondell's stock reply.

He cursed his mistake of letting the scars be seen and knew in the instant that Pancardi was smart enough to deduce that he was lying. He had to think quickly.

"No, before the Foreign Office I was in the services," he offered.

Pancardi nodded.

"Northern Ireland, I took some shrapnel when we had our tour of duty."

"That was bad luck," replied Pancardi.

"Yeah, lost my spleen and had some rebuilding of the colon, but hey I was pensioned out and here I am. Lean fit and a detective no less." He tried to make light of it.

The younger man watched the detective's face, there were no signs of disbelief but he knew that the story had not made sense. It had probably sparked more questions than answers in Pancardi's thought processes. Why had he said Northern Ireland? He tried to think of back–up detail and work out timings of tours of duty. Which regiment he had been with and how long in hospital. He began to wonder about whether the troubles in the province had been over before he had been old enough. It was a poor lie but Pancardi asked nothing.

"Fifteen minutes then," was all he said. "Come Mostro."

And the little dog leapt from his play on the bed with Magdalene and trotted off through the narrowing gap of the closing door his tail high and pert.

"You never said anything about military service to me," said Magdalene, turning on her side and propping her head with her hand. "And you said you had never seen anybody shot, until today." She paused thoughtfully, a wounded expression on her face, "That's not the truth is it?"

"I don't like to talk about it."

"But which story is true then?" she continued, "an accident as a boy or the services?"

He knew he had to think fast, "We were on a patrol," he lied, "four of us near Londonderry, me and three others. The jeep was blown to pieces. I caught some shrapnel and well, the others, they," he slowed as if recollecting the event, "they weren't so lucky."

"You don't have to say anymore," she said. "I understand."

He knew that his luck with Magdalene would hold but was not so sure of Pancardi with his powers of deduction. The detective knew that shrapnel and normal gunshots would not make the scars he had. Pancardi would know that they were high velocity bullet holes; made by bullets so fast and so precise that they passed clean through the target, him. The loss of spleen would be easy to see but the reason for it, a sniper from long range, would be another matter. From those facts Pancardi would deduce that he, Alex Blondell, had been a subject to be sniped at and then would come the why? He knew he should have told the truth.

Duane Rightman in his security van and uniform drove straight through the centre of the city through two road check points and out onto the eastern Motorway the A6.

The police road block officers had thought him no more than a late night security patrol and their checking, in consequence, was minimal, at one point they simply waved him through.

At the first Motorway service station he parked the van in the most obscure corner of the parking area underneath some over hanging trees. In a car a few spaces away a couple were dozing. Taking the uniform jacket off and throwing it into the back of the van he locked the door and walked casually toward the lights of the shop and food hall, unheeded by any onlookers. He needed a shower, a change of clothes and something to eat.

In the lorry park at the back of the Heineken brewery Alice Parsotti knocked on the window of a large road transporter which was parked up for the night. A fine drizzle had started and she looked soggy and forlorn. The driver wound down the window and looked at her on the footplate.

"What do you want?" he asked.

Making the biggest doe eyes that she could she smiled, and speaking in English said, "I'm in trouble."

"What sort of trouble?" continuing before she could answer the driver said, "and what's that got to do with me I'm trying to get some sleep here. I have to make a living."

"I need to get out of Amsterdam and I don't have any money and I could do with a lift."

"Come back in the morning," he snarled, and started to wind up the window.

"I could stay the night too," she said, "I don't have anywhere to sleep and we could have some fun."

The driver studied Alice. She must be desperate, he thought, to offer sex for a bed. She looked clean and vulnerable, he made an assessment that she was probably truthful. He wondered if her breasts were big, with pert nipples like the small glace cherries on a bath bun, he liked big breasts but couldn't decide if they were. If her nipples were pert he would play with them, he thought, as his eyes drifted down her body. Small feet, long legs and a tight muscular frame perfect for his needs. She had nice eyes he thought, honest eyes, and she looked desperate. Anyway he was doing her a favour and what the hell, he could do with some comfort on the road; his wife would never know - no one would ever know. He wound down the window to check if there was anyone else around. He'd seen hitchers do this before, send out a pretty girl to get his wagon to stop. Then they would pile out and all demand a lift, but this was different this was a lucky break for him.

"You need somewhere to sleep?"

She nodded.

"I only got the one bed in here," he said, confirming his intention.

"I know," she said, "and I bet it's warm."

"What's your name then girl?"

"Alice."

"You're not Dutch?"

"No English and I'm trying to get home. I had an argument with my boyfriend and the bastard left me here with nothing and I've run out of Euro. I want to get home. Are you going to the ports?"

She seemed genuine and distressed.

As he stuck his neck out to crane along the side of the vehicle to check for bystanders or wind up merchants the blow which broke his neck and cracked the back of his skull was heavy, sudden, decisive and silent. Paul West lying on the top of the cab had hit him once from above with a small scaffolding tube.

Alice leapt up reached in through the window and pulled the door lever – it popped the door open. The body fell onto the gravel as West simultaneously swung himself from the roof of the cab and landed on all fours like a cat beside the body. Taking the keys from the ignition Alice threw them to West and then busied herself by drawing the curtains at the windows. West dragged and then threw the body into the container on the trailer, breaking the security seal as he did so.

"Get down," he hissed at Alice, as his keen eyes spotted movement.

A Police car moved into the lorry park and West made out that he was urinating at the foot of the door. The car swept the area and West acknowledged them as they then proceeded out of the park. He knew it had been routine but he continued to scan the area for movement before jumping into the cab alongside Alice.

"Police! Have they gone?" she asked.

"Yeah, just a routine sweep I think. I made out I was taking a leak. The lazy buggers didn't even stop to question me."

"Just as well or I would have shot them both." She laid the .38 calibre on the dashboard cup-rest.

"Christ Alice!" he exclaimed, "we'll end up dying in this city in a hail of gunfire, we're not Bonnie Parker and Clyde what's his name. If we gun them down then the whole place will be swarming with cops."

She smiled, "Well I for one am not going to jail for this. If you kill someone they give you fifteen years, but the great train robbers Ronnie Biggs and all those they got given thirty. See it's worse to steal from the rich than it is to murder the poor."

"Fuck me you really are …"

"Ruthless?"

"No hard."

"Well you go to jail for years if you like, get kicked around like some football and then let some pig get up your arse and then tell me not to be ruthless."

"Alice…"

"Never mind Alice," she chided, "I'm not being some bloody Lesbian bitch – toy. They can kiss my sweet arse."

"I thought you didn't want that."

"You know what I mean," she laughed, realising the tension of the moment had been broken. "In the morning we get the jewels and we head out, together or separately?" she asked.

"They'll be on the lookout for us anyway so we might as well stay together. Cover each others back so to speak."

"Agreed," she replied. "But first we need to eat. Has that driver got a gas thingy in here?"

She started rummaging through the dash board and under the seats; then she moved into the sleeping compartment which was laid out with one sleeping bag, a double, well what passed for a double in camping circles. Alice found nude magazines, a contact magazine for whores, condoms, two empty coke cans, some sweets and some cigarettes.

"There's no burner here," she said. "Looks like cold food for us tonight. But at least we'll be warm. I hate the great outdoors – it plays havoc with my nails." She formed her hand into a claw shape as she spoke.

"Well my little Tigress we've got a bed for the night," West replied, "and beggars can't be choosers. It'll probably piss down later and this is better than any park bench. Let's listen in on the radio to see if the cops have picked up Rightman. I bet this has a tuneable frequency CB in here somewhere. Anyway what gourmet delights do we have in store then?"

Chapter 29

Sitting alone he had ordered fish and a salad, coffee and cake. The clean white tee-shirt shone in the fluorescent overhead lights which stung late-night drivers' eyes. He had torn the cuff from the soiled shirt and the rest he had stuffed into a bin. His hair was still damp and the freshness of a shave and clean underwear made him feel as if he had slept for hours. The disposable razor had been sharp and he had lightly nicked his chin but the bleeding had soon stopped and he looked less dishevelled now. The trousers were those he had worn all day and his socks too could have done with a change but he could not find any in the shop. However, he had found a nice chunky zip fronted sweater with deep pockets which was good insulation against the night cold and also concealed the handle of the pistol tucked into his waistband at the small of his back. He was drinking coffee and watching. He scanned the people as they entered, the tourists in ones and twos, the students hitchhiking and the couples on holiday. He lit a cigarette and blew idle smoke rings into the chill air. The clock in the main hall chimed twice.

"Jesus Alice!" exclaimed West, "there's no room to swing a fucking cat in here."

"I don't want to swing a fucking cat," she mocked, "just a normal one will do; anyway it's something, or would you rather be under a bush in the rain?"

"I'd rather be under your bush," he laughed.

"No chance," she replied. "If we can't swing a cat then you won't be swinging me."

She changed the subject as they nestled into the three quarter size bed area. It was hard on the back and West needed to sleep diagonally to avoid having constantly bent knees. The Driver had been shorter and fatter and, as Alice noted, less clean. His sweat was noticeable in the fabric and Parsotti was thankful that she had not been required to get naked with him. The man had been stupid enough for her not to have to degrade herself as she had done with Dalvin.

"Can you drive this thing?" she asked.

"Yeah, no problem," replied West. "When we were on a tour we drove these ten tonners."

She heard the word tour and immediately thought of a rock band and Paul West as a roadie. The vision of him testing equipment for popular boys with over inflated egos made her smile. Thinking of him separating packets of smarties to make sure only red ones were on a dressing room table made her snort. She imagined the tantrums of stars that had come from nothing to bask in fame and she could see that Paul would not have lasted long. He had never mentioned it before, perhaps it had been one of those short episodes of the past, an episode of youth best forgotten.

"What tours?" she asked nestling her wriggling backside into his receptive lap.

She turned on her side and drew his arm over her waist.

"Northern Ireland mostly – Royal Armoured Corps, or as we called it the shit brigade."

"I didn't know you were in the army, you never mentioned it."

"Best forgotten my lovely, nothing much to it really, a boyhood mistake. When you come from where I came from you didn't really get much choice. See I'm not posh like you."

"So what did you do?" she continued probing.

"Like I said shit brigade!"

"I don't understand."

"Well we used to have these fucking great trucks and some of the barracks on the border had cesspits which needed emptying. It was all temporary, nothing left now not even a border, but back then, well it was hell. So we used to drive these great tankers full of shit that we had collected to the sewerage plant. We were nick-named the shit brigade by the other guys. It was a shit detail too."

"Oh!" she exclaimed.

"Oh, indeed," his voice became bitter, "those bastards had a mock medal made for us, a turd on a brown ribbon. Even had an inscription put round it, like the George Cross, services to shit it read – wankers. Just because they got to parade around in armoured jeeps with stirlings we were treated like…"

"Stirlings?" she asked.

"Stirling sub-machine gun. Many of the guys had these, especially the tankies."

"Tankies?"

"Yeah Tank Regiment and the old cavalry boys, Blues and Royals. Stuck up pricks, especially the officers. Thought they were something special. All public school and full of awfully, awfully. You know the type, come from nowhere and going nowhere but thought they were somethin' cos they'd made lieutenant. Not a bean to their name just like me. Only they had a few more chances along the way." His voice was loaded with venom.

"How come you never said anything about this before?" she asked.

"Well I was only in three years thank Christ; just long enough for me to get an HGV. If I'd stayed longer I would have ended up shooting one of those toffee nosed pricks."

"And?"

"And nothing," he continued, "came out, got a job on the lorries and then … Well the rest is history. Didn't want to be nobody all my life. "

There was a silence and Alice knew not to pursue the subject of West's past any further.

"So," she said, "if we get the jewels then we can leave in this." She hit the roof over her head.

"Now that's the problem. How to get to our jewels? The whole city's crawlin' with the filth."

"Easy," she replied brimming with confidence. "I go wandering and get them on the way, cool as you like. Who's going to be looking at a woman tourist? The police will think we've done a runner and if we hadn't then I certainly wouldn't be sight seeing now would I?"

"What about image change?"

"Leave that to me," she said confidently.

Their conversation tailed into grunts and mild yeahs as the two of them drifted into an uneasy sleep peppered with dreams of police sirens, ambulances, and undertakers' hearses.

The police patrol vehicle swept the car park for a second time following the reports of a shooting in an old derelict building a few streets away. They were looking for a gang of youths who might be loitering or joy-riding a van. The officers noticed that two further Lorries had parked up and that all the vehicles had blacked-out for the night, there was no van. The lazy patrol swept by with only the sound of gravel being crushed beneath the wheels barely audible to the lorry occupants. They didn't get out as the rain was falling steadily now and they would have another four hours to sit in wet uniforms if they did.

"The equipment in the car," said Magdalene, "it struck me as strange."

"Why so?" asked Pancardi.

"Well," Magdalene continued, "first it was all English, nothing Italian at all and it was old, out-dated. Now this is strange because why did they bring the equipment. It must have been shipped? They could have got far better here – more modern."

"Maybe they brought it in the boot of a car, like holiday makers?" quipped Blondell.

"No!" exclaimed Alaina, frustrated at the interruption. "If you let Magdalene finish!"

Pancardi smiled at the rebuke.

"The valves on the Oxygen tank." Magdalene expected an interruption there was none. Blondell remained silent and Pancardi simply nodded knowingly. "These valves, they are old, all imperial sizes and they will not connect with the metric of Europe. Not only that, but there are some flippers which are marked and coded with a bar code which has been moulded into the rubber. Why did they not get rid of the code or the flippers?"

"A mistake?" asked Pancardi.

"Maybe, maybe not," snapped Alaina, "we traced the bar code to a supplier in Scotland, Andersons of Dundee a diving specialist. The only problem is that the place closed down three years ago and there are no customer records now. Perhaps the person who left them knew that?"

"A Scotsman!" Alex exclaimed.

"But how does this help us?" asked Pancardi.

Magdalene thoughtfully tilted her head to one side. "Well it could mean that our diver is a Scot or that he has equipment bought in Scotland, or that someone gave equipment to them from Scotland and that they got all their oxygen before they came to Italy. Or that they trained in Scotland," she replied.

"A lot of if and maybe," said Pancardi.

"We could track and trace all the divers and diving schools in Scotland," said Blondell."

"We could," said Magdalene, "but there are too many. How many years do we have?"

Blondell's shoulders sank.

"There are the divers on the oil rigs," she continued, "they come from all over the world and they are many. Then there are the schools and the retired. With a thousand men it would take us ten years."

Pancardi's mind was clearing, "The real question is why," he said, "why was this left in a car that we would obviously find?" He reached for the dauphinoise potatoes before continuing, "Was this left as a clue? A blind alley for us to run up like a set of trapped rats-just as before. Or was it an attempt to get someone caught? If these were placed in the car - by whom? Which one of the gang? Someone who wanted us running all over Scotland while they slipped away. Maybe they wanted us to trace someone in the team, but why and who? We don't even know who we are after. It's a very clever ploy. " He placed peas next to his steak, "Someone threw us a bone, someone who was the driver of the car," he concluded.

"Alice Parsotti!" exclaimed Blondell.

"That's the DNA match of the driver," chirped Alaina.

"But why?" asked Magdalene.

Pancardi did not answer but placed a forkful of steak between his lips and chewed, the juices of the rare meat melting onto his tongue. He watched the others as his silence overwhelmed them.

"Precisely?" asked Blondell.

She was tall, alone and rather dowdy. A frump with heavy spectacles and an uncommonly poor dress sense and Rightman spotted her immediately. He watched her go to the toilets and then glance at her wrist on her return, obviously checking the time. She seemed to be dithering, thinking, calculating as if she had an appointment and then impulsively decided to go for a coffee. The waitress refilled his mug.

"Two refills only," she said, in the unconcerned manner which only those in a truly dead end job could employ.

"OK," he mumbled.

"That's your second," she affirmed.

"Fine."

"I was just saying if you want any more you'll have to pay."

"Right," he replied.

The frumpy woman sat a long way from him staring out into the gloom of the night, she yawned and stretched. Rightman checked to see that she truly was alone.

When she got up to leave he followed her quickly catching the door as it swung back against him as she passed ahead. She walked slowly and fumbled in her handbag for her keys. There were a few people about. Some were stretching their backs as they stood upright, some were preparing to leave, and others were making their way into the café area. Rightman was behind her now no more than three strides; she was heading toward a small blue Ford. She passed between the unoccupied cars and lifted the key, it clicked and all the lights flashed once - the vehicle was open. Rightman barged into her like a rugby player and she fell headlong to the ground between the cars, her spectacles smashed and slid under a vehicle to her left as her head bounced on the tarmac. The keys fell from her hand in the instant that Rightman grasped her hair and forced her head back with his body weight against the nape of her neck. Bones loudly snapped and she lay lifeless underneath him. Rightman scanned the car park, his breath was short and sharp, there were no people watching and the slip road was empty. He looked to the light and saw the CCTV cameras and wondered if anyone had seen his actions and raised an alarm; he knew that time was short.

Working at lightening speed he dragged the lifeless corpse dumping it in the boot, took the purse from the hand bag and got into the drivers seat. Shuffling through the purse he retrieved 84 Euro, a credit card and then threw the rest onto the rear seat of the car. As he fumbled for the seat adjuster to give him more leg room a police motorway patrol vehicle appeared and parked thirty feet ahead of him. The driver noticed him and Rightman smiled as he reached toward the small of his back; his fingers found the handle of the pistol and withdrew it unnoticed onto his lap.

The police passenger got out of the car and began to walk slowly toward him. Then he checked and returned to the driver's side.

"Remember no sugar," the driver called to the standing officer, "I'm on a diet, so low mayonnaise."

The walking policeman laughed and then resumed a confident stride toward the food hall. Rightman watched and waited until he had passed the Ford before turning the ignition key and swinging the car out toward the exit. In the rear view mirror Rightman glimpsed the driver reading a magazine and he slipped the gun from his lap into his pocket and changed gear to enter the flow of traffic heading north into Germany.

Chapter 30

The early morning mist rose from the canals and the air was still and hushed. It was dawn and the chorus of birds had begun. The smell of the air was sweet and fresh tinged with salt blown in from the North Sea. Traffic was still and only a few early morning windows were illuminated by the early risers. Alice Parsotti was leaning out of the nearside window as Paul West urinated against the front wheel of the lorry cab.

"Very impressive," she said, bleary eyed and yawning. "Now how are you going to get it back in? What time is it anyhow?"

He looked at his watch, "6.34 am. I could always fold it." he replied.

"Why are we awake so early?"

"We're not," he said, "I am and I needed a piss. Duck in baby here's the filth."

A police car approached from the driver's side of the lorry and by the time it arrived beside West, Alice had disappeared back inside and re-drawn the curtains. It pulled up alongside the wagon as West was adjusting his dress. The policeman did not move from the car and winding down the window called over. He spoke in Dutch, "Good morning sir, have you been here all night?" he asked.

West nodded. He was using his knowledge of German to guess what the answer should be.

"Have you seen a van or a gang of boys?" he continued.

West had to come clean, "I can't speak Dutch," he said.

"OK, English?"

West nodded.

Remembering the number plate he realised that the vehicle he was in had a Dutch registration. He hoped that the cop was a little less observant and anyway perhaps that company used English drivers to go back and forth across the channel. If he checked, then he checked, there was no time to fluster and panic now.

"Last night there was a shooting," the policeman stated, "over in the old brewery."

"Don't know it," replied West, nonchalantly.

"Well just checking to see if you saw or heard anything last night."

West shook his head.

Alice Parsotti was inside the cab with her Smith and Weston .38 trained directly at the driver's head. The gap in the curtain was less than half an inch but she knew that despite being three feet behind the window she could blow a hole in his face where his nose should be. He was alone but she had made her mind up that if he stepped out of the patrol car he was a dead man.

"I heard nothin'," said West. "Mind you I was out for the count. What time did it happen?"

"In the early evening, they think," the policeman replied.

"Well I didn't get here till late and then went straight for the bed down," said West.

"Where are you off to?" asked the cop.

"The hook and then Britain via the ferry."

"Have a good day then sir, and safe journey."

The police patrol man then drove over to other vehicles parked at the far side of the gravel and stepping from his vehicle tapped at the window of one of the other two lorries which had parked up. West could not make out clearly what was being said but he sensed from the body language of the driver and the odd word which drifted over on the wind that he was not pleased at being woken. West busied himself checking the tyres and the air brake hoses as if he were preparing to start a journey. As the policeman started the same routine on the second vehicle the driver of the first vehicle started his large diesel engine which drowned out the conversation altogether.

West hopped into the cab and started pulling back the curtains.

"Leave them," hissed Alice, "make it look as if you're going back to bed."

"They've found the security guard," West said, as he closed the door. "And they're still looking for the van. They think it's kids on a joy ride. We'll be safe for an hour or two."

"I need a little more time than that," said Alice. "I've got to get to the museum and get the jewels and get back. It doesn't open until nine and I don't want to be hanging around outside. I'd like a few tourists to be about."

"No need to get back," he replied, "I'll pick you up."

"Where?"

"Outside the Rijksmuseum?"

"That's just a few minutes from the Van Gogh – great," she said.

"The less time we are out and about the less likelihood of being seen." He smiled at her, "See, I don't think that in their wildest dreams they would think that we would still be in the city, and a lorry, well that's perfect cover."

The telephone in Pancardi's room sounded for the early wake up call. It was 7.15 and Mostro reluctantly jumped from the bed as Pancardi walked toward the shower.

His movements were slow, stunted and arthritic – he stretched. These days he found the beds in hotels hard and unforgiving and he would much sooner have his own bed; the aging process had made him learn the love of home.

As he stepped from the shower there was a soft tap at his door. When he answered Alaina stood grinning at him, he was dripping and wrapped in a towel. Her hair and make-up were perfect and he wondered at what time she had started her toilet.

"Some excellent news," she said enthusiastically.

"Oh, excuse the dress I have only just got up," he replied. "Could you do me favour and let Mostro onto the balcony."

She did as she was asked and ushered the little dog onto the concrete pad which overlooked the canal below. A gust of fresh wind entered the room and freshened the dull and heavy air of the sleeper. When she returned Pancardi had hastily pulled on his trousers and was buttoning a shirt. It was obviously straight from a pack as it carried the square lines of folding which were now interspersed with the damp patches where the detective had tried to dry himself too quickly and failed.

Mostro, after studying the crowd below, cocked his leg against the furthest stanching and released the stored flow of the night. Pancardi hoped there was no one on the balcony below. He listened for a complaint and as none came he assumed his little companion had caused no offence.

"We have confirmed that the woman in the room was the same one as in the Volkswagen – Alice Parsotti," she affirmed.

"Fantastic," he replied, fastening a tie around his neck. His collar was up like the extended neck of a turtle. "So we know we are on to them," he continued.

"It gets better."

Pancardi stopped and turned to face her. His tie now straight but his feet still bare.

"Udo Richter," she continued, "confirmed match to the rag and the room and the blood at the nursing home."

Pancardi stood still, "Anything else?"

"Well we also have DNA on the other man the one Dalvin called West. Semen on the bed sheets; if we find him then we should be able to lock him into the murder and the robbery, which leaves you just one other. We have a positive for a male as the third man, your American? Interesting development too we came across something unusual, well almost unique in fact." She hesitated as if she didn't wish to say, "I think it's an error, but Ennio is convinced."

"Go on."

"Well you said there was one other man," she said hesitantly.

Pancardi pulled on his socks and shoes quickly fastening his laces, he made a mental note that they needed a polish. Sensing that she was unwilling to go into further detail, he pressed her on the subject.

"Why the hesitation? What do you not wish to say?" he asked.

"Ennio seems to have a DNA match," she slowed as she spoke, "that doesn't make sense," she hesitated again.

"Well what's the problem?"

"Ennio thinks there is a partial match," she slowed again.

Pancardi became irritated, "Can it help or not?" he asked.

The detective offered Alaina a chair at the small desk while he sat on the unmade bed.

"That's debatable," again she hesitated, "I don't think it can be possible. I suspect Ennio was tired, and he probably got the family match mixed up."

Pancardi was confused, "Family, are these people connected? Are they brother and sister?" His mind was postulating. "Parsotti and the man who did not turn up here, they are related, are they brother and sister?"

Mostro trotted into the room, defusing the growing tension, tilted his head at Alaina as if to ask her when his breakfast might arrive and then jumped into her lap.

"Well…. There could be a possibility that they…" she hesitated again, "the chance that they are not related in some way is very rare. If Ennio is right," she tried to qualify her statement.

"How rare?" he asked.

"1 in 7.3 million, give or take a .003% variable."

Pancardi whistled an exclamation through his teeth.

Mostro was attempting with all his might to get his head under Alaina's left hand. She grabbed his ears and shook his head as a diversion from the insistent questioning which Pancardi was levelling at her. Her nose was making contact with the white ball of fluff, in fact they were almost nose to nose, but Pancardi was not so easily put out of stride, he continued to delve.

"A match then?" he said.

"Yes, but I don't understand how I missed it," she was perplexed. "I couldn't have missed it. I never miss such things. It makes no sense for Ennio to find this now. "

"Go on, give me detail," he said.

"As I said Ennio may have this wrong, so I think we had best check the results thoroughly first."

Pancardi looked at her intensely, "You are not being truthful, first the cryptic clues then the reticence to say anything at all, then you will not say. This is most unlike you. You are the professional and mistakes do get made but not by you, something big troubles you."

"It does," she replied, "that is why I want to be sure. It could be the fourth man. But I don't know how I missed it. Or it could be something else which has plagued my dreams for most of the night. So I will run the…"

Her voice was cut short by a loud knock at the door. Pancardi rose and answered, at the door stood Alex Blondell.

"Breakfast?" he asked and smiled knowingly at the sight of Alaina in Pancardi's room. He deduced that some form of liaison was underway and he could not resist a quip. "Did you sleep well Alaina?" he asked.

"Yes very well thanks," she replied.

"Comfortable beds aren't they?" he continued.

"Angelic," she said innocently.

"Soft and inviting?"

"Very inviting and big – just what I needed."

Pancardi caught Blondell's eye and opened his own wide in response to the younger man's puerile mentality. He raised his index finger gently as if giving a warning.

"One good turn and all that," said Blondell.

"And two and two do not always make five remember that my young apprentice," Pancardi returned.

Alaina picked up on the cryptic inferences and despite a blushing face, which Blondell misconstrued as an admission of complicity, she strode forward to meet Magdalene who had appeared behind Blondell's right shoulder.

"Well all this activity has given me an appetite," she said. "How about you Magdalene?"

Standing on a toilet seat inside the public toilet cubicle Alice Parsotti could just reach the bottom of the cistern. She was listening intently for the footsteps of the cleaning woman, who had been mopping the floor. She could hear her talking to passers-by while she smoked her cigarette, a fowl smelling Turkish brand which stank like burning bus tickets. Parsotti had removed the cast iron lid and was now extended on tip toe her hand walking inside the metal flush box. She thought she felt something but could not be sure. She extended herself one more inch and then with her other hand flushed with the chain. Immediately the water disappeared from the box and rushed between her feet. Her fingers met a stone and then bubble wrap and she lifted and stepped down in one flowing movement. In her hand she held the package containing the jewels. She untied the stone and placed it on the floor, the jewels went into her handbag. Her fingers clasped the handle of the .38 as she opened the door and walked out of the toilets.

As she left a museum official called to her, "Hey Lady the entrance is this way," he said in Dutch, "toilets are for museum entrants only."

She shrugged but kept her hand firmly on the revolver inside her bag.

"I just wanted to pee," she said loudly in English, and turned confidently to go out into the open air.

"Bloody ignorant American," the guard muttered under his breath.

He knew the toilets should have been placed after the entrance kiosk and not before it. That way people had to pay to use them. It was a design fault on the part of the architect and the bane of his life.

Alice Parsotti turned left and started the exposed walk from the Van Gogh museum.

Crossing a small bridge she turned right then left and continued on toward the main road. Ahead at a corner shop she saw two police officers looking at fruit and talking with the shop keeper. Her grip on the revolver tightened; she was only a few metres away now and the police had seen her.

"Gut tag," she said cheerily as she passed the group, avoiding eye contact.

The shopkeeper repeated the phrase in return and three strides later she had passed them. One of the policemen noticed her long red hair and the sway of her hips before the shopkeeper snapped him back to reality.

Alice Parsotti continued languidly and then turned left into an alley and stood behind a set of garbage bins her heart beating like a drum. She listened for people following and could faintly hear the continuing conversation of the shopkeeper. Taking stock she walked down the alley and then turned right, left and right again. Ahead she could see the ring road and the large open area in front of the Rijksmuseum, there was no lorry.

A woman opened her door ahead and a pushchair appeared with a grizzling child in it. Parsotti smiled as she passed and the woman made a comment in Dutch which she nodded recognition to even though she had not understood the language. She slowed her pace and scanned the area for a bench or bus stop. There were two police cars on patrol and the occupants were nonchalantly looking at the people on their way to work; scanning the crowds but not looking. She stopped and took off her shoe at the same time looking for the lorry to appear. She pretended she had a stone in it; shoved her fingers into it as if to clear an obstruction and then bent to replace it on her foot. As she looked up, the lorry drew up as if to ask directions and with a few quick strides she was up to the door and talking to the driver.

"Got them," she said, "we being watched?"

"There are a couple of patrol cars over there," he replied, "but I don't think they clocked me, can you see?"

"Yeah, but I think we are safe enough. They're not even looking are they?"

"Nope not a movement, stupid fuckwits, they'll think I'm after directions," he replied. "In ya get girl let's fuck off before the cement comes."

Alice Parsotti walked around to the far side of the truck and with a nimble step hopped in and slid over the co-drivers seat and on into the sleeping compartment.

Drawing the curtain around the bed area she spoke softly as the wheels began to bite the tarmac and the diesel engine roared into the ring-road traffic.

"I'll stay out of sight for a bit," she said, "until we're on the motorway at least."

"Here we go," said West, as he passed the police cars. "Let's see if they move."

He looked into the near side rear view mirror as one of the patrol cars joined the traffic behind them.

"Heads up," he said, "one of those bastards is behind us."

"Did they see me get in?"

"Don't think so, but I can't be sure," he said.

"Christ they probably think I'm on the game or something and they're going to give us a pull."

"No I don't think so," he replied confidently.

"Trust us to find the only diligent cop in this rat hole city. If he stops us I'll blow his fucking head off."

"I don't think you'll need to my lovely," he laughed. "He's filtering right - we're clear."

Chapter 31

"So what do we know?" asked Pancardi, as he poured a large strong coffee for Blondell and himself. He was taking stock, "We have names, nationalities, DNA and one of them in custody. Things are looking up for us no?"

"Richter won't say a word though," Blondell interjected. "He knows that if he does he's a dead man."

"But not if we get them all," Pancardi replied. "The whole nest in one go?"

"That's hoping. In fact," Blondell continued, "it's a vain hope, because we'll probably never know who this mystery man is, the one that got away – the brother."

"Probably not," Pancardi shrugged, "but what can we gather from the evidence we already have?"

He smiled at the waitress and ordered two soft-boiled eggs and some crispy bacon.

The bacon he had decided was for Mostro and the little dog seemed to be aware of this decision as he looked up at his master whose hand fell casually to stoking the top of his head.

"Then there is this wonderful development," he continued, "of Alaina and the blood relationship between the girl and the missing man. If this can be proved then we know at least that we have some chance of finding them."

"That could lead us to Scotland?" Magdalene piped up.

"Then it is to there we shall go," replied Pancardi. "We will catch them, if we must go to the ends of the earth. But I do have one niggling problem," he paused thoughtfully, "if this man is

Scozzese and the girl she is Italian how can they be of the same blood?"

"Perhaps it's just another clever red herring?" Blondell smirked.

"Just like Jersey?" Pancardi agreed. "She is cunning and she tries to put us off the scent, maybe she is not Italian at all, or he is not Scozzese....But," Pancardi continued wryly, "as clever as they think they are we are cleverer, no?" He laughed and clapped a heavy hand upon the table, "We will catch our slippery eels," he said, "of that I am certain."

He took a deep draft of coffee and smiled at the others around the table. He was so positive that virtually nothing would throw dejection into the mix and his attitude was infectious. Mostro barked loudly from under the table adding his voice to the sudden exuberance of those above him. In return Alaina passed him a small morsel for his trouble which he accepted all too willingly.

Blondell was studying Alaina and she reddened at the intensity of his stare.

Pancardi became aware of what Blondell might be thinking and returned the favour of embarrassment by asking Blondell if he needed pancakes to keep his strength up.

"You look tired my young friend," he chirped, "a bad night?"

Magdalene's faced began to glow. The two women let their eyes meet and in that split-second glance they realised that both had sexual feelings for the man they sat next too.

Looking directly at Pancardi Alaina vented the frustration of both women, "Isn't it about time you two stopped trying to embarrass each other?" she asked. "And just to clear matters up Alex," she turned to Blondell, "I did not spend the night with Carlo, though I wish I had."

The moment the words left her lips she knew it had been a mistake, but the statement had the desired effect, in that the professionalism of both men returned as if an elastic connector had suddenly retracted.

"What will they do next that is the real question," Blondell barked in an attempt to regain the momentum.

"Precisely," said Pancardi, as he took another piece of bacon and passed it to Mostro under the table. "Good boy," he said.

"You will have your food soon, though you like this better eh?" Once again he petted his dog.

"Where have they gone?" asked Alaina.

"They will not be in Amsterdam now," replied Blondell. "They will be long gone."

"The sea and airports are sealed so they cannot get out," quipped Alaina in reply.

"They must either take a train or car out and go back into Europe, but where?"

"Inspector?"

The large Dutch detective approached the breakfast table apprehensively. Pancardi continued to pet Mostro and barely acknowledged him.

"Inspector?" the man repeated.

Pancardi looked up.

"We have a strange incident which took place late last night or in the early hours of this morning." Pancardi nodded. "It seems that a security guard was shot last night, in an old brewery." Pancardi's ears pricked up. "It may be totally unrelated, probably drug related, but," he hesitated, "a guard and his dog were shot by what might be two different weapons and the van he used has gone. Most likely for joy riding."

Pancardi waited expectantly – he knew there was more.

"Traffic CCTV footage of the slip road entry to the motorway shows the van heading out of the city."

"You think this might be related?" Blondell asked.

"It is too early to say. We are checking the brewery and…….."

"And you will find nothing," Pancardi affirmed. "Our birds have flown, this must be our team. Who else would shoot a guard, steal a van and head out onto the motorway. Drugs, ha nonsense. This is our quarry."

He took a final gulp of coffee to signal he was finished at breakfast, stood erect and smiled.

"First," he ordered, "all CCTV footage must be checked from all the exit slipways. Second get a car to every service station and parkplatz and find this van. I think they would have dumped it somewhere, and where better to find another vehicle. If they have not dumped it then it should be easy to trace. Next check all enquiries about stolen cars from motorway services, and missing persons, or people telephoning hospitals in the area. They took that – then they would have to change vehicles and we need to know what that next vehicle is."

"What do you want me to do?" asked Alaina.

"Re-run the tests of Ennio," he replied, "you are the best in the whole world," he flattered her, "now you must give us absolute proof."

She smiled and visibly rose in stature as he spoke. It was clear that there was an admiration on Pancardi's part and attraction on hers.

"How can we be sure?" asked Blondell.

"We can't but we can think like them and guess no? What would you do?"

Blondell nodded and felt, rather than thought, that Pancardi was probably closer to the truth than he would like to agree. Magdalene, who was still sitting as the others began to move, suddenly blurted out one word.

"America!" she said.

Blondell thought she had said Eureka and to Pancardi she might as well have.

"One of them is American?" she continued, "and when we are in danger we run to home. To be safe, to be with the ones we know who can protect us."

She was looking directly at Blondell as she spoke and he could feel the hairs at the back of his neck stand to attention. It was clear that her revelation was intended for two recipients and not just one. Pancardi was nodding as she repeated his own reasoning.

"He will try to get to an Airport and fly to America."

"See," said Pancardi, smiling broadly, "the girl she thinks."

"But what about the others?" asked Blondell, "Scotland, Italy?"

"Well I just thought that it was a good guess," she replied.

"An excellent guess more like," chirped Pancardi. "It is such a shame that you must be here with Alaina and Alex he must go with me. I want you to try and trace this diving equipment, use anything and everything." He turned to the bemused Dutch Inspector, "She must have all the facilities at her disposal. She will need a high speed computer link and a direct Interpol phone line." Pancardi turned and smiled at Magdalene, "Nothing must get in her way," he barked as a final command, with his back to the Dutch Inspector.

The Dutchman turned to some uniformed officers who were already deep in conversation with Alaina, issued some sharp orders and one of the men left rapidly.

Pancardi turned to Blondell and spoke under his breath, "Damn bloody idiot," he hissed, "but that girl of yours she has a brain, no? And she has a fine ar..."

"Everything will be set up in the next few minutes," said the Dutchman as he returned from listening to Alaina.

"Good," replied Pancardi, "then we shall go to this brewery until you find the van. Then we shall go there. We are so close that we can touch them."

The Dutch Inspector looked at the Italian and noted his total inability to accept that he might be wrong. It was in his eyes which burned as if candles had been lit behind them. He was convinced that the security guard murder had been this gang of jewel thieves, there was no proof, no logic, but even he began to feel that the Italian was probably right.

"If they did kill this guard and it was only last evening or night, the time of death will give us how far behind we are. Ha!" Pancardi exclaimed, "we are the bloodhounds after the foxes."

Duane Rightman lit another cigarette and blew smoke rings as the small Ford rumbled northward through Germany. His eyes were heavy and he knew that he needed to sleep. The thought of the flight to Montreal sustained him and then the short hop across the border back into the states. He was looking forward to getting out of Europe. He had been driving most of the night and traffic was beginning to greet the dawn dew. He knew he would need to rest soon, get some sleep before moving on, but he had to dump the car and get further away first. He wanted somewhere big in a city, a multi-storey car park somewhere where lots of people came and went, a rail station; a place where a car could sit for days without seeming suspicious. By the time they found the body he would already be home. It was a dull and dreary dawning; he wondered how long it would be before anyone had noticed that the woman in the boot had not arrived and started to think about an accident or contacting the police. His mind wandered to her life before their paths had crossed. Perhaps she lived alone, perhaps she had no one and it would be days before she was missed. He considered fate and the chaos theory. Perhaps her body would rot and stink until it was finally discovered bloated and maggot ridden by some over zealous parking attendant. He imagined the boot being forced and the attendant vomiting over his newly polished shoes as the maggots crawled out of her eye sockets and into her nose, and he laughed at the vision. His mind wandered unchecked.

The run across the border had been uneventful but he knew that he had best ditch the car in Bremen and get a train. Time might be on his side but he was not going to take chances. His eyes were heavy and the lights ahead danced as he forced himself forward. He needed the dawn to break fully, to wake him. His mind was wandering, drifting from subject to subject, and he felt his eyes get heavy as the lids began to close and the car moved gently toward the central barrier.

"Two teas," said West at the truck stop café, "and do you do English breakfast?"

"Full fry up?" asked the man in the greasy apron behind the counter.

"Too fucking right," replied West in a heavy London accent.

Alice returned from the toilet and the man at the counter gave a knowing lecherous smirk at West, "Hitchhiker?" he asked.

West shook his head, "Wife," he said.

The man behind the counter had already noticed that the girl wore no wedding ring and he knew many of the girls that came into the café were girls who plied their trade from driver to driver. Or they were girls who needed to get from A to B and had no money but were prepared to drop their knickers to get there. He had seen them all before, Poles, Romanians, Lithuanians, running from little one room hovels; no work, no prospects, no education, no life except being with a man who drank too much and filled their bellies with arms and legs rather than good food and fine wine. He looked at Alice Parsotti and noticed her green eyes and red hair and wondered just what she might do for a passport and a new life. He imagined her naked and bent over one of his tables as she walked away from the counter, before turning back to the fryers behind him.

"Don't give us any fried bread though," called West, as the two made their way to a table near the door and far enough away from ears that might overhear.

They sat with two mugs of tea and an encrusted ketchup bottle between them. The table was covered in a pale blue plastic cover which had been stapled crudely at the edges and the surface was slightly tacky.

"My God," said Alice, "what a dump."

"Yep," replied West, in his most derisory tone of affectation, "we are lorry persons now. Anyhow the best place for us to be is here. The cops won't be looking for a lorry yet."

"It's hardly the Ritz though is it?" she replied. "Not exactly clean either." She ran her finger over the table edge, "I don't want food poisoning."

"You'll be fine," he replied, "besides these places save on the décor my dear and not the grub. Not your posh nosh, half a pea on a plate with a square of bacon called some fancy French name," he chuckled. "Anyhow old greasy Joe over there was clocking your arse – I think he might fancy a twirl."

Alice took a mouthful of tea and shuddered, "I needed that," she sighed, "really needed that."

West smiled as he spoke, "We'll have to dump the truck somewhere. Best to just get to a parking area and then close up the curtains and fuck off. When people see us go they'll think we're off for a meal or something. Leave the body in the back."

Alice nodded and as the greasy waiter-come-cook approached cast her eyes down to avoid eye contact and saw the grubbiness of his clothing instead. She could smell the mixture of stale sweat and old cooking fat on his skin and it revolted her.

"Two erm …afternoon… erm evening breakfasts?" he joked, looking at the clock. It read 5.32pm

"Thanks," said West.

"Where you two from then?" he questioned.

"England," replied Alice.

"Me too," he said, "came over here with the BFPO mob in the sixties and seventies and got tied up with a German lass. Fuckin' loved it and ain't been back 'cept for a visit. We got divorced though, a while back, but I still don't fancy blighty.

I'm not surprised you're divorced thought Alice as her mouth served up, "Oh well we live in Orpington, do this run all the time. I just come along for the ride really."

He noticed that her accent was not eastern European but he could not place it. He thought her too posh to be driver's moll. Her hair and nails were well kept and she had an edge to her voice. He was sure they had not been in before, he knew he would have remembered that hair and that arse.

Chapter 32

The horn on the car was blaring and Rightman could feel something warm trickling down his nose and dripping onto his chest. The safety belt dug into his shoulder and his right knee was throbbing. There were lights and people and glass and someone was pulling him out from under the airbag. His arm was wrenched and he fell face first onto the tarmac. His head swam and he struggled to adjust his vision.

"You're ok," the voice reassured. It was a sweet voice high and resolute, "Try to move your legs and step out."

It was a woman smiling and helping, supporting him under his armpit. She was small, frail even, but she helped him hobble to the side of the motorway embankment where he sat down-instantly she was gone.

Rightman studied the blue Ford, every panel was dented and he knew it must have rolled several times. He saw the windows blown and the roof and doors battered. The passenger side door hung limply from its hinges and the driver's side was deeply dented. The boot was open and the body gone. He tried to stand and felt numbness in his knee and was forced to sit. The little woman was now at a grey BMW which lay overturned some fifty yards ahead. He felt dizzy, sick and disorientated and he knew he had fallen asleep at the wheel, he cursed his stupidity. He raised his left hand to his face and felt the blood oozing from his nose and at his mouth he felt his own touch sting. Running his tongue along his teeth he felt the pulpy gap at the front where the two teeth had been. The taste was sweet and fleshy with the texture of an over ripe pear. His upper lip was swelling and he could feel a bump the size of a chicken's egg growing above his right eye. He checked his fingers for movement then his neck and spine, everything seemed fine. Trying to gather his senses he stood and attempted to move toward the woman as other cars began to arrive on the scene. He could see her directing operations while another man was examining a lump which lay in the road behind the blue Ford. Rightman could see a bare foot and knew it was a body. The man rose and spoke into a mobile phone and then seeing Rightman moved toward him with athletic bounds. The little woman was directing traffic now which had slowed to watch the curious pantomime of carnage. Cars slowed in the hope of seeing a corpse or two and then once assured there were none on display they sped on into the dawn, thankful and content that it had not been them but disappointed that the spectacle had not been worth the effort of slowing down. The athletic man spoke in German at first and when no response came shifted to common English.

"Sit down," he said, "there's nothing you can do for her now. An ambulance is on its way. The Police will be here in a moment too."

Rightman fought with the dizziness. He wanted to run but knew he would not get far. The Police would have a helicopter out after him and ......Rightman sat down, his mind was resigning itself to captivity. He needed a smoke, needed to clear his head, had to think. There was no way he was going to jail, especially for murder. He imagined himself as an old man locked in a cockroach infested cell with the smell of piss stinging his nostrils. He touched the centre of his face and felt the tackiness of blood from his nostrils but knew his nose was not broken. Sirens stung his ears and blue lights flashed as he lay back against the bank, it was only a matter of time now. He needed a cigarette and reached into his cardigan pocket only to find the handle of his revolver. He slipped it from the pocket and held it at arms length concealed in the long grass and weeds beside him.

"Nothing, absolutely nothing," Blondell remarked, "a waste of time us being here."

Pancardi studied the murder scene and then sat on the bench from where Parsotti had delivered the fatal head shot. Mostro was in his lap and he was thoughtfully stroking the top of the little dog's head.

"How so?" he asked casually, as he looked around him.

"Well it could have been them or it could just have been somebody else," Blondell replied.

"But it was them," said Pancardi confidently, accentuating the was. "And you know this to be true Alex, come look at the door."

Blondell stood with his back to the Italian.

"Look," Pancardi said, softly from behind him. "The first shot at leg level. Obviously the person thought there might be a dog, so they first shoot through the door."

Blondell nodded in acceptance.

"Then the door is opened and the guard is shot with clean precision."

Blondell nodded again.

"So what can you deduce?" asked Pancardi in triumph.

Blondell stood and visualised the scene, his mind entering a state of grace.

"The first shot," he said, "is lucky." He paused thoughtfully, "It kills the dog and stops the guard in his tracks."

"Yes!"

"Then they open the door, because the guard would not have opened it once the first shot was fired," he added, "and he would have been falling and in pain, his last thought would have been to open the door."

"Yes, go on."

"So they open the door and bam his head is blown off."

"But why would they have acted so quickly," Pancardi asked, "so without thought?"

"Gut reaction," blurted Blondell in his reply. "The guard turns up and they are skittish."

"Skittish?" Pancardi questioned the colloquialism.

"Means jumpy," Blondell explained.

"So why were they skittish?" Pancardi asked again.

"Good grief yes," Blondell hissed, "they saw us at or near the hotel and they made..."

"For here?" Pancardi completed the thought process.

"Yes for here. They had this place as a fall back but they never expected to need it. Then the guard turns up and bam he dies, they get lucky by killing the dog outright and the guard – he's yelling and the noise and confusion and bingo one clear, calm, shot."

"To the head no?"

"It had to be them. It was clinical designed to stop the noise."

"So the last shooter, she must have been calm?" asked Pancardi.

Blondell spun to face the Italian who was sitting with his chin resting on the backs of his hands. Mostro was examining the corners of the room, checking for a good spot.

"She?" he questioned.

"Yes she," Pancardi confirmed. "She is cold, methodical, and what she did is what I would do. What you would do?"

"But…"

"There is no but Alex. She is a very worthy adversary. A dangerous adversary."

"If I didn't know better Carlo," he used the Christian short version for the first time, "I'd say you admired her."

Pancardi's face tilted at the use of his name, "She is the enemy," he said almost casually before leaping to his feet and saying, "now we go outside and examine."

"Where the van was?" interrupted Blondell,

"Si," said Pancardi, "come," and he swept past Blondell, stepping over the brown blood stain in the doorway as if it were a mere puddle on a rain-soaked street.

"It had been raining for days before we arrived," said Blondell examining the ground.

"But there are tyre tracks no?" said Pancardi.

Mostro was busying himself at the far edge of the compound, sniffing intently at the ground.

"Yes, one set." Blondell considered before making a summation, "So how did they get here? One set of tyre tracks and one set of footprints near the gate – the guard's I suspect."

It was Pancardi's turn to nod.

Blondell examined the ground like an Indian tracker in a poor 1950's B movie.

"So the van driver opens the gate drives in and releases the dog from the back, and starts to make a circuit."

Pancardi nodded for a second time.

"Then he walks the perimeter and hears voices and then gets shot in the doorway."

"Excellent," laughed Pancardi. "But there are no other footprints in the soft earth. No women's feet marks? So did they just fly away?"

Blondell returned to the site of the parked van, "Shit," he said, "just the one set of prints, male. I don't understand it there must be more prints."

Pancardi waited, allowing Blondell time to flounder, then said, "Sometimes you think like them and sometimes..." he checked himself and continued. "After they have killed the guard one man comes to the van and opens the driver's door and drives away. There are too many prints for one guard, on the driver's side. Then the driver leaves and the second man locks the gate from the inside and he and the woman leave by another route. Maybe they joined up with the driver of the van, but would you?"

Blondell shook his head, "No of course not, they split up," he said. "Shit, shit and floured eggs!" he exclaimed.

Pancardi sucked his tongue on his teeth.

"Fuck and double fuck!" Blondell exclaimed. "They could be anywhere now, anywhere in Europe. We've lost them and all because of that dumb smuck Dutch cop. All that and Roberto.... all for fuck all."

A flashing light and siren appeared around the corner and a police car sped into the compound. The Dutch Inspector stepped out of the car and rushed toward them.

"We've found the van," he blurted out.

He waited for a reply, Pancardi caught Blondell's eye as he spoke, "On a motorway services?" he asked.

The Dutch Inspector nodded, "I can take you there right now," he said, half bowing in a courtly style gesture.

Blondell listened as the Dutch Inspector was relaying the events of his investigations. He told Pancardi that every service station had been checked and double checked. That CCTV footage had been examined and how a squad car had found the van tucked quietly into an out of the way corner. During the report Pancardi gave no reply but listened intently. The Inspector went on to say that everything had been left exactly as it was and that he had the Italian forensic team on their way to the scene as well. He was looking for Pancardi's approval - none came.

Blondell heard the screaming siren outside the car as it reached the motorway; it swerved and entered the outside lane. His stomach churned as the car reached speeds of 150 mph, the noise of the Inspector rambling, the siren screaming, and the scenery rushing by gave him the image of another world. He felt his vomit rising as the police car swerved, braked and accelerated away again briefly halting the incessant chatter of the expectant Dutch policeman, who was now turned sideways to face them in the back seat. Pancardi had said nothing in reply and as the Inspector turned to face the windscreen and speak to the driver Pancardi turned to Blondell and hissed under his breath.

"Bloody cops and robbers show case."

Pancardi smiled as the police car sped toward the parked van. Incident tape had been placed around the vehicle and a small crowd of onlookers had gathered to see what might be happening, their lively respite to dull motorway driving.

The Dutchman hopped out of the car and in booming tones was ushering people back in a fashion of superior command.

"See," said Pancardi to Blondell, "il cretino."

The police driver turned to the back seat and smiled. Blondell raised his eyes and the driver nodded in acceptance of the shared evaluation of his commanding officer.

"Come on," said Pancardi, as he opened the door, "might as well give the tourists their show."

As he and Blondell stepped out of the car the Dutch Inspector continued to busy himself.

"It's men like that," Pancardi nodded in the Dutchman's direction, "who give us a bad name. What a showboat time waster."

The driver was out now and Pancardi spoke to him sympathetically. The conversation was brief and effective and the driver laughed as Pancardi thanked him and clapped his hand upon his shoulder.

"What did you say?" asked Blondell.

"Nothing really," Pancardi replied, "well nothing he didn't already know."

"The Inspector?"

"Need you ask?"

"No wonder he was laughing then."

Blondell turned and viewed the man as they spoke. He was ushering another car through the increasing crowd as a newspaper reporter arrived and a camera flashed.

"Why does everything have to be a circus?" he muttered, not intending anyone to hear.

"Promotion!" exclaimed Pancardi. "He can smell it. He wants to be a Chief Inspector. Look at the fool, he could not catch a butterfly with a net, but he will be a senior officer one day."

The Dutchman was talking to the reporter who was jotting like a student in a meaningless lecture. Notes which would be distilled until the Inspector's words would seem as if they had emanated from the mouth of an alien. He had seemingly forgotten his charges in the media glare, while they had made their way to the van with the police driver.

"Time?" Pancardi asked the driver.

"Just thirty minutes ago. We don't know how long it's been there. No sign of a struggle and it's locked," he replied. "Seems as if it was abandoned, but not in a hurry. It's been tucked away nicely out of sight. Not easy to see unless you're specifically looking for it. Calm very calm operator this one – methodical."

"Let's have a quick look inside then,"continued Pancardi, pulling on some surgical gloves from his pocket.

Blondell wondered where they had come from – he had not seen them before.

The police driver nodded to another officer who popped the door lock with half a tennis ball and Pancardi opened the door as Alaina exited the newly arrived car and walked toward them. She smiled broadly at Blondell and he noticed the swing of her hips and the click of her heels as she covered the few metres which lay between them.

Mostro was the first to respond to her arrival and he sped to greet her by standing on his hind legs to raise himself, she patted his head as she passed.

Pancardi was kneeling on the passenger seat as she arrived, "Nothing," he said, "not a damn thing."

"He's a smoker," said Alaina as she approached, "the ashtray will be full of butts, just like the VW."

"Magdalene?" asked Blondell, "is she with you?"

"Researching," was her single word reply.

Blondell involuntarily turned to check the car Alaina had arrived in, it was empty, there was no Magdalene, his disbelief evaporated.

"Put it in here." Alaina was holding a poly bag as Pancardi tipped the contents of the ashtray into it. "I am sure we will confirm it is the same man from these," she said.

"There, nothing else," said Pancardi, as he straightened himself and stepped out of the vehicle. "Some mud on the driver's side carpet. Which will confirm he or the security guard was at the compound?"

"So where did he go?" asked Blondell.

"Deduce Alex deduce!" Pancardi snapped. "He is a clever boy this one, he takes his time, holds his nerve and never ever hurries. So he will have found a way to leave too. Any news on the diving equipment? Are we after a team in kilts?" he asked Alaina.

"None, Magdalene thinks that the equipment may be older and the stockists have gone out of business so the records are not easy to trace," she replied. "Though she is still trying to find us a link. I think we have a breakthrough in another area though."

"Well?" Pancardi was furtive, "are we looking for a team who once worked on the oil rigs?

"The DNA match, Ennio was quite right though I can't believe it myself really. These people," she paused, "they must be related. The probabilities of them having the same matches are too close for them not to be."

"Are you absolutely certain?" Pancardi quizzed. "We have run up enough blind alleys."

"What's that," asked Blondell, interrupting and pointing at the poly-bag which held the contents of the ashtray.

Before Alaina could stop him he had opened the bag and retrieved a small screwed up slip of paper.

"What do you make of this?" he asked handing the unfolded item to Pancardi.

"A now useless piece of forensic evidence?" Alaina announced in reply.

"Numbers and letters, a code?" Pancardi became immersed

in thought. "There's a digit missing, look the end of the slip she is burnt off, what else was on here?

"Could it be a car registration, or a phone number? Or it could just be a scrap of paper left in the ashtray," proffered Blondell. "REW 383 what the hell does it mean?"

Chapter 33

Paul West jumped down from the foot plate at Heikendorf Wagen Parkplatz 21 and swung an arm around Alice Parsotti's narrow waist, before kissing her hard on the mouth.

"What was that for?" she asked.

"Luck," he said, "you're my lucky charm."

The truck windows were curtained and any passer-by might think the driver was sleeping prior to taking a ferry north. The Parkplatz was on the main road so traffic would turn over quickly and West thought it the perfect place.

The couple began to walk back toward the centre of the small town. As they passed some roadside bins they dumped the weapons they carried wrapped among garbage and food residue.

"Fuckin' weeks," he said, "it'll take them weeks to work it out. Dumb bastards, I'll chuck these keys." He dropped the lorry keys into the wide grill of a roadside drain. "Home and dry, home and dry," he laughed, when he heard the splash.

He grabbed Alice by the waist and kissed her again.

"Boy aren't we romantic today,"she said.

"See I can be," he retorted, "if I want to be."

"Mmm well I'd like it to be, more often."

"Well when we are sunning ourselves in the Maldives and living the high life, we can fuck like honeymooners and stay in bed all day if we want to."

"I'm not sure your idea of romantic and mine are the same, fucking is not necessarily a romantic activity."

"Well what is it then? Is it to keep the class divide going? You toffs are all the same, but we in the lower orders are going to outbreed you lot to extinction. See you get romantic and loving and we," he paused, "well we just fuck. Viva la C.H.A.V."

He waited for a reaction, none came, "That's why," he continued, "all our people start breeding and stealing by the time they're fourteen. See if you were a nice east-end girl you'd have been face sitting at thirteen and clubbed at fourteen. By the time you are as old as you are now," he paused, "you'd be a fucking granny. Hell you're nearly old enough to be my granny. "

Alice laughed in reply at his lunacy and looked at her watch, it read 10.18pm. She knew that they would make the Oslo ferry easily and after sleeping in a cabin overnight would wake refreshed for the train journey to Stockholm. They would, she calculated, be nearly a day early for the flight. She pondered on Rightman.

"How far to Kiel from here?" she asked.

"About five miles."

"That's a long walk," she sighed.

"You walk if you want too," he joked in reply, "me I'm going in a cab - come on."

He crossed the street jovially, his spirits were high, and went toward a taxi rank. Outside the Koenig's bar they took a cab from the town to Kiel docks. As foot passengers they bought two overnight tickets to Oslo with a cabin. West calculated that they would be in Oslo by early morning. There they could buy some clothes and luggage and still make Stockholm nearly a full day before the flight was due to leave. It was all falling into place quite nicely, he thought, after the German's capture had thrown things into disarray.

"Rightman," said West, as he stepped into the cabin, "is a prick. I want to make sure he hasn't screwed up."

Alice closed the door, "Surely he won't," she said. "Anyhow he would warn us, wouldn't he?"

"What like that fuckwit German?"

"I see what you mean," she said, as she lay on the bed. "I'm whacked! I need to sleep and I need a shower. And I've got to wear these clothes again tomorrow and they're filthy. I hate wearing dirty knickers."

"Well go without then," he laughed.

"Yeah, you'd like that wouldn't you? You'd be trying to get your hands up my skirt all day long."

"Well in Oslo we can get some clean and then we can have time to check-out and scope the airport in Stockholm." His tone became serious, "If we are early then we can get into a Travel Lodge. Those dumb cops will increase activity if they're on to us, they're so easy to spot; and we, my lovely, we can simply disappear again and the Yank can take his chances."

"Do you think he made it?" Alice reflected.

"If he dumped the van quickly. He's a loud mouth but he's not a total fool, and he's greedy enough, he'll have made it." He paused thoughtfully, "Speaking of dumps."

"Oh no you don't," said Alice, rising rapidly, and moving toward the bathroom. "You're not going to stink out the bathroom before I have my shower. That really takes the biscuit. No, nope, no way José, go to the public ones on one of the decks, and you could get us a bottle of wine and some food while you're at it." She closed the bathroom door behind her.

"Fine," he replied loudly enough to penetrate the door, "I'll see if they have any knickers too shall I?"

"Oh you are a sweetie aren't you," came her muffled reply, as she turned the shower on to full.

"So REW 383?"

Blondell was pondering as the three of them sat in the car on the way back to the Doupelein Hotel. Mostro had managed to ensconce himself on Alaina's lap and she stroked his head with broad sweeping motions.

"Are you sure that this dog of yours is not part cat?" asked Blondell, as he watched the pair next to him on the rear seat.

"Ah my friend he is just affectionate and he knows who loves him best."

"Well if I fed him and pampered him he would love me too?"

"Then why does he not run to you?" asked Pancardi, "every time you appear."

"Because he has good taste?" Alaina cuddled Mostro close, "I love this dog,"she said, "absolutely love him."

It was at that moment Blondell realised the true extent of Alaina's feelings for Pancardi, though the Inspector, for all his deduction had failed to see it. The answer was so simple, Alaina admired Pancardi, respected his mind; but more than that, she loved him and he, he could not see it at all, even if it was right in front of his eyes. Blondell considered the age gap and thought of Magdalene. His mind moved back to the code, the van, the shooting, and a proverb about old dogs and new tricks, which, in turn, was quickly replaced by a good tune on an old fiddle. He snorted a laugh.

"A penny for your thoughts then," said Pancardi, without turning round.

"Oh, I'm afraid you wouldn't like them," Blondell replied.

Pancardi reached for the sun visor and using the mirror on the back of it fixed a stare on Blondell.

"So this bird has now flown and we have a cold trail," he said. "So now we must become like them, think like them, no?"

Blondell did not react.

"Alex, do you agree?" he continued.

Blondell caught the eyes in the mirror and nodded.

"So we have a van and he parks. Then he must move on. To hitch hike is too risky with the police on the look out. There is no train, no bus and to take a taxi too easy to trace?" Pancardi paused thoughtfully and looked directly at the driver now separated from his bungling promotion seeking superior, "What would you do?" he asked him.

"Steal a car," was the curt reply.

"Precisely, precisely, but how? And why has no one reported one stolen?"

"Because they are in the car with him?"

"Yes," said Pancardi, "the others are with him? No, we only found one set of footprints in the mud near the van. There is just the one man surely? The others are leaving by another method, unless they met up somewhere on the motorway."

"But how did they get there?" Alaina questioned, "and wouldn't it be too risky to meet up. They would be better to stay separate surely."

"But," said the driver and then checked himself.

"Go on," Pancardi requested.

He hesitated and Blondell caught the scent of a man whose ideas were rarely considered and often overruled. He wondered if this man had counselled against the show of force at the Doupelein but had been overruled by his Inspector. He deduced he had and probably on more than one occasion, and he had, in consequence, learned to hold his tongue and ideas for a more advantageous moment.

"Go on," chirped Blondell, "all ideas gratefully received. No honours, no blame, and no bullshit here, we're all on the same team."

There was a brief considered silence and then he spoke, "Well," he said, "what if he, not they, kidnapped someone, at gun point and they drove off. No one gets reported as missing, the car is not stolen and we cannot trace a car and person who are not missing. I also think this gang did not meet up they are far too clever to do that; this man is working alone but they could meet up later."

"This would be the clever thing to do, I agree," Pancardi asserted

"Well I've had the CCTV camera footage for last night checked and we have the numbers of every car that left the car park. I have a time window allowing for a high speed run from Amsterdam and officers are now on the phones checking the addresses of every single one."

Pancardi knew that the young man had policing in his blood and while his superior dealt with the high-profile media to his own advantage, this man had worked on the grind of the investigation. Pancardi knew that if the man were caught this way the Dutch Inspector would gain promotion and he, the driver, would gain a ,"well done," in some closed anti-room office. Pancardi was glad that the Inspector was not in the car.

"It will take time, but we may just get lucky," said the driver.

"It is a clever method. If someone is missing then this may be the only way to check it," replied Pancardi. "But we have to see what the night brings. The Inspector he is coming to the hotel?"

"He will be later," said the driver, "I think he is giving a TV interview."

"Are you alright sir," asked the paramedic as he approached.

"Hell yeah, but my wife?"

"American?"

"Yeah, so you'll have to speak in American, sorry."

"No problem sir, we all study it at school here in Germany. Where does it hurt?"

"Everywhere," replied Rightman, "but the leg feels the worst."

"Let's take a look at it then." The paramedic slit Rightman's trouser leg and felt the knee joint, "I don't think it's broken," he assessed, "but you'll have to have an x-ray to be sure."

Rightman reached for his nose and upper jaw as the medic examined the wound. The paramedic asked him to lie down as they needed to brace his neck before they lifted him onto the stretcher. He was to go to hospital in the ambulance and have a set of check overs. He might feel fine but it had been a fatal impact and he might have concussion.

"She must have fallen from the vehicle during the impact," Rightman's voice crackled like a scratched record.

He lay back against the grassy bank and pushed the pistol deeper into a clump of grass to conceal it.

"She is alright though?" he continued to question. "I need a cigarette they're in my pocket." He fumbled for them.

"We don't advise smoking sir," said the paramedic discouragingly.

"Well I need something."

As the paramedic turned to talk to the ambulance crew, Rightman lit one. He drew a deep breath which made the cigarette tip glow in the dark and accentuated the deep red of the blood on his chest.

"Besides," he continued as he exhaled, "it's not like I'm gonna die from cancer. My leg hurts the worst," he lied. "Caroline is she alright? Where the hell is she?"

"My colleague will be in a better position to answer that a little later. They are with her now. Please extinguish the cigarette."

The paramedic knew she was dead, her neck was broken but

he was following procedure. A stretcher was being brought over and Rightman knew he had to remain conscious as he was fitted with a neck brace and painkillers were administered. If he wanted to escape before the police arrived, he had to remain conscious; he fought with the feeling which was forcing him toward sleep. He had heard the word fatal and that would always draw the police to investigate, but his eyes were getting heavy. A tall police officer came over to the paramedic and spoke in German. Rightman tried to glean some information. The woman on the road was dead, the car was registered in Holland to Krista Clemens and the driver, the man, this man, was an American. The other driver in the BMW was dead too. Half of his face had been torn away as the steering wheel smashed upward into his chest and then travelled under his chin removing the lower jawbone completely. His family would have trouble identifying him. The paramedic thought that Rightman had used the name Caroline, rather than Krista but did not bother to tell the police investigator. Many couples used pet names and it was not really that important. In the instant that it came into his mind to mention it, it was gone; overridden by far more important things, two bodies and an injured man who might have concussion. The investigator, he thought, could do his job later at the hospital. This man wasn't exactly going anywhere.

In listening Rightman knew he had to play the part well. He had not been arrested and was obviously being taken to hospital. The confusion was working in his favour and he could see the traffic slowing to take a look as he lay on the stretcher. There was plenty of blood and the early morning drivers were enthralled by the pantomime of death which they had been lucky enough to see. The dawn was up and the half light was now increasing visibility for passers-by. After all it broke the monotony of their dull bureaucratic lives to see someone fighting to save theirs.

"My wife?" Rightman shouted.

The police officer came over as Rightman was being lifted via stretcher into the back of the ambulance.

"I'm afraid sir, she is dead," he said.

His voice was cold, methodical and to Rightman it sounded almost bored.

Rightman started to mumble incoherently.

"Were you the driver of the Ford sir?" asked the policeman.

"Yes and my wife she was asleep and then this arsehole hits us and the car's turning and then it's all …"

He became emotional and for good measure spattered blood from his mouth by coughing toward the cop. He thought his performance rather good as the cop stepped back to avoid blood hitting his tunic. Rightman's mind was racing and he knew he only had a few seconds before a decision was made.

"That guy in the other car I'll kill him. Where the hell is he? Driving like a fucking maniac," he said angrily.

Rightman tried to lift himself from the stretcher as if making to stand and the paramedic restrained him.

"I'm afraid," said the policeman, "the other driver is also dead. In fact it's a miracle that you survived. You've been very lucky."

"Lucky, my wife?"

Rightman began to cry as the paramedics lifted his stretcher into the ambulance. The policeman said he would have to ask further questions and a traffic incident investigator would need to come to the hospital. Rightman knew the investigator would probably work out that he had fallen asleep at the wheel. The real question would be if he could establish that the body had come from the boot and not the passenger side. All he could think about was the safety belt. How did that not hold her, he needed an excuse and then his mind began to drift. He was tired and the painkillers were kicking into his system. Married, suddenly he tried to remember if the dead woman wore a wedding ring; he tried to visualise her hands but he couldn't remember, the picture was fuzzy. The ambulance was moving now and an oxygen mask was being placed over his face. The heart monitor was bleeping rhythmically and his eyes closed.

Chapter 34

Duane Rightman woke with a start. His neck was not braced and his legs moved – painfully. The blood and his clothes had gone and there was a bandage around his head. He looked at the wall, there was no clock, and he fumbled with the drawers of the bedside cabinet as the nurse came in.

"How long have I been here?" he asked, and without waiting for a reply continued, "have I been out for long? Where is my watch, my passport and my cigarettes? Where the hell am I?"

"Good evening Mr. Rightman," the nurse calmly replied.

"How did you know my name, and what time is it?"

"Well," replied the nurse, "I'm a detective really."

Rightman stopped talking immediately.

"Your passport is in the middle drawer, with your mobile, wallet and watch, which is smashed I'm afraid and doesn't work. An Omega too and gold so you are a man of good taste. Your clothes, well they had to be laundered, all soiled with blood but we have a service department which can find you something to replace them until your relatives arrive. You've lost your front teeth and your head will be sore for a couple of days, you took a nasty bump to the head. You seem to have lots of bumps and bruises but there are no broken bones. It's now," she looked at her fob watch, "8.36pm precisely, and my shift ends at nine. Oh, the police traffic investigator wants to interview you but the doctor sent him away until the morning. You're not really up to it yet what with all the sedatives, and you cannot smoke in here, it's a hospital. Your ciggies are in the bottom drawer though," she smiled and winked at him.

Rightman lifted the bed covers to see he was clad in nothing more than a surgical gown.

"Oh and yes I gave you a full bed bath," she continued, "you're my first American."

Rightman wondered what else she had examined while he'd been sedated and then gave a wry smile.

"Thank you," he said, though it sounded like thab whoo with his teeth missing. He winced at the effort of speech.

"I know," said the nurse sympathetically, "it will take some time to heal and it will sting a bit," as she took his wrist in her hand to check his pulse. "It may be a few days before the swelling on your gums recedes. Best not to try and talk too much. Everything else," she winked again, "is in perfect working order."

Rightman could smell cigarette smoke on her clothes and he liked that. He watched as she lifted a ball point from her tunic breast pocket and filled in the chart at the end of the bed. Rightman noticed that her breasts were ample and that she was not a slight woman. He imagined her throwing him around the bed like a dummy as she sponged away the blood. She was tall with bright blue eyes and blonde hair, typically North German with that slight pinkish tinge to her skin. He imagined she would burn easily in the sun but that she wore neither wedding nor engagement ring.

She noticed him observing her hands as she worked, "No not married," she said, "never had the time," she qualified the statement.

"Moo nither," volunteered Rightman, realising in the instant the blundering mistake he had made.

"From the deep South? I can tell by your accent," she continued.

"Yep Scarlet O'Hara country, a real Johnny Reb," he laughed and then winced again.

He watched carefully for a reaction on her face. She laughed, but seemed not to know he had been in the car with a woman, a woman he had named as a wife to the police. His heart rate lowered and he realised that he was not really thinking straight, the sedatives needed to wear off.

"Rhett Butler too?" she said, "I always liked Clark Gable, but he had rather enormous ears I thought, great big ones in fact. But he did have a way about him and that voice, well that could melt ice."

She was flirting with him and he knew that she could not possibly know the details of the accident. She probably did a good job, worked long hours, and never really got the chance to socialise. So once all the doctors had taken their pick she had to wait on the sidelines for the next best thing, a needy patient. She wasn't a great beauty but she had sex appeal, a soft and sensuous nature which the right man would bring out in her and benefit from. He tried to imagine her naked.

"I've always wanted to go to America," she said as she tucked the sheets in at his side. "Would you like something to eat?"

Rightman knew he was hungry but his face felt as if it had been pulverised with a baseball bat. At first he nodded and then shook his head pointing at the swollen top lip.

"Can they get something liquid to me at this time of night?" he asked. "I don't think I can chew anything, no teeth," and he grinned at her, wincing again as he did so.

"Try not to smile too much," she chided, "those stitches might burst."

"Shit!" he exclaimed, closing his mouth rapidly. "Stings like a bastard too."

"Soup perhaps? I'll see what I can do," she said as she started to leave, "but don't expect me to feed you."

"Christ," hissed Rightman after she had left, "she's a real flirt."

He tried to gather his thoughts. Once the nursing shift changed he needed to get some clothes and leave. Where was the spare clothing kept? He'd quiz the girl when she got back. They had his name now and the traffic cop would be back in the morning; he had to be long gone before they tied him into the dead woman. His legs were sore but workable - he moved them. Alone now, he sat up, reached for the jug of water on the dresser, and then placed his feet on the ground. His mouth was dry and after two glasses he could feel the dehydration begin to clear. His head became less fuzzy and he knew that he could stand and walk.

"Oh no you don't," clucked the nurse, as she returned complete with a Porter and a tray. "Back into bed if you please Mr. Rightman." Her voice had become formal.

"But, I just wanted to use the toilet," he boyishly replied.

"There's a bed pan in the bottom drawer and the orderly will take it away if you buzz."

She spoke to the porter in German and he left the room. Carefully pinning the tray across Rightman – now back in the bed, her tone and voice noticeably softened.

"You Mr. Rightman, are a very naughty boy," she smiled. "I've got you some soup and some very soft white bread which you can dunk into it. Sit up please."

Rightman drew himself into a sitting position and she began to spoon mouthfuls of warm soup into him, carefully blowing each spoonful to cool it. He watched her pout as she blew; she knew her art well and her eyes gleamed. She knew she was reasonably attractive and he wondered how many times she had worked this ploy to entice. Her breasts heaved and he read the time upside down on her fob, it was 9.21pm she was well over her departure time.

As she was feeding him he gleaned information from her. He was in Lubeck and not Hamburg as he had at first guessed. She volunteered that Hamburg emergency unit had been full to bursting last night, some sort of chemical fire in a warehouse on the outskirts and in consequence he had been transferred to Lubeck even though the others in the traffic accident went to Hamburg. She knew there had been some deaths but that was all the detail she had.

Rightman guessed that the morgue in Hamburg was the only place available for the corpses and as he only had superficial injuries he could be transferred elsewhere, a spot of sheer luck for him. When the new shift finally came to see how Rightman was doing he had found out all he needed. It was 10.10pm when the blonde nurse went and only minutes after that he slipped into one of the adjacent rooms to pilfer some clothes. From a comatose old man he stole a watch and a jacket and from the third room he entered he managed to procure a pair of trousers, socks and a clean shirt. The trousers were slightly short and the shirt was tight across his shoulders but they would do until he had managed to get replacements elsewhere. He even managed to steal a few Euros.

Back inside his own room he telephoned and found a taxi

firm that would pick him up outside the main entrance of the hospital. Holding his shoes he left quietly as the night nurse dosed at her station. He hoped she was as lazy as she seemed and his disappearance would not be noticed until the morning, when the blonde returned.

The taxi driver took him to the Trelleborg Ferry entrance but the next departure was a roll on roll off car ferry leaving at 2.00am. The taxi driver had joked about him being in the wars and he had responded by saying that the girlfriend's brother had given him a good seeing to and if he didn't get away he'd end up dead.

In the Ferry all night shop he bought a tee shirt, some ibuprofen, some plasters on a strip and had a strong coffee, which stung his mouth. He caught sight of his face in a reflective door and could see the pronounced swelling of his top lip. In his pocket he had a bag of boiled sweets and some chocolate and a fresh pack of Marlboro. He had forgotten the ones in the hospital which sat in the lowest drawer inside the bed pan, he guessed his lighter was there too. Outside in the cool night air he drew deeply on a cigarette and thought carefully of what to do next. He examined his wallet, his credit cards were there, the flight reference was there and he had some Euro.

In the toilets at the Ferry terminal he examined his face in the mirror and removed the bandage from his head. There was a cut on his forehead and a bump which was turning blue but the bandage needed to go – it drew too much attention. His eyes looked clear and as he swilled his mouth, he knew that if he didn't smile the lost teeth would hardly be noticeable. Back in the states he'd get them fixed and no one would be the wiser. He ran his tongue around the inside of his mouth and felt four stitches. A couple of snips and they'd be gone; he wished he bought some mouth wash to keep them sterilised. He swallowed four ibuprofen with a handful of water and then went into a cubicle.

Inside the cubicle he sat, his trousers around his ankles, straining and feeling his ribs. They were bandaged but he could breathe well so his diaphragm was working and the ribs were not broken. All in all he thought he'd been very lucky, just a few more hours and he'd be away. He just needed to have one more piece of luck and he had about an hour and a half to pull it off.

Giancarlo Pancardi looked drawn, his face was long, despite the shower and change of clothes. Alaina had obviously said something to him which had totally shocked him, he seemed thrown off stride. Mostro was no where to be seen and Blondell guessed he had already plumped for his bed in Pancardi's room. The small white investigator had given them Richter but even he had to stop sometimes.

Blondell marvelled at Pancardi who seemed to take fresh injections of energy every time pieces of evidence fell into place or the trail warmed. He was at the bar with Magdalene getting pre-dinner drinks and was just about to go over to the seated couple when Magdalene quietly stopped him.

"Not just yet," she said, "give them a little space."

"But why?

"Oh Alex really, look at them she is saying something which has shocked him."

"Right," Blondell's mind jumped several grooves, "she's told him she loves him."

"Yes, and about time too the old fool is long overdue some affection. Why are men so bad at this? Just say it if you feel it. What can a person say but no."

"It's not as easy as you think you know," he replied.

"For you maybe, but he is Italian and we Italians we are hot blooded. Not like you English who wish a love and then do nothing when it blows past you in the wind. She is seizing life, there will be time enough for us all to talk when we go over."

Pancardi was leaning in and Alaina was whispering intensely, after a few more seconds Pancardi shook his head and moved back upright in his seat.

"Now we go, come," said Magdalene.

"One dry Martini, and two Campari bitter and a Gin and Tonic for me," Blondell spoke as he approached the table. He looked at his watch it was 10.23 pm. "It's late to eat," he said, drearily, "but I for one am starving and I need a good sleep too."

Pancardi was smiling broadly, "To sleep in the arms of a lover is good," he said, "but Gin Alex, it stinks. The foul smelling liquor which you English love. How can you make love after such a beverage?"

Blondell nodded, took a deep swig, sighed and then asked calmly, "Have you ordered food?"

"Not yet," replied Alaina, "I was just telling Carlo about…"

Pancardi placed a finger to his lips in a sssshing motion and Alaina stopped mid-sentence, and in response Magdalene grasped Blondell's thigh under the table as if to say, see I told you so.

"We can talk of that later," Pancardi interjected merrily.

Clearly he had been told something which enthused him. On his face was a broad grin as he spoke, "First we feast and then we see how far we have got. It will be after midnight before we birds can crawl into our nests."

"Not very far, we've not got very far at all," chirped Blondell. "The birds we chase have flown and we have lost them."

"But," said Pancardi, "all things that fly must come to land and there we will set our traps."

"Except the Albatross," Blondell quipped, "those buggers never land. They even mate on the wing don't they?"

"But even they must land to have their eggs," Pancardi chirped triumphantly, "and there we shall be, with our big nets." He turned to Magdalene, "What of the equipment?" he asked.

"All Scottish supplied," she said, as the waiter arrived with his note pad to take their order.

"Are you sure, absolutely sure?" Pancardi interrogated.

"Absolutely! Some of the stuff is over ten years old. The suppliers have gone out of business. The only real lead I can give is that it looks like ex oil rig equipment. So the diver may be from that area but I cannot narrow it down further."

"Well at least we have tried this avenue," Pancardi concluded.

"And we also now know that," interjected Alaina, "that Alice Parsotti is related…"

"Yes," interrupted Pancardi, shooting a piercing look at Alaina which silenced her.

"So we know," said Blondell, "that one man is a Scot, that the other man is an American and the German will tell us nothing, especially if he dies, but he hasn't done that yet. What about the big players where are they? This Vaughan or Verechico or whatever his name is where the hell is he? And Drecht he's vanished too."

Blondell was clearly despondent.

"Patience Alex," said Pancardi, as he ordered food, "our Dutch Sergeant is no fool he will give us a lead. These thieves are not God's even they make mistakes, and you, you MI5 should know this."

The atmosphere around the table changed immediately. Magdalene shot Blondell a fierce look and Alaina stopped chewing on her bread stick. Blondell caught Pancardi's eye and realised that he must have known all along and the scars had merely confirmed his suspicions.

"You don't deny it then?" asked Pancardi.

"Would you believe me if I did?"

"No," Pancardi's reply was short.

"So why should I deny something which you know is fact?"

"I hope you won't. Would you like to know how Alex?"

"I know how."

"Then we need not talk of Northern Ireland and shrapnel. High velocity? Long range?"

"Yes," Blondell replied, "but you forgot one thing," he paused, "intense pain, invasive surgery and being sidelined until this Romanov thing came up. I was lucky, studied Russian history at Cambridge, so I suppose I was the natural choice. I was never a field agent just in the wrong place at the wrong time. A British Embassy employee who happened to be in the way of an assassination attempt – funny really for a pen pushing graduate. "

Both women sat in stunned silence as the two men entered into a conversation which neither had been vaguely party too. Alaina wondered why access to Interpol data bases had been so swift and now realised that Blondell carried far more influence than she had estimated. No wonder he and Pancardi combined could instil fear in all of the other police officers. Magdalene however, stared at Blondell and her eyes were fiery with anger. Before she could utter a word Pancardi said exactly what she was thinking.

"No more lies," he said, "we must know we can trust each other and not have secrets."

Magdalene's nails bit into Blondell's inner thigh and he winced. He understood what she was saying though she didn't speak a word.

"Mistakes?" Blondell changed the subject, but knew that

Magdalene would deal with the matter more closely later. "Well they don't seem to make any, other than by choice," he paused thoughtfully, "and then it's a red herring designed to fuck us up."

Magdalene dug her elbow into his ribs, her anger was apparent for all to see.

"Sorry for the language," he said.

"That's not the issue here is it?" she mumbled in return.

"But," said Alaina, "we are far closer than you think. The pieces are finally falling together. All we have to do is think of their next move."

"Yeah and REW 383," said Blondell flippantly, "once we've decoded that then we're there I suppose."

Magdalene was chewing a mouthful of rare steak, "There's no need to decode that," she said nonchalantly unaware of the significance of what she was about to say. "It's a flight booking reference. All you have to do is match it to the airline and you'll know exactly when and where they are." She continued chewing and preparing her next mouthful without looking up.

The other three at the table sat as if stunned – it was so simple, and yet as Pancardi had predicted they had made that one mistake.

Rightman knocked on the cab window of his tenth truck in line for the Trelleborg ferry. The window was wound down by a woman.

"What you want?" she said.

"I'm looking for a lift," he replied. "I need to speak to the driver."

"I am the driver," she said, "what you think a woman can't drive this heap of mechanical shit?"

"Err no," he struggled for words, "it's just that women don't often drive these."

As the words came out of his mouth he knew he'd said the wrong thing and blown any chance of a lift. He wanted to exit stage left and thought that he might have to buy a ticket afterall – a ticket that could be traced. He was turning away when the woman spoke.

"You American?" she asked.

"Yeah."

"Where from?"

"Birmingham," he lied

"Ah, Alabama," she said, "that's where my brother-in-law comes from. Lynard Skynard, sweet home Alabama. Where you want to go?"

"Stockholm?"

"You got a ticket for the ferry?"

"Yes," he lied.

"What's your name?" she asked. "Step into the light so I can see you better."

He did as he was asked and allowed light from the overhead street lamp to illuminate his face.

"Who the fuck did that to your face?"

"Duane. A jealous husband," he replied.

"Well Duane," she said, "you like to pussy whack?"

He nodded, it didn't matter now what he said, she hated him, hated him just because he was a man. He'd try the last two lorries and if they didn't give him that lift, he'd take the train. He knew he'd have to use his credit card to pay and that might give away his location, but he didn't need this shit from some fat feminist.

"Find me when we get to Trelleborg," she said, "and I'll give you a ride to Stockholm."

As the words of thanks came from his mouth he saw the woman winding up the window. The thought of having to have sex with her appalled him. He imagined her to be a real ball breaker, weighing in at 300 pounds and demanding doggy style sex for hour after hour in some roadside lay-by. He began to wonder if he had chosen a good method to leave Germany unnoticed.

"Hey Duane!" the lady driver called, from the re-opened window. "There ain't gonna be any pussy whackin' in this cab. Got it? So you keep them Southern hands to yourself."

He saluted in response.

"Keep your dick in your pants - got it?"

He saluted again, "Will do ma'm," he shouted in reply.

As he walked away he knew luck was on his side.

What should have been a refreshing meal before a good nights sleep turned into instant chaos. Pancardi rose and left his meal half eaten, within minutes he was with the Dutch Inspector and the Interpol team.

"I don't care how late it is find the departure airport," he barked at the Dutch Inspector. "Wake up every executive in every booking centre, in every airline. Don't you dare mess this up," Pancardi continued, looking directly at the Inspector. "You do nothing without my authority do you understand. No circus, no bears and no clowns, I don't care about your promotion and neither do MI5." He looked at Blondell approaching before continuing, "If I so much as smell a hack within 5 miles, I will personally make sure you are a traffic cop for the rest of your days. You messed up once don't mess up again."

Blondell joined him, "I've left the ladies eating what can I do?"

"Nothing Alex, nothing," he replied, "I want those bastards, they killed my friend and you know I will not let this pass? We have them now. Can MI5 have covert surveillance, no police? If they can then we can catch them." He turned to the now smiling Sergeant who had been their driver, "See," said Pancardi, watching the Inspector scurrying away, "it works no, fear – have you any leads?"

"My men are working on it at the moment. There was a blue Ford which left the Motorway services at the right time last night. The same car was reported in an accident near Hamburg at around dawn. The registered owner was killed but there was a passenger, an American, he's in Hospital in Lubeck."

"That's him," said Pancardi, "I don't want local police or your idiot Inspector involved in this." He looked directly at Blondell as he spoke, "MI5?"

Blondell simply nodded.

Pancardi was excited now, "I want the hospital," he said to Blondell, "surrounded sealed and the American lifted without any fuss. He will then lead us to the others and I want them all." Pancardi spat his words out, "I want to see their faces when we take them all," he paused, "welcome to the parlour said the spider to the fly."

Chapter 35

The knock at the door was very loud and as Magdalene struggled to open her eyes Blondell let the light and Pancardi in. She wanted to go back to sleep, especially after the late-night argument which she and Blondell had on the subject of lies. She knew the things she had said hurt him and it took a long time for their discussion to terminate in passionate love making.

"It's," Pancardi looked at his watch, "5.58, time we were out and about."

Blondell was clean shaven and dressed in his customary suit but he looked washed–out, his eyes were red from lack of sleep and his skin sallow and drawn. Pancardi caught a glimpse of naked thigh as Magdalene defended herself from Mostro who had jumped onto the bed and was digging at the duvet and barking to get in with her.

"Good grief, that dog," Blondell said.

"Yes he is well rested," Pancardi replied thoughtfully, "and you two lovers are not?"

Blondell turned and looking directly at the older detective said, "Oh please, and I suppose that you and Alaina, you, went quietly to your separate rooms? Pull the other one. Do you think that after watching you with her last night I'm going to believe that old chestnut? You must think me green as grass."

Magdalene had turned on her side to face away from the two men and had tucked Mostro under her arm in a cuddle, she appeared to be going back to sleep. He however, was more keen on playing than sleeping, and he was winning.

"We have men at the hospital in Lubeck," said Pancardi in triumph. "Or should I say your government has. Wonderful how MI5 react when Interpol and one of their own is on the case. We have also been in touch with several airlines but we do not have destination details yet, though there are many more to try. Come we must go."

"American only flights," said Magdalene dreamily.

Pancardi's face shone in a smile for a brief second but in the instant she spoke he realised his own stupidity. He knew his search had been too narrow.

⁕

Regimental Sergeant Major Richard Clove, an Irishman, was to be in absolute command and there were no officers involved.

"I want NCO's only Clove," the Colonel had said. "We can't afford to have one of those wet behind the ears school-boys get this wrong. Pick your five best Clove, get in, get the job done and get out. No names no pack drill."

The entry of the six Royal Marines into Lubeck hospital was swift and silent. They had travelled direct from exercises on the Luneburg Heath with rather peculiar orders. Apparently the exercise involved penetration of western defences by a Soviet sleeper disguised as an American. Orders for the six man team were simple, take and extract, no shooting – under any circumstances. It had to be a stealth mission.

RSM Clove had made the team check their weapon clips and leave them with the driver of the jeep. Two men were deployed on the fire escape in case the spy had spotted them and tried to run. It was a test, they had been reminded, so there could be some sort of trap to see how they did and the Colonel wanted no mess ups.

The night nurse had been interviewed and she had confirmed that the American was called Rightman, a traffic accident victim who had gone to sleep last night. His light went out at 11 ish and she had done her rounds twice that night, as she always did, and he had been sleeping. RSM Clove looked at his watch it was 6.00 am. He and the two others had fifteen minutes to take the man out and report to the Colonel direct.

Silently the three men entered the room – it was empty. Clove felt the bed – it was cold. Personal effects had gone too except for a broken watch. That he surmised had been put there for the team not to miss. Clever he thought to make us get proof, as he slipped it into his pocket. The other men checked the bathroom – there was nothing. Clove gave the aerial wind-up signal and the team retreated silently down the corridor. The same signal was given to those on the fire-escape and they too retreated back down toward the jeep. The Sergeant Major stopped at the nurse's station and asked when she had last seen Rightman; she said 4.00 am, but he knew she was lying. That, he guessed, was also part of the hoax, she was probably a plant too.

Regimental Sergeant Major Clove had followed his orders to the letter and back in the jeep radioed the Colonel as it left the hospital grounds.

"Gone sir, probably some time between 11pm and 5am. Though the nurse claims he was there all night."

"Mission accomplished RSM return to base."

"Yes sir and I have the watch."

"Good," the Colonel replied, not having the foggiest notion why Clove had said it.

Clove smiled, "See lads, officers," he chirped, "they think we're all berks, but we're on the ball this time. Well done, now let's move."

As the jeep sped down the main highway back to Luneberg the RSM and NCO team were quietly chuckling to themselves. It had been so easy, if there had been someone there and it had not been an exercise then they would have the man captive now and the whole thing would be done and dusted. Back to camp for a fry-up and game over.

The night nurse was not sure if the whole incident happened at all or if it had been a vivid dream. As the morning broke not a single patient had seen the mysterious soldiers and she began to doubt her own exhausted consciousness. Only one thing was really true the American had gone and she hadn't even seen or heard him go.

❧

"Alice," West chirped as he re-entered the cabin, "I've been

268

for a Tom."

"Charming," she replied as she left the bathroom. "There's not enough room to swing a cat in there, and the water's cold, and you regale me with tales of your bowel movements, is nothing sacred? Just look at my hair, is there a hair dryer in here?"

West shrugged.

"Well look in the drawer then," she snapped.

"They got room, cabin service. Two pepperoni pizzas and a bottle of pink plonk are on their way. I know it's not much," he sang, "but it's the best I can do, my gift is my pong and this one's for you."

"Ha bloody ha," she snorted. "Don't you ever take anything seriously? Just look at my hair and I've no conditioner. It's like straw."

"Red straw? Mmmm unusual."

"Fuck off, just fuck right off you bastard," she playfully returned.

"A few hours and you can have all the conditioner you want, honey. One more day and we'll be in Montreal complete with the extra stash and the money transfer completed. We've done it."

"So how do we get the jewels through customs?" she asked.

"Not we, you."

Parsotti looked at him thoughtfully, "Not inside surely?" she asked.

"No," he teased, "but if you want I could get one of those Cuban cigar thingy tubes.

"On your fucking bike you."

"Seriously," he interrupted, "you have them under your hat and as we go through I'll misdirect. Look, they're bored most of the time, a little slight of hand and confusion and you're through, leave that bit to me."

"And what if it doesn't work, I suppose I spend seven years in jail for smuggling?"

"I'll write you," he replied.

"Right that's it," she said, as she tried to swipe a blow at his nose with her fist, before falling onto the bed as he side stepped.

"See," he said, "there is natural justice."

There was a loud knock at the door and a voice declared the arrival of room service.

Rightman lay on a reclining couchette, his mind replayed the details of the road accident. He felt his face which was still swollen but the ice from the bar bucket, now wrapped in a polythene bag, was soothing. He had told the barman he'd walked into a door but the barman knew he'd really been in a fight. Rightman didn't care what he thought as long as he got the ice. He had three and a half hours to Trelleborg and he knew he could rest where he was for a while. Thinking of the blonde nurse his imagination turned her into the lorry driver, they were hav...

"He's gone?" said Blondell. "When? How? You told us he was injured." There was a pause as Blondell listened on his cell phone, "So when did he leave?" he questioned. "In the night? What time?" there was another pause, "so he just flew out the window I suppose, he what?"

Pancardi was listening to Blondell's conversation and directing enquiries at the same time. There were ten officers making phone calls to airlines in rapid succession. There were several more who were working on Interpol laptops, all were trying to match the elusive number REW 383 to a flight. It was more like a call centre than an incident room.

"Concentrate on airlines which fly to the Americas," Pancardi had said. "North or South and include Alaska and Canada."

He knew it was a gamble to widen the search. If they could find the flight before it took off then they had them, if not, Pancardi knew they would land and vanish. The woman, she might, just might, return to Italy, especially if she had family ties there. If she did Pancardi thought there might be an off chance of a further lead, so far nothing, though he had a sense that Magdalene's hunch was right. His mind was still trying to assimilate what Alaina had said to him at dinner. He could hardly believe it - it made his heart race and it blurred his judgement. He hoped she had said nothing to Blondell, he could not afford emotion to get in the way of his reason. He tried to clear his thoughts. She was the right age for him and he was old enough to be her father. She had that wonderful colouring and she was beautiful – he could hardly believe it. At his age to find such a thing was a miracle, and yet in such dark circumstances how could she allow this to happen to her?

"They fucking lost him," said Blondell anxiously as he approached. "Can you even think it...a team of Royal Marines in and out like a surgeon's knife and the bastard's gone? It's like sixth sense, they seem to be one jump ahead, all the time. If I didn't know better I'd say someone was tipping them off."

"Ridiculous Alex," Pancardi snorted, "they are just lucky and as with all luck it runs out eventually."

"Fuck," was Blondell's reply as he slumped into a chair. "Fuck, fuck, fuck."

His shoulders rounded and he knew that unless the flight number yielded results they had probably lost them for good.

Pancardi knew better, "All this fucking, ah ha and yet we are still on the scent?" Pancardi laughed, "Come not so despondent. Think ! He is in Lubeck on foot where can he go?"

"Any fucking where," Blondell replied.

"No, think," chided Pancardi, "he was heading north on the motorway past Hamburg."

"But there's only the sea."

"Yes and."

"Bloody hell he's on a boat going north to Scandinavia."

"Yes," said Pancardi, "so we need to check flights to America from Scandinavia."

Blondell sprang to his feet, "Right, let's….." he said.

"No need," Pancardi interrupted, "we have all the operatives working on it now. If there is one they will find it. You and I," Pancardi continued, "will have some strong coffee, we shall walk along the canal with Mostro to get some air and then we shall have breakfast."

Blondell nodded in capitulation. He looked at his watch it was 6.45 am.

❧

Alaina's heels clicked on the cobbles as she walked beside Pancardi, her arm interlinked with his. Blondell thought they looked the perfect couple and he marvelled at the older man who, despite the frantic activity inside the hotel had remained totally calm. He was clearly flattered by Alaina's attention and Mostro too seemed to approve. He sped along the canal edge stopping only to sniff and urinate against pillars and trees. The morning air was crisp and Magdalene had joined them, tired but in good spirits. It appeared that she and Mostro had fallen asleep after Blondell and Pancardi left and it had only been Alaina on the phone which had forced her into the waking world. As they turned the corner to make a return circuit to the Hotel a detective raced down the street toward them. He was waving a piece of paper.

"News from Cologne sir," he panted as he handed Pancardi the note. "It's your man Richter," he said, "he's dead."

"What, how?" Blondell shrieked. "He was under close surveillance, who, how?"

"By all accounts he did it himself," said Pancardi, "by disconnecting the intravenous drip and blowing air into the tube."

"What blowing air into his own blood stream, but why?"

"To give him heart failure I presume. Not much left to live for was there? Arrested for killing a cop and for a huge robbery. He'd have ended up rotting in jail or worse." Pancardi reflected, "I think I might do the same in the circumstances," he continued, "mother like a cabbage, shot to bits and guarded from myself. Death is a way to go free."

"But we have no other leads. No other hopes except to wait for the code to be broken. They could be anywhere by now. They could even be airborne." Blondell sounded anxious.

"If they are up they must land," was Pancardi's short reply. "Anyway breakfast, I know he wants some," he pointed at his dog, "and so do I, come."

⁂

At 11.51 Pancardi ordered coffee. There had been no confirmation of the REW flight.

"Perhaps it's not a flight at all," Blondell suggested.

Magdalene's face tightened. She was on borrowed time, in fact she had taken some annual leave to spend time with Blondell

272

but things had not gone to plan.

"Then we have a real problem," was all Pancardi said.

He stroked the top of Mostro's head as he looked around the room at the frantic activity. No one was moving but there was a clatter of key-boards and printers while other officers spoke into telephones in a variety of languages. Ennio and the forensic team were already on their way back to Italy. Alaina had stayed as long as she could but eventually she too had to leave. Pancardi suddenly felt old. This he surmised, as he studied the room, was the future face of policing and his did not fit. At that moment he was glad he had retired when he did.

At 1.10 Pancardi exclaimed loudly that they should have lunch. So sandwiches were brought into the room, along with a water bowl for Mostro. There were several silver platters bedecked with the customary buffet food. Sandwiches cut into triangles, and then garnished with lettuce and tomato, and bits of pastry filled with assorted mass. The Italian hated buffets, the paper plates and the standing and eating and the whole fake friendliness of the activity, but as a working lunch it sufficed. The thing that really rankled was the fashion of making buffets healthy, he thought the whole thing an oxymoron by adding fresh fruit and then counterbalancing that with full–fat cream. He despised fashion almost as much as he did television. He watched the Dutch Inspector fill his plate, as he spoke platitudes with his mouth full, and wondered what the next generation would do when they realised they had been conned. How they were being socially engineered into thinking, or not thinking at all, by those things which the TV blurted at them. That Inspector needed his fifteen minutes, just as Warhol had said they would. It was his opiate, his religion, his downfall. Pancardi sensed he was having an out of body experience as he studied the room, perhaps, he thought, he was already dead, just another ghost in the machine. He stuffed another piece of meaningless mix into his mouth and looked for the coffee. The last honest thing in the room, as long as it was not fashionably decaffeinated.

At 1.39 one of the computer operators broke the silence.

"That's it," was his first remark. "Oh so clever, but then so am I - encryption to avoid detection. That way the code doesn't show up on the main frame, clever, very clever."

Pancardi picked up on the voice immediately, his senses as

honed as a Tiger Shark smelling blood.

"Got something?" he asked, a sandwich in his mouth muffling his enquiry.

"It's scrambled sir."

Pancardi was out of his seat now, alert and moving.

"Well," explained the computer operator, "the code is not REW 383 it's scrambled to stop anyone tracing it and linking it to a credit card, very clever idea to stop identity theft. So if it's scrambled the combinations have to be replayed in various permutations, which are only known to the airline. Well as I was going through I thought what about if we change the sequence. WE 338 R seems to have thrown up a series of flights, all going to Canada but with one digit different, like we had a digit missing. The black spot on the slip where something might have been burnt off?"

Pancardi and Blondell were behind the man now listening to his reasoning as his fingers tapped the instructions for the hard drive to vary the combination sequence.

Blondell noted the security pass on his lapel, Bronowski and involuntarily registered - Polish.

"So I thought Canada," Bronowski continued, "let's try a (c) as the first code digit variation and hey presto." He was leaning back now as his hard drive worked on the WE 3C38 R combination. "10.25 tonight – only it's been delayed to 11.00. That's a bit of luck, Stockholm to Montreal. There are no others though the programme may take an hour to give full permutations."

Pancardi nearly poured his coffee down the back of the computer operator's collar as he whooped.

He was cut short by Bronowski who was watching the cascading number combinations moving down the screen at hyper-speed; correcting himself, he said, "It seems there's another one WER 338 C 11.20pm on the 23rd and there might be some more."

"Today is," Blondell looked at his watch, "the 14th they won't wait over a week - too risky. They know we're on to them now, they'll want to be gone as fast and as far as possible."

"How long for the whole sequence to run?" asked Pancardi.

Bronowski looked at the clock on the wall, "By three, at the latest," he said. "That will give all the possible permutations."

Chapter 36

"What the hell happened to your face?" asked Paul West.

West sat down opposite Duane Rightman in the executive lounge of Stockholm airport. He had spotted him as he arrived, though Rightman had not seen him. West had watched him, seen he was injured, but more importantly, that he had not been followed. West had sat with a pad on which he had scribbled a variety of notes; numbers and times but the level of police presence had remained unchanged all day. When Rightman arrived there had been no significant changes and West deduced that they were safe to approach him. Alice was making a final sweep and had bought a hat for the security gate.

"You look like shit," West evaluated.

"This," smiled Rightman, showing the gap in his upper jaw, "is courtesy of a Ford steering wheel, and this beauty," he showed the bandages at his chest, "is the result of a motorway spin."

"But you made it and they have no men on the ground here. Weird though, I get the feeling we're being watched. "

"Hey man," said Rightman quietly, "you're getting paranoid. No one knows we're here, and what's more no one gives a shit. Take a look around it's all families off on holiday. We're fine and in half an hour we're gonna be airborne. On the way home. Fucking A baby, Fucking A."

West wanted to use the old cliché about just because you're paranoid it doesn't mean they're not out to get you, but he couldn't be bothered. He felt uneasy but he could not explain why. It was a gut reaction, a reaction which had served him well over the years. A reaction which had saved both his liberty and life in the past and now his antennae were picking up some strange signals. It was all too easy and he didn't like it.

A female voice announced the boarding of flight WE 3C38 R to Montreal and both West and Rightman began to move. Alice Parsotti was nowhere to be seen.

When she did arrive near the security gate there were no niceties.

"Well?" asked West sharply.

"As far as I can see nothing," she replied. "Everything is as normal as can be. I think if anything there are less cops this evening than this afternoon. They're not on red alert that's for certain. I even got to chat to one of them, I think he thought I might fancy him. Flashed his big gun and uniform and he was a total gobshite. He gave me nothing unless you count this." She produced a slip of paper with a telephone number scrawled on it. "If anything is happening the cops know nothing, and that is good for us." She flicked the piece of paper into the bin, "Best place for that," she laughed.

"I still got a feeling about this," said West, "it's like it's too easy."

"I don't," she disagreed, "I think we're clear, so let's get boarded and ..."

"Go home?" splattered Rightman through his mushy gums.

Alice Parsotti studied his face for the first time and raised her eyebrows quizzically. The tinges of blue bruising were now deepening to purple and yellow and a casual observer might think him a prize fighter who had just lost a title fight

"Later," the American replied to the silent question, "it's a long story."

The air in the conference room was thick with the smell of stale smoke and male sweat.

"Thank you," said Pancardi, and the room fell silent. "I would like to thank the Dutch authorities and Interpol for the speed of this operation, which is now over." There was a round of applause. "We have our targets placed in Stockholm. It is likely that they will board a flight to Montreal later today." Another round of applause. "So thank you gentlemen for your involvement and I look forward to working with you once again."

There was a little cheer which was followed by some mumbling as the gathering began to disperse.

Pancardi raised his voice, "You of course understand that everything is still confidential so nothing goes out of this room." He shot an intense look at the Dutch Inspector – a look which said just you dare.

The room cleared and only Blondell, Mostro and Pancardi remained.

"We have to play this very carefully Alex," said Pancardi thoughtfully. "We cannot have the same mess as before. I must not go to Stockholm, this team can smell me. You and Interpol must be anonymous, if they suspect anything they will run and we will lose them for good. We must do as my friend Stokes says, slowly slowly catchy monkey. "

"So how do you figure to do this then?" asked Blondell.

Suddenly the conference room door flew open, "So what happens now," asked the Dutch Inspector as he returned with his stoical Sergeant?

Pancardi stood quietly, "For you nothing," he said, as he placed some papers into a file.

"But surely," rejoined the Inspector, "you are going to Stockholm to arrest them as they board?"

"No, no one is going to Stockholm," said Pancardi, "no newspaper reporters, no TV, no one. I don't want anyone at Stockholm, least of all you. They are under surveillance now and I want them to take off without suspecting a thing. I want them to relax – to think they got away and then we tighten the net. We shall check the flight list, make sure they are on board and when they land we will take them – quietly with no fuss."

The Sergeant smiled at Pancardi's calm cunning.

"So is there anything I can do?" the Inspector repeated solemnly.

"There is one thing," Blondell interjected. "The time now," he looked at his watch, "is 3.10pm, can your man get us to the airport in forty minutes?"

The Sergeant nodded.

"Then what would you like me to do?" repeated the Inspector.

"Go home," said Pancardi.

At the door Magdalene appeared with two small bags. She had packed Blondell's shaving kit, a couple of shirts and some underwear. The exercise had been repeated for Pancardi.

"Shall I look after Mostro?" she asked.

Mostro barked as if he knew what was coming and was raising his objections early.

"Thanks that's very nice of you Magdalene," Pancardi replied, "but he always goes with me. He has his own pet passport so he can travel and this time we're going special class so he doesn't even have to go into the hold."

Blondell nodded at Magdalene, "About two days," he said, as if answering her silent enquiry.

"Don't get him shot," she blurted in a sudden panic at Pancardi.

"My dear girl," he laughed in reply, "neither I nor Mr. MI5 here have the faintest intention of being shot at. In fact I shall be in Montreal a full four hours before them, despite having to get a helicopter to get over the border. The Canadian Police are already setting up the runway and the landing gate so it will be like taking sweets from a baby."

"That's fine for you," she replied, "but what if they spot Alex in Stockholm?"

Into Magdalene's mind there flashed a picture of the holes in Blondell's abdomen and she imagined Calvetti, blood bubbling from his mouth as his body twitched like a landed fish. Her reaction was swift and the kiss she gave was strong and deep. It was a come home to me kiss, the kind only a woman who is truly in love can give.

At the departure gate Alice Parsotti wore a felt beret over her long red hair. The jewels were inside the edging held in with black gaffer tape. She placed her bag and shoes on the rollers for x-ray and walked toward the body scan.

"Oh, silly me," she said, removing the beret and shaking her hair loose provocatively.

She wanted the men to notice her and they did. She casually placed her hat on top of the x-ray machine and walked through – there was no bleep. The seated operator would have noticed the hat but for the sudden diversion from West.

"What do you mean take off my shoes?" West shouted aggressively behind her, "why?"

Attention rapidly turned to the barking man as Alice retrieved her hat unnoticed and placed it back on her head. With her bag over her shoulder, she lifted her mobile phone from the plastic tray and rolled her eyes heavenward at the seated male x-ray operator, who smiled back before she passed unhindered into the departure lounge.

"It's standard airline policy," the security guard said to West.

"Jesus Christ this is ridiculous," he raged as he saw Alice pass the point of no return. "What next exploding shoes?" he snapped, "has the world gone crazy, who has exploding shoes?"

"Your shoes sir please?" the guard calmly repeated.

A woman in the queue behind him was becoming anxious and the boy she was with was trying to calm her. She was obviously a nervous flyer, even the sound of the word explosives was sending her into paroxysms of fear. West was grateful that she was there it gave him something to work with.

"Hey lady," he said, as she passed him while he was being body searched, "you got any explosives in your shoes?"

As West made a significant fuss Alice Parsotti moved into the duty free shopping area and vanished with the jewels in her hat. The security guards at the desk had swallowed the misdirection, just as West predicted they would, but the scruffy cleaner had seen everything.

An unshaven Alex Blondell watched carefully broom in hand – Parsotti was good, very good. She used her beauty and sex appeal like it was a loaded revolver. Being this close to her he finally understood; the bank in Jersey made sense and Dalvin made sense. He had to work hard to remember how ruthless she really was. She was one of those women who made sense, the type that command attention just by being there – a Marilyn. If she was armed, he thought, the gun was in that hat. The man creating the obvious diversion was West, tall and blonde and English. Blondell was feet away from him and he could have taken them

279

both but he had no idea where the second man was or if the fourth, the diver, was there too. He wanted the victory, could almost taste it, but thought better of it and continued to sweep and observe as the boarding gate closed.

On Board KLM flight 721 Giancarlo Pancardi was reading The Times with Mostro on the seat beside him. His white head was in Pancardi's lap and his eyes were closed. The little dog had already become a favourite with all of the stewardesses and had managed to trot into one of the front flight attendant compartments only to be carried back bodily. A fat man opposite Pancardi had reclined his seat into a sleeping position and his grumbling snore was filling the air. A pretty stewardess arrived, she had no idea who the man with the dog was but she had been instructed, by the company chief executive no less, that he should have everything he wanted. And when he said everything he meant everything, and if she looked after his needs there would be a cash bonus in her pay that month. The Pilot had said he was so important that if he asked her to sleep with him she had better do it. The other stewardesses were ribbing her and she hoped she didn't get asked to sleep with him. He wasn't good looking; she tried to place his face, who was he? He wasn't famous so she thought he must be exceedingly rich.

Air Canada flight WE 3C38 R took off from Stockholm at 11.03pm it carried Paul West, Alice Parsotti, and Duane Rightman. The pilot had shortened the safety checks this one time because of the tight scheduling and because it was his wedding anniversary tomorrow; and he had promised his wife he'd be home in time for the meal she had planned. It was tight and he couldn't afford a long delay by being banked at Montreal. He hated the way that they had to hit certain time windows to get in and out of anywhere. The company did not allow enough turn around time and he wanted to do something else. He had always wanted to be a pilot but in reality he was nothing more than a coach driver in the sky.

At 22 thousand feet he levelled out and handed over to his co-pilot.

❦

Pancardi's phone bleeped in his pocket – it was Blondell.

"They are on the plane," he said. "Paul West, Alice Parsotti and Duane Rightman, that's our American. He's the only male US passport holder on the plane so it's got to be him. The fourth, the mystery man, the Scot, I don't think he's there with them; I don't think he ever was. He must have left by a different route. There's no one who fits the bill on the manifest and there was no ticket bought under the same encryption."

"Well done, Alex," said Pancardi, "a professional job."

The phone call woke the fat man opposite and Pancardi smiled at him as he continued, "That man has long gone, but the others will lead us to him," he said. "Take the next plane out to Montreal we'll have them by then....You're breaking up... Phone me when you ge..." He was gone – Pancardi snapped the phone shut.

Chapter 37

Alice Parsotti sat drinking a large glass of Bollinger from a bottle which Paul West had pre-ordered. She was washing down Belgian chocolates she had purchased in the departures lounge after rejecting the pre-packaged airline food. She smiled and joked as the steward opened the bottle – life was good.

"Easy so easy," said West, "I told you security would not pick it up."

"It was so simple," she agreed, "almost too simple. No wonder people get scared of terrorism, just one simple mistake is enough." She lowered her voice, "What do they say, they only have to get it right once and the authorities have to get it right every time? Well they got it wrong that time." She laughed and quaffed a mouthful of the expensive fluid. "What ever you say Paul from now on," she laughed again, "is fine by me."

Duane Rightman sat near the back of the plane between a nervous red-haired American woman, who chattered incessantly with anyone who might respond, and a small computer geek who nodded and spent most of his time glued by his nose to a laptop screen. The woman had a son in the row ahead and he kept popping his head between the seats to chat back to her. Rightman thought about grabbing the annoying child's ears and ripping his head off between the seats or shoving his mother through the back of the seat to shut them both up. They both had window seats but why they had not sat together he could only guess. Perhaps it was to cause the most annoyance to passengers who happened to be travelling next to them. He even thought of swapping with the boy so that they could be together but in the end his only respite was to stare aimlessly out of the window or pretend he had dozed off. Reaching into a pocket he took out some ibuprofen and popped four from their silver backing into his palm.

"Not good for you," the woman remarked, placing her palm over his to stop him throwing them into his mouth.

She was a nurse she told him, "Too many painkillers of the wrong sort won't help, you need to target the pain.

"Dental surgery is painful," he replied, "got to have something to help me sleep."

She noticed his mouth and the toothless gap, "Stitches?" she asked. "Hey Bobby get Mamma's bag down from the overhead there's a good boy."

The boy did as he was told and a few seconds later the noisy nurse was fumbling in her bag as she spoke, "I got some real doozies in here," she said. "I get these bad migraines and then I really need something which works. Do ya wanna try some?" she asked.

"Do I, had a bad traffic accident in Holland," he said. "My car took a real tumble and they patched me up but I just wanted to get home. Get some of mamma's chicken soup and get a real dentist take a look at it. Hurts like hell."

She looked at the man as he swallowed two of her pills. He looked decent, kind and homely, he couldn't be a bad man if he wanted to get home to his mamma. Not like her ex–husband who had been a marine. He had no time for her or the boy and he hated his own mother to boot.

"Is it hard to talk?" she asked.

"Got some stitches and a busted rib or two but I'll live till I get home."

"And home, where is home?"

"Well I'm a North Carolina boy but I live in Burlington now."

"Burlington, Vermont?"

He nodded.

She couldn't believe her luck. The man was resident less than fifty miles from her, it must be destiny, or fate, or some such, she said. He cursed his choice of lie. She peppered him with constant questions. He tried to keep track of the lies he was telling until he had to feign drowsiness to avoid strangling her. His mind imagined what sort of man she was married too and what sort of mother she might be to the uncontrolled child from hell in the row ahead. His head was aching and her voice was becoming a drone like the buzz of bees on a hot summer afternoon.

"I don't want to be rude," he said politely "but those pills really work and I need to get some sleep. Thank you the pain's going."

She visibly rose in stature as the man smiled and thanked her for her kind Christian deed.

"The name's Duane," he said offering her his hand to shake.

"Hi," she took it, "Rosalie Pattern," she said, "and over there's my boy Bobby, Robert Pattern."

"Well thank you Mrs. Pattern," he said, "for being a good Samaritan to a stranger."

Alex Blondell flipped open his mobile telephone and dialled. The ringer sounded and he was told the person he had called was not available, and that he should leave a message after the bleep. He didn't and flipped the phone shut. I'll call later he thought. Within seconds his phone rang, it was Magdalene, her voice was breathless and yet chirpy.

"Where are you?" she asked, "I was taking a shower when you rang."

"Just getting ready for departures," he replied. "Our targets are airborne and I have had something to eat and a shower – I'll sleep on the plane."

"Well just as long as you do. But I'd rather you were sleeping here, between my legs," she laughed.

"Well at present," he said, "I could do just that sleep and nothing more. I'm knackered."

"Nockered? What is this nockered?" she asked, not understanding the slang.

"Not nockered, knackered. It means to have copulated, shagged, or fucked until you have reached the point of exhaustion. To be so tired you cannot fuck anymore."

She laughed coquettishly, "That sounds really lovely," she said. "That is just what I need, to be fucked until I can't fuck anymore."

"Well my little sex-kitten, don't you ever get tired of cock?" he asked.

"It's what I need most," she growled huskily into the receiver.

"Well," he responded, "it's not what I need. I need to curl up and recharge."

"I could re-charge you with my mouth," she teased, "over and over again."

"No doubt," he said, "you could make me blow a fuse, but I'd be dead or crippled."

"You don't know what you can do until you try," she teased. "I'm standing on the bath mat all dripping and naked."

Blondell visualised her nudity as he moved toward the boarding gate. A stewardess shot him a look and a hand signal mimicking a mobile phone to his ear as a warning and he held back in the queue.

"Got to go," he said into the receiver, his voice suddenly serious, "boarding."

"Phone me when you get there," she said.

"It won't be until late morning I'm nearly four hours behind them so it's down to Pancardi from here on in. I'm just the back-up really. I'll see you soon."

Alex Blondell made a kissing sound as the stewardess came toward him and he snapped the phone shut. Magdalene heard the line go dead.

Rightman closed his eyes to get relief from the awful woman and her demon spawn. The thought of spending many hours with the pair filled him with horror but it was a small price to pay for freedom. He wished that she would be struck dumb or that her tongue would stick to the roof of her mouth. Failing that he fanta-sized about digging a plastic spoon into her eye until she was finally silenced. As for that grinning baboon of a boy in the seat ahead he was a discipline nightmare. Up and down like a flag on a pole, the mother laughed when he annoyed and the passengers next to him were so obviously English – they said nothing. Rightman noted, as with most parents, this mother believed that her child had the right to do anything and that all adults had to pay the price for her orgasmic progeny. He hated parents who expected others to make allowances for their children, when in fact the converse should be the case.

Rightman wanted to grab the boy by the throat and squeeze until his eyes popped out, or tell the mother to control the little fucker before he drowned him in the toilet and flushed him away like a shit. In fact he wanted to tell her that it would have been better if the boy had been flushed away many years ago. Perhaps if he pretended for long enough, he thought, they might both go away and he could get some sleep. His mouth was sore, his eyes were heavy and his ears were nearly ready to bleed.

Rosalie Pattern looked at the man next to her in the reclined seat, with his eyes closed, the good Christian man who had thanked her for being a Good Samaritan. She liked his style and his quiet honesty. He wasn't handsome and he smoked, she could smell it, but he could give up if she wanted him to, she knew that. She imagined him to be an athlete or at least someone who worked out, he had a muscular frame. He had a flat stomach and a taut chest and most important of all there was no ring. She guessed his age at around 38, five years older than herself – perfect. She hit the overhead call button and asked for a travel rug. When it arrived she threw it over Rightman leaving half for her to get under. She could feel his warmth next to her and smelt his manly scent. It had been a long time and she could so easily have slipped an arm around the man and drawn herself to him but she resisted. That could wait until they were back in the States and they exchanged contact addresses and phone numbers. Bobby had his own seat and blanket tonight, there was no room next to mamma.

Alice Parsotti waited until everyone around her was asleep before going to the lavatory cubicle. She took her bag and her beret and sat transferring the stones to a small pocket in her bag. She lifted the diamonds to the light and made an assessment of their worth. There was enough here to see them set pretty for years to come. Dalvin's money had been set aside for those personal little shopping trips – her escape fund, should she ever need it. She stared at two identical Emeralds the size of her eyes and lifted them up to look at her image in the over sink mirror. The whole world was refracted into shards of yellow, green and ...

"Hey lady," came a knock at the door, "there's other people on this plane."

"Just coming," she said, as she flushed.

A sweating fat-faced Mexican greeted her at the door and she had to squeeze past him to get by. As she did so he could feel her nipples rub against the blubber of his chest and he wondered if he should ask about mile-high club membership. If she complained of harassment though, then his wife would surely make his life hell, so he thought better of it and stared at her fluidity. She was going back down the stairs to the lower level; he watched her arse as it went and wished he was fifty pounds lighter and twenty years younger.

In Rome Alaina lay unable to sleep, she was thinking of what she had said to Pancardi. She had to do it but the effect had been devastating. It had completely taken him by surprise, stunned him. She thought he might at least have had some idea but he seemed genuinely mesmerised by the whole thing. Perhaps she should have saved it for a better moment; she cursed herself for being such a fool. Now she was in Rome unable to sleep and he was on a flight to Montreal brooding about the whole thing; trying to work out how and when it happened. She knew his mind would re-play the facts until he had extracted every minute detail from his memory bank mind.

Perhaps, she thought, I ought to phone him. She flicked the bedside lamp to on, her clock said 3.14. She couldn't phone now – she switched off the light. She pondered on the nature of love, life, and birth and thought of Magdalene who was now hopelessly in love with the English MI5 man. The man she had seduced on a whim and look how easily that happened. She could be pregnant right now all the fucking those two got up to. Life was simply not fair to some people but it seemed to her in that desolate darkness that Pancardi had received a very raw deal. All that pain, all that trouble and now this. She really did wish she had kept her mouth shut until this whole jewellery thing was over. It had been a big mistake.

Chapter 38

As KLM flight 721 was landing at Montreal airport police activity suddenly became intense. The men on the ground knew that the Italian officer was supremely important, and that both Interpol and MI5 officers were jumping through hoops to please him. The local Chief Inspector looked nervous and the District Attorney was sweating under the warmth of the neon lights blazing in the airport waiting lounge. The man arriving was renowned and he was expecting them to perform a simple task in isolating a plane after it landed. Apparently he was a stickler for detail; rumour had reached Montreal, rumour of a fiasco in Amsterdam, a fiasco of such proportions that one Inspector had probably been side-lined for the rest of his career. It was a mistake which neither of them was prepared to make and certainly one which this powerful Italian should not witness. The District Attorney knew only too well that publicity came after success and not during or before an event. That was why he had the press on standby and not actually there – he too craved notoriety but not for failure. His blaze of glory was going to last far longer than some loud-mouthed Dutch buffoon, he had a career to develop and this Italian might just be one of those who could throw every possibility into his lap.

Pancardi was swiftly whisked from the plane, without the formality of customs or security checks, a full 6 hours and 13 minutes before the flight carrying West, Parsotti and Rightman was due to land. Mostro trotted confidently beside him, his tail high as Pancardi talked with the operations police. They were Mounties but they did not wear the traditional red tunics.

Pancardi thought of their reputation for always getting their man and smiled.

"Something wrong Inspector?" asked one of the officers as he passed, noticing the Italian's wry smile.

Pancardi shook his head and reminded himself not to let his thoughts show.

"Inspector Pantrardi?"

"Pancardi," he replied, "it's Pancardi," he continued, slightly irritated by the puerile mistake.

A friendly hand was being extended, "Bellows," the man on the end of the hand said, "Michael, Mike, Bellows I'm the District Attorney and this is…"

"Jacobsen," the second man swiftly interrupted, "Chief Jacobsen."

His handshake was firmer, it spoke of assured power, and was underpinned by self confidence and intelligence which shone from the man's eyes.

"You are in charge?" asked Pancardi, "are things fully set up?" he continued, completely ignoring the District Attorney.

"The plane will land at runway thirteen. It will be totally isolated and the passengers will then be loaded into a bus for the terminal. It's all quite usual and no one will suspect a thing. We are keeping the whole situation very low profile. No fuss, no increase in security, and no press – in fact everything should work smoothly. Once inside the customs hall we can arrest them all. "

Pancardi smiled, there were no airs and graces with this man, he cut through irrelevant niceties and got straight to the point – Pancardi liked that.

"And is every exit covered?" he asked.

The Canadian nodded, "With fully armed officers," he said, "in plain clothes. Not those monkeys you had in Amsterdam, these boys are the real McCoy."

Pancardi tilted his head, clearly a reputation had preceded him from Holland. He wanted to smile but thought better of it and merely cast his eyes down to his shoes.

"They will do the job," the voice continued, "and then vanish like a virgin on prom night. You won't find them craving glory, they are my very best, not a single idiot among them."

Pancardi nodded and smiled, he really liked the man's style, quiet and efficient – no needless bullshit, no great thirst for popularity, a policeman first and foremost.

※

"What do you mean hydraulic fluid leakage?"

"Well the instrument panel says that the fluid in the wing adjusters is low and falling."

The pilot tapped the instrument panel and knew in the instant that he should have left the plane and checked all of the external fittings when they were on the ground; but that would have taken him twenty minutes and he wanted to get home, that now looked liked an impossibility. His mind raced forward to the landing in Montreal. What if the landing gear only came down on one side, what if the wind breaks failed? He cursed his luck and looked at the instrument panel once again as if that alone would change the issue.

"Fuck it!" he exclaimed.

"And," said the co-pilot, "the weather is turning nasty and looks like a thunder storm on the horizon. Can we fly over it?"

"Nope we only have a flight ceiling of 22,000 feet in this band. So it looks like we have to fly through the bastard."

"Shit!" the co-pilot retorted.

The pilot knew that one strike from lightening would probably be enough to end their chances of landing in Montreal. The plane felt heavy, almost leaden as he wrestled with the control of the aircraft. He knew that they were in for a bumpy night but that if push came to shove he might be able to fly under rather than over the storm. Cursing his luck he turned the plane thirty degrees west into the oncoming thick cloud. The horizon was black only interspersed with occasional forked lightening.

"Time to fucking pray," he said, "pray like a prick on Sabbath night. It's all fucking luck and bullshit from here on in."

With his free hand he flicked the intercom switch to on.

※

"Coffee?" asked the Police Chief. "Apparently there's a heavy storm coming in over the mountains and we may be in for a doozie. They'll keep the runways clear but there may be a diversion if …"

"Diversion, what sort of diversion how much of a diversion?" Pancardi coolly interrupted.

"Could be 500 miles."

"You are joking," Pancardi hissed incredulously. "If they get that far away then we'll certainly lose them. Talk about giving them a head start, this whole thing is becoming my worst nightmare .They'll slip away and then we might as well give up."

"The problem," replied the Canadian, "is that we won't be able to get to where they land ourselves but we can get officers there to detain them until we arrive."

Pancardi gave a smile which showed his teeth like a crocodile and the Canadian knew that within his inner thoughts he too realised that the whole issue might become another Amsterdam.

"Ladies and gentlemen," the pilot announced, "we may experience some turbulence as we are entering a storm in a few moments. There is absolutely nothing to worry about but we ask that you refrain from using the toilets and fasten your safety belt as sudden turbulence is always a possibility."

The murmuring chatter in the fuselage died to a nervous hush when a fork of lightening narrowly missed the plane and fell to earth somewhere near Nantucket Sound. To the very receptive ear the chant of Hail Mary full of grace was just audible in its repetition.

He turned to his co-pilot and spoke with quiet resolution, "We'll need the luck of the Irish in this. Don't have any Irish blood in me but today I wish I was called O'Neill – here we go."

The cabin lit up as the lightening struck and the plane dropped twenty feet like a stone. The effect on the passengers was instant. Some became silent, while the less travel hardened vomited and the sound of small talk was replaced by the rich smell of human bile.

Magdalene was woken from deep sleep by a resonating buzz – it was still dark. She automatically reached for her mobile phone, it was switched off. The buzz continued and she looked at the alarm clock. It read six thirty but she had not set it – the buzzing continued. She struggled to sleep. Thinking she was in a dream, she tried to roll over but the noise would not go away. Her ears began to hurt and when finally she lifted the receiver a familiar voice resounded in her ear and she began to come to.

"Magdalene," Alaina said down the phone, "turn on your TV."

The caller's voice didn't make sense, maybe it was a dream, a vivid nearly awake dream - but it went on.

"Turn on your TV now. Have you got Alex's number? Call him. Call him right now."

Magdalene reached for the remote control and the room was filled with a cacophony of sirens, blue lights and emergency company spokesmen; statements with news that a plane had gone down on a remote mountain side. There had been a storm and chaos at airports and one plane had been lost. It was a plane en route from Stockholm to Montreal. The newsreader boldly explained that the authorities had no idea about survivors because it had gone down over the Ungava Peninsula somewhere between Fort Chimo and Gagnon. There was talk about a freak storm and remote regions and mountain rescue teams and not being able to get people into the mountains for days.

Radio contact had been lost and they could not get a plane over the area because of the storm. Relatives were being given a contact number.

Magdalene was wide awake now.

Reaching for her mobile she spoke into the receiver at her other ear. "Is it the plane Alex was on? Holy Mary please no," she squealed as her own reply.

"That's why I said to phone him," Alaina said.

"Nothing, it's dead," said Magdalene, suddenly realising the importance of what was happening.

"It's probably just turned off," Alaina's hopefulness was feigned. "If he was on the plane then his phone would be off. Or maybe the battery…"

Magdalene knew it too, "But he's got flight safety mode," she blurted, "he never turns off."

"Maybe the reception is poor?" Alaina sensed she was clutching at straws as she spoke.

There was a long pregnant pause.

"Maybe he's …"

"Or maybe the plane just crash landed," Alaina interrupted, "nobody really knows what's happened ….and he's fine and his phone has been lost or damaged."

There was silence at the other end of the line and Alaina knew that Magdalene was crying.

"I'll try to get some more information," Alaina said quietly to placate her.

Silence.

"Magdalene?"

Silence.

"Get on the phone," Alaina said, "and see if you can find out…"

The line went dead...

Chapter 39

The sound of grinding, searing, metal split the silence of the cold winter air like the wail of a banshee. Screaming people being thrown from a disintegrating fuselage was followed in less than a minute by total silence. A swathe had been ploughed across the mountain side and the plane had broken into three major sections. The wings had been torn away by the heavy pine trees which flanked the fuselage, and those passengers in the central section had been dashed against the rock and ice like biblical infants, while many others had been smeared across the mountain face like raspberry jam. The wind howled and the storm and snow intensified. It would only be a matter of hours before the whole scene of carnage was re-painted in a glorious fresh white emulsion and the smell of aviation fluid and death would be replaced by new crisp stillness.

"Yes en route from Stockholm to Montreal," said Alaina.

A muffled voice replied down the line.

"I'm calling on behalf of Inspector Giancarlo Pancardi of Interpol, I am his personal assistant."

This time the voice changed from sympathy to alert reply mode.

"I want to know if an Alexander Blondell, British, was on that plane when it left Stockholm?" She continued, "It is a matter of international importance that Inspector Pancardi knows this fact."

"I'll have to put you through to my supervisor," the voice replied, "please hold."

Alaina could hear the sombre music which was piped and imaged the chaos she had caused by using Pancardi's name. After a few minutes a Scandinavian voice asked, "Can I help?"

"Can I have your name please, for future reference?" Alaina asked calmly.

"Bjorn Johansson," came the terse reply, "I am supervisor of the telephone enquiry centre. I am in direct contact with all of the authorities, concerning this accident, how can I help?"

Alaina reiterated the full outline. She could hear the manifest pages being flipped before the dispassionate reply came, "There is no one of that name listed."

"Is there an Alice Parsotti or West, Paul West?"

Again the pages were ruffled, "Both of those names appear on the manifest. I am so terribly sorry for your loss…" He began to switch into condolence mode as his voice became noticeably softer and the harsh edge of seconds earlier was replaced by a smoother drone.

"Thank you," said Alaina and hung up.

She dialled Magdalene immediately and as she heard her pick up the receiver she almost yelled down the line, "Good news, it's not his plane," she yelped, "it's the other one. The one they are tracking. He's safe so there must be a problem with the phone and he can't answer. I'll speak to Carlo as soon as I can."

There was silence which was followed by rapid sobbing. She could hear Magdalene crying at the other end, only this time the whine was more relief rather than distress.

A voice could be heard in the distance, it was soft and yet it had the resilience of a traffic siren, "Help me," it repeated. "Help me please, help."

When Paul West woke his eyes were filled with blood. The gash along his forehead yawned across his brow like a razor blade smile. "Fuck," he mumbled as he unbuckled his safety belt and fell forward. The effect was immediate and he fell onto the seat ahead. He knew the plane was at angle and that only the safety belt had saved his life. The seat next to him was buckled and empty; he was glad that he had not chosen a window.

"Alice!" he called.

He tried to stand but the angle of the floor was too steep. The fuselage was torn away and he could not see the front section of the plane at all. The tail was behind him and wind was ripping through a great gash where the wing should have been. The rear end was exposed to the elements, a whole section bodily at a 90 degree angle. It was light and he could see snow falling into the compartment and he suddenly became aware that he was intensely cold. He saw the body of a man, well at least the half that was left looked male, exposed and draped like a bloody throw across the torn opening.

"Alice!" he called again.

"Help me," came a reply.

Clambering up toward the tail compartment the voice became stronger. Once past the searing gash in the side of the aircraft the floor levelled out and he found he could stand. He followed the voice, "Where are you?" he called.

The voice did not change and he had to home in on it.

The ginger haired boy was lying on his side a large gash opened in his leg. Blood was steadily pumping from the wound and West thought that his artery might be severed. He pulled the belt from his trousers and made a tourniquet to try and stem the bleeding. He evaluated that the boy was in shock and that his help me call would soon cease. The boy screamed as the tourniquet bit into his leg at the thigh and then promptly stopped all noise as he passed out. West looked at the row of seats immediately behind the boy and found Duane Rightman. His head was leaning to the right and it seemed as if his neck might be broken. The woman next to him was dead. Her red hair was matted with the already coagulating blood which had drenched the seats. Her right eye and a portion of her skull were torn away and the whole body looked crumpled like a balloon with the air taken out. West leaned over the corpse and grabbed the still lump that was Rightman.

"Wake up you piece of shit," he yelled, as he slapped the American's face.

There was no reaction.

"Don't you die on me you fuck."

Rightman stirred and an intense pain stabbed his right side, "Jesus Paul," he mumbled, "my fucking ribs man. Fuck I need a doctor man. "

"Never mind that you have to get up, we have to find some shelter or we'll die."

Rightman nodded involuntarily and his arms had the direction-less and clumsy quality of a marionette.

"Where's Alice?" asked West.

Rightman shook his head. He felt sick and retched – blood fell to the floor.

"Have you seen her?"

Rightman shook his head again, coughed and blood hit West's shirt. West knew from that Rightman's lung was probably punctured – most likely by one of his own ribs.

A female voice called weakly from below, down in the exposed belly of the plane, "My leg, I think my leg's broke," it said.

Alex Blondell landed in Montreal to find Giancarlo Pancardi waiting for him at the terminal gate. He had not heard the news of the accident; it was not the sort of news which airlines liked to broadcast to in flight passengers.

"Well, did you get them?" he asked as he approached the Italian.

"Mmmm," replied Pancardi, "not exactly but we know where they are."

Blondell's heart sank and he could feel his shoulders sloping, "What the hell went wrong?" he asked.

"Their plane crashed."

"But that's ridiculous, outrageous, mad."

"Ridiculous but totally true, I'm afraid."

The men started walking as Pancardi relayed the facts.

Blondell listened intently before speaking, "We'll have to go out there then," he said, "however remote it is. They could take off into the mountains and we'll never catch them."

Pancardi laughed.

"Good grief," exclaimed Blondell, "what is so funny? The whole thing has turned pear shaped, and not for the first time, and all you can do is chuckle."

"But Alex!"

"Never mind bloody buts," he chided in return for Pancardi's flippancy. "They will be away off into the Canadian Rockies or something."

Pancardi paused and took a deep breath before speaking, "If they are alive," he said solemnly, "and it is a very big if, this storm is set to last for three days at the least. They are in a remote part of Canada but it is not the Rockies - geography Alex geography. The mountain rescue teams are standing by and as soon as the sky clears we shall be up there with them, by helicopter. You can walk if you like but I'll ride, they are not going anywhere in a hurry."

Blondell could see the sense of what Pancardi was saying and realised that he was tired, "I need a shower and a freshen up," he suddenly said, changing the subject completely.

"There is a hotel booked right here, on the airport," Pancardi replied, "so we don't even need to go far from the transportation. All we do now is sit it out and wait, wait for the storm to abate and then go get them – all too easy really."

"I'm glad you're so confident," replied Blondell. "They seem to slip through every net we cast. It's almost like fate."

"Well fate this," Pancardi threw him a key, "209," he said, "I'm in 210."

"Where's Mostro," asked Blondell, "you could train him to scent out Parsotti and West."

"I expect he's asleep on my bed," Pancardi replied. "And how can I train him when we have nothing to scent. No, this time Alex we must trust to luck and ourselves."

In room 209 Alex Blondell finally switched on his phone and picked up the frantic message from Magdalene; he returned her call, for which he received due warning about allowing his phone battery to die. Magdalene vent all her frustration and anger upon him before telling him how much she was upset that he hadn't phoned to put her mind at rest. He tried to explain that he didn't know as it was not the sort of thing that might be broadcast mid-flight, especially as it was the same route. She accepted his reasoning, had cried out of sheer relief, and he, in turn, vowed to leave his phone on and charged whenever possible. With the air cleared he showered and afterward lay on the bed. The wind whipping across the terminal carried the sound of death upon it and Blondell knew that Pancardi was right in his assessment of survival.

"Alice?" called West.

He called again and began to clamber down the rows of seats as if he were descending the branches of a tall tree. He passed a woman slumped in her chair, her safety belt still tight around her waist; he could tell her neck was broken by the angle of her head.

"Alice?"

There was no reply, he called again.

At the bottom of his decent he found a woman. She was small, a size six or eight. She was jammed between two seats with her legs protruding into the darkness. At first he thought they were outside the plane and then realised both of her legs had been severed below the knee and the carpet was soaked in blood. She was weak and he knew he could not help her. West left her to bleed out.

"Alice!" he shouted out into the night through a gash in the fuselage.

There was no reply though he thought he saw something like green eyes only a few feet away in the blinding snow. Eyes which stared at him, eyes which were not human, cold eyes, predatory eyes; he looked again trying to discern a body shape and then they were gone. West studied the seat numbers above him they started at row 9; he and Alice had been in row 4 she should be in the seat ahead he reasoned.

"Paul?"

The voice of Alice Parsotti was clear and clinical. It came from behind him, from where he had just been. He turned to see her covered in snow standing at the gash in the fuselage with a medical kit and some kitchen knives in her hands.

"I thought these might be handy," she said, throwing the items on the ground. "We need to check all the overhead lockers for clothes, coats and things to keep warm."

"Where were you?" he asked.

"I found my way to the cockpit. The pilots are dead and the radio is smashed. But there's an emergency light flashing red on the fuselage so maybe a rescue team will get to us."

"But I was just here," he said incredulously, "how come I didn't see you?"

"Must be all the blood in your eyes," she said. "That's nasty let me take a look." She examined his head wound, "Perhaps you've got concussion. I was just there."

She pointed to a place which he was certain he had checked.

He looked at her and wondered how he could have missed her, "Rightman's in the tail end, up there," he pointed, "and there is some reasonable shelter and it's flat. There's a kid there too. I put a tourniquet round his leg and there's a woman."

"Let's go back up then," she replied. "I get the feeling that we are being watched by something."

"Yeah, I saw some eyes in the snow too," he confirmed.

Giancarlo Pancardi sat talking to the helicopter pilot in the bar. He noticed that the pilot only drank coffee, strong coffee the kind he preferred.

"Keeping a clear head?" he asked casually.

"Yeah," was the terse reply.

"Are you expecting to fly the rescue helicopter tonight then? In this storm?"

The pilot turned toward him, "Foreign ain't ya?" he said. "Can tell that by the little white dog. If he was out in a storm up here both you and him would be as dead as Dodos."

Pancardi knew already that he wouldn't like this man. Foreign to him would be anyone who lived more than fifty kilometres away. He had an air of self righteous arrogance borne out of years of prejudice; a prejudice based upon air lifting city folk off the mountains when they had no right to be there in the first place. Pancardi knew that if he continued that would be precisely what the man would say.

"So how long have you been doing this air rescue?" asked Pancardi.

"Too long," he replied.

"Twenty years?" Pancardi continued.

"Hey, why all the questions?"

"Well I just thought with you and the coffee that there might be a way to get out to the crash tonight."

The man laughed, "Listen," he said, "no one is going nowhere tonight. Nor tomorrow for that. By the time we get out there we'll be bringing everyone home in bags. It's gonna be colder than hell and then there's the wolves. And I like coffee tha's all." He took a large gulp, "Foreigners," he muttered into his cup as he drank.

"Me too," chuckled Pancardi. "In fact we Italians all do." There was a pause, "Wolves you said?" Pancardi questioned.

"Yeah, big grey hungry devils. They'll just love all that fresh meat delivered to their door, it's a kind of nature reserve where they are. But if it was me I shoot 'em all and let the buzzards have a feast." He took another gulp of coffee, "But them old wolves, they like the warm too and they ain't gonna be out in a hurry neither. They'll wait and either me or Johnny Ainsco had best be there PDQ. If not it'll be dinner time for fido." The man laughed heartily.

Pancardi was beginning to detest him, "Who's Johnny Ainsco?" he asked.

"Johno? Why he's the other pilot – flies out of Cupforge."

"Sorry Cupforge?"

"Yeah, Cupforge air club, small bi-planes and such."

"So he flies the helicopter, chopper too?"

Pancardi's continued questioning was clearly beginning to irritate the man.

"Look there's two choppers," the man snapped. "Johnny flies the one and I fly the one."

"And how far away is Cupforge?" asked Pancardi.

"About 250 clicks give or take?"

"250 kilometres?"

"Miles, miles. This is Canada."

"And where is Cupforge then?" Pancardi asked.

"Other side of the mountains, but he ain't flyin' neither. So you won't get him to take you neither. Anyways how you gonna get to Cupforge?" He paused, "You wanna get out there you're gonna need dogs, good dogs. That's if anyone I'll take ya. Be the best part of two days in the clear – snow like this could be upwards of a week lessen you die tryin'."

Pancardi decided that there was no point in continuing any conversation and excused himself by walking to the toilet. As he urinated he could hear the wind wrapping the silent blanket of snow around the airport and briefly he thought of passengers who might be stranded without a hotel room. The comfort of emergency blankets and soup was nothing compared to a warm shower and a dry bed. As he zipped and washed his hands he wondered how his quarry might be – wondered if they were even alive now.

Chapter 40

Paul West kicked the door of the baggage compartment open.

"Hey Duane!" he said, "help me move these cases down to the opening we gotta block off that wind."

Duane Rightman coughed loudly and a large sticky wet lump shot from his lungs as he spat against the floor before rising slowly. He would rather have lay still but he knew, as West and Parsotti knew, that they had to survive the night and the extreme cold. Light was failing in the storm and Parsotti had taken a kitchen knife and climbed down the ladder of seats to find what clothing she could from the overhead lockers and galley.

As she returned she saw West slash open a soft suitcase only to find underwear, towels and beach gear. She hoped they were on more than a connecting flight for Florida, otherwise the majority of bags would contain lightweight clothes totally useless to all of them.

"Jesus fucking Christ!" he exclaimed, "all bikinis and panties. Fucking useless, totally fucking useless."

"That's not what you used to say," said Alice, "I thought you liked me in that sort of thing."

West scowled, he had no time for frivolity. Rightman laughed and then coughed more blood.

"You got those suitcases piled up high? Make sure it's a good wind break," Alice Parsotti continued, in a more serious mode. "Down below I've got the medical first aid stuff and some airline food, some bottled water and bottles of wine. It's all I could find; I'll need a hand to get it up here though." She could sense that

West had lost his sense of humour.

Rightman laughed again more blood rose, "Hi diddly dee it's picnic time for me," he snorted. "Go see Alice when you're ten feet tall," he chortled.

Alice scowled at the man, "There's blankets in the overheads and coats and I thought we could use the baggage hold to sleep in," she said. "At least we can block the door if anything gets up here."

"Wowa!" Rightman's face lit up. "What the fuck do you mean if anything gets up here?"

"Well we are in a remote area," Alice confirmed.

"What like a bear maybe? Holy shit." Rightman's voice showed panic. "We're fucked man, truly fucked, if a bear gets in here." He coughed again, the agitation making the blood flow more quickly.

"What I meant was that we ought to be careful. You know just in case," she continued, "they can smell blood from twenty miles away, I think."

"Just in fucking case – in case the fucker gets up here?" Rightman coughed again and blood spurted from his lips and swirled around his teeth as he spoke.

Alice smiled a toothy grin, "He'll probably eat you first," she smirked, "cos' you can't run baby," she paused, "you're a lunger now." She taunted him, "Anyhow you probably don't taste too good all those fags an awl." She drooled the words out deliberately accentuating the awl in a mimicked southern accent. "Bet you could do with a real good smoke now," she laughed.

Rightman coughed in agitation, his lungs were painful and getting worse.

"I think you better rest up for a bit Duane," said West sympathetically, he was using his Christian name now, "you seem to be coughing up more blood than before."

He nodded a reply and rasped a deep cough which shook his whole being.

Alice Parsotti reckoned on two days without medical treatment.

"Help," called the now conscious boy, who everybody had forgotten.

Alice Parsotti moved over to him and then she and West

lifted him into the baggage hold. On a bed of coats and laundry he was laid down – Parsotti inspected his wound.

"It's bad Paul," she said, "real deep. We might be able to stitch it but the artery looks cut."

"Well I got that tourniquet on," West remarked.

"Yeah?" Alice rebuked him, "But you're going to have to release it every now and again or he'll lose that leg."

The boy was fluctuating in and out of consciousness and asking about his mother and where she was.

"What's your name?" Alice asked him.

The boy was delirious.

"Name, what's your name?" she asked again.

"His name's Bobby," Rightman coughed.

"Bobby," Alice called quietly and the boy's eyes opened in recognition.

"Mom?" he said, mistaking Alice.

"Where's mom?" he asked, and then drifted out again.

"Yeah, his fucking endless chattering mother," said Rightman, "sat next to me she was a real talker. Didn't know how to shut up, made my ears bleed."

"Well she isn't going to be talking anymore, she's dead," said West. "Half her head's been ripped off."

"Best thing for her," replied Rightman, "nearly did it myself when she went on and on…and that little shit." He pointed at the boy. "Is the spawn of the devil. If I had my way," he coughed, "he would have been strangled at birth. The best part of that little bastard ran down the inside of his mother's leg. Hey, I can do the little fuck right now, snap his neck like a chicken save us all some trouble." He advanced menacingly.

West stopped him. "You're not thinking straight man," he said, "listen if there is a rescue team it would be better if it were not just us left here. Sure we'll throw all the other bodies out for the wolves but…"

"Wolves, fuckin' wolves!" exclaimed Rightman, "nobody said anything about god damn wolves. Are there fuckin' wolves here too? Holy angel shit."

"Well there's something out there in the snow," replied West, "and it isn't frosty the fucking snowman. So we need to stay cool."

"Stay cool, you son of bitch!" Rightman exclaimed. "We're so cool we're gonna freeze to death and now you say there's wolves too. Fuck man, hey double fucking jeopardy fuck, fuck, and fuck."

"So what are we going to do?" Alice interrupted coldly, sensing Rightman's nervous anger. "We are all stuck in the same boat, either we keep clear heads or we all end up as hot snack food."

"Precisely," West affirmed, "we can't walk out of here and someone will come to find us. We just have to have good cover stories. No one knows that we're on this plane so no one is looking for us. When they come to find this crash we just get back to civilisation like normal people and vanish."

"Vanish," squealed Rightman, "we'll fucking vanish alright. We'll be found as wolf shit spread all over these goddamn mountains. We should have flown straight for the States, you and your clever little backwater detours. Well I ain't goin' outta here in no wolf belly give me one of them galley knives." He snatched a weapon from Alice. "Anything comes for me I'll gut it like a barn pig."

His eyes were full of fire and his mouth was gritted which gave him an unworldly look with the two front teeth missing. He coughed up more blood as he spoke but his eyes were lit with fight and vengeance.

"I don't like this Carlo," said Alex, as he fed another small piece of bacon to Mostro.

"Then give it to Mostro," Pancardi replied.

"No, not the bacon, the situation."

Pancardi smiled knowing full well what the Englishman really meant, "So what do we do?" he asked.

"I'd like to go out there after them."

"Why?" Pancardi spoke through a mouthful of food.

"Every time we get close they slip away."

"Ah and you have a death wish too."

"Don't be absurd," Blondell snapped.

"Absurd. It is you who is absurd my friend. Just look out of this window. All the planes are grounded. It's a freak storm and a bad one too. Look not a soul is out. "

"But they'll find a way out of it, they always do."

"Not this time, not this time eh Mostro?" The little dog barked once in reply as Pancardi stroked his head. "You see," continued Pancardi, "he knows."

"What can he know?" asked Blondell sarcastically, "he's just a dog."

"Well he has sense enough to know that if we went out in this weather we would die. He also knows that here we are warm and well fed – they are not. That is if even they are alive. They may all be dead – in fact that is the most likely scenario no? When the weather she is clear then we will go and collect the bodies."

"I want to get the whole thing over and done with and I know that they'll have some way of slipping …" His phone rang, he stopped suddenly, it was Magdalene, "Fine, yep fine," he said, "later today. Yes I know but you have to have patience." He hung up.

Pancardi tilted his head to one side and then back to upright and then to the other side.

"What time is it Alex?" he asked.

Blondell looked at the clock above the doors. It said 8.51

Pancardi caught sight of his eyes, "No not here Alex, at home in Roma?"

Blondell looked at his watch it read 2.50, "Shit," he said.

"The girl she cares so much that she phones in the middle of her night, half across the world to see if you are alright – this is love no? To think of the other more than yourself? She could have phoned in your middle night not hers," he paused and then thoughtfully added, "she knew you were more the tired no?"

Blondell looked out of the window to see the snow falling more heavily. Pancardi was right he needed to acknowledge that fact and be less reserved. He cursed himself inwardly for being an insensitive fool.

"I must take Mostro to walk," said Pancardi. "We wait and we prepare and we relax and we are ready, like the greyhounds before they chase the rabbit." He patted the small white dog on the head. "And you," he continued, as if giving an order, "you must phone your woman back, if you wish to keep her. She is

308

Sicilian no? You English you have no idea." He rose and left the breakfast table, "Come Mostro," he commanded.

As the Italian turned to leave the dining area he glanced back at Blondell who had flipped his phone open and was busy talking to someone. His face was smiling so the call must be pleasant Pancardi deduced. As he headed down the corridor for the lobby, Mostro trotted confidently alongside him and gave one single bark as they started down the staircase.

Pancardi had hated lifts ever since that case in Milan where the damn thing jammed and he had to spend seven hours locked in with two women in a six by four steel box. They couldn't get the thing down, and it was so hot; all three of them sweating like pigs in the broiling heat and down to their underwear and walking in their own piss by the end of it. He wasn't ever going to let that happen again, nowadays he always took the stairs.

Paul West wiped the blood from his right eye as it seeped from the bandage loosely wrapped around his head. He looked at his palm it was bright red.

"Ok," said Alice, "we can rest up. First I'll stitch that and dress it and you Duane need to take a morphine shot for those ribs."

Rightman nodded, he had no strength left to argue. As the liquid bit into him his breathlessness eased and he sighed in relief.

Alice Parsotti pushed the mother's body down the sloping aisle, it slid like a sledge of potatoes and then crumpled in a heap with a soggy thud. She rubbed her hands together and realised a pair of gloves might be useful. She hadn't wanted to spend her last moments seeing the one eyed mangled woman in her dreams. It was bad enough that she had red hair which was similar to her own, though shorter, and it was obviously from her that the moaning boy got his colouring. It could have been me she thought. It could be my body that they were dropping. It could be me that hit the ground with half a face and... She cleared her thoughts and began searching the overhead lockers again for useful items.

Duane Rightman now sat propped against the side of the

fuselage. He had dragged himself into a sitting position because it was easier to breathe and lying next to the vile devil spawn only irritated him the more. The morphine had helped and both he and the boy were sleeping.

Paul West was awake, the blood in his right ear irritated him and he examined the tip of his little finger as he removed it. He was stiff and cold had managed to penetrate into the body of the plane despite his best efforts. As he stood, his head swam, by sheer force of will alone he moved out of the baggage hold.

Alice Parsotti was sitting in a seat near the opening wrapped in a mass of coats and pillows.

"Ah you're awake then?" she said. "Do you want to take a look at my handy work?"

She passed him a small vanity mirror and a plastic cup. As he looked at the stitches across his forehead he could see white cotton ties protruding.

"Jesus," he said.

"Wine?" she asked. "It's a particularly fine vintage."

"I'm going to look like Boris fucking Karloff after this trip," he said, taking a deep gulp of red plonk.

The fire of the alcohol bit into his tongue and only then did he realise that he must have bitten it during the impact. He could taste dried blood in his throat.

"I feel like shit," he said.

"Get under here with me," she coaxed, "keep warm."

He clambered under the vast mass of coats and felt the comforting warmth of body heat revive him.

"Sorry about the head," she said, "I had to use normal cotton, but I sterilised it in brandy. The morphine knocked you out so I worked while you were under. It's going to be an ugly scar but you can always get that fixed later. It's not like we can't afford it, anyhow at least the bleeding's stopped. There's plenty of morphine and brandy, have some in your wine."

She poured brandy into his cup which he threw back with one massive gulp.

Rightman coughed deeply in his propped sleep and several large spots of bright crimson appeared on the cabin wall next to where he sat. Parsotti looked at West and he too knew that Rightman's lungs were very slowly filling with blood and that eventually he would drown in it.

"Where is our stuff," asked West.

Alice lowered her voice so that no one else could hear, "Overhead locker 21c," she pointed to it, "in the black handbag bag that's up there. It belonged to that kid's mother, Rosalie Pattern"

"I think he's gonna die," West replied.

"And that yank too... If we're really lucky," she replied.

"Then just you and me Alice, like always."

He rested his head against the reclined seat back and as he did so she noticed the fresh blood in his ear.

"I got this," she said, and produced an automatic pistol taken from the cockpit. "It's only got five rounds though," she continued, "so the other four must have been used at another time."

"Strange not to reload the clip, but it's a God send," he replied leaning over to kiss her.

"And we've got the galley knives," she confirmed, "the trouble is I heard snarling a minute ago just before you woke. It came from below that's why I came out here, just in case."

He wondered why she had placed herself in a seat near the entrance and now he knew – she had been standing guard.

"We could do with a fire," he suddenly said, "I'll get some wood from outside."

"But the wolves?"

"Give me the gun," he said confidently. She handed it to him. "I'll stack as much as I can in the area below. Then we can at least get some heat. If you hear shots you know I'm in trouble – wake up Rightman but don't come looking for me."

With that he slipped out through the blanketed entrance and began to slowly descend the ladder of seats. The woman with the severed legs had gone, so too had the red head with half a face. He could see the marks where the corpses had been dragged through the torn fuselage and out toward the tree-line. They passed over the brow of a hollow and disappeared. He looked out through the driving snow and thought he briefly saw some green eyes in the wooden darkness. He decided to stay close to the plane and collect as much wood as he could. As he gathered, he listened intensely for movement, for a snarl, but all he could hear was the sound of the wind. Briefly he surveyed the devastation, the torn wreckage and the other parts of the fuselage. Everything was being covered with a fine powdery snow and he could not see the cockpit though it was less than 30 metres away. He wondered how Alice had managed to find it.

In the baggage compartment Duane Rightman woke with a start, there was a needle going into his arm and he could feel himself sliding. He was losing consciousness and he fought to remain upright. Something was pulling his legs and he was sliding onto his back, he was dreaming a pleasant, painless dream. He tried to cough but the fluid was too heavy, he decided to leave it till the morning, when he could get some coffee. There was a coffee shop he could use when they landed which wouldn't be long now; he snored and gurgled as his chest tightened and his breathing became restricted.

"Bobby Pattern," the boy replied.

"Well Bobby," the nice voice said. "You're in hospital now and mom is fine. I expect she'll be in to see you soon."

The boy smiled.

"We're just going to give you a little jab," the voice soothed, "you won't even feel it."

He winced and then passed into a deep sleep. He hardly felt the needle and it was warm all around him. His leg hurt a bit but the nurse would see to him. He had been to hospital before and he was very brave then just like now.

Alice Parsotti released the tourniquet and the artery began to allow a deep crimson flow from the wound. The stitches crudely held the flesh in place but the artery needed really careful work. After two minutes she retightened the tourniquet and returned to her outside couch area.

Paul West watched the tree line as he collected firewood. The whole area was strewn with dry timber some of which had been torn away by the plane as it crashed, but mostly it had fallen naturally in the desolate hillside fir forest. His feet scuffed away the loose powdery covering as he gathered armful after armful. Occasionally he stopped to listen – he was certain he could hear a pig snuffling and those green eyes kept haunting him. They were watching he could see that. He thought about a shot but knew that would panic Alice and Rightman. Besides, he needed the five shots just in case a whole pack attacked at once. He stared into the snow and followed the eyes, they appeared quickly and vanished quicker only to reappear somewhere else. Feeling faint, the blood in his ear was hurting and the driving snow was blurring his vision.

His fall backwards was soft and precise like children making snow angels in a park.

"Paul, Paul," came the voice.

It was less than a few feet away but he could not see the person.

"Come on, dozy," said the voice – a voice he knew. "You don't want to be late for school again do you?"

"No mum," he said, as he rolled over and got to his knees.

It was a lovely voice, an encouraging voice and he knew it and trusted it.

On his feet again, his head swam, his skull ached like it was going to explode. He reached for his ear and then something heavy hit the back of his head. He swayed and fell forward, face down into the cool river where he always swam in the summer. His dog Dillon had jumped in after him and they were going under the surface, down, down, diving down to the bottom. There was a gunshot, someone was hunting, then another and finally silence.

Chapter 41

Mostro cocked his leg against a southwest facing wall and turned east away from the sharp wind which cut Pancardi to the marrow. The sky was heavy with clouds as they passed two Mounties who had stepped outside for a cigarette. Pancardi noticed their skins which were white yet as thick as Whale skin.

"We Italians," Pancardi joked, "we like the warm."

"Hey so do we," replied one of the men, "only up here it gets as cold as hell."

"I notice," replied Pancardi.

"Every once in a while though, we get a freaker, and this one's a true freaker."

"How long do you think it will last then?" Pancardi asked.

May be over by sun up," said the second man, "might stay a week. Sometimes it clears on the other side of the mountain first, sometimes here. Either way this one's bad."

Pancardi nodded thoughtfully and then wondered if Blondell would go mad in the vast expanse of soft white.

"Anyhow I'm going in," he said, "before my dog gets frozen."

In the lobby Pancardi checked for messages – there were none. His mind wandered to Alaina's revelation and now for the second time he considered the full implications and he could not quite believe it. It made a form of sense but not totally. It would however, explain the level of cunning; everything was planned in fine detail almost nothing was left to chance. Was that inherited or learned behaviour, it was the same old chestnut, nature versus nurture, he had never really made his mind up on it.

As a team they were without doubt the best he had ever seen, the woman in particular was as ruthless as she was cunning, but had it not been for the fiasco in Amsterdam then things might well be concluded right now. There were of course the red-hair and green eyes, not normal for an Italian. He knew that was what she was now – he could sense it more than deduce it. He asked the clerk to put a number through to his room and turned toward the stairs.

"I'm so certain," she said.

"Absolutely?"

"Carlo face the truth," Alaina was pleading for acceptance now, "DNA does not lie, however hard it might be to swallow such a bitter pill." She changed the subject, "The Dutch police have found a body, which they think might be connected to you."

"How so?" Pancardi asked.

"It was found in an office block not far from the Doupelein Hotel."

"And?"

"The body was wrapped in a carpet. A cleaner discovered it after a smell was reported – it wasn't pretty."

"Go on."

"It looks like the sort of thing your team could be responsible for."

"But it could just be another murder. You know what Amsterdam is like for drugs and people trafficking."

"I know but what if it's Verechico?"

"It won't be," he said with certainty and then murmured, "but it could be," he paused to think, "the Scotsman, the one that has not been accounted for. How did he die?"

"A shot to the head."

"Can you do the forensics?" he asked imploringly.

"I've only just got back and already you wish to send me off again. I'll send Ennio he can deal with a ballistics match, that's if there is one, after all he discovered the family tie." There was an awkward pregnant pause. "Anyhow how are you?" she finally asked.

"Fine, fine," he lied. His mind was catapulted into a future of what ifs.

"Magdalene was going frantic with worry when that plane went down. Alex doesn't seem to understand what…"

"I know, I told him," Pancardi interrupted.

There was another awkward pause.

"Perhaps he ought to realise when someone cares for him," Alaina chided. Another awkward pause followed. "What do we have to do," she asked, "to get through your thick skins?"

Pancardi nodded.

"Are you still there?" she asked.

"Yes," he coughed.

"Well aren't you going to say anything?"

"What would you like me to say?"

"You really are the most exasperating man Carlo. You know what to say. How long must I wait?" He swallowed. "When you come back to Italy we must talk about this."

"But," he replied, "I am old enough to be your father."

"But, but, but, always but," she continued, "not too old to be my occasional lover though? I want more."

"When I am back in Rome?"

"When you are back in Rome, Giancarlo Renaldo Pancardi," she used his full name, "you had better be prepared to do something honest or ….." she stopped herself.

"What do you want?"

"You, you," she said, "you," she paused, "you silly old fool."

She slammed her phone into the cradle and Pancardi cupped his receiver for a full minute before putting it back in his cradle. He knew he should phone her back, tell her how he felt. But fear and self–loathing took hold of him and he lay back on the bed his arms folded behind his head. Mostro jumped up and lay next to him.

"Well Mostro," he said, "the woman she is serious and Pancardi he is..." his voice trailed off into a barely audible sigh.

Mostro licked his paw to remove some path clearing salt which had jammed itself between his toes. Pancardi rubbed his ear and the little dog responded by rolling onto his back to get his stomach rubbed.

The phone rang, "Yes," he said.

"It's me," said Alaina.

There was an awkward silence. Pancardi expected her to rant

and rave and curse and swear – her reaction was the opposite, she was totally calm.

"When you get back to Rome we will talk," she said.

He nodded.

"We will talk about all the things we have learned. Your past and this…"

"Alaina," he blurted.

"Don't interrupt me," she said forcefully, "I only have one further thing to say to you Carlo. If you cannot see it then you are worse than Blondell. I love you, and you can't even see it, can you? I," she paused, "love," she paused again, "you."

She repeated the words slowly, pounding them home like hammer blows to his thick skull, hoping they would register somewhere. He was about to reply but she had cradled the receiver again.

When finally he got through there was no reply, either she had left the office or she was not picking up the phone. Perhaps, he thought, he'd try her home phone later. He cursed and wished he still smoked, he could do with a cigarette right now. He was too old for this sort of high emotion and he needed to tell her that. In the end he was glad he had not got through.

Paul West felt sick, he was inside the fuselage wrapped in an airline blanket and a roaring fire was at the mouth of the gaping havoc-made entrance. Duane Rightman was sitting opposite him rubbing his hands in the heat and coughing in the smoke.

"What happened?" asked West, his head fuzzy.

"I don't fucking know man, I don't know," he replied. "I was sleeping and then bang, shots and wow I could hardly breathe. Lucky for me I heard 'em, stopped me from choking. I was having really weird fuck off nightmare dreams and then bam and then I coughed man, like really coughed, all this blood and shit." His eyes rolled in their sockets and his speech slurred, "We're all gonna fuckin' die baby. We're all fuckin' werewolf food," he began to slobber.

Rightman was ranting and making no sense. He seemed strung out with eyes that stared and then suddenly darted from place to place like a frightened animal. His pupils were dilated, his speech slurred and West wondered if he was on something, something from the medical bag. His own ear hurt and his head felt like it was inside a goldfish bowl – he was finding it hard to hear and sometimes his vision blurred too. His head was splitting. He tried to remember but only half of it came back. He was outside and then he saw the eyes and then a paw or something hit him, a log, on the head and th....

"You're awake then," said Alice, as she came through the door, her arms laden with firewood and the heavy coat she wore covered with snow. "I got a fire going."

"Wha... What happened?" asked West.

"You were collecting firewood," she replied.

"Yeah I know."

"Then this wolf jumped you from the back, landed both paws on your head. Jumped clean from the fuselage above. I heard something on the top of the plane so I came down grabbed the gun and fired – it ran off. I think I hit it."

"Fuck," said Rightman.

"Fuck indeed," said Alice. "Then I lit this fire and we have to keep it going day and night to keep them away. They're going to run out of bodies soon and they'll want some fresh meat and I for one am not going to be eaten."

"Fuckin' A," Rightman interjected. "We can't let one of those fuckers in here."

His eyes glinted with anxiety.

"Absolutely," Alice agreed. "But I can't be on guard forever, I need to sleep too, so we'll have to take it in turns. Sleeping Beauty you can have first bash," she said to Rightman. "How's the head Paul?"

"Sore," he said, "like I've been hit with a shovel."

They sat in the warmth of the fire. Alice made a snow bag out of her stocking which she hung on a tripod near the fire. The steady drip of water hitting the steel of the pot below ticked the moments away. Paul West lay with a surging throbbing pain at the rear of his skull. His eyes closed he dreamt in a half sleep of pain and anxiety. He dreamt that he was out in the snow, that he was injured and that Alice was walking away. She was laughing, calling him a fool and wishing him well with the wolves.

Dehydration was the enemy as much as the cold and Alice knew that water allowed the brain to function adequately. She wasn't about to let lack of fluid cloud her judgement, she slurped the now semi-full container of luke-warm water to the drains; she had to keep a clear head and she had to sleep too. Her last waking thought was an image of Rightman sitting by the fire, the pistol in hand, watching the drifting snow outside for any sign of movement; she rolled into her mass of coats and slept deeply.

⁂

"The Romanov jewels are you sure?" asked Blondell.

"Totally," replied the female voice on his phone.

"They are out on the open market already, that's extremely bold, who's the seller?"

"Well," said the female, "it appears to be a family by the name of Alsetti, through an agent, one Michael Vaughan. Very aristocratic, very influential family and there is a provenance story on these jewels being passed down father to daughter, since the revolution. A very plausible story considering that Baron Alsetti had given considerable chunks of money to finance the white counter revolution in 1919. There was talk even then of laundering cash, gold and jewellery onto the open market. The connections within the Alsetti family go back to the 1700's and it seems when the old matriarch died, the family felt that they had to put the jewels onto the market, death duties and all that. And if you believe that then you are Mickey Mouse and I'm Donald ... "

"Duck," Blondell hissed, "they're the stolen ones."

"I know that, you know that, but how can it be proven? This story ties in nicely with the death of this woman who supposedly ruled the family, including distant cousins, aunts and uncles with a rod of iron. She died last year and the documents show that her father the Baron had been given jewels by Alexandra. There is also talk of an Anastasia connection and an escape."

"And people believe this crap?" asked Blondell.

"If the Alsetti family, Mr. Blondell, claimed the moon was made of cream cheese and that their relatives were black moors from Turkey there are very few people who would go against them, well publicly at least."

"My God," said Blondell, "it's over. We're screwed, they have turned us over completely."

"Not quite," said the woman reassuringly, "the Foreign Secretary has been in contact with the evaluations people in Holland and several historians and just about everyone else."

"And?" asked Blondell despondently.

"The owners of the safe deposit box will say nothing, poor political image and all that. What with the Sicilian connections, Mafia, and the interconnection with the church it's a total mess I'm afraid."

"But it always was! I said that would be the case." Blondell's temper was rising.

"Well," the voice calmly continued, "and this is not to be passed to Inspector Pancardi."

"Why?" Blondell interjected.

"Official secrets and all that. So only for your ears please?"

"Fine," Blondell replied, though he felt a sense of divided loyalty.

"It seems that some of the jewels are not on the market at all. We can only guess why not. We hope," she accentuated the we, "that some of these are on that plane."

Blondell was thinking about telling Pancardi.

"If they can be proven to be Romanov jewels then the whole tissue of lies collapses and the Alsetti family will be exposed."

"And the Mafia?" asked Blondell.

"Well that is between the Alsetti and them."

"Meaning if the Alsetti family is exposed then they get thrown to the wolves so to speak?" Blondell felt uneasy.

"Precisely."

Blondell remained silent.

"For that reason Mr. Blondell the Foreign Secretary requests you find any jewels at the crash site. In particular there are two large Emeralds which were Russian cut. There is clear irrefutable evidence to name these as Romanov jewels. We will be faxing you a seating allocation as at take off, that should narrow your search area."

There was along pause.

"Like looking for a fucking needle in a fucking haystack," he said under his breath.

"That may be so," said the voice, "but they will most likely be concealed on the body of ..."

"The team? They could be spread all over that mountain."

"You will inform this office immediately if the items are recovered."

There was a loud click, followed by a short quiet one a few seconds later.

Blondell knew immediately what the second click meant – the phone call had been both monitored and recorded.

"Wake up man!" Duane Rightman was shaking West from his deep sleep. "It's your fucking turn man."

West struggled to his feet and then walked stiffly to the opposite side of the fuselage to urinate.

"Hell man," said Rightman, "we gotta sleep here, and you piss."

"Well you piss outside if you want to. Maybe you want to go out there in the dark with your dick in your hands but me I want to live. How much wood is left?"

"Just that," replied Rightman, pointing to a depleted stack of timber.

"What the hell have you been doing?" West questioned.

"Keeping us alive," Rightman replied. "I keep the thing high, to frighten the fuckers away."

"Well what do we do when it runs out?"

"Get more? Or burn some seats and stuff."

"You stupid yank," said West, "it's a plane, fucking plane seats don't burn."

Rightman was wrapping himself in blankets at the far side of the fire.

"Fuck you," he snorted.

"No fuck you," West replied under his breath. "I'll make sure you're the first to go."

In the fire light Paul West sat with a small trickle of blood running from his ear. He could feel the throbbing in his head and noises were being carried on the wind, noises like voices, hideous voices, goblins, demons and wolves. He could hear them now in the distance baying, baying for his blood. He checked the clip of the pistol – three rounds. He felt on the ground for the large carving knife, it was gone and then he remembered that Alice had it under the covers. The two smaller ones were close to hand standing up on the arm of a seat like two sentries. Throwing more timber on the fire he surveyed the darkness and his eyes began to feel heavy. The relentless snow was almost hypnotic drawing him toward sleep.

When Alice Parsotti woke the fire had almost died and the cold had become intense.

Rightman was gargling blood, Paul West lay slumped on the ground and the injured boy was moaning above. Throwing wood on the fire she began to scramble up the seats.

"My leg hurts," the boy said, "where's mom?"

"She'll be here soon," Alice replied calmly, as she administered another shot of morphine.

"I want to go home," he said helplessly.

"I know dear," she said, as she released the tourniquet.

The boy bled heavily onto the blankets, his heart slowed and his breathing became shallow.

Clambering down the ladder of seats she carried a rolled blanket to the opening in the fuselage allowing drops of blood to fall from it at the threshold. Then she dragged it out, out into the darkness beyond the fuselage. Returning she slid quietly under the mass of coverings and lay still for a moment or two.

Suddenly she screamed and shouted, "Paul, Paul, shoot."

"Immediately West raised his gun hand and fired. One shot then another into the darkness beyond the fuselage.

"You got it," she squealed, "you hit it."

West could see nothing, his head was spinning and his eyes blurred. Rightman was awake too, spitting, coughing, and choking.

"Look," she said to them both, "you hit it, there's blood and look the others dragged it away."

"Fuckin' A" Rightman coughed, leaning over the blood stains and adding more of his own. "But now we've only got one shot left," he said, "just the one."

Chapter 42

"Yeah, right," the American was indignant, "you have got to be kidding me."

"I'm not," said Alice.

"She's right," said West. "If we don't have more wood we're all going to die."

"Well you go fetch boy, like a good little retriever," Rightman snapped.

"Listen we take turns," said West, "that's what we flipped for and you lost. So you go with Alice first, then I go with Alice – Jesus Duane," he used his first name, "Alice gets to go twice."

"Well I get the gun then," he said.

"Fine. It's only got the one round. Let him have the gun Alice."

Paul West watched as the two of them disappeared into the thickly falling snow.

The first to return was Rightman his arms laden with wood, Alice followed close behind.

"Nothing," she said.

"Not a goddamn sound," Rightman confirmed, "just the wind. We're gonna go again." His confidence was high now. "Until we got enough for the night. Those fuckers have to sleep sometime and I reckon tha's what they're doin' right now man. If I see anything I'll blow it away," he coughed more blood and his breathing was heavy.

"Don't you want me to go?" asked West, "it's my turn."

"OK," he replied, handing over the gun.

Alice Parsotti and Paul West moved out into the storm. West followed her footprints but the wind bit into his head and he could hardly see a thing. He felt faint and he found it hard to speak. Physical exertion made his head ache and near the edge of the tree-line he lost sight of her and became disorientated. He wanted to sit down, wanted to sleep; he could just roll in the soft inviting snow, lay his heavy head down and curl up, but as he did so Alice found him.

"Come on," she urged, "back inside, it's going to kill you otherwise, take these." She handed him an armful of heavy logs. "And send Rightman out. Give me the gun though just in case."

Paul West trudged back toward the plane and did as Alice instructed. His brain was bubbling and he needed to lie down. It was like the migraine from hell and he thought that unless he lay down he might vomit. Everything was a blur of wind and snow.

"Just walk in a straight line," shouted Alice, "a straight line."

"Gentlemen, good news," said the District Attorney. "It looks like the storm may be lifting. Forecast is for another four to six hours, then blue skies for about a day. That should give us a big enough window to fly you guys up there and get a rescue team in place."

"What about bears and wolves?" asked Blondell.

"What about them?" came the smiling reply.

"Well isn't it dangerous to go up there, with them about?" Blondell continued.

"Oh yes of course," laughed the Canadian, "but all the wolves we have are in the national nature reserves and that plane is not inside that boundary. The chances are they'd be more scared of you than you of them anyway. They're wild and wild things spook real easy, unless they're starving. In fact that plane is nearer some ski runs rather than anything else, it'll be found by a skier first.

Duane Rightman became a dead snow angel the instant the bullet penetrated his left eye and removed it through the back of his skull. His feet lifted from the ground and he fell backward without a single cough leaving his lips. Alice Parsotti dragged the corpse into the nearby hollow and quickly covered the body with snow. She listened for the approach of West but heard nothing; then smearing some of Rightman's blood on her hands and face she ran back to the plane screaming.

When she arrived she found West slumped near the fire, his face was ashen and he was semi-conscious. The concussion had taken hold and she knew she had wasted her time with the charade. A tank could have passed him three feet away and he would not have noticed a thing. He did not see the heavy log which came down upon the back of his skull, but he felt the impact. Blood spurted from his eyes and nose as the second blow fell, at the third his skull cracked like a boiled egg. He fell forward landing face down in the fire edge; the smell of burning hair filled the compartment and he instinctively struggled forward and up to avoid the heat. Alice Parsotti punched the carving knife into his left armpit and his eyes opened wide. For a brief second he recognised her and what was happening. He tried to call but she pushed hard and the steel shaft bit through his lung and disappeared up to the handle in his chest. As he tried to get up and fight back the wolf was on him, on his back, pushing him down with its body weight. Blood was in his eyes and he couldn't see, couldn't fight it off. He could hear it snarling in his ear; he wanted to live but it kept biting. Deep bites that made his lungs fill with blood.

"Now you know what a fucking feels like Paul," she said, as she twisted the blade and his eyes opened wider. "Just like taking it up the arse. Only this time it's your turn to get fucked."

She grit her teeth as she twisted the blade a second time before withdrawing it. Blood was bubbling from his lips and he clutched at the wound to stem the flow. He wanted to scream, to fight back but no sound came from the wide gash in his throat. He sank his teeth into something and there was a yelp. But there was no air and his strength was ebbing and the wolf on his back was so heavy. He tried to lift himself, turn over, he pushed with his arms and then collapsed. He was still, but his corpse made an awful bubbling noise – a noise like a man gargling mouthwash before bed. Then, as Alice Parsotti rolled off the corpse, catching her breath, a final expulsion of air came from his lungs and he was dead. Alice Parsotti was alone.

"How long?" asked Pancardi.

"One hour, maybe two," said the pilot, surveying the sky.

"That's too long," he snapped in reply.

"Well that's how long it's gonna take sir, I don't give a damn about you and your special fugitives. You may be the best Mountie in the world but up here you're Joe Smoe. If we take off too early then we won't get there at all. The boys from Cupforge are on their way, anyhow, things are clearer on that side of the mountain."

"And," interjected Jacobsen, "one of my best men is over there. He'll be on the chopper when it takes off and he'll cover everything."

"I hope for your sake you're right," said Blondell. "We don't want another Amsterdam on our hands do we?"

The Chief of Police looked at the younger man and wanted to spit in his eye but thought better of it. He wanted to say that he had been handling investigations when Blondell had been playing with himself as a teenager, but he didn't. Instead he noted the threat to his career and resented it. Politics had taught him much, that defeat could be snatched from the jaws of victory, that small men could indeed make much noise and that revenge could be honed. Most of all he had learned the greatest lesson in politics – when to say nothing at all.

Cupforge mountain rescue helicopter took off at 12.22pm. The pilot estimated thirty five minutes to the crash site. He said he was going to land about two minutes away. He'd been on a fly over earlier in the morning, as soon as the storm had blown out and he thought he could set down in a spot close to the wreck. The wing of the plane had carved a convenient landing pad out of the forest which seemed flat though covered in snow it was hard to tell from the air.

The pilot had informed Billy Patterson of mountain rescue team 7BC that there were no tracks, so he presumed no survivors, but there must be someone inside the plane. There had been smoke coming from the tail end of the fuselage, clear visible smoke, so someone had a fire going. There was no way the fuselage could smoulder for so long.

Billy, Frank Dilo and Doc Thorpe would be the team. They were all local men used to the terrain and Billy Patterson had been famous ten years back when that small by-plane had gone down. It had been front page news, he was hero, and on the TV and all. It was Billy who walked in and it was Billy who kept those people alive long enough to walk them out. The pilot respected Billy Patterson and the local climbers and skiers knew his knowledge of the mountains was second to none. If Billy couldn't get people out alive nobody could. His only problem was his looks, which tended to make girls shy of him. In the fall of 82 a grizzly had gone crazy and Billy, well, he had been in the way of the rampage. Some skier, a girl, was trapped and Billy, he tired to scare the thing off but it turned on him instead. Old man Tunnock shot it in the head but Billy was badly mauled, he nearly lost an eye and the right side of his face still carried the horrible scars. These were matched by even worse ones on his chest and back. If anyone came by to visit he always quickly put his shirt on when he'd be chopping logs and working, and he never went swimming, though he was great at it when he'd been at school, had cups and all.

Billy liked girls but girls didn't like Billy, so he became a kind of recluse. Lived in a cabin at the foot of the mountain with just his two dogs for company. But every man in Cupforge knew he was the best. He sat in the chopper with Patton and Monty his two Newfoundland dogs. The best ever generals he told everyone, they could win when others quit and his two boys were just the same, could find a body in thirty feet of snow.

Frank Dilo had come to Cupforge one winter, a bit of a drifter looking for work and he and Billy hit it off. One night in a bar in town a young guy taunted Billy, called him a cripple, said he was deformed. Billy didn't seem to mind but Frank took exception and threw the kid out the door and the young guy up and stuck a knife in his gut in reply. That was his last ever night as a barman and the start of a twenty year friendship. Billy Patterson trusted the man with his life and he was always the back-up.

Doc Don Thorpe hated flying but had to go on the rescue it was part of the job. He nearly always felt travel sick and would much rather be dealing with troublesome schoolboys and pregnant women.

Detective Sergeant Jack Flanders was the worst nightmare that Mountie money could buy. He was old school, difficult, hard boiled and very thorough. He hated authority figures, had little regard for politics and his career had no where left to go except retirement. Once he had even struck a superior officer when the man made too many mistakes. Some people said that officer deserved to be hit, because he got a guy shot by mistake, but it was kind of hushed up. That officer was a Chief now and Flanders had managed to keep his job but his ability to make enemies made others dislike him. Jacobsen had chosen him personally, not out of like but out of necessity - he was good at the job and there was no margin for error here. On the phone he had briefed the detective fully. Two men, one English, blonde, tall, the other an American. A woman long red hair, pretty, they would have a haul of stolen jewels. All the survivors had to be searched carefully he had said, without exception. Check everything twice and be certain, were his final instructions.

When the Cupforge helicopter landed powdery snow lifted in a tumult of swirls and resettled in silence. The three man rescue team jumped out ducking beneath the rotating blades as they slowed. The two large dogs followed Billy Paterson waiting for instructions. They made for the smoke and as they did so out came a woman. She was waving madly, shouting. Flanders noticed her red hair, short, unkempt, probably a bob when it was styled. She looked dirty and her face was a mess but she was pretty; she was shouting in an American accent, shouting about a boy, and she was agitated.

"He's here," she said, as they got closer, "next to the fire. He's got a cut and I put a tourniquet on it, but there was so much blood, please help us."

"What's his name mam?" asked Thorpe as he felt for the boy's pulse.

"Bobby, his name's Robert, Robert Pattern."

The Doctor shook his head, and as Dilo threw a blanket over her shoulders, she started weeping, sobbing uncontrollably. Flanders checked her purse – her passport said Rosalie Pattern. She looked like the photograph – he checked the side pockets.

They were empty except for a mobile phone some lipstick and a photograph or two.

The woman had collapsed to her knees now and the heavy coat gave her the appearance of a snowman, a black snowman; if anything she looked frumpy rather than pretty. He evaluated quickly – this was not the woman they sought, despite the coincidence of hair colour. He tried to ask her questions but Patterson shook his head to discourage him.

"Shock," he said.

"Rosalie? It is Rosalie isn't it?"

The woman nodded.

"We're going to make a quick check to see if there is anyone else."

"There isn't," she sobbed. "There's just me and Bobby. There were two men they went for help in the storm but they never came back."

"When did they go?" asked Patterson"

"Yesterday sometime, but they never came back and it got so cold and the fire went out. How's Bobby she sobbed?"

Doc Thorpe told her the simple truth.

She collapsed.

"We have to get this woman onto the chopper and the boy too," the doctor said. "She needs medical attention in hospital and the nearest is 50miles from the airbase. She may be........"

Flanders nodded but checked her pockets and the pockets of the boy before he was satisfied – they were empty.

"Right we take them now?" ordered Thorpe.

The body of Bobby Pattern and Alice Parsotti were loaded onto the helicopter. Billy Patterson noticed her striking green eyes as he lifted her into the belly of the helicopter. He tried to avoid it but she made eye contact with him and fixed her mouth on his and then kissed the terrible scars on his face.

"You are a beautiful man," she said to Patterson, as the doctor climbed beside her and the helicopter took off.

Patterson watched as the rotating blades lifted, he wondered how she had known of his fears and the results of the bear deformity, those piercing green eyes. The helicopter nose dropped before the whole thing sped off at high speed over the horizon and he wished he was not deformed and she not married. Life, he decided, was cruel. With a single whistle he set off Southward toward a sunken hollow near the tree-line. Patton and Monty were working the ground ahead in sweeping arcs as Patterson had trained them to do.

"Those men," asked Flanders, "how far could they get?"

"Depends what they know about survival skills," replied Dilo.

"How far would a novice get?" Flanders quizzed.

"What someone like you?"

"Really?"

"Well if it was me and Billy we'd dig a snow hole and bed down, wait for the storm to clear. A greenhorn city boy, maybe a mile, If he was fit and knew what to do."

"Right," said Jacobsen, as he Pancardi and Blondell took off.

Mostro sat on the floor, being used to the motion of helicopters he wanted all four paws to balance with as they swung around various valleys and bends.

"My man on the ground says that there are two survivors a mother and a boy. He's checked their passports and they are genuine. He's searched them both and he's certain it's not them."

Pancardi said nothing and Blondell felt sick at the thought of his quarry being plucked from his grasp.

"But," Jacobsen continued, "the woman says there were two men who got the fire going and then set out yesterday to get some help. They never came back and we have no tracks."

"That's them!" exclaimed Blondell, "I would put money on it."

"Well," said Jacobsen, "if they did go off, chances are they froze to death. We may have to wait for a thaw before we find the bodies."

"How long till we get there?" shouted Pancardi over the noise of the engine.

"About ten minutes," the pilot replied. "If you think someone is walking off the mountain you had best look for track. I'll drop down lower and fly just above the tree line."

Blondell took the left and Pancardi the right while Jacobsen played political gooseberry in the middle. He knew that the men had died and wasn't going to waste his time looking for tracks that didn't exist. Even blundering novices knew they needed to stay under shelter, warm, and remain in the area easiest to find. Jacobsen was amazed by the two men next to him, why did they rate this gang of incompetents so highly. To say he was stunned would have been an understatement.

Frank Dilo had checked the cockpit – the flight crew were all dead. All the bodies were in a crumpled heap as if none had been wearing safety belts, which he found really strange. The pilot was still in his seat and his head was slumped forward, his neck was broken.

Flanders was inside the main body of the aircraft now. He had climbed the seats to the luggage compartment at the tail, found the shelter of bags and coats and blankets and in the semi gloom the blood which had been let out of Bobby Pattern.

"Why did she move him?" Flanders asked.

"The fire?" Dilo replied, as he climbed to join him.

"Yeah, but why not start a fire up here then?"

"Ventilation?"

Flanders nodded but he was not convinced by the logic. He would simply have opened the rear door, after all it was not jammed, he had opened it easily. They could have set a fire. Granted they would have had to carry the wood up and wedge the door, and then it struck him – one or both of the men were injured. If they were and the woman was right, why would they strike out in the storm? It just didn't make logical sense unless they had the jewels, it must have been them.

At the entrance to the fuselage Flanders studied the ground and then the threshold. There seemed to be no other bodies. Where were they? It didn't make sense. Lots of blood, lots of compressed snow, lots of foot prints. This had been a thorough-fare but there was only the woman and the boy. So who made all the footprints? He began to think that the woman had been covering something up. Perhaps she was afraid that they would do something to her – so had lied to cover their escape. Perhaps the woman Parsotti was alive and she had lied about that too.

The helicopter from Montreal Airport landed in the rotation snow storm. Alex Blondell was the first out followed by Mostro, who sank up to his belly in snow.

Pancardi lifted him and carried him under his arm. Inside the fuselage he put the dog down. He extended his hand to the Canadian detective.

"Pancardi," he said, "this is Mostro and that is Alex Blondell."

He nodded toward the Englishman who had begun to climb the numbered seats without the slightest interest in introductions. He scrambled as if he were searching for a specific location.

"Well, anything?" Pancardi yelled up.

"Loads of blood. Someone must have died in this seat. It co-responds. Shit." He lost his footing and his hand strayed onto the blood soaked seat back in an attempt to steady himself – it felt spongy, sticky.

"The overhead," Pancardi called, "check the overhead."

"Empty," called Blondell, as he began to descend.

"And what do you think happened here Sergeant Flanders?" Pancardi turned a question upon him.

"Something and nothing really," he replied. "It seems they set up upstairs and then built a fire down here. For some reason best known to themselves they built a fire here. Then they brought the boy down to the fire and they …the pilot … the pilot. Of course it's all wrong, all wrong."

Pancardi was bemused.

"Come with me," Flanders said suddenly

In the cockpit he showed Pancardi and Blondell the bodies and the pilot still in his chair.

"I think they killed them after they landed the plane," he suddenly blurted. "Look this is no random scattering like you would find in a crash they've been piled. Why?"

"To hide something?" quipped Blondell.

"But what, give me a hand will you?" Flanders asked.

Together the men moved the top two bodies which were solid with the frost and ice.

"Look," said Blondell, "bullet wounds."

"Shit!" was Flanders single word reply.

Mostro began barking furiously. Blondell had seen him do this at the nursing home the day that they caught Udo Richter. His tail was up and he was barking out into the expanse of snow. Frank Dilo was waving to Billy Patterson and the two big dogs were sniffing the ground in between.

"He can smell something," Blondell said.

"Yes a rat," Pancardi replied."

Chapter 43

Alice Parsotti was in the morgue – alone.

"I just want to see him," she had pleaded with the attendant.

"Hey lady I'm just the night janitor," he had said, "I don't make the rules. I just get to..."

She had started weeping loudly as people walked past the entrance, "He was my only baby," she had howled, "and you won't let me in to see him, it's not... Yo...u... mon...st...er."

Her voice had risen and the howl become a wail. Her breathing had been intermittent between words and the night porter only wanted to get away.

"Hey lady," he had tried again.

Her wailing had increased.

He knew it was against the rules but he wasn't about to get into an argument with a woman who had a dead kid. She wouldn't go away whatever he said and as his manager was not there why should he be lumbered with the decision, they only paid him a few bucks an hour. What the hell, he had said to himself, she'll just cry a bit and after he had had his coffee and a smoke he'd come back and calm her down – take her upstairs and the nurses could sort it out. They'd give her a pill and knock her out and he could get some peace.

As soon as the attendant left Alice Parsotti stopped the wailing and found a post mortem scalpel in a drawer. Throwing back the sheets which covered Bobby's body she opened his shirt. His stomach had been stitched shut with white cotton; a crude blanket stitch which she slit open easily. Having done so she reached inside his corpse and retrieved a small bag which she washed quickly and stuffed into her robe pocket. She refastened his shirt and threw the sheet back over the boy. The corpse lay on the refrigeration unit shelf, like a slab of butcher's meat. Alice smiled and took a deep breath, she knew the attendant would soon return. A toe-tag protruded from under the sheet with the name PATTERN in capitals and Robert in lower case attached to his left big toe.

The swing doors opened and the attendant entered gingerly, "I have to ask you to leave now Maam," he said.

"Of course," Alice replied, she was quite calm now. "You were just doing your job."

The man nodded.

Alice turned and with a, "Thank you for being so kind," left the morgue.

The attendant casually slid the boy's body into the storage refrigeration unit. Usually his job was to strip the corpses, clean them down for post mortem. But it was not his shift in the morning and Jones could do this one. He didn't want to waste his time when he needed to phone his girlfriend. He was on his own and he could stay on the phone for ages. No one would check and he had done enough for the shift, they weren't paying him to be a martyr. He closed the door of the refrigeration unit and walked over to the desk and picked up the phone, dialled nine, and got an outside line.

"Judy," he said cheerfully, the weeping woman already forgotten, "yep, later when my shift is over. I need a bit of creature comfort." He could hear the giggle on the other end of the line and he knew he had something nice to come home to.

In the morning, Alice thought, some doctor would do a post mortem and then they'd find the hole and Alice Parsotti would be classified as a monster. But it had been a great hiding place, her own personal jewellery bag. She reflected as the lift rose; the Canadian detective had checked her passport and her pockets too; he knew what to look for, but he had also thought her genuine. Someone guessed they were on that plane, they had made a mistake somewhere – the Italian. She cursed and then decided she had to move quickly. The kid had been far more useful than Rightman could ever imagine. Well that's one in the eye for him then, she thought, and smiled at her own joke. She imagined the American shouting his mouth off about the best thing for the kid anyway and she almost laughed. She wanted to dance and sing from the rooftops but she restrained herself. Life was going to be great, she was going to live the high life, just like her grandparents had done. She had the emeralds. Everyone probably thought she had died in the crash – it was perfect. Lots of the bodies would never be found, they would be spread all over the mountain. West and Rightman could have argued and one killed the other but she wasn't going to rest on her laurels – in about an hour she would be gone.

At her bedside she said, "Thank you," sombrely and that she would, "like to sleep now." The nurse had given her a sleeping pill which she feigned taking by holding it under her tongue for a while.

As she pulled the robe cord tight around the nurse's neck she felt the pill begin to disintegrate; it caused a nasty taste in her mouth and she mockingly spat it at her choking victim. The lifeless body fell to the floor and the bitter taste was making her nauseous, she needed to swill her mouth out before she did anything else.

Mostro was waist deep in the snow but his senses were working overtime. Pancardi was studying him, as the small dog sniffed the air. He stopped at the brow of the hollow and started to bark. Billy Patterson and Frank Dilo started probing. Patton and Monty were sitting some distance off watching the small city dog in their environment.

"They didn't get far before they dug in," Blondell said to Flanders as he approached, "maybe two hundred yards?"

"Dug in?" questioned Pancardi in reply.

"A snow hole," Dilo replied. "A shelter from the wind."

Billy Patterson was the first to find a limb, a leg, cold lifeless. A few minutes of snow moving and they found Paul West, his skull had been shattered and his throat cut.

"No accident then?" Pancardi remarked.

"Nope." Blondell was examining the body. "He's been stabbed too. This was a messy business, must have been loads of blood, yet the snow here is pure white."

"He was killed somewhere else then and the body moved," said Flanders blandly.

"That's how Mostro got the scent," Pancardi smirked, "the blood near the fire. That little dog will surprise many people yet with his cleverness. He is the spider to catch our flies."

Patterson said nothing but knew that the real advocates had been his two animals.

Less than two metres away they found the one eyed body of Duane Rightman.

"Right through the eye," said Blondell, as he examined the corpse.

"You know of course what his must mean?" said Pancardi.

"The woman, with the boy," replied Blondell, "that woman was Parsotti."

"Impossible," Flanders interrupted, "I saw her passport – it was an exact match."

"Exact or near enough?" Pancardi snapped. "We leave now. Get the hospital surrounded no one goes in or out and do it quietly." He turned to the helicopter pilot, "Get us right into the grounds," he commanded.

"Hey Billy," the pilot called as he began to walk back with Blondell and Pancardi, "gotta take these guys to the Portman."

Patterson nodded.

"Frank, me and the boys we'll have scout around see if there's anybody else," he shouted in reply. "You make sure you come and get us though my generals get a mite tetchy if they don't get their feed of a night."

The pilot laughed and gave a thumbs-up in reply.

Alice Parsotti tried to get the foul, bitter taste out of her mouth. The bra had been useless, far too big and she had decided not to bother. She hoped there was a coat out there somewhere. The shoes were big too but at least they were lace up comfy ones which would make it easy to walk. Soon as she could she'd buy new stuff anyway.

She opened the door a crack and checked the corridor: it was clear. The overhead lights were bright and showed that her hair was wet. That was good she thought as it appeared darker than her usual red. She passed the nurses station, stopped to check the drawer for a purse, grabbed a coat from the stand, and began to walk toward the exit signs. From the corridor windows she saw the flashing blue lights of the approaching police cars. She halted briefly, observing, evaluating, then she made her decision.

The helicopter landed and without ceremony Flanders, Pancardi, and Blondell ran across the lawns. Mostro sped into the entrance ahead of them.

"Its room 203," said Flanders breathlessly. "One of our men has checked the room and she is still there sleeping. I don't think she suspects that we are on to her."

Blondell drew a pistol from the small of his back. The 9 millimetre Browning felt heavy in his hand. He hoped he would not have to use it but he knew that Parsotti carried a .38 snub nosed Smith and Weston and he did not want to end his life like the security guard at the brewery.

"No need for that," said Pancardi, "Flanders searched her."

"Yeah and there was no gun," he confirmed.

"Then who shot that guy in the eye then? The bloody tooth fairy? I don't intend to end up like Roberto Calvetti, or that security guard and his dog," he scoffed.

"Through the double doors," said Flanders, "third on the left."

Pancardi stopped them, "Slowly," he said, "now we walk."

They passed the nurses station. Two female armed officers were standing guard dressed in plain clothes as if they were visitors.

"Where is the nurse?" whispered Blondell.

Both women shrugged in unison.

They all scanned the corridor, there was no movement.

Blondell's face appeared at the oval window set in the door. The window which the nurses used to check on patients without having to enter the rooms.

"Asleep," he said, "she doesn't seem to know we are on to

her. This is going to be so easy."

Leaving the hospital at the rear was so easy. The security guards were checking for people trying to get in, not out. All Alice Parsotti had to do was watch where the other nurses went and then tag along. She followed a small laughing group – not one single person spoke to her. No one challenged her and she felt secure knowing that she, Rosalie Pattern, was fast asleep in what should have been her bed. When the authorities came for her they'd think her sleeping, it might, she thought, buy her a little more time

Outside the hospital she turned right, saw a police car approaching – it slowed as the nurses passed but then went on to secure the rear exit. She did not stop nor turn her head but flicked the collar of the coat up against the cold. Casually she turned into an alley, walked into a side street, took a left and then a right and melted into a crowded street.

Blondell, first in, stood back from the prostrate woman in the bed, his senses were on red alert. His firearm was cocked and he had every intention of firing if he had too. Pancardi entered the room with the two plain clothes officers and without speaking switched on the light. A woman lay on her side facing away from them, her brown hair scattered over the covers.

"Shit, oh shit!" exclaimed Blondell lowering his aim, "she's gone. How did she know?"

"She didn't," replied Pancardi calmly, "she's just playing the percentage; she is so very good she anticipates. We will not find her now, she has the jewels and the money. All the others must be dead."

"You admire her !" exclaimed Blondell, the pitch of his voice rising.

"No, far worse," Pancardi muttered, so as to be inaudible, "much, much, worse."

Flanders pulled back the covers and the naked female body

of the duty nurse was exposed. Her skin was tinted blue and her purple tongue hung from her mouth.

"Gone," said Pancardi, "the best I have ever seen."

He walked into the corridor and Blondell followed replacing his pistol to the small of his back.

"We've lost her haven't we?" he said, "she's gone and the stones have too. She's got the Dalvin money and the profits from the sales." He sighed, "It's over," he said, "and we've lost her. Good lord we were so close, so close."

Pancardi's reply was choked, "For good this time," he said, "she is gone for good. She is the best – awesome."

Chapter 44

It was a frosty morning and five years since that marriage in Palermo.

The ancient cathedral of Monreale on the hillside overlooking the city had been breathtakingly bedecked in flowers which gave it an air of opulence, white orchids-expensive white orchids. The contrast with the gold of the crusaders roof had been stunning as the sun pierced the windows and bounced light around the couple who gave their vows in Italian. Pancardi had thought of the many crusaders who worshipped there before taking boats to the Holy Land. He imagined them praying for their God to keep them safe, and he thought of the Muslims under Saladin doing precisely the same in their fashion and his mind had wandered to the meaning of life. Religion had never interested him despite his Catholic family background. He did not enter churches as a rule but Magdalene and Alaina had asked him so sweetly that he found it hard to resist. Pancardi had thought the whole thing stunningly beautiful but had felt strange as he sat among the Mafioso, and the dregs of the affected English middle classes. Magdalene's eyes smiled, her face beamed and the old Italian had seen love sparkle through her.

Alexander Thaddeus Newton Blondell, ex Harrow, ex Cambridge, advantaged and privileged had tied himself to a dark eyed Sicilian beauty with criminal connections. Ancient criminals tied to new criminals it would be a perfect match thought Pancardi.

Alaina had been with him, she too wanted a marriage and Pancardi had genuinely thought that the time was right, he wanted to have the happiness of Blondell but nerve had got the better of him. He did not doubt that Alaina loved him and he her, but his life was ending and hers was still vibrant and alive. She was an eminent forensic scientist and he a crippled old wreck – it would not be fair. That was all in the past now as Alaina had moved on and he and Mostro remained, though the old dog began to move slowly and heard less than he should. They were inseparable and they both knew that the partnership was for life – Mostro's.

Pancardi turned the collar of his overcoat up and Mostro walked rather than ran among the tombstones, returning periodically to see if Pancardi had moved – he had not. The man sat with a rug across his knees and his face buried in a copy of the English Times newspaper. His head was covered with a large brimmed fedora hat and his face shrouded with a black woollen scarf. He sat inside a three quarter shelter which gave him protection from the wind, a thermos of strong coffee next to him on the bench. The shelter was surprisingly clean and graffiti free; it did not stink of urine nor have prophylactics scuffed into the corners, but most importantly it did have a clear view of the graveyard and specifically the family mausoleum. An ancient structure which spoke of wealth and taste. Pancardi estimated the age at three hundred years. The names of the family members were engraved upon it while lesser members were buried in graves nearby. It was one of these graves that Pancardi was studying.

The vigils of the last four years had produced no result at all and Alex Blondell with his new wife had told Pancardi that it was a pointless exercise – a waste of time. He had a better way to find her he claimed. The case of the Romanov jewels was not over, he had said; they had lost for the moment but he was more determined than ever to track her down.

Pancardi had replied that he was certain she would come eventually, if not this year then the next and if not then, the year after.

That morning he had carefully checked the grave – there were no flowers. He even sought out the grave digger who was working nearby and questioned whether anyone had been lingering at the site – he received a firm negative. It was the right date and hoping this would be the right year, he had taken up surveillance in the bench hut.

Pancardi recalled his conversation with Blondell and winced. "She's a ghost, we're chasing a ghost," Blondell had said. "She has laid so many false trails, that we have to unpick each one systematically. It could be a very long ride."

"Every year she sends flowers and the tag always says the same," Pancardi had replied, "and there are kisses too. That much we do know – who is she really?"

"But she won't dare to show her face." Blondell had been adamant, "She is far more cunning than anyone," he had repeated, "you said she was the best you had ever seen didn't you? Well would you show, think logically?"

Pancardi had nodded a silent reply, but secretly he had hoped some sentimentality had surfaced in her genes too.

"Well," Blondell had continued, "she will not risk her life and liberty to go to this grave – when she sends flowers every year? What if it is not her, what if you are after the wrong flower sender?"

"But I must for the sake of Roberto at least try," Pancardi had replied in defence to the admonishment.

Pancardi had surprised himself with the sentimentality of his own deductions. Alex Blondell had simply shrugged and let the matter drop – his pride would not allow him to do the same.

Magdalene was a mother now and Alex had other fish to fry. Pancardi had not seen him for over six months but they spoke on the telephone and Magdalene was enjoying life in Chelsea. Pancardi had been retired for good, but this case was sticking in his throat like a fish bone. Alaina had been sworn to secrecy and she had stuck to her word and said nothing; this was his last chance to get things right – to set the record straight. Pancardi looked at his watch it read 1.15pm. Mostro was on the bench beside him now; he had climbed under the rug to avoid the biting wind and he snored in his doggie dreams.

At 2.00pm Pancardi poured a coffee and ate a pre-made sandwich. He had read the Times from cover to cover and wished he had brought a good novel along. Something English and classic, he fancied Villette by Charlotte Bronte as he had never read it. Jane Eyre had been a great read and he would have given everything to have what Jane and Rochester had – to find it and keep it would have been marvellous. He cursed his stupidity and resigned himself to a thoughtfully sullen reflective afternoon.

At 3.30pm he knew that the vigil would soon be over for that year. The sky was darkening and clouds which threatened overnight rain hung like pall clothes over the coffin of the sky. His supply of coffee was nearly depleted and Mostro was feeling the cold. They had both been for a quick leak behind the bushes and soon they would need to go again.

At 3.41pm the delivery van drew up at the gates of the cemetery as Pancardi adjusted his dress and reappeared from behind the bushes. Quickly the pair slipped back into the bench hut unnoticed by the driver. The white florist van was emblazoned with green writing, it read *Intrigo Fiori Roma* and the telephone number was clear next to the interflora symbol: It seemed genuine. The driver hopped out and at the back doors removed a wreath, which he casually placed onto the roof of the van.

Looking around the graveyard as if checking for a location, he picked up a clip board, made some note, then threw the clipboard into the back, slammed the doors, retrieved the wreath and started walking.

"Shit," said Pancardi, quietly. "Again she does not come Mostro, but she sends a wreath."

He stroked his dog and watched the approach of the driver. He was in a blue boiler suit which was loose about the body – like sagging skin. Pancardi noticed the driver was slight though tall and the walk was quick and impulsive. He was obviously making for the family mausoleum and then suddenly it dawned. The driver was a woman not a man. The walk was languid, leggy, and sophisticated. Pancardi could tell that the figure beneath the oversized boiler suit was young and athletic and immediately his attention refocused. Mostro too sat up watching and raised his nose into the air to sniff for a familiar scent.

The woman wore trainers and a baseball cap which shrouded her face. Through the gap at the back of the cap hung a bleached blonde pony tail. Pancardi followed her with his eyes, he estimated her height at 5ft 10ins, about the right height and about the right build. He watched the woman as she went directly to and laid the wreath at the grave of Margarite Alsetti – Pancardi knew it well. He had stood before it many times in silent contemplation. He watched the woman standing at the grave as if in silent prayer and suddenly realised that she was no delivery person – this woman was praying.

Quietly he slipped from the shadows and approached across the grass. His step was quick and his cane could not be heard against the soft earth but the woman knew he was coming and Pancardi spotted the tension in her shoulders as she braced herself for a possible attack.

At a distance of ten feet he spoke confidently, "I knew you'd come," he said.

The woman did not move. He hoped she was not armed. Mostro sniffed the air and caught her scent, his lip curled in recognition of an odour remembered but he sat quietly, waiting for a command.

"I knew that today of all days you would come," Pancardi said again. "There is too much history here is there not?"

The woman had her back to him but she nodded.

"She was a wonderful woman," he continued, "so full of life and zest. She showed me how to love," he paused, "no, she taught me how to love. Then she broke my heart."

"How did you find me Inspector?" the woman asked casually.

"Our forensic expert got a DNA match Alice," he paused, "your fingernail and some skin in the Volkswagen, you should have been more careful, and some unexpected blood on a rag made it absolutely certain. The thing is," he paused again, "no other living soul knows."

The woman turned to face him, in her left hand she held a .38 Smith and Weston which was pointing at his head. Her face was radiant, beautiful, just as he remembered. The hair colour was all wrong, but that, that was the bleach and he'd know her anywhere. Her face was printed on his memory like a tattoo – it had spread with time and some of the crispness had become jaded around the edges but it was there and always would be. The complexion, and the hands, confident hands, and the same striking green eyes – those were her mother's eyes. It was as if Margarite had returned from the grave.

"Are you going to shoot me?" asked Pancardi.

"I might, why shouldn't I?"

"History Alice, history."

Chapter 45

When the little dark-haired girl picked up the letter at the front door she had raced her small white puppy to get to it before he shredded it. She giggled and swooped upon the letter as her mother appeared at the top of the stairs – she was holding a new baby in the crook of her arm.

"Charlotte, take that to your father please, he's in the study and let Noodle outside he needs to go to the toilet, I don't want him to wee on the floor again," she said.

"Si Mamma," the girl replied.

"English please," called the mother in reply.

The girl lifted her Bichon pup into her arms and stroked the white curly profusion of his furry head as he tried to lick her face and simultaneously get to the letter she was the victor of. She laughed as he jumped to the ground and sped ahead of her barking as he did so. A high – pitched bark which carried the joy of youth and announced the arrival of the duo at her father's study.

Her father sat at a large oak desk, a telephone receiver pressed to his ear, papers were strewn before him. Charlotte handed him the large brown envelope which he noted carried an Argentinean stamp and he smiled at her as he reached for the letter opener and spoke to someone on the line in Italian. His face looked grave as if he was receiving unwanted and shocking news and the little girl knew better than to ask. She raced into the garden to play with her dog.

"When?" he asked.

"At least three months ago?" the woman replied.

"Where the hell is he?" Blondell continued, his face ashen white.

"You know he always does things alone, never relies on anyone." Alaina was emotional now, "He didn't want to be wrong and he never told a soul?"

Blondell could hear the anguish in her voice.

"His confounded pride Alaina," he confirmed, "always so proud, so strong a man, you above everybody should know that. In his way he loves you, but he always told me that it would not be correct to get you to become his nursemaid in his old age."

"He's an exasperating, pig-headed, egotistical, and wonderful man," she laughed.

"Do you want to tell Mags yourself or shall I?" he asked. "He gave Charlotte that puppy you know. I think he did it to get back at me for teasing him about Mostro."

"I love him you know," the woman on the line continued, suddenly becoming serious. "He should know that if I never see him again. Where is he the doddery old fool? Off on some wild goose chase no doubt, with Mostro in tow."

"I know," Blondell replied, as his hands worked on the package his daughter had produced, "if there is anything I can do," he said. "Thanks for telling me."

The letter inside the larger envelope landed lightly upon the desk as he spoke, it was sealed with cello tape. Alex Blondell opened it carefully, the contents were beautifully written in a fine scrolling hand which gave any reader the sense of a well educated writer-someone who took the time to select and craft their words.

It was a fine morning in Chelsea, bright, crisp and light. Autumn was turning the leaves gold and auburn on the trees outside and the Copper Beech in the garden was on fire in the sunlight. Magdalene was changing the baby and he could hear her humming as she did so and he knew – he was content. He took a deep thoughtful draught of strong black coffee, and began to read.

Buenos Aires 17th September

Dear Alex,

It might seem that fate pieces a life together in haphazard ways but I think everything has a purpose, even if circumstances are separated by oceans of time, don't you?

Life cannot just be chance and chaos – can it? Look at you – you're so lucky, so very lucky to have something so precious.

In this world there are very few truths. Love does exist – you should know that now. I know that, and if you don't believe me read some Yeats poetry and maybe you'll get to understand. Love exists but how strong is it, is it stronger than death?

The only absolute truth is death after all. It comes to all of us eventually only most of us don't get to choose when; in the end will you be able to choose?

Me, well, I want to die in bed, but hey what do I know? I know all about you.

Please cease this charade of trying to find me, you won't be able to.

Perhaps you should consider young Charlotte she is a very pretty young girl and you wouldn't want any unfortunate accident to befall her, would you?

Let us agree that if you leave me alone, well I'll leave them alone. There must be enough space in this world for us all to rub along.

Take care now – Alice.

Instinct drew Blondell to the window of his study and he scanned the street for observers of his home. On his face he had a broad smile – he knew now that his method was working.